THE HUNTING

THE HUNTING

Matthew McCain

This is a work of fiction. All of the characters, names, incidents, organizations, and dialogue in this novel are either the products of the author's imagination or are used fictitiously.

Any people depicted in stock imagery provided by Getty Images are models, and such images are being used for illustrative purposes only. Certain stock imagery © Getty Images.

Cover design by: Anthony Vitukevich

Print information available on the last page.

Rev. date: 09/17/2019

To order additional copies of this book, contact:
Xlibris
1-888-795-4274
www.Xlibris.com
Orders@Xlibris.com
784484

For:
Ricky West
"Young and reckless then, now it's all different."

PROLOGUE

"Run!" Sam Rainey shouted.

"I am!" Tyler Benton yelled back.

Out of breath from running so far—further than they've ever had—the two stayed side by side as they pushed deeper in the woods.

"Faster!" Sam shouted.

"I can't!"

"Well, try!"

For ten-years-old, both boys were in good shape, but as the footsteps stomped from behind, Tyler and Sam started to panic, screaming at the top of their lungs, hoping that somebody in the town of Hunting, Pennsylvania would hear their pleas for help and come to the rescue.

But no such event happened; the part of town they were near was full of vacant houses with no-one in sight—nearly everyone on this side of town had either relocated to another part of the state or left altogether when the steel mill closed twenty years back. All Tyler and Sam had was each other and what energy that was left in their little legs.

"Jump!" Sam warned as they crossed a fast-moving stream and approached a rusted out truck that had been placed there back in the early forties.

Following Sam's lead, Tyler jumped, leaping as high as he could to make it over the water and past the truck. Despite nearly losing his footing from the jump, Tyler grabbed onto Sam's extended hand and landed on his feet.

Out of breath, the two charged up the steep hill cluttered with broken branches and headed toward the outline of what appeared to be the exit of the woods. With nothing but the last rays of the evening sunshine penetrating periodically through the trees, the two boys kept running, hoping they were heading in the right direction.

"Faster!" Sam shouted when he realized Tyler was starting to slow down.

"I can't!"

The footsteps behind them were growing louder, only adding to the rising tension.

"Come on!"

They ran.

The footsteps got louder.

The light got dimmer.

The footsteps closed in.

"Hurry!"

Tyler started sobbing.

Sam looked over his shoulder, paying no attention to the steep slope he was charging straight into at full speed—he lost his footing and plummeted down. Tyler did the same, also unable to spot the slope in time to stop.

They screamed as they stumbled downhill, crashing into everything from broken tree branches to sharp-tipped rocks sticking out of the Earth's crust. Tyler cried out in agony as a piece of bark from a pine tree sliced a large gash across his face after slamming into it, sending blood spewing onto the wet sticky leaves and moist dirt beneath him.

Sam suffered the same fate as he rolled down and smashed his head onto a large boulder, the hit nearly knocking him out as his ears rang like a church bell. Even though the fall lasted nothing more than a few seconds, to the boys, it felt like hours. Over and over they rolled, shouting and bouncing off everything the woods were made of.

Landing first, Sam crashed onto the bottom of the slope and into a thorn-bush face down. He lost what little breath he had when all of Tyler's weight landed on his back. Unable to shout from the lack of air, he kept still and closed his eyes, hoping—praying the pain would dissipate.

Silence came over them with nothing but their heavy breathing being the only sound around. There were no animal noises or the sound of water moving.

There were also no footsteps.

Tyler got to his feet first, his back cracking in three different places as he stood. He began to panic when he looked down to see Sam entirely still. "Sam!"

Hurt and clearly in pain, Sam rolled onto his back, allowing Tyler to see the scrapes and dirt across his best friend's face.

"Sam."

Sam—once again—extended his hand. "Help me up. Quick."

Grabbing his hand, Tyler used what muscle he had in his little body and began pulling Sam up.

"Ow, ow, ow," Sam mouthed all the way to his feet.

The two boys kept their hands clenched together even after Sam got up. They looked up at the slope they had tumbled down; it was a lot steeper than either of them thought, but neither acknowledged. Instead, despite their bruises and cuts, they knew they needed to keep moving, no matter how much pain they were in. The silence was comforting but questionable at best.

Ready to push deeper in the woods, Sam squeezed Tyler's hand, forcing him to look up.

"We need to keep going?"

"Why?"

A loud painstaking scream from the top of the hill shattered the silence. It is followed soon by footsteps. Only it wasn't footsteps; it was running steps.

"Go," Sam said.

They ran.

There was sudden crash.

"Faster!" Sam warned.

Another crash.

"Come on!" Sam shouted again.

The further they ran, the less light there was. The floor of the Earthy ground was rigid and unstable, almost to the point of unbearable. Rain from the last two days made the wet leaves covering the ground slippery—both Sam and Tyler tripped numerous times, and yet kept running for they knew that if they slowed down, even for a moment, they would be killed.

CHAPTER 1

The last glimpses of sunlight were fading on that late September evening as Officer Tyler Benton drove down Lancaster Street in Hunting, Pennsylvania, nearly twenty years after his experience in the woods. The sky was clear, the wind was calm, and the headlights to his cruiser were bright as day, and yet he couldn't shake off the unsettling feeling that was forming in the lower half of his gut.

The street of Lancaster was on the outskirts of the depleting steel town that once occupied over fifteen thousand people. Now that the population had nearly been cut down to less than a third, due to the lack of work and deindustrialization, Lancaster Street was saturated with rundown houses and massive potholes in the road. Nothing more than a few street lights accompanied Officer Benton on his journey down the street, keeping him quiet and on edge. Lancaster was also only three streets away from where he entered the woods all those years ago, but the young officer did everything he could to avoid that thought.

Because he was working the night shift for the week, Tyler was responsible for responding to every incoming call the station received. Typically, other than a few reports of a car crash—usually in the center of town between Main Street and Torque Street, his nights consisted of speeding tickets and multiple cups of coffee to get him through the predawn hours. But when he got the call from eighty-one-year old Clarence Grzywacz saying he needed the police at his house right away, Tyler knew it was going to be another dramatic night at Old Man Claire's house.

"I'm on it," Tyler said when he heard the call come in from over the radio.

The eighty-one-year-old war veteran had lived in the town of Hunting for his entire life. He was one of the first to see the old steel mill in town open and was the last to clock out the day it closed. He also was one of the most foul-mouthed blue-collar workers in the upper mid-west. Old Man Claire had spent the last years of his long life criticizing and objecting to America's changing demographics, especially after the mill closed. Many in town—those who still remained—chose to ignore him when he would wobble into Mary Ann's Diner—the last restaurant in town, and go off on one of his racist rants. But, several years back, that was not the case.

Old Man Claire found himself facing off against Juan Mitchell—one of the only African Americans in town. It got ugly fast and resulted in him with a black lip and Juan in handcuffs. Ever since, people did their best to stay away. Except for Tyler.

Since the old man called the police about every little thing, from cars speeding to trees in the woods falling, Tyler always had to be the one to drive down and take care of him—mostly because he was the only one who wouldn't get offended by his racist remarks. He dreaded heading down to see him because he knew he was in for a night filled with drama.

As he reached the end of Lancaster Street and pulled into the driveway of Old Man Claire's rundown home, Tyler flipped on his siren lights to alert Claire that he had arrived. He stepped out of the cruiser, keeping the lights on so he could try and avoid the giant potholes entrenched in Claire's driveway.

Since Old Man Claire was the only person living on the street, darkness surrounded the entire area. Shadows loomed largely and every noise that was made in the night sent chills down your spine. Tyler rested his hand on his pistol as he approached the old house.

When he reached the farmers porch of the two-story home, the outside light flipped on and the door swung open. Because of the late hour, Tyler wasn't surprised that Claire answered the door dressed in a blue bathrobe, brown slippers with his walker resting in front of him; all accompanied with a sour look of disgust on the old man's unshaven face.

"About fucking time you got here! I called over a half-hour ago!" Claire shouted through his toothless mouth even though it really hadn't been that long.

Tyler chose not to pick a fight, hoping to keep the visit as short as possible.

"Sorry, big fire down at the fire station," he lied.

"Fire, huh? Probably some spooks from across the county causing trouble!"

Tyler waved his hand. "No, it was just an electrical issue."

Skeptical, Old Man Claire tightened the strap to his bathrobe. "Uh-ha. If that's what you wanna call it." He stepped out of the house and slammed the front door shut. "Follow me."

Rolling his eyes, Tyler stayed behind Claire as he slowly went down the few steps and started leading him to the back of the house. Claire put his hand over his face to cover his eyes from the blue and red strobes lights on top of the police cruiser. "Jesus Christ, can your lights be any fucking brighter?"

Tyler said nothing; he just kept following him while counting down the hours he had left before his shift was over. When Old Man Claire got onto his lawn, he picked up the pace. The feeling of isolation loomed like surround trees, leaving Tyler feeing uneasy. In an attempt to end the feeling, Tyler started acting like a police officer. "So what kind of noises have you been hearing?"

"Helicopters! A bunch of them, too."

The answer surprised Tyler. "Helicopters?"

"Yes, helicopters! What're you deaf?"

"No, just curious. How long have you been hearing these helicopter noises?"

"Years!"

Tyler rolled his eyes. *Jesus Christ, out of all the people in the world, this is who I get stuck with. God, this night needs to be over already.*

Despite not believing a word the Old Man was saying, Tyler kept up his persona that he was interested. "Really?"

"It's been getting worse, too!"

The backlight kicked on when the two of them reached the backyard, revealing a small sized yard that desperately needed to be cut.

"Huh, and is this why you called?"

"No, but feel free to look into that, too." Claire pointed to the metal fence on the outskirt of his lawn. "That's why I called."

Tyler looked in the direction of where Old Man Claire's curled finger was pointing, only to see darkness. The porch light mounted on the back porch was no match for the surrounding shadows.

"What? I don't see anything," Tyler said.

Claire pointed again. "What, you need my reading glasses or something? Right fucking there! Right in front of us!"

Tyler pulled out his flashlight resting on his hip, clicked it on, and started toward the fence, keeping the beam of light on the tall thick grass in front of him. The feeling of dread grew larger as he approached the end of the yard. Slowly, he placed his left hand back on the butt of his pistol.

Nothing appeared.

"I don't see anything!"

"Keep going, goddammit!"

Growing impatient by Tyler's pace, Old Man Claire resumed his walk and started to catch up to him. "Gotta do everything my fucking self!" he grumped.

Keeping his flashlight pointed to the ground, Tyler started to feel exposed, almost as if something or someone was watching him. The feeling allowed the memories of his last experience in the woods to come rushing back. When he reached the metal fence at the end of the yard, he spotted something in the grass.

He couldn't make it out at first—the beam of light wasn't strong enough to penetrate through the brush. But whatever it was, it stuck out like a sore thumb. The grass surrounding the area was yellow with a few spots of green mixed in, but the object—or thing in front of him—wasn't yellow or green. What he was looking appeared to be red.

Curiosity became him, and before he knew it, he realized the red splash of color was all around the ground, even underneath his shoes. He stepped back, gasping by his lack of awareness. He jumped when Old Man Claire walked up to him.

"Fucking pussy! Get out of the way."

Groaning with each step he took because of his arthritic legs, Claire stepped into the ray of light and walked over to the source of the red substance, which Tyler now assumed was blood. In a spite of rage, Claire tossed his walker to the side and reached down.

"What're you doing?"

Placing his hands on something that blended in with the grass, Old Man Claire began pushing, thrusting his body weight into whatever was in front of him.

"Are you gonna help me or stand there with your dick in your hand?"

Sprinting into action, Tyler walked over to Old Man Claire's side and reached down. He shined the flashlight down on the thing in front of them.

It was an animal.

A deer.

A dead deer with its head face down in the Earth, or what was left of his head. Tyler couldn't see much, but he was able to confirm his suspicions about the red substance being blood; the animal was covered in it. Tyler reached down and put his hands on the back end of the deer.

"You shoot this thing?" Tyler asked.

Claire didn't answer. Instead, he started pushing on the animal. Tyler joined in.

"Holy shit," Tyler muttered as he started pushing.

"Put your back into it!"

Listening to Claire, Tyler used the muscles in his legs and shoulders and pushed his left shoulder into the deer.

It started to roll.

"That's it! More!"

Tyler pushed more. So did Old Man Claire.

Working together, both men were able to muster enough strength to get the deer to move and eventually roll onto its broken back, exposing its white belly and front of its body.

"Holy shit!" Tyler shouted.

He stood up and stepped back, placing his hand over his face. Old Man Claire did the same thing, only slower. A sense of nausea turned in Tyler's stomach. Hoping to avoid breathing in any of the nearby air through his mouth, he cleared his throat as the beam to his flashlight lit up the grisly sight.

"Is…is that deer missing…" Tyler started.

"Its face," Old Man Claire finished. "This deer is missing the skin on its face."

Tyler winced before taking another look. "Jesus."

From the neck up, the animal was skinless. Nothing but its eyes and flipped tongue remained—even its nose and ears had been pulled off, leaving behind nothing but blood and smell so foul even Old Man Claire couldn't stand.

"How the hell did this happen?" Tyler asked, keeping the flashlight beam on the animal.

"Beats the piss out of me. I've been on this Earth for almost a hundred years, and in all my time, I've never known an animal do this to another animal."

Tyler did what he could not to focus on the head, and instead focus on the large bone sticking out of the neck.

"Looks like the neck was snapped, too."

Claire agreed.

Silence grew among them before a soft snap coming from directly in front of them broke the stillness. After looking at one another—both with a look of uneasiness—Tyler lifted his flashlight quickly and shined the bright light into the woods directly in front of them.

Nothing out of the ordinary could be seen. There were large trees and thick looking brush, but nothing more and yet both of them sensed their eyes were being deceived. They were unable to put it into words, but neither of them could shake off the feeling like something was with them; something that was staring back at them through the darkness.

On an isolated road deep in the woods behind the old cemetery, on the outskirts of town, sixteen-year-old Mike Eaten and his girlfriend Kimberly Wilson sat together in the darkness, listening to the sound of crickets chirping all around them. The dirt road was nothing more than a dead-end that led about two miles into the woods only to stop abruptly for no reason at all.

Many in town—those who left and those who remained—knew the history of what the road was typically used for; either "mudding or fucking." Many of the more youthful citizens in the town of Hunting had either lost their virginity or came close to it on that road, despite only being able to access it from inside the eerie cemetery. To anyone who lived outside of town, it seemed more like the type of place that would give you the chills than make you aroused.

Because Mike and Kimberly were in their mid-teens, in love and closing in on the final year of high school, they met the qualifications to become another young couple looking for fun just to regret it nine months later. But to their surprise, they weren't having sex or even making out. In fact, the idea never crossed their mind—at least not Kimberly's.

Instead, they were leaning back in their seats, looking up at the stars through the opened sunroof of the truck as the windows fogged up from the heat of their bodies with the coolness of the night keeping them company. It wasn't the first time they'd been out to the old dirt road and more than likely wouldn't be the last; at least not until they graduated and moved out of state.

"Oh, I think I saw one!" Kimberly shouted, pointing to the night sky.

Her excitement spooked Mike, causing him to jump, yet he looked up right away. Nothing seemed to stand out.

"I don't see anything," he replied.

"That's because you didn't look in time, you bozo."

"Bozo? Wow, that's really nice."

"Yep, bozo. A blind bozo," Kimberly joked.

"Why am I a blind Bozo?"

"Because I've seen three shooting stars and you've missed all of them."

Mike smiled, ignoring the urge to check his phone to see if he missed any calls because he feared it was time for them to head home. "Oh."

Kimberly rose from her seat and let out a big yawn as she normally did when it got late into the evening. Remaining still, Mike decided to be a smartass. "Oh, I'm sorry if I'm boring you."

"Well it's not your fault; I chose to be here," Kimberly shot right back with the same sarcasm Mike fell in love with instantly.

"Ouch. You know, if I had feelings, they'd probably be hurt."

"If I had feelings, I still wouldn't care—whoa!"

Mike jumped up. "What?"

Kimberly pointed out the windshield which hadn't completely fogged up yet. "Look at all the fireflies."

Despite his back cracking, Mike pushed the back of the seat up and took a look for himself. "Whoa."

Before them, piercing through the darkness were an overwhelming amount of small yellow lights flickering off and on in every direction. The two lovebirds remained still in the truck, amazed by the majestic view as the tiny lights poked holes through the darkness that engulfed the woods.

"There must be hundreds," Kimberly whispered.

"At least," Mike replied.

The excitement from the sight brought Kimberly back to the good memories of her childhood when she would try to catch a firefly in a glass jar when she was on her father's ranch back in Ohio before he died.

Typically, she would become disheartened—even upset at time—when she thought about her father, but not on that fateful night. The void that usually held sadness filled with enthusiasm.

Mike reached for her soft hand, lifted it to his lips, and gently kissed the knuckles. She smiled from the sweet gesture, squeezing his hand as she embraced the romantic moment. The two made eye contact and exchanged looks of happiness. A boyish grin emerged on the left side of Mike's face—the very grin she'd fallen in love with instantly. They lean in for a kiss, ready to make the romantic moment complete—a loud crash came before them.

The roar was loud, quick, and worst of all, close—very close. So close that the vibration of the bang made their sodas resting in the cup holder shake. Like the drinks, both Kimberly and Mike jumped as they were taken entirely off guard by whatever the sound was.

The echo left behind from the noise dissipated as fast as it came, leaving the two grief-stricken in the dark with the silence of the night returning.

"What the hell was that?" Kimberly asked in a panic.

Mike trembled. "I—I don't know."

Kimberly—being smart for her age—locked the doors to the truck before Mike even got his hand on the button. They looked at each other, both incredibly scared, but also incredibly curious. Everything inside told them they should heed the warning and leave without thinking twice, but instead of being rational, Kimberly chose to be daring. She reached into the glovebox and pulled out the yellow flashlight with black trim Mike kept way in the back. She turned it on and shined it through the windshield.

Something was in front of them—something massive. Possibly more massive than the truck. The beam of the flashlight was nothing more than a candle in the dark compared to the unforeseen blackness that entrenched the forest.

"Mike, what is that?"

Unsure of the answer, Mike reached down slowly, grabbed ahold of the headlight switch, and flipped it up.

Light lit up the last of the road and surrounding woods. The bright LED headlamps dissolved the shadows in a matter of seconds and pushed the darkness into the woods, making the two teenagers feel somewhat safe. The light was also able to illuminate the object that was in front of them.

"Oh, shit," Mike muttered.

A sizeable thick tree branch laid before them. From what the two teenagers assumed, it appeared that the branch must've snapped high up because of the force of its landing. The smaller branches attached to the main one reached out like helpless hands; some of the larger ones were even in striking distance of the truck. Mike and Kimberly started to feel incredibly lucky while also horrified because had Mike pulled up another three or four feet, they would've been crushed.

"Oh my, God," Kimberly whispered.

"You okay?" Mike asked, despite already knowing the answer.

"Fine," she replied before lifting her head and shining the flashlight beam up into the tree. "What the hell made that happen?"

Curious himself, Mike also looked to the sky. "I'm not sure."

While it was true that Kimberly was much more intelligent and wiser than many her age, curiosity got the better of her, and before she knew it, she was pulling open the door to the truck and stepping out.

"What're you doing?"

She didn't answer. She remained focus while keeping the source of light pointed on the branch as if her life depended on it.

"Kim? Kim…goddamn it."

Following his girlfriend's lead, Mike hopped out of the truck and walked to the front and stepped in front of the headlights. The two then focused on the branch; both following the light from the flashlight as Kimberly moved it along the entire length of the branch until she reached to where it snapped.

"This is a big ass branch," Kimberly thought out loud.

"That's an understatement," he replied.

The echo of the crash was now a distant memory, leaving nothing more than a few crickets chirping and a light breeze coming down from the north. Even though they would've been crushed if the truck was inches closer, they didn't feel scared. They felt at peace if anything.

Kimberly took in a deep breath of the Earthy air as the wind picked up a little. The smell brought her back to when she was in middle school and would sneak out into the woods despite everyone from her parents to her teachers warning her and the rest of the children in Hunting to stay out at all times.

The warnings scared many of the children—nearly all of them. There were only a few exceptions, and Kimberly and Mike happened to be two of those exceptions. They loved the woods, and no warnings or scary stories—many they dismissed as old folk tales to keep the young kids in line—would keep them out.

Without thinking, Mike pulled out his phone from his pocket and checked to see if he missed any alerts. The first thing he spotted was the time: 8:39 pm. "Oh, shit."

"What?" Kimberly asked, taking a few steps into the woods.

"It's getting late! I gotta get you home before your stepdad kills me. I promised I'd have you home by nine."

She took another step into the woods, keeping her attention on the darkness just beyond the headlights. "He's probably already sleeping. He won't even know I'm gone."

"You said that last time."

She took another step.

"What're you doing?"

She stopped. "Yesterday at lunch, I overheard James Nelson talking to some of his friends; his only friend, actually."

Mike chuckled. "The same James Nelson who's in sped classes?"

"He said he was out here when he was younger, and he claims to have seen some type of structure or building out here."

"A structure, huh?"

Kimberly kept the flashlight shining directly in front of her, holding the shadows at bay. "Yeah."

Mike walked over to her. "Well, the kid is beyond weird. I mean, how many times have we gone to lunch and he's sitting alone in a corner and talking to himself? Rumor has it he was in a mental hospital for like four years before he was allowed to go to a public school."

"Yeah, well…" she began.

"Oh, don't tell me you believe him!"

"He's one of the only people that's been out here, right?"

Not getting anywhere with her, Mike renewed his calls for getting her back home before it got any later. Again, she dismissed. She turned to him, a strange smirk covered her face.

"I'm going in."

"What?"

She started into the woods, keeping the beam of light pointed at her feet, lighting up a path for her to walk. Knowing how stubborn she was, Mike didn't see any reason to try and talk her out of it because it would just be a wasted effort. He ran and caught up with her. She smiled.

"I don't think this is a good idea," Mike said, pulling out his cellphone and opening the app that turned his camera flash into a flashlight.

"I'll note that in the log."

A chuckle squeaked out of him before he playfully elbowed her on the shoulder. "Smartass."

His flashlight beam joined hers on the ground as they pushed slowly yet steadily through the trees and darkness with nothing more than the sounds of the forest keeping them company.

The landline rang only twice before Sam Rainey picked it up on that last night. Even for him, being at the office this far into the evening was uncommon, but between the piles of paperwork he needed to go through and getting sidetracked from the beautiful view of the Pittsburg city skyline, he had fallen a lot further behind than he wanted to. Typically, if his office phone rang late in the night, he would ignore it and deal with it the next day. But when he read the caller ID and saw who it was, he picked it up right away.

"Rainey."

He recognized the voice of his boss—Jess Sowa; leader of the research and development department, right away. "Are you on a secure line?"

"Yeah, I'm still at the office. Why?"

"We have a massive problem on our hands."

The feeling of exhaustion he'd been struggling with since lunchtime was replaced with dread not a moment after she spoke. Sowa had been his boss for close to three years and never once in that time did she sound more worried than she did on that phone call. It was obvious something substantial was happening.

"What's going on?" Sam asked with worry as his ears started to focus on what sounded like an alarm bell ringing in the background of the phone.

There was silence. A silence so deafening that Sam thought Sowa had hung up on him. "Jess?"

"He escaped."

Sam leaped from his chair.

"Wh—what?"

The alarms on the other end of the line intensified, almost as if they were chasing after Sowa on the other end of the line.

"He fucking escaped!" she shouted through the blaring alarms.

The phone dropped from Sam's hand, landing on his glass desk with a loud thump. Sowa winced from the loudness of the clatter.

"Sam? Sam?"

Her muffled voice cried out into the office, only to be met with nothing. It was apparent to her that Sam's reaction was the same as hers when she found out the news. Assuming Sam had already left the office, she hung up the phone, placing into her pocket.

Unsure of how to react, she remained still with her heart beating inside her like a drum. It only grew worse as Sam's warning replayed in her mind like a bad memory she couldn't shake. Any sense of calmness she had at the beginning of the situation was now gone; the void was now filled with horror so potent, the thoughts sent shiver down her spine.

There had been breaches at the facility before; some rising to the level of serious, but nothing like this.

This time was different.

Much different.

The multiple dead guards's throughout and the broken down gate that led into the restricted area only confirmed how dire the situation was she for her and Sam. Sprinting into action, she raced toward her office as the facility remained on lockdown.

"Did you hear that?" Kimberly asked.

Mike, who was only a few feet behind, keeping his focus on the darkness behind them, stopped just short of banging into Kimberly. He leaned over her shoulder and listened for anything that sounded out of the ordinary.

The light coming from the truck headlights had vanished about a half a mile back, leaving Mike and Kimberly vulnerable to their flashlights.

The app that turned Mike's camera flash into a flashlight was eating away into his half charged cellphone battery, but paying no attention to that, he kept his focus to the forest in front of them, waiting for his eyes to adjust to the darkness.

Kimberly shut her flashlight off.

"What're you doing?" Mike asked.

"Turn your phone off," she whispered.

"Why?"

"Just do it!"

Listening to his demanding and most times stubborn girlfriend, he lifted the phone to his face. But, he didn't shut the phone off. Kimberly noticed immediately.

"What're you doing?" she barked.

He turned the screen to her. "I have full service out here."

She thought nothing of it at first. "So?"

"Why would I still have service all the way out here?" he asked.

Giving the question some thought, she became curious as to why that was. So much so that she reached in her pocket and checked hers. "I have full service, too."

"How is that possible? We must be at least a mile out."

Unsure of the answer herself, Kimberly stayed quiet, kept still and remained concentrated on the blackness in front of her. Mike shut his cellphone screen off, leaving both of them standing together in dark.

Crickets were chirping, bugs were buzzing, and the wind was softly flowing, but either than that, nothing else sounded out of place. After a few moments of remaining still, Mike leaned in. "I don't hear anything."

She didn't hear anything, either. The more Kimberly thought of it, the more she started to question what exactly it was that she heard. Or even if she heard anything at all; it wasn't lost on her that she was deprived of sleep from staying up so late the night before. The silence made her hesitate, even taken her off guard— a light appeared.

"Look," she said in a loud whisper.

Mike's eyes followed Kimberly's fingers toward the direction of where she was pointing. His eyes hadn't entirely adjusted to the darkness yet, but when they did, he spotted the light too. He squinted, trying to make out what they were seeing.

The yellowish light was dim and small, so small the leaves flapping in front of them from the sudden gust of wind blocked it out at times. It could've been a number of things, but whatever it was, both of them knew it wasn't a natural light. The moonlight flickering in between the trees above them let off a soft crème color, like a newborns bedroom, but this small light was yellow. But, it was also too big to be a pair of eyes staring back at them.

Kimberly began running. Mike chased after her. "Kim. Kim, wait up."

She didn't listen; she focused on the small circle of light and kept pushing deeper into the woods—almost running. Following her exact footsteps, Mike made sure he stayed very close for fear of somehow getting split up. He reached into his pocket to pull out his cellphone but stopped short when he heard a soft gasp.

He looked up. "What?"

Kimberly didn't answer. Instead, she let the view speak for itself.

She stepped out of the way so Mike could see for himself. "Whoa."

Before them was a small ledge with an incredibly steep drop and a beautiful view of the forest beyond. With no tree branches in the way, the pale moonlight was vibrant and it cast a glow across the distant horizon that was nothing but miles and miles of forest. But, despite the majestic sight, neither of them paid any attention to it. Instead, they focused on the large one-story building that rested at the base of the hill.

Unable—or unsure—how to react, Mike and Kimberly dropped to their knees and took cover behind a large, dying oak tree. They looked at one another, both with the same expression on their face: confusion. Knowing neither of them knew what the building was, they popped their heads out of opposite sides of the tree to take another glance.

It didn't take long for them to realize the building looked like a military base. With large spotlights aiming in the direction of the nearby woods, large Humvee's and convoys scattered throughout the front of the building and a large watchtower overlooking everything, it was more than apparent that it was at the very least a government facility.

The tall barb-wire fencing all around the lit up building led Mike to the assumption that the building was the home of *something* that was meant to be kept a secret. Kimberly thought the same thing as her curiosity led her eyes from one part of the building to the other. Both hid back behind the tree when they saw at least half a dozen armed men dressed in military gear come rushing out of the front entrance.

They turned to each other, surprised and confused by what they had stumbled upon as their consciences grew heavy because of all the times they made fun of James Nelson. From what they could see, it was now apparent that James Nelson, the 'slow' kid nobody believed or listened too, was indeed right.

"Holy shit," Mike whispered. "What the hell is this?"

Kimberly shrugged. "I don't know."

Staying low to the ground, watching as the military soldiers sprinted to the Humvees followed soon after by what appeared to be men in long white laboratory coats. Because they were at such a great distance, Mike and Kimberly were unable to make up what any of them were saying, but they were able to hear a few muffled shouts once they listened carefully.

When the soldiers reached the Humvees, they piled into them with fire under their feet, like a packed caravan headed to the boarder. Mike started looking around the perimeter of the building. "How the hell did they get out here? No road leads out here."

"I'll be damned if I—" she pointed. "Look."

Mike snapped his attention toward the left side of the building. At first, he didn't see anything, but when bright LED headlights emerged from the forest just off to the side of the main entrance, he gasped. Mike had grown up in this part of Pennsylvania his entire life; he knew the area like the back of his hand, so if anyone knew if there were some type of road that led out into the heart of the woods, it would've been him. But, the more he watched as the vehicle drove up to the building, the more he realized it wasn't coming from a road.

The vehicle was coming from a tunnel. A large, clearly manmade, tunnel, complete with a paved road and hanging lights—almost like a tunnel you'd find in Manhattan or California. Having trouble taking everything in, Mike didn't know how to react when he watched the vehicle emerged from the tunnel, pull up to the front of the building and reach the security checkpoint.

"I'll be goddamned. This is unreal," Mike said in awe.

Paying no attention to the spotlight on the watchtower starting to turn their way, Kimberly slowly stood, trying to get a better angle.

Mike looked up as the engines of the Humvees powered on. "Kim, get down."

She didn't. She rose to her feet. Mike jumped to his feet and grabbed her arm.

"Kimberly, dammit!"

The spotlight shined on them, lighting them up in a brilliant white light.

"Oh, shit," Kimberly muttered.

"Run!"

Grabbing onto her hand, Mike jetted into the direction they had come. With her heart racing, Kimberly took one last look over her shoulder as the spotlight fixated on them and the shouts of the soldiers and roar of the engines from below amplified and started in their direction. Along with gunshots.

After finishing the last of his fifth beer, Old Man Claire crumpled the can with his arthritis ridden hands and threw it across the room toward the trash barrel on the other side of the living room. He missed it.

"Goddamn."

Even though Claire was in the final stages of his life and his memory was mediocre at best, he always remembered the whipping he would get from his mother back when he was a boy if he so much as attempted to make a mess. Those memories of getting his behind whipped with a belt forced him to get out of his rocking chair that overlooked the backyard, grab his walker and head over to pick the can up from the dirty floor.

Being in the comfort of his own home, he didn't care how long it took him to move; his mind was focused on Family Feud; he was surprisingly good at it. Because he was so focused on the old fashioned square T.V., he didn't even notice his cat, Haley, sitting in the middle of the room.

She screamed when the leg of his walker came crashing down on her overweight belly. Claire jumped as he lifted the walker back up. Letting out a low growl, Haley bolted out of the living room and into the kitchen.

Claire's heart fluttered for a moment when he started losing his balance. "You fucking cat! Jesus Christ!"

It took him a second, but when he did, the old man took several deep breaths when he got his balance back and proceeded over to the other side of the room.

"Back in the day, if you ever pulled something like that, we'd grab your ass by the tail, put you in a bag, throw you in a dumpster and light your fat ass on fire!"

When he finally made it to the other side of the room, after successfully shouting out the correct answer to the jeopardy question, Claire slowly bent down, grabbed the can with his veiny right hand and threw it in the trash. Sweat formed in the creases of his forehead as he straightened himself up. He turned and looked at his pet of seven years as he made his way back to his rocking chair.

Claire had stepped on her many times, and she usually would hide under the kitchen table and hiss for a while every time Claire spoke to her, but this time, she didn't. Instead, she sat in the middle of the kitchen with her tail wagging and her pupils dilated, almost as if she was about to strike. Claire returned the look, growling at her as he turned and flopped back into the chair.

He reached for the unopened can of beer resting on the table next to him that was just below the window that overlooked the yard. He cracked it open and lifted it to the cat. He scoffed. "Here's to you, kid."

He started to bring the can up to his lips but stopped when he noticed Haley wasn't moving. He lowered the beer from his face and fixated on her. Her eyes were black and still while her tail pounded the floor.

"What?"

Old Man Claire had many traits that qualified him as elderly, but his eyesight wasn't one of them. In fact, except for reading glasses, his sight was 20/20 in both eyes. That blessing allowed him to realize that Haley wasn't looking at him. She was looking out the window behind him.

He turned around. "What're ou—?"

A pair of hands broke through the thin layer of glass in the window and reached inside. Dropping his beer and trying to get up, Old Man Claire continued shouting, but the massive hands had latched around his neck and started squeezing.

The grip was paralyzing as the large hands wrapped fully around the old man's neck and successfully closed off his windpipe. Intense pressure started taking over Old Man Claire as his face turned from pale to beet red in a matter of seconds. With only the ability to move his eyes, he looked to the window and his attacker. His eyes began to blur from the pressure around his neck, but they widened when he saw the intruder had some type of mask on. A mask that mimicked the face of a deer.

The veins on his forehead started bulging. He opened his mouth for air but letting out nothing more than a horrific screech. His body started jerking as his eyes lost all focus. Panicking, he opened his mouth one more time, but when he did, the left hand of the person strangling him swooped in and grabbed hold of the roof of his mouth while the right hand remained on his neck.

The hands started pulling away. Old Man Claire started groaning. His body started violently convulsing as the fear of death took over. The hands pulled harder, causing the skin on Claire's neck to stretch out before finally starting to tear.

He screamed.

The hands pulled harder as the sound of ripping pieced through Claire's hearing aid and the silence of the night. He started crying and closed his eyes as the hands sprang out, ripping the top half of Claire's head from his jaw, killing him instantly.

CHAPTER 2

Using the secret tunnel that led out to the facility, Sam sped up to the front of the building and screeched the tires to an abrupt halt. He swung open the driver side door and started over to the entrance where Sowa was impatiently waiting for him. She turned around when she heard the car pull up.

He walked up to her as he put on his white surgeon coat and straightened out his bright red tie. "What do we have so far?"

"Security is pulling the tapes now."

"How much of the woods have been searched?" Sam quickly followed up.

"They just started now. Movement was spotted up the hill, so the search party is going to start there."

Taking in the news, Sam started for the entrance of the building. Sowa followed him, staying only a few feet away from him as he walked up to the security booth. The glass window to the small hutch had been shattered, with specs of blood were scattered about. Sam's distaste for germs led him to put on the pair of rubber gloves he had in his coat pocket.

He focused on the blood. "Is that his blood?"

"Some of it."

Sam looked at her. "What do you mean *some* of it?"

Sowa nodded in the direction of the security station. Picking up on the hint, he walked up to booth and peered in through the broken window to see the two security guards—Bill and Rich—lying face down in large pools of blood. He looked away quickly after spotting large bones sticking out of their necks.

"Are their others?"

Sowa pointed. "Inside."

"Show me."

Sowa sighed. "Hope you don't have a weak stomach."

They started for the entrance of the facility. Dawn was nowhere in the distant horizon, the night hung over the sky, making it difficult for Sam to avoid stepping on anything that could be considered evidence. Sowa, on the other hand, paid no such attention to her steps. Her mind was clearly elsewhere.

Shivers rippled down Sam's spine when they reached the entrance of the facility, and noticed the steel door meant to keep everyone, and everything inside was bent and snapped off its hinges. It brought upon great distress to him—more than the others who were there.

Sowa stopped when she noticed Sam's footsteps had come to an abrupt halt. "You coming?"

"Yeah…"

Sowa waited until Sam had caught up to her before she continued. "Brace yourself."

Sam entered another hall. "For what?"

They stepped inside.

He eyes widened.

"For that," Sowa answered as she tried to avoid looking down the nearby hall.

Because Sowa's germ phobia was so uncontrollable, she kept her distance from the hall, but Sam—being the investigator and scientist that he was and always had been—did the exact opposite. He started down the hall, trying to keep his emotions and sensitive stomach at bay.

The long metal hall that led to the elevators that went down to the research and development lab were draped with dark red blood that started at the beginning of the hall and ended more than halfway down. Most of the bodies scattered throughout the hall appeared to have been mangled; from what Sam could see, many have limbs either snapped off or faced a direction they shouldn't have.

He turned away, looking back up at Sowa. He prepared to tell her how screwed they were when a military general—Dylan L'Heureux—stepped up to the entrance. "Miss. Sowa, you're gonna want to take a look at this."

Sam ran over when he heard L'Heureux's stern voice.

"What is it?"

"There's no sign of him, but we did find tracks."

"Where?" Sam intervened.

"East side of the base."

"That's in the direction of Hunting," Sam warned. "Oh, Jesus."

"What's our next step, ma'am?" L'Heureux asked Sowa, despite the look of hesitation across her face.

She turned to Sam. "What should we do?"

A bit surprised that Sowa would be so blunt and pass off the leadership role to him, Sam gave real thought to the answer before he spoke. His mind was racing, trying to use every bit of smarts he had to come up with a serious plan that would keep the situation as contained as possible. But, since the tracks were heading in the direction of Hunting, Sam knew no such containment would take place.

He turned to Sowa. "We need reinforcements…a lot of them."

"What for?" Sowa asked.

Sam shrugged. "Because we're heading to Hunting."

After spotting the truck headlights still illuminating through the trees, Mike and Kimberly picked up speed as they ran toward it, holding each other's hand. Deciding not to wait until they reached the truck, Mike pulled out the keys, aimed the clicker to the vehicle and double clicked the top button. The doors unlocked instantly.

With the sounds of footsteps following from behind, their hearts raced. Despite not knowing who—or what—was coming after them, they knew it was not a friendly force following them. Kimberly let go of Mike's hand when they reached the front of the truck.

"Quick, get in!" she barked.

Racing to opposite sides of the truck, both opened the doors and jumped inside nearly at the same time. Mike started the engine before Kimberly even had her door closed.

The engine started right away, leaving no need for suspense. Without thinking, Mike slammed the truck in reverse and pressed hard on the gas. Kimberly—while still on edge—took the time to put on her seatbelt without Mike telling her to.

Keeping his arm wrapped around the back of Kimberly's seat and his head twisted toward the back window, Mike watched as the truck barreled down the long dirt road. Kimberly—putting trust in Mike's driving abilities—fixated on the woods in front of them, waiting for whoever was after them to emerge from the dense woodland.

"Hold on," Mike warned before turning the wheel counter clockwise, hoping to spin the truck around as fast as he could because of the sharp turn vastly approaching. *Come on, turn. Turn, you bastard.*

Kimberly grabbed ahold of the handle on the roof just above the passenger door as she lunged forward from the force of the sharp turn. Because the truck was an extended cab and the dirt road was so narrow, Mike was unable to spin around all the way; he was forced to put the truck in drive to pull forward so he could get enough room to make the turn.

Clinging onto the handle for dear life, Kimberly watched as multiple lights illuminated from the woods in front of them. Her eyes widened with fear. "Mike, hurry. Hurry!"

"I'm trying!"

When the nose of the truck was only inches away from the tree in front of them, he put the truck back in reverse and backed up again.

More lights emerged. Kimberly reinforced the need for them to get out of there as fast as possible.

"I know!"

Both jerked forward as the back end of the truck hit the pine tree with enough force to leave a significant dent, but due to the adrenaline running through him, Mike paid no attention to it.

A flash came from the woods.

Safire sparks exploded out of the driver side headlight and went dark. They jumped.

Darkness had now engulfed the driver side windshield. It hid most of the left side, but the passenger light was still bright enough for Mike to see the tree in front of them. He could tell the frontend of the truck was to close for comfort, but instead of backing up again, he pushed the gearshift into drive and pounded on the gas pedal as he spun the steering wheel to the left.

Dirt flew up from the ground as the wheel spun, creating a horrific screeching noise that pierced through the stillness of the woods as the truck turned and headed to the exit of the cemetery and back toward town. Without saying a word, the two remained still as they sped down the dirt road and toward the exit until Mike looked in the rearview mirror and saw another quick flash. Suddenly the entire back window of the truck shattered, sending hundreds of pieces into the truck bed and backseat.

"Holy shit!" Mike shouted as the truck drove over a large bump and shook the entire cabin so hard, it knocked their drinks out of the cup holders.

"Fast, Mike! Hurry!" Kimberly cried.

"I am, I am!"

Taking his eyes off the rearview mirror, he refocused on the dirt road, spotting the sharp turn rapidly approaching up ahead. He jammed on the break, against Kimberly's wishes because he knew the truck wouldn't turn in time because of the speed. The truck speed reduced from forty to under thirty in seconds as Mike pushed hard on the breaks.

Another spark went off in the woods behind them before the sound of a loud thud struck the backend of the truck. Kimberly watched on the side mirror as more sparks began emerging through the woods. Her eyes widened with fear, unable to take them off the danger behind them. *Oh, my God. Those are gunshots! They're trying to kill us!*

Make slammed on the gas the second he made it past the sharp corner.

The exhaust of the powerful diesel roared as it hurdled toward the entrance of the road.

By the time Tyler made it to the other side of town to patrol the safest areas, he was in desperate need of another coffee. Many of his night shifts seemed to drag on forever, but this night was particularly draining. There had been many times where he almost fell asleep at the wheel but never completely did. Static coming over the radio in his patrol car made him jump.

"Benton," the woman's voice said.

"Yeah," he replied through an unannounced yawn.

"How are you doing?" the voice asked.

Tyler smiled. "I'm doing good, Lois. How're you?"

Lois, picking up the sarcasm in her partner's voice, also smiled. "Oh, just great. Just watching life pass before my eyes."

Her bluntness got a laugh out of him; like always. "Glad one of us is looking on the bright side."

She chuckled. "Yeah, the only problem is I don't know which one of us is."

Tyler did a California stop at the red light on the end of Monarch Street. "Where you at?"

"I'm out over Viking Hill—figured I'd scope out the area and then make my way back into town."

Being a lifelong resident of the depleting town, Tyler knew where she was exactly. He took comfort in knowing she wasn't far away in case either one of them tumbled into trouble. He took a glance at the radio clock, keeping the radio inches from his mouth.

"You wanna meet up for coffee?"

Lois looked down at the clock on her radio. Usually they would meet up a little later in the night, but she could tell from Tyler's mellow—almost lifeless—voice that he was in desperate need of a fix.

They had been partnered up on the night shifts off and on for almost a year. They both hated the nightshift and bitched about it regularly, but chose to keep the hours on behalf of how well they got along. Over that time, the habit of meeting each other for coffee around the half-way mark turned into a tradition within the first week. It wasn't much on the surface, but it was enough to provide them with something to look forward to on those long nights that seemed to drag on forever.

"Yeah, sure. Let me do a drive around, and I'll meet you there," Lois replied without hesitation.

Tyler smiled and spun the steering wheel to the cruiser to flip the car around. "Alright, be careful out there. You know how creepy that damn cemetery gets at night."

"Copy that."

"10-4."

Smiling from the sound of a second wind emerging from Tyler's voice, Lois placed the radio on the passenger seat of her messy cruiser and continued down the road to the outskirts of town. While she appreciated Tyler's warning about keeping her guard up, there was no need for him to remind her; because that area of the town was nearly abandoned, she always kept on her toes in case the night came where she wasn't alone. She tried not to think about it, but she developed chills when she would find herself realizing that if anything happened, she would be on her own.

With only a handful of street lights that worked on Viking Hill, only the headlights to Lois' cruiser kept her company and lit the way forward, which wasn't unusual at all. Over time, it got to the point that anything more seemed out of place. But a light emerging from the far end of the street felt out of place. She noticed it instantly. Briefly, she thought maybe it was just someone with a flashlight taking a midnight walk, but as it grew closer and larger, she thought again.

Straightening her posture in the driver seat, she eased off the gas but stopped herself from pressing the break. Keeping her eyes on approaching light, she reached for the mounted laptop resting off to her side and closed it, allowing darkness to engulf the inside of the cruiser.

The more she watched, the more she realized it couldn't have been a flashlight because of how quick it was coming at her. *That's a vehicle. Great.*

She gripped the steering wheel tight as her car gradually reduced speed. *Wow, they're going fast...holy shit, they're going really fast!*

The vehicle zoomed by at record-setting speed, sending a sonic roar and brush of wind so strong as it passed the cruiser, Lois rocked in the seat, leaving her almost stoic as her eyes moved from the vehicle driving past her to the rearview mirror.

As the vehicle passed by her, she was able to make out it was a truck, but she was unable to figure out the make and model of it. Finally, after what seemed like minutes, she looked down at the radar gun mounted next to the computer.

61 was lit up in a vibrant red.

Her tires screeched as she made a U-turn and flipped on the siren lights. Once the cruiser was in the other lane and straightened out, she stomped on the gas, sending the RPM of the cruiser to the red line. She reached for the radio. "Tyler."

"What, did you get scared?" he joked.

"No, I'm still on Viking Hill, but I'm making a traffic stop. I got someone in a dark-colored truck doing almost seventy."

Tyler lost his smile. "You need backup?"

"I'll let you know; I'm pulling them over now."

"Copy," Tyler replied as he picked up speed in his cruiser and went racing passed the coffee shop and in her direction.

The flashing blue lights from the top of the cruiser lit up the street with a strobe-like effect as the siren pierced through the night sky and echoing into the distant horizon. Taking in deep breaths to control her anxiety, Lois watched as the speedometer sored past 40 and closed in on 50mph.

The truck didn't appear to be slowing down. There was still a large gap between the truck and the cruiser, but Lois figured the lights and siren were more than enough to get the driver's attention. The lack of response from the truck was overpowering to the point of chilling. She pressed down harder on the gas pedal and began closing the gap.

She reached for her radio. "Tyler."

"Yeah."

"I am gonna need back-up."

"On my way. ETA: five minutes."

"Copy th—"

Her pause sent panic down Tyler. "Lois? Lois, you alright?"

"Yeah…yeah looks like they're slowing down."

"Alright, listen to me; I want you to stay in the car until I get there."

Lois took her foot off the gas and placed on the break. "Copy that, but hurry!"

"I am."

Tyler flipped on his patrol lights and picked up in speed as the truck pulled off to the side of the road followed soon after by Lois. She pushed hard on the breaks when the truck came to a complete stop, keeping a reasonable distance between her cruiser and the truck. Without thinking, she reached for the switch that turned on the spotlight on the side mirror. It powered on instantly.

The bright LEDs lit up the truck, revealing both the color of the truck and the damage to the back taillight; that was the first thing Lois noticed, but it was the holes in the tailgate that grabbed her attention most. Despite being at a greater distance than she usually would be for a traffic stop, she was able to make out that the round holes easily pierced through the metal of the truck. There was no doubt in her mind that bullets made the holes.

She drew her pistol as she reached down for her radio again. The truck towered over the patrol car, but the spotlight was bright enough to reach the cabin of the truck. Movement inside the truck took her attention off the holes in the tailgate.

"Tyler, hurry."

"I'm coming."

She looked at the radio clock briefly while resting the service revolver on her lap. Unlike Tyler, she had never used it and prayed she never had too, but while she waited for Tyler, a sense of fear overcame her like never before. But, the more she kept her eyes on the truck, the more she started to wonder if she had seen it before. Typically, she would've already run the plates and know who it belonged to, but given the circumstances, she wasn't about to take her eyes off the vehicle.

The driver side door to the truck flung open.

Lois cocked her gun.

A figure emerged from the truck cabin and started right toward her.

Feeling venerable in the sitting position, Lois mustered the courage her father taught her at a young age and engaged. With her gun pointed in the direction of the truck, she pushed open the driver side door, jumped to her feet, pulled out her small black flashlight, and took aim at the figure approaching her. "Freeze!"

The brightness of the flashlight beam forced a hand to emerge and cover the face of the person in front of her. She kept her gun aimed at the person. "Don't come any closer!"

"Lois, it's me," the person said.

The familiar voice resonated right away. She lowered her gun quickly. "Mike Eaton?"

Keeping his hand over his face, he nodded. "Yeah, it's me."

The two had met several times—mostly for traffic stops. Because of Mike's likeability and status as the star quarterback for the high school football team, he always drove off with nothing more than a warning even though Lois would constantly warn that a ticket was coming next time she caught him. She holstered her gun. "Jesus Christ, you scared me. What the hell are you doing out here? Do you know how fast you were going?"

Like an outraged parent, she could've gone on and on, but trailed off when she saw the look of horror across his young face. She then pointed to the tailgate. "Please don't tell me those are bullet holes in your tailgate."

Mike didn't answer. He kept still, trembling as Lois began taking a few steps toward him.

"Mike," Lois said firmly, clearly demanding to get a response.

He looked up from the ground. "Yeah."

She raised the flashlight to the tailgate. "What the hell happened?"

The passenger door flung open suddenly.

Lois reached for her pistol and pointed the flashlight in that direction. "Hold it!"

Kimberly entered the flashlight beam with her hands raised.

"It's me, it's me," Kimberly whimpered.

Lois rolled her eyes and let out a sigh of relief. "Goddamn it. Are you both trying to give me a heart attack or what?"

Kimberly, while feeling somewhat relieved to see Lois, lowered her hands and walked over to Mike. Lois spotted she had the exact same look as Mike did. "Now, what the hell happened?"

"Somebody shot at us," Kimberly answered.

"Who?" Lois replied quickly.

Mike shrugged. "I don't know."

"Where was this?"

Neither of them answered, forcing Lois to raise her voice. "Mike, where was this?"

He swallowed hard, preparing for the long speech about the warnings they received. "In the woods...behind the cemetery."

Tyler's patrol car came screeching onto the street before Lois could respond. The blaring of the approaching sirens forced Mike and Kimberly to cover their ears until Tyler pulled up alongside them and shut them off. He quickly stepped out of the car.

"Lois, you alright?" he shouted.

"Yeah, it's just Mike."

Tyler walked over to them, turning on his flashlight as he approached them.

"Mike Eaton...awfully late to be out on a school night. What're you doing out here?" Tyler asked, echoing Lois.

"They were out behind the old cemetery," Lois began.

"In the woods?" Tyler shot back.

A hint of angry was noticeable in his response, but Lois stopped him before he could say anymore. "Tyler."

"What?"

Lois answered by pointing to the back end of the truck. Picking up on the hint, he walked over to the tailgate and spotted the bullet holes right away. Kimberly looked at Mike when she felt his hand grab a hold of hers.

Tyler bent down to get a good look at the holes, gliding his hand across where they had penetrated the metal. Any doubts they were bullet holes were wiped away instantly though he didn't have much doubt to begin with. He kept his focus on the back end of the truck as he shifted his eyes to the taillight that had been shot out.

"Did you see who did this?" Tyler flatly asked.

Mike shook his head.

"No," Kimberly replied.

Tyler straightened himself up and walked back around to the front of the truck. The look of worry was more than apparent on Mike and Kimberly's faces. He turned to Lois, who looked unsettled herself. Rather than responding quickly like he would, Tyler thought about it, trying to come up with the best way to proceed.

He wiped his forehead as he took a deep breath. "This was out at the cemetery?"

"Yeah," Mike quickly replied.

"Out on that dirt road behind it," Kimberly added.

Tyler sighed. "Of course, it was."

There was a moment of silence between the four of them with nothing but a light breeze and flashing blue lights surrounding them. Sleep deprived already; Tyler could feel a headache pressing in the middle of his forehead and the thought of how long of a night it was going to be didn't help matters.

"What do you wanna do?" Lois asked, finally breaking the awkward silence.

Tyler and Mike made eye contact.

"You two head home," Tyler began. "You go home, and you stay there. You don't leave the house for anything until Lois, and I get there. Is that understood?"

Mike nodded. "Yeah."

Tyler shut off his flashlight and dismissed them. "Go."

Sprinting into action, Kimberly and Mike raced into the truck, both getting in at the same time. And without worrying about following the speed limit, Mike started the truck and ripped out the tires and sped off down the road, leaving Lois and Tyler behind.

Tyler rubbed his eyes as he placed his flashlight back in its hostler. Lois shut hers off but kept it in her grip. They looked at each other. The look of inundated uneasiness swelled Tyler's face, hinting at what he was thinking.

"Oh, don't say it," Lois sighed.

"We have to go check it out, Lois."

"Yeah, but—goddamn it!" she grunted.

The last glimpses of Mike's taillights faded into the darkness, symbolizing they were on their own.

Tyler sprinted over to his cruiser. "Follow me."

Lois' short response that was intended to be filled with sarcasm was overwhelmed by a sudden roar from above followed soon after by a humming noise that started from behind. Tyler and Lois stopped short of getting in their cruisers and looked at each other; both just as taken aback from the noise, trying to figure out what it was.

Lights emerged in the sky on the distant horizon. Lois spotted them. "Look!"

Tyler managed to look up as the roar reached its peak. By the time the lights and sound were above them, both realized the noise was coming from a helicopter. At first, the darkness from the night hid everything but the flashing lights on the chopper, but as it closed in, they were able to see how low it was.

The humming of the blades spinning in the sky echoed throughout the area, waking many of the remaining citizens who still lived on that part of town. As fear trickled down his spine, Tyler kept his eyes on the dark colored helicopter as it closed in.

Lois pressed her hands over her ears as it flew overhead. "Jesus Christ!"

The humming made Tyler's ears pop, but he kept still and watched as the helicopter glided by and flew in the direction of the outskirts of town before it suddenly banked left, away from the center of town and toward the direction of the woods, allowing silence to return to the area.

Lois lowered her hands from her ears. "What the hell was that?'

Tyler stuttered. "I—I don't know, but look where it's heading."

Lois glanced back at the blankness of the sky and in the direction of where the helicopter had disappeared, quickly realizing it was heading straight toward the area of the cemetery.

"Come on," Tyler jumped into his cruiser.

Lois wasn't far behind. In synth, they turned the sirens back on and started the same direction of the woods as curious residents on the streets peered out their windows.

CHAPTER 3

The humming noise from the helicopter echoed throughout the town, waking even those on the far side of town, but James Nelson was not one of those people. Instead of sleeping at that late hour of the night, like many of his classmates were, James chose to spend his time looking out of the telescope in his bedroom window and wondering about life on other planets.

James had been in special needs for most of his school life. Unlike some of his other classmates in the special need classes—or slow classes as many on the football team would say, James, on the outside, appeared normal. He was not wheelchair bound, nor did he need assistance for the physical demands of life; his disabilities were more internal than external.

He had a hard time reading, but he could keep up with the subtitles on when he watched T.V. He struggled with words, but not ideas. He couldn't spell but could lay out an entire movie plot in one breath. It got to the point where some teachers thought he was faking it, but his grades in Math and Science proved them wrong.

James had been labeled a lot of things, but when it came to movies, books, and ideas about space, the only way to describe him was extraordinary. He could barely remember what he had for breakfast two days ago but could remember every single line of dialogue from the book he was reading or every quote from a movie he was watching. His mind worked in a way that made him extraordinarily brilliant and incredibly debilitated at the same time.

When he was younger, it was movie and books that kept his mind occupied, but as he grew older—and finally moved out of the small bedroom downstairs and up to the roomier attic—he found himself looking past the T.V. screen because of the large window that overlooked the street.

Like every other street in Hunting, Merrin Street—his street—also had decaying houses scattered about, only just not as many as other streets scattered around town. The lack of humanity meant less noise and less light to hide the sky. And the first night James stayed up there, he realized what he had been missing for the first part of his young life.

The Nelson house was in the area where many of the wealthier residents lived. Nearly every house on the dead-end street was two stories high with a large backyard, but James' house was the only one to have three stories with a large picture window in the dead center of the top floor, which overlooked the nearby mountains and woods.

When his parents bought the place—right around his third birthday—the neighborhood was full. But, as time passed and more and more people left for either nearby cities or Sunbelt states, all but a handful still live on the street. Many of the kids in the neighborhood that James had become friends with were the first to leave, which left him all alone. It wasn't hard for his parents—Jack and Molly—to see that the lack of friends was difficult for him to process.

Desperate to lift his spirits, Jack and Molly decided to use the bonus Jack had gotten from working overtime at the factory on a telescope for James. James was a massive fan of sci-fi movies and had dozens of boxes filled with Star Wars comics, so they figured the telescope would both keep him busy and allow his mind to roam wild.

It did the trick.

Every night as soon as it got dark, James would shut off the T.V. and spend most of the night peering out through the eyepiece. Because he was so high up, he was able to see everything; he even had a good view of Bridget Ashlee's bedroom. Bridget was one of the most popular cheerleaders in the school, and everyone wanted to date her, including James, but despite the excellent view of her bedroom where he would be able to watch her change every night, his attention was focused on the stars, although there were a few times where the temptation was borderline overwhelming. The focus on the stars and surrounding woods allowed him to see everything from shooting stars and large hawks high up in the sky searching for prey.

At first, he would only spend an hour or two looking through the telescope before going back to watching T.V. or even falling asleep when he could, but as time went by, he found himself using it later and later into the night. Staying up late allowed him to see many shooting stars and it also allowed him to see the lights from the facility off in the far distance.

At first, he thought it was nothing more than the city lights from Pittsburg. But once he realized that there was no way it could be because of how far out Pittsburg was, he grew curious. His father dismissed the lights to be nothing without providing a good reason for what they exactly were. Not satisfied with the answer he got, James continued to hammer away at getting a reasonable explanation, but when his father threatened to take the telescope away, he let it be.

As time passed by, he started coming up with theories as to what the light was. His original thought that it was a couple of cars on the abandoned road behind the cemetery, but the light was too bright to be coming from just a group of vehicles. After giving it much thought, he concluded that the lights were coming from a UFO. It seemed like the logical reason and explained why the warning of staying out of the woods was so enforced.

The UFO conclusion nested in his mind and became an obsession for him. He started collecting books and printing out every webpage he found about unidentified flying objects and their origins. When he tried explaining his theory to his parents, they once again dismissed him, saying it was all in his imagination. He kept firm to his belief to the point where it would become a shouting match every time the subject was brought up. Therefore, he decided to keep his ideas to himself.

That night was no different. When he heard the soft humming approaching from the East, he spun the telescope in that direction in time to spot the large black object swoop in and start to descend into the woods near the lights. It wasn't the first time he had heard such a noise, but it was the first time he saw what was making it.

A light turning on in Bridget's room caught James' attention, sending a spike of adrenaline through his underweighted body. He lowered the telescope down to her window just as she stepped up to the window and started looking up in the sky. James concluded that she must've been woken from the humming vibration. And if the noise was loud enough to wake her up, it was loud enough to wake up others.

A sudden rush of panic combined with a bolt of energy struck him as he watched the helicopter slowly lower into the countryside. He kept still, frozen in place as if he was unsure how to react. Part of him wanted to run downstairs, pound on his parent's bedroom door and demand an apology while another part felt fearful of the thought that something *really* was out there in the woods.

He kept his eyes in the telescope and focused on the descending object until it faded into the trees and disappeared.

The truck was quiet as Mike and Kimberly drove down Henniker Street. Mike kept still with both hands on the wheel while Kimberly sat stoically with her hand tucked between her legs, keeping her eyes on the darkness outside the passenger window. Neither of them said a word since they were ordered to head home.

Kimberly felt the truck picking up speed as they headed down the old abandon street. A street once filled with little shops and a diner was now a hallowed out ghost town. Many of the shops had been torn down, and the restaurant had been completely deserted. To many in the outside world, it would seem strange that a street so close to downtown would be so empty, but those who lived in town were used to it.

The street was divided up with the shops and diner on one end and large suburban houses on the other. Many of the homes were large, grand, and majestic, and yet, all of them were empty and rotting away; nearly all of them had even been condemned, too. It was just another reminder of how much had changed in the town within the last twenty years.

When the truck started to shake from driving over the cracked and pothole-filled street, Kimberly looked at the speedometer. The speed limit was twenty-five. Mike was closing in on forty. She looked at him.

"Mike, slow down."

Mike neither lowered his speed nor acknowledged her; he stayed focus on the road. The silent rejection struck a nerve in Kimberly.

"Mike, goddamn it!" she began.

"What?" he shouted, taking his eyes off the road.

"Slow down; you're going to fast."

"You heard Lois and Benton!"

"Yeah, we need to get home, not killed on the way there!"

Looking away from the road, Mike looked into her eyes. Kimberly was always one to put up a good front to cover what she was really thinking, but Mike could see the worry behind her deep brown eyes just as she could see his.

He took his foot off the gas and looked back at the road, taking in a deep breath. "I'm sorry. I didn't mean to get pissy. I just…I don't know what to think or even say right now."

Kimberly agreed. The night had changed so drastically; it was hard to get a sense of what they were going to do next. Because the two had been together for so long, she knew how vulnerable Mike could get when he gets nervous. She could see how unsure he was, and she felt an obligation to try and make him feel at ease like he'd done for her on many occasions.

She slid her hand across the bucket seat and took hold of his.

"It'll get better once we're home. We can figure out the rest there."

Her words were simple, but they were enough to ease the tension building inside him. He lifted her hand up and gently kissed it as they made eye contact. She smiled and turned back to the road.

"Watch out!"

Mike turned back to the windshield, but by the time he thought about jamming on the breaks, the front of the truck reached the figure in front of them and barreled into it, sending a large dark shadow across the hood and slamming up and over the windshield.

As the figure slid up the front of the car, the windshield on the driver side cracked, and the top of the roof slightly caved, revealing the force of the hit. The dark figure disappeared into the darkness behind them as it slid across the bed of the truck and rolled off onto the cracked pavement with a loud thump.

"Hold on!" Mike shouted as he clung onto Kimberly's hand and slammed on the breaks with both feet.

Because of the speed, they were going; by the time the truck came to a complete stop, they were at least three hundred feet from the impact zone. The truck wobbled from the forceful stop, rocking the two teenagers inside.

Everything became silent. The echo of the tires screeching disappeared into the air, leaving nothing but the sound of the engine running and Kimberly breathing intently as she would typically do during sex. Mike was also breathing heavily but slightly more measured.

"Are you okay?" he finally asked.

Kimberly let go of his hand and started feeling her body for anything that felt unusual. She shook her head. "I think so. Are you?"

"Yeah, I'm okay," Mike replied before looking up at the caved in roof above him. "Shit."

When she was sure that she was okay, Kimberly straightened herself and looked out the back windows of the truck. Nothing but darkness could be seen. The street light they had passed was on, but the light was mediocre at best.

"I can't see anything," she said.

Mike sighed as his eyes moved from the roof to the cracked windshield. "My fucking truck."

Kimberly slapped him on the arm.

"Ow!"

"Really? We might've just hit somebody, and you're worried about your truck?"

Mike shrugged off her criticism. "I don't think we hit somebody."

"How do you know that?"

Mike pointed. "Look around. Nobody is here. You know this area is a ghost town."

Kimberly kept her eyes on the darkness that surrounded the outside of the truck. While Mike was uninterested with finding out what they hit and even brought up the idea of driving off, Kimberly answered by opening the glove box, pulling out the flashlight and stepping out of the truck.

The passenger door opening spun Mike's head in her direction. "Oh, come on, Kimberly!"

"We have to look," she shot back.

"We've done enough investigating for one night. Look what happened last time!"

She turned and looked at him. "I'm going to look; you can either go with me or stay in the truck."

She slammed the truck door before he had the chance to respond. Not liking the idea of her being by herself, Mike rolled his eyes, accepted that he was going to lose the fight and got out of the truck. While Kimberly started walking toward the back of the truck, Mike walked to the front to inspect the damage.

With her flashlight beam aimed down the road, she continued even though she heard Mike's swearing upon his own inspection. Her mind was so set on figuring out what it was they hit, she didn't reply; all she wanted to do was figure out what they could've hit.

Mike's eyes slid down along the truck. The more he looked, the more frustrated he became. Aside from the roof and windshield being damaged, both the hood and driver side fender were beaten to shit with scratches all along it that were deep enough to reach the metal below the paint.

He threw his hands in the air. "Great. Just great."

He was about to head to the back of the truck and regroup with Kimberly to tell her about the damage—even though he knew she wouldn't care—when he stopped and noticed a large black spot on the front of the truck.

Huh, what the hell is that? Oh, so help me God, if that's something that fell off, I'm going to be pissed. It was hard for him to make out what exactly it was, which forced him to take out his cellphone and turn the flashlight app back on.

Fear trickled down his spine as his mouth hung open in dismay. He started taking a few steps back, trying to grasp the gravity of the situation they found themselves in. With his heart pounding in his chest cavity, he kept the flashlight still.

The black spot was a large splatter of blood that ran from the front grille and straight up to the hood. The nighttime sky made it difficult to see just how much there was, but the flashlight was bright enough to reveal all he needed to know.

Blood started drizzling on the ground, creating a horrific dripping sound as it crashed onto the cracked pavement. Hyperventilating, he lowered his cellphone and ran to the back of the truck as fast as he could. "Kimberly!"

She didn't reply. Instead, she kept her flashlight point down the road as Mike's footsteps approached from her right side. She turned frantically when she spotted him from the corner of her eye.

"What?" she asked.

Out of breath, he replied, "Blood. The whole front of the truck is covered in blood."

"I told you!"

He grabbed her hand. "Come on, let's get out of here."

She pushed his clammy grip away. "We can't."

Mike looked around, spotting nothing on the dark empty street. "We can. No-one is around."

She spun her head around. "Yeah, and what if we hit someone? That's called hit and run, Mike."

"We'll tell Benton and Lois when they get to the house."

She nodded quickly. "No, we can't do that."

He grunted in frustration. "Why do you always have to fight me?"

"Because I don't wanna be in jail before I finish high school!"

Trying to remain calm, Mike took in a few deep breaths, but was unable to stay silent, even though he knew an argument would follow. "I love you, Kim. I really do, but you can be so dramatic sometimes."

Kimberly scoffed. "What's that supposed to mean?"

And just as Mike predicted, an argument pursued. With each response, their voices grew louder and echoed throughout the abandon street. Glaring at one another with each response, neither backed down and kept focus on who would get the last word while completely ignoring the man standing in the middle of the road about a hundred yards away.

"I'm not leaving until I find out what we hit," she firmly said.

Knowing when to walk away before he said anything he would regret later on, Mike put his hands up and took a few steps back.

"Okay, fine," he began. "If you want to go looking around, then, by all means, go for it. I'll be in the truck."

Kimberly scoffed as Mike turned and looked down the street. "You know what, Mike? Let me tell you something—"

She paused, waiting for Mike to look at her, but he kept his widening eyes in the direction of the opposite end of the street. Frustration emerged in her voice. "Um, hello? Mike?"

He didn't reply. Instead, he pointed.

"What?" she asked.

He started breathing heavily. "Look."

Picking up on the sense of absolute dread on Mike's face, she lowered her head slowly and carefully turned around. She gasped as a sensation of numbness emerged within her thighs.

Standing beneath the only working street light on the road, the bulky size stranger stood tall, keeping just as still as Mike and Kimberly. While the street light was bright enough to show his outline, it was ineffective too reveal anything else. The only thing they could see from their distance was his outline and something being held by his right hand.

The night air came to a standstill, leaving nothing more than an emptiness on the empty street. There were no headlights or streetlights in sight; all they had for light were their flashlights and the one working streetlight.

While Mike tried to figure out what the object was in the man's hand, Kimberly focused on his head. It was incredibly difficult for her to make out, but it almost looked like the man was wearing an Elmer Fudd hat with two large, what appeared to be ears standing up—a deer's ears. The awkwardness of whatever the man had on only added to the razor-sharp tension.

"Jesus," she began before tilting her head to Mike's direction. "Did we hit him?"

Mike nodded quickly. "We couldn't have. No man would be back on his feet from getting hit as hard as that."

She turned back to the street. "What the hell is on his head?"

"I can't tell," he whispered while keeping his eyes on the stranger down the road.

She didn't reply, the overwhelming sense of horror encapsulated her body to the point where she felt like she was unable to move let alone speak. Her pulse raced.

"Why the hell would someone just be standing out here like this?"

Mike shrugged. "How the hell should I know?"

Fearful, Kimberly remained still as the night air sent shivers down her. She started feeling lighten-headed; almost as if the sight of the stranger was too much for her to grasp because of all the stress from earlier in the evening.

The wind picked up, allowing the chill of the air to blow in both their faces—a sure sign that winter was on the doorstep of the industrial Midwest. As the wind started to move, both Mike and Kimberly began shivering while the stranger down the road remained still.

Trying to use the cover of darkness to hide his actions, Mike took a step closer to Kimberly to get her attention. "Kim, we need to get out of here…"

Keeping her eyes on the outline of the person, she swallowed hard, finally realizing that Mike had been right all along. "Yeah."

When Mike heard her reply, the overwhelming silence grew even quieter. He turned around, checking to see how far he was from the truck before looking back at the man. Kimberly, not taking her eyes off whoever was standing in the street, tried to discreetly take a step back.

The man charged.

"Go!" Mike shouted. "Go, get in the truck!"

They rushed back to the truck.

Kimberly raced for the passenger door only to find it locked. She yanked on the door handle. "It's locked! Mike, it's locked!"

Tripping over his untied shoelace, Mike stumbled and felt his keys slip through his fingers. "Shit."

Kimberly—despite her fears, looked back in the direction of the street. She cried out in horror.

Coming straight at her, the man ran, almost at lightning speed, like the person chasing her in her darkest nightmares would. The stranger started running faster, closing the gap between them by half within a few seconds.

Kimberly yanked on the door handle.

"Mike!" she screeched.

Trembling in fear, Mike bent down and picked up the keys as the footsteps of the stranger approaching started getting louder.

"Mike!"

Unlocked the driver-side door as quick as he could, Mike pulled open the door and pressed the button that unlocked the passenger door. When the lock popped up, Kimberly flung open the door and jumped inside at the same time as Mike.

The footsteps grew louder.

Mike closed his door.

The footsteps got louder.

Kimberly slammed her hand down on the lock. "Go, Mike! Go!"

Mike shoved the key into the ignition.

Kimberly looked in the side mirror.

Mike started the truck.

The man reached the truck.

The engine roared, sending a loud grunt into the sky as the working headlight lit up the road.

Kimberly grabbed hold of the handlebar on the door as she felt the truck get into gear—a large hand smashed through the window and reached inside.

Screaming as shards of glass fell on her, the man stepped up to the side of the truck and started to grab at her.

"No! No!"

The man's grip was overwhelmingly firm as he clawed at her clothing, stretching it to the point of ripping once he grabbed a hold of it.

She struggled to get free and started to lose consciousness when she felt the man starting to pull her out of the truck, when flashing lights lit up the inside of the truck, illuminating the interior, and the strangers face in a brilliant strobe effect.

The man let go, using the hand to shield his face from the flashlight strobe effect. When she felt his hand pull away, Kimberly sprung up and prepared to strike her assailant when the stranger suddenly lowered his hand, revealing dark brown eyes behind the deerskin flesh over his face. She screamed as the eyes glared at her with uncontrollable hatred that would haunt her dreams for years to come.

The man stepped back up to the truck.

Kimberly lunged forward, striking the man in the face with her right fist, knocking the attacker onto the ground.

"Go, Mike! Go goddammit!"

Mike slammed his foot on the gas pedal and sent them flying back onto their seats and down the road.

The lights could be seen in the woods even before Tyler pulled onto the road that lead to the cemetery. He slowed his patrol car down to almost a crawl as he spun the wheel to the entrance of the cemetery. Lois—following her partners lead—followed right behind, keeping the front of her patrol car only inches away from the back end of his.

Once he was on the road and his wheel was straightened, he glanced up in the rearview mirror spotting Lois—more particularly the look of worry as the taillights to his car lit her face up in a haunting red tint. He reached for his radio. "Hey."

"Yeah," she responded instantly.

"You alright?"

He watched her take a deep breath from the rearview mirror.

"Yeah, I'm fine. Just trying to figure out what the hell is going on here."

Once he got her response, he accelerated on the gas, sending his car jerking forward—a little faster than he intended—toward the bright lights at the far end of the cemetery.

They were still too far away for him to make anything out past the lights, but it was obvious, the lights were too bright and too high up to be just headlights—they were something else. Something bigger.

Keeping his eyes forward, Tyler placed the radio down and drew his service revolver. Even though the situation called for it, he was hesitant at first. Not even the gift of time had been able to wipe away the horror and regret he still carried with him from last time he was forced to use it.

The cold dead weight of the deadly weapon pierced his hand with a stinging cold sensation as thoughts of him having to use it again replayed like a bad memory he couldn't shake. Once it was out, instead of taking the safety off like he was trained to do, he chose to leave it on and placed it next to him on the seat before picking up the radio again.

"Stay right behind me," he ordered.

"Copy that."

Neither one said it, but it was clearly apparent that both were well outside of their comfort zone. They had each other's company, which was very much welcomed, but they couldn't shake the feeling like they were over their heads no matter how hard they tried resist.

At first, Tyler started to wonder if the attack on Mike and Kimberly had anything to do with Faith Rothacker. While the name was new to the area, many outside the Rust Belt knew her name and reputation as a rising leader in the mafia trade up in New England. Reports had come down from New Hampshire that she was planning on expanding her business interest and the Rust Belt seemed like the most logical place for her to do so. That idea stayed in his mind as the lights in front of him drew closer. But it slowly dissolved the more he approached the scene in front of him.

Tyler was still a couple of hundred feet away, but he was able to make out that the light was coming from a massive spotlight like the ones used on the football field on the other side of town. It was complete with a trailer hitch and large black wheels beneath it. The brightness of the lights snatched his attention first, but it was the multiple military Humvees and soldiers walking about that left him in disarray.

"What in the hell?" he muttered to himself.

He flipped his police lights on, lighting up the forest with a Florissant red and blue tint. Lois did the same. Her lights joined in synch with Tyler's as the siren from her car bleeped twice, getting the attention of Tyler and everyone in the forest.

Jamming on the breaks, Tyler put the cruiser in park, grabbed his pistol and got out of the car. When Lois saw the driver side door fling open, she did the same; only instead of using her service revolver, she grabbed the mounted shotgun resting beside the laptop displayed in front of the passenger seat.

Tyler extended his pistol and aimed. "Police freeze!"

Lois cocked the shotgun and also aimed at the dark shadows in front of them, but both broke a sweat when suddenly nearly a dozen men dressed in military uniforms drew their assault rifles and aimed back.

Lois' pulse began to uptick. *Oh, shit.*

The blinding light blasting directly into their eyes made it difficult to see, but both were able to see the large number of people—and weapons in front of them. Well out-numbered, Tyler and Lois turned to each other. Both had the same blank expression on their face, but nevertheless, stayed true to their oaths as officers. They stood their ground.

"Drop your guns and get your hands in the air!" Lois ordered.

A chuckle echoed from the nearest soldier until the soldier felt a tap on his shoulder.

"It's alright," Sam Rainey said.

Dylan L'Heureux turned to Sam. "You sure?"

Uneasy about the situation, Dr. Sam Rainey didn't have to think long for his response. "What're we going to do, kill a couple police officers?"

L'Heureux—also feeling unsettled—agreed with him.

"How many are there?" Sam followed up.

"Looks like just two," a voice answered off to the side.

Sam sighed. "Alright, let me handle this."

"You got it, sir," L'Heureux said before he turned to his fellow soldiers. "At ease!"

L'Heureux's voice echoed into the night like a howl, loud enough for all to here, including Tyler and Lois, who continued to remain still and keep their weapons at bay. They glanced briefly at each other when they saw the soldiers lower their weapons.

"It's alright," Sam's voice said over L'Heureux's voice as he squeezed his body through the space between him and another soldier.

Putting his hands up to ease the tension, Sam stepped out in front of the line of soldiers; his white surgeon coat stuck out like a sore thumb amidst the surrounding darkness on all sides. Tyler aimed at him.

"Not a step further!" Tyler ordered.

Sam stopped short of another step, keeping his hands at bay. The spotlight behind him casted a deep shadow over his face that the patrol headlights were unable to offset, which kept Sam's face—along with his identity—in the dark.

Lois remained still, keeping the shotgun drawn on Sam. Tyler did the same but started questioning if they were really in danger. Sam held his hands up and looked at Tyler.

"Hello, Tyler."

Lois' head snapped in Tyler's direction.

Tyler didn't acknowledge her. Instead, he stepped away from the cruiser and took a few steps forward. The blank expression on his face confirmed that he was confused.

He kept his gun drawn. "Who the hell are you?"

While the steps were not enough for Tyler to make out Sam's face, they were enough to reveal more of an outline of him.

Another spotlight kicked on behind Sam, sending a bright beam of neon light blasting into Tyler's direction. The brightness was strong enough to force Lois to turn away, but instead of looking away, Tyler kept his attention forward and slowly started to realize who he was looking at. *No…it can't be. It's impossible.*

Years had gone by since they last spoke and a decade had passed since they last saw each other, but not even that lapse of time was enough to fade the memories they once shared as kids.

"Sam…?"

A large Humvee pulled up behind Tyler's patrol car, forcing Lois to take her eyes off Sam and the dozens of soldiers behind him.

Sam took a step forward. "Yeah. It's me."

A soft chuckle hiccupped through Tyler; he was clearly confused about what was happening and how to even react. He lowered his gun slowly once he realized he was aiming it at his best friend came to him.

Lois spotted the action from the corner of her eye. "Tyler."

He looked at her over his shoulder. "It's okay."

"You sure?"

Tyler turned back to Sam, making eye contact with him again. "Yeah, I'm sure."

Sam watched as Tyler holstered his rifle before looking back at L'Heureux. "Scout the area, but make sure no one wanders off to far. We need to stay close."

"You got it, Rainey," L'Heureux said before turning to his military squad. "Let's move out, boys! Let's go!"

Following their captions orders, the soldiers scattered into the woods instantly, resuming their search. The abrupt exit of their presence left Sam, Tyler, and Lois alone with their thoughts.

Tyler and Sam made eye contact again. Sam nodded. "Been a long time."

Tyler kept his guard up. "Yeah, it is...what the hell is this?"

Lois asked the same thing when she walked up to them only with a little saltier language Tyler spotlight used.

"I'll get to that, but first, I need to know how many other officers are with you?"

Tyler and Lois remained looked at each other.

"What?" Lois asked.

"How many other officers are on duty with you?" Sam rephrased.

"Just Lois and I," Tyler answered.

"You sure?" Sam asked, clearly pressing for confirmation.

"Yeah," Tyler reaffirmed. "Why?"

"Who are you?" Lois quickly added.

Sam stopped shy of speaking. He hesitated.

Tyler and Sam had been friends since pre-school. Back then, they knew every single thing about each other—they even knew how each other reacted on many occasion. Neither of them believed in fantasy or the supernatural, but during that time when they were young boys, the way they seemed to interact without muttering a word resembled a type of psychic ability to communicate. It may have been a very long time since they last spoke, but on that fateful night, through all of the chaos, those old familiar feels came rushing back.

"Somethings wrong," Tyler blundered out. "Somethings *really* wrong and you're not telling us."

The look on Sam's face as he glared into Tyler's deep blue eyes revealed that he hadn't forgotten about their close bond and gift, either. It was apparent that he wanted to break away from the situation and take Tyler off to the side so they could catch up—Tyler resisted the same urge—but the looming danger overpowered that from happening.

Sam wiped the sweat from his forehead. "Look, its best, for the both of you, if you just stayed out of this."

"No!" Lois said. "This is our town—our job—to protect."

Tyler agreed, forcing Sam's hand. He sighed, clearly he was getting nowhere with the two stubborn officers. He thought about pushing back, but since it was their jurisdiction, he felt his authority was limited at best.

He sighed. "Can you keep a secret, Lois?"

Lois quickly snapped her head in his direction. "What?"

He repeated his question.

Caught off guard, she turned to Tyler, who nodded at her.

"It's alright," he said softly.

She looked back at Sam. "Yes, I can keep a secret."

Believing her answer, took a deep breath.

"Follow me then."

CHAPTER 4

After putting on the aluminum foil helmet he made a number of years ago in science class, James Nelson returned to the telescope and peered through the eye scope. The lights in the woods had disappeared, leaving behind nothing but a darkness so thick, not even the tips of the trees could be made out.

What the heck? James muttered to himself out loud. *They were just there! The lights were just there!*

He didn't have a clock near him, but he was sure he couldn't have been gone longer than a minute or two. His aluminum helmet was always in the same place—on the bottom drawer of the nightstand next to his bed—so there was no need for him to go searching for it. A sense of annoyance took control of the young boy.

This hadn't been the first time he had lost the lights after walking away from the telescope. In fact, this was just another brick to a pattern that he slowly started to comprehend. The disappointment began taking over that feeling of annoyance as he moved the telescope back and forth, holding onto the hope that he'd be able to find the ambient illumination again.

James, you stupid idiot, the voice echoed in his head. Only it wasn't his voice. It was the voice of Zach Dempsey—the bully of Hunting High School. *You're such a loser! I bet your mum and Dad regret even having you. You're nothing but a piece of shit loser.*

The voice brought James on the verge of tears, just like they had when Zach said that to him the first time. In his kind heart, he knew they weren't true—he knew his Mom and Dad loved him very much, but the words were difficult to overcome. Especially given that he was in special education classes and knew that was part of the reason why Zach picked on him.

James' search turned up empty. The woods were encapsulated with pure blackness. Nothing but the pale moonlight casting down on the trees was in sight. He sighed, shaking his head before squeezing down on the aluminum helmet.

The light in Bridget's room had gone out, too. While he only looked briefly, it was easy for him to come to the conclusion that his crush of three years had dismissed the noise as nothing or the remaining echo of a bad dream she had awoken from. The view of both lights being out cast a feeling of isolation on James, feeling more alone than ever.

He thought about going to bed. He could feel the tiredness building up within him, putting James on the verge of sleepy. But, he wasn't ready to call it quits just yet. In one last ditch effort, he scanned the telescope back and forth thinking this time he would find the lights.

Nothing.

Nothing even close to resembling lights.

God…dammit! I knew I shouldn't have left. James, you idiot! Zach's voice returned. *Oh well. Time for bed.*

In a brief act of anger, he took his helmet off and threw it across the room. He would've shouted, but didn't in fear of waking his parents who were just below him. He rose from the metal chair he stole from the shed out back long ago and walked back over to his bed. He spun the alarm clock around and looked at the time blinking at him.

It was the time of night he dreaded—the time where it felt like the night stood still; almost as if no matter how much time had passed; the sun would never come up again. This added another layer of grievance to his already flustered mind. Knowing there was nothing he could do, he began stripping out of his blue shirt and grey shorts, which desperately needed to be washed—and prepared to hop back in bed.

A sound emerged.

He stopped halfway into taking his shirt off and turned back to the window.

The sound was growing louder; much louder.

He dropped the shirt out of his grip and bounced back over to the window and stuck his eye through the scope once more.

The sound was coming from the street. He turned in the direction of the noise and spotted a single light heading straight up the road and right in his direction. The closer the headlight came, the more James realized what it was.

It's Mike…yeah, that's Mike and his truck coming up the road. Or at least it sounds just like Mike's truck. But it can't be. Mike doesn't get home this late.

He kept his eye on the road, even looking up from the eyepiece from time to time with the suspicion that it was Mike's truck. Lord knows he's heard the sound of the loud exhaust plenty of times. His parents even filed a complaint because of the noise. Out of fear, that was one of the reasons why he tried to avoid Mike when he would see him around the neighborhood every chance he got.

His suspicions about the approaching vehicle proved to be true. When the vehicle pulled into the driveway two houses down from him, next to Bridget's house, he was sure it was Mike. He turned back to the clock, double checking on the hour of the night.

It is that late. Why is Mike just coming home now? And why does he only have one headlight?

The question stayed with him as he kept his eye in the scope, watching, trying to see what was going on.

The truck was as close to the garage door as it could be without hitting it when Mike put it in park and shut off the engine, allowing silence to overtake the once wealthy street. Wasting no time, both he and Kimberly sprung out of the cabin, slamming the doors as soon as their feet hit the ground.

Because his parents were out of town, his two-story house was dark— not even the nightlights in nearly every room of the house could be seen through the windows. Typically, when it got dark out, Mike's Mom would flip on the porch light just before she went to bed, but because he was more focused on seeing Kimberly, the thought to turn it on before he left didn't even cross his mind.

He raced around the other side of the truck to Kimberly; his approaching footsteps spooking her. "You okay?"

"Yeah, I'm fine."

He took her hand. "Come on, let's get inside."

He started for the door but stopped when he felt Kimberly resist.

"What?" he asked.

She remained quiet as she stood motionless. The light from the moon on the driveway was dim at best, but it was enough for him to see that something got her attention. Her hand slid out of his grip, allowing her to start toward the back of the truck.

"What?" he asked.

She took in a large breath of air. "You don't smell that?"

He shrugged. "Smell what?"

Before she answered, Mike watched as she reached into her back pocket and pulled out the flashlight that had kept them company all night. She turned it on and aimed the beam down to the pitch black pavement.

He walked over to her. "Come on, Kim. I've had enough of this playing detective for one night."

Rolling her eyes—even though she felt the same way—she reached the back of the truck, keeping the beam of light fixated on the tailgate. The smell was growing stronger with each step she took, and by the time she got to the back, the smell was overpowering to the point where it started giving her a headache. But, she stayed persistent, and when she realized the smell was coming from beneath the truck, she dropped to her knees and took a peek under. "Oh, shit."

Mike walked over. "What?"

She pointed. "Look for yourself."

Trying to remain calm, he followed Kimberly's lead and got down to his knees. "Now what?"

Because of how bright the flashlight was, and how strong the smell was, it wasn't difficult for Mike to see what Kimberly was looking at. There was a crack in the gas tank—a decent size crack that sliced across the lower half of the tank, which was allowing a constant stream of gas to come flooding out.

"Goddamn it! How the hell did that happen?" he shouted without thinking about how his voice could easily awake the neighbors.

"Shh!" Kimberly ordered in a whisper. "It must've been when we hit those potholes on Henniker Street or hit…" she trailed off.

Mike wiped the sweat from the forming age lines on his forehead. "God, could this night get any worse?"

Staying focused on the crack in the gas tank, rather than paying attention to Mike standing back up, Kimberly watched the gas drizzled out before she slowly started moving the flashlight down to the freshly tarred driveway and started following the small, yet consistent trail. Her eyes followed not long behind the LED glow.

The stream of fuel was heading down the driveway and straight toward the road. In the dark, the fuel looked like nothing more than a small flow of water during a gentle rain, the type of rain that would create a day of lying around the house and watching movies all day, which Kimberly liked to do, but the smell only seemed to be getting thicker. She started coughing.

Mike patted her on the shoulder. "Come on, Kim. We need to get inside."

Hesitantly, Mike's words resonated, forcing her back on her feet. She knew he was right, though she would never admit it to him out of fear it might get to his head and start to have him think that she was beginning to become less independent.

She raced toward the front door of the Eaten's house and stepped inside the moment Mike slid his house key into the doorknob and unlocked it. Any sense of security she had after the sound of the front door getting locked back up was overtaken by fear.

Inside the large house was just as, if not darker than what it looked like on the outside. Granted, some of the blinds in the front windows of the living room that overlooked the bit of grass in front of the mailbox were opened enough for cracks of moonlight to come in, but it was less than enough to feel at ease. She started searching for the nearby lamp—a light from above the staircase suddenly flickered on.

"Jesus!" she screamed, her heart resuming its intense pumping from where it left off back on the road.

Mike put his hand up. "Sorry, sorry, sorry."

Breathing heavily as if her life depended on it, Kimberly placed her hand over her heart, trying to calm herself. "Goddamn it, Mike."

He stepped away from the light switch and entered the living room. "Here, just take a seat and try to relax."

The large living room consisted of hardwood floors, ambient lighting just above the fireplace, a mounted flat-screen T.V. hanging peacefully on the wall and two citrus pink sofas facing each other—the couches being some of the ugliest yet most comfortable things Kimberly had ever seen. While she was sure they were new, considering everything in the house looked like it was just bought, the design of it was unmistakably a throwback to the old style couches of the early thirties. She was not impressed in the least.

"How the hell am I supposed to relax?" Kimberly blurted out as she flopped down on the nearest pink cushion.

Mike raced over to the windows and pulled down the blinds, trying to create some sort—*any* of security he could get. It proved to be enough even though he was sure more windows around the house were probably open, allowing anyone or anything to peer inside.

"I—I don't know."

Kimberly scoffed, shrugging her shoulders, clearly offended by the answer. "I don't know is not an answer, Mike. Not tonight!"

Mike closed the last blind, keeping his eyes on his truck in the front yard, wishing now more than ever his father would've let him park it in the garage instead of the 65 Mustang, often regarded as his pride and joy. While Kimberly's heart rate started lowering back to average speed, Mike's insecurity was on high alert. Panic was just a couple of heartbeats away.

Kimberly kept her eyes on the back of Mike's head. "Mike? Mike!"

He spun around. "What?" he screamed.

"What're we supposed to do?" she demanded.

"I don't know!" he replied, throwing his hands up. "I don't know! I'm just as scared as you are, okay?"

Mike's voice echoed in the room for a few seconds before evaporating into the walls, allowing the stillness that engulfed the house all night to return with force.

The response wasn't the one she was hoping or expecting to get. It didn't settle her nerves like she wanted, either. It was clear, just by looking into each other's eyes, they we're both equally terrified. She looked away, unable to take in his look of horror any longer.

"I'm…I'm sorry," she said in a voice barely above a whisper.

Feeling guilty for raising his voice, too, he walked over to her and sat down at her side, placing his muscular arm around her torso. She fell into his chest.

"I'm sorry, too."

He felt her take in a deep breath; she was trying to get her breathing under control. Her body was tense, almost like it was the first time they had sex, on that very couch; he could tell she was uneasy. Hoping to reassure her, he began gliding his hand down her brown shoulder-length hair, caressing it with each stroke.

Silence filled the room. Typically, either the T.V. was on because Mike's father was watching a football game or the radio in the kitchen was on because his Mom was cooking—plus she hated overhearing the football games. Mike had gotten used to all the noise. Its absence was noticeable.

His phone suddenly vibrated.

Kimberly—along with her pulse—sprang back up from Mike's lap.

"It's alright, it's just my phone," Mike reassured as he dug into his pocket and pulled it out. He turned on the screen. '*Chicago Police Officer slain laid to rest. Here's a look at his life:*' displayed under a news alert banner. "It's nothing."

Feeling as if she'd never shake off the feeling of paranoia ever again, she pointed to his hand. "Make sure you charge that. The last thing we need is for it to be dead."

"Good idea, I'll be right back."

He stood.

She looked at him. "I'm going with you."

An unattended chuckle squeezed its way out of Mike's belly as he approached the kitchen table and placed it onto the wireless charger. "The charger is just right here. I'm not going anywhere."

She nodded, pleased to see he wasn't leaving her sight. "How long do you think it'll be before we hear back from Tyler and Lois?"

Mike shrugged. "I don't know. Probably not very long. I hope."

Taking Mike's answer with the little optimism she was able to muster, she turned away from him and remained on the couch. With the hall light on, it was only really able to light up the stairwell, leaving much of the living room still in the dark. The foreboding feeling left both of them feeling uneasy. Mike turned the small pink lamp that matched the sofa on in an attempt to brush the dreadful feeling away. The LED bulb took some time to reach its peak of brightness, but even at first, the light was enough to shrink the shadows, leaving only very few in the corners near the kitchen.

The look on Kimberly's face was unlike anything he'd seen before. It was a look that made him feel a bit on edge because she was scared. In all the years they'd known each other, Mike had never seen Kimberly look as frightened as she did at that moment. She was always a strong independent woman, who refused to be like all the other girls at school, but on that night, that independence he discovered on their first date was nowhere in sight. He didn't like that.

He returned to the couch and wrapped his arm around her and squeezed, not hard, but enough for her to know that he loved her. She returned the gesture, placing her hands around his muscle laced stomach, both refusing to let go.

Bright lights pulling up from behind, grabbed Lois' attention, spinning her around to see what the illumination was coming from. Surprise overcame her when she realized it was another military-style Humvee pulling up behind to the entrance of the dirt road.

She rolled her eyes, not because she was annoyed by the presence, she actually didn't mind more reinforcements coming to assist, but because she was sure that it was only a matter of time before the station started getting flooded with calls about large vehicles driving around…if it wasn't happening already. She turned back around and started sprinting to catch up with Tyler and Sam as they approached a grey van parked off to the side of the dirt road which had been cleared of debris.

The darkness that once overtook the road and the surrounding forest was long gone, replaced with dozens of headlights and blue police lights keeping the half a dozen spotlights company. Typically, when he patrolled the area, Tyler would get a knot in his gut from worrying about being on this side of town when it came time to patrol, but no such feeling was in him. Instead, he was more focused on Sam while trying to figure out what was going on.

The trio stepped up to the grey van. The engine was off, but the LED headlights were lit like a Christmas tree. Sam knocked on the side door twice. The door swung open immediately.

"I was just looking for you," Jessica Sowa said in a panicked yet condescending voice. Her eyes shifted to Tyler and Lois when they approached. "Who are they?"

"This is Tyler Benton and…" he trailed off, giving Lois the chance to answer since he didn't know her name.

"Lois Tanguay."

"They're with the Hunting Police Department," Sam explained, trying to avoid getting Jess, even more, wound up than she already was. It was ineffective.

She threw her hands in the air. "Jesus Christ, Sam. What did I tell you about keeping this thing quiet?"

Unlike his partner, Tyler leaned in, hoping to hear the conversation clearer without taking steps closer to make it look obvious. Lois, on the other hand, was less concerned with the conversation and more focused on the interior of the van.

Inside was a state of the art work station complete with a large desk filled with paperwork, a small flat-screen T.V. and an entire wall of below average size monitors illuminating the interior in a clear glow mixed with the abundant red light on the roof just below the work station. It looked like something out of a sci-fi movie. She fell in love with the work station almost immediately.

"Jesus Christ, what the hell did you want me to do? Tell them there's nothing to see and hope they believed me?"

Jess sighed, clearly Sam's attempt to prevent her from getting frustrated fell flat, like it typically did. The expression on her face was hard to judge incorrectly.

"Plus, this *is* their jurisdiction," Sam added. "Having people who know the area might not be a bad thing, either."

The more Sam talked, the more memories flooded into Tyler's mind. Everything from the first day of pre-school to the last day of high school returned, taking him back to a time when life was at its easiest. But, with the memories came their secret—their secret they promised to keep forever. Those fond memories of childhood were overtaken quickly by darkness when thoughts of that promise emerged from the dark corner of his subconscious.

"Fine," Jess sturdily said, bringing Tyler back from memory lane and into reality. "But this is on you. They're your responsibility."

"Fine," Sam agreed before turning to his once close friend as Jess slammed the van door shut, the loud bang echoing into the nearby woods.

He shrugged. "You gonna tell me what's going on here?"

"No, it's probably best you see for yourself," Sam warned. "Follow me."

Confused by Sam's cryptic answer, Lois turned to Tyler. "What the hell does that mean?"

Feeling unwelcomed by Jess—and everyone else around them for that matter, Tyler started following Sam. "I don't know, but stay right behind me."

More Humvees pulled up to the entrance of the cemetery, blocking the entrance. Following their sergeant—Dylan L'Heureux's order, several lower classified ranking privates started taking steps to close off the road the cemetery was on, creating a perimeter around the area.

Had Tyler and Lois remained at their vehicles, they would've seen the significant military presence expand. Instead, they kept close to Sam, hoping he could clarify what they were now a part of. Trying to remain focused on the situation, Sam did his best to ignore Tyler's voice until they were far enough away, so he didn't have to shout.

"What do you know about Quimby Research?" Sam shouted over the sirens of the Humvees and military soldiers shouting back and forth at each other.

The roar of the Humvee's and helicopter above drowned out Sam's voice, forcing him to ask again.

"The name sounds familiar, but I'll be damned if I can remember where I heard it from," Tyler answered as they approached what appeared to be a large metal trailer hitched behand a late model Dodge Ram.

"I've heard about them," Lois responded within a second after Tyler's answer. Even though they were surrounded by noise, Tyler could tell her response wasn't one of enthusiasm, but one of annoyance. Sam picked up on that too. "It's all over the news. They're currently being sued for unlawful practice. They're being called the Nazi's of the twenty-first century."

Her sharp and flustered answer brought Sam to a conclusion that—unlike his childhood best friend Tyler—Lois was much more aware of national news. The emotion in her voice wasn't the first time Sam had heard such passion when it came to the heated topic of Quimby Research.

In fact, her tone was no different from co-workers to the Vice President of the United States when he was cornered several months back. On any ordinary day, he'd get his boxing gloves on and fight back, explaining how much good their research does dispute the small yet incredibly high risk of danger, but on that chilly September night, there was no time. The comparison did get a chuckle out of him, though.

Keeping his fast pace, Sam walked up the two black steps and opened the door to the metal trailer, holding it open long enough for Tyler to grab it. He started up the metal steps, holding the door for Lois, who kept her promise of staying close.

Sam looked away from the wall of monitors and to Lois when he heard her unsuccessfully attempted to close the door. "That door sticks sometimes, so you might have to pull on it to stay closed."

Being the strong woman she was, Lois grabbed hold of the cold metal knob with both hand and with one soft grunt, she slammed the door close—the force of the door sending minor tremors throughout the narrow trailer. Neither men paid attention to it, though. While Sam was focused on logging onto the desktop, resting peacefully on a large shelf that had been converted into a desk, Tyler focused on the interior of the trailer.

Just like the van Jess was in, the trailer was loaded with state of the art technology with everything, but not limited to wireless Bluetooth Internet and cellphone reception to hand print and facial recognition security and software. While the technology had been around for quite some time—in the world of technology anyway, it was the type of futuristic hardware and accessories Tyler and Lois had only seen in the movies.

No such technology could be found anywhere in Hunting, Pennsylvania. Many of the residents—those who were left—still had box T.V.s and cable boxes, including Old Man Claire, who bitched about the changing way of life every time he called Tyler to his house. Hell, even the school buses were camera-less.

Once the computer completed scanning Sam's face and confirmed it was him, all the screens across the wall powered on, lighting up the interior so bright, Tyler and Lois turned away so their eyes could adjust to the neon light. Undeterred to the brightness, Sam sat down in the chair in front of the screens as a hologram of a keyboard illuminated across the surface in a bright blood red.

Tyler's eyes adjusted first, allowing him to look at Sam first. His once best friend forced out a smile and even prepared to engage in what would be their first real conversation in quite some time until Lois looked back at the screen.

"Holy shit, look at this!" the geek in her shouted.

Her reaction—that of an excited child, got another laugh out of Sam. It was a nice change of pace, allowing the tension to dull a bit, but Sam transition back to the task at hand fast.

"Before I go any further, let me stress the point of complete secrecy on this. Under *no* circumstance are either of you allowed to talk about what you're about to see. Is that understood?"

The two officers shook their heads.

"Alright," Sam began before Tyler interrupted him.

"So what the hell is all this?"

Sam cleared his throat. "What if I told you we were on the cusp of the cure for cancer?"

"I'd say you're full of shit," Lois replied before Tyler even had the chance to think about the answer.

Sam sat back in the chair, the backrest squeaking from the pressure and weight he applied to it. "Why do you say that?"

"Because my father was diagnosed with liver cancer. We did every treatment in the book, and he still died less than a year after begin diagnosed," Lois explained as her voice grew louder yet began to crack toward the end. "We were even able to get him into an FDA study, and that didn't work, either."

Sam sympathized, although not with many words. Tyler also remained quiet, but he didn't have to say anything because he was at Lois' side all along during her father's treatment. The story brought back painful memories for both of them, but it also brought back the realization of how resilient Lois was in the face of adversity.

"Why are you asking us this?" Tyler asked, trying to get to the point.

"Because I *do* work for Quimby Research," Sam revealed.

Lois' expression changed drastically as Sam assumed it would. But, rather than let her get a word in, he continued. "And what you've heard about us is true. We conduct experiments, yes, but only after years of research has been done."

Lois shook her head with disgust. She could feel her temper starting to slip away as her face started turning bright pink, mimicking the holographic keyboard in front of Sam. Tyler could see it, too; which is what prompted him to take a few steps closer to her, preparing to try and calm her down for when she erupted.

Her cellphone started to ring inside her pocket before she was able to muster a word. Tyler let out an undetectable sigh of relief. Wrestling in her pocket, Lois answered before the third ring ever had the chance to start.

"Yeah…okay just a second," she lowered the phone from her face and met Tyler's eyes. "It's dispatch. Should I take it or you?"

Because of how small the town—and budget for that matter—was, the town on Hunting shared the same Dispatch office with Rockville—the other once prosperous steel town next door who also was in financial hardship because of the deindustrialization occurring across the Rust Belt. Typically, it was Tyler who would respond since Lois patrolled the opposite side of the town, but because he desperately wanted answers from Sam, he told her to take the call.

"You'll have better reception outside," Sam added.

Because of how quick the situation was, Lois was unable to adequately provide an answer to Tyler or start the dispute about the history of Quimby Research. Instead, despite not wanting to do anything Sam said, she stepped out of the metal trailer and took the call from dispatch, leaving Sam and Tyler to themselves.

Silence took over the trailer, leaving nothing but the sounds of computer hardware and military vehicles outside humming through the isolated walls of the trailer. The two men glared at each other, both with a blank, pale, emotionless look. Neither of them knew what to say; a far cry from where they were as kids.

Tyler tried as hard as he could to find some way of breaking the ice, but no matter how hard he did, he couldn't find the right words to say. Sam felt the same way, but fortunate enough, he was able to end the awkward silence. "So…it's been a long time."

Tyler forced a smile. "Yeah, yeah it has."

The awkwardness was debilitating, but Sam plowed through it. "You know; I've meant to get in touch with you…it's just I've been really…"

"Busy," Tyler finished for him. "Yeah, same here. The days just get away from you, you know?"

"They do," Sam agreed.

They paused.

"How's your mum?" Sam asked without thinking.

The question caught Tyler off guard; his mind was clearly somewhere else. "She's…she's good."

"Good…she still in Hunting or…?"

"Ah, no. She retired and moved to Miami about a year ago."

Sam nodded. A smile emerged on his face—the first in quite a while. Sam had always been a fan of Tyler's Mom. She was, in his opinion, everything that a mother should be; smart, funny, and easy to be around. A far cry from his parents, especially his father.

"Good. Glad to hear."

Even though he was doing everything he could to keep the conversation going and willing to talk about pretty much anything to do so, he was out of ideas to ask about next. The lack of questions and look on Tyler's face proved he felt the same way. Things felt awkward. Awkward in a way that neither of them ever thought they'd be.

Work kept Sam so busy; he barely had time to think, let alone go out and leave the office behind. Sometimes, on nights where he found himself unable to fall asleep, he stared up at the ceiling, completely surprised by how many years had gone by in his life. Tyler also felt the same way when he had free time on his hands, too.

There was much they wanted to say; much they needed to say, but the years as a police officer taught Tyler to leave his personal feelings at the door every time he clocked in and this night was no different.

"So, you gonna tell me what the hell is happening now?" Tyler asked.

Sam rubbed his forehead. A headache was forming in the back of his mind. He tried not to focus on it as best as he could though it was hard to. Instead, he kept focused on his once best friend. His best friend that he was now about to bring into a dangerous situation.

Sam crossed his arms. "Do you remember our secret?"

Dread shot through Tyler's muscular body—a muscular body Lois was dying to see. The expression on his face changed so drastically; it was as if someone had struck him with a two by four. Sam felt the same way but was able to control his feelings like the expert he was.

"Swear to it!" the nine-year-old Sam shouted at him twenty-years ago. "Swear that you'll never say anything. Not to your Mom or Dad and anybody!"

"But—but—"

"But nothing!" Sam screamed at him, grabbing him by the shoulders and began squeezing. "We saw nothing; we know nothing. Understand?"

It was difficult, but he, even at that young age, understood.

"...What about it?" Tyler finally asked.

Sam sat down in the computer chair and spun around to the hologram keyboard. "Have you told anyone about it?"

Confused by the, almost interrogational tone from his friend; or once friend—Tyler was unsure what to say. He paused before answering. "No... why? Why are you asking me all this?"

"You gotta swear to it!" the ten-year-old voice of Sam returned in his mind. "We don't know anything! Anything."

"But, Sam...we can't just leave him in there," the ten-year-old voice of Tyler pushed back. "We need to get help."

"No!" Sam shouted, his voice echoing in front of the then recently abandon steel mill. "You know what will happen if anyone finds out we were in there."

"Bu—But—"

"But nothing."

Sam was carefully listening, taking in Tyler's response. But, he was focused on the computer screen in front of him while pounding away on the table. It was clear, he was looking for something, but what was the question. At least, to Tyler, it was.

A prolonged length of silence—longer and arguably more awkward than any of the others emerged between Tyler's answer and Sam responding. So long, in fact, that he gave thought to stepping out of the trailer and taking the call from Dispatch after all.

Sam rose from the seat. "Here."

Tyler looked up, noticing the snowy white noise filling the screen almost instantly. This—like everything else so far in the night—raised more questions.

"What?"

Sam stepped back from the desk, pulling out the chair as an invite for Tyler to sit. "There's something you need to see."

Tyler approached with caution, keeping his eyes on Sam's emotionally-filled face; the type of look he used to make when he would get yelled at by Tyler's father, Steve Benton, when he was caught doing something that he wasn't supposed too.

"Am I supposed to do something?" Tyler asked.

"All you need to do is watch."

Keeping his guard up—like he had all night, Tyler slowly sat down in the chair and faced the computer monitor in front of him, admiring the hologram keyboard inches away from his elbows. Once in the chair, Sam walked up from behind and typed in the security code, towering over Tyler, and invading his personal space.

The screen beeped twice, faded to black and then transitioned slowly to a shot of a security camera overlooking the front gate of the research facility, guarded by four men dressed in military-style equipment, two of them enjoying a butt.

"What's this?" Tyler mustered out, keeping his attention on the screen.

Sam's cryptic yet meaningful answers remained. "This is what we're dealing with."

CHAPTER 5

Today

Camera 1: Main Gate
5:02

Joe Catalano—the head security officer standing in front of the research lab entrance—finished up nearly half his cigarette when he decided he had enough for one day and flung it on the ground, trying to control the urge before he officially took the first step toward quitting the awful habit. "Wow, is that hard to do."

Surrounding him were his three other parolees working the shift; Tom Burke, Garrett Auclair and Jonah Manning. With the exception of Manning, Catalano was still getting to know Burke and Auclair while trying to keep Jonah—his ex-boyfriend—at bay but not make it visible. Up to that point, his efforts to do so were practical, but he knew it wouldn't last—he could tell by the look in Johan's eyes every time they looked at each other that water under the bridge remained and they would have to address at some point.

"Whoa, never thought I'd see you waste half a butt before," Burke said as he finished up his. "You feeling okay, boss?"

Burke's sarcastic tone—well executed tone—got a laugh out of Catalano.

"Yeah, I'm just getting ready for when I start to quit."

"Ha! I've heard that before. I'll believe it when I see it!" Burke shouted.

Unlike Burke and sometimes even Johan, Garrett Auclair—the newest hire—was more measured in his tone. In a way, he stuck out like a sore thumb compared to the other three who very easily could be described as loudmouths.

"My brother just quit recently, so if you need any support, I'll be happy to help," Auclair offered. "I know it can be a bitch."

"Thanks, Auclair," Catalano said before glancing up at Burke, who had his typical smart-ass smile. "Fuck you, Tommy."

Burke shrugged his shoulders. "What did I do?"

Rather than answering, Catalano, instead, decided to end their break and start to head back inside the off the grid facility. The four men—all under the age of thirty-five, with Catalano being the oldest at thirty-three, followed him back inside.

Camera 2: Lobby
5:09

There were two doors one had to get through in order to get inside—three if you count the seven-foot-high electric fence near the security booth. Both doors were made with the highest grated steel on the market. When the doors sealed shut and the guys were inside, all of them, except for Catalano, felt secure.

All of them were equipped with handcuffs, combat training, and nine-millimeter pistols, which also added to the sense of secureness. Being there the longest, Joe Catalano was always on edge for when the day came where that training and pistol would be needed.

Being the ringleader of security for the nightshifts, his orders from Jessica Sowa herself were as straightforward as could be: 'monitor the lab and under no circumstances allow anyone in 'Section D.' Her voice was loud and menacing—she couldn't have been more serious. And because she was the one that got him the job, he felt obligated to keep her happy.

"Alright, where do you want us, Joe?" Burke asked.

Catalano looked down at his watch.

It was early. Wicked early; a long night was clearly on the horizon. The thought did little to improve his mood. Finally, after Burke asked again, Catalano replied, "You and Auclair, head down to Section C. Johan, you take Section B, and I'll take Section A and the offices. We'll meet back here in about…an hour. Does that work?"

To his surprise, everyone nodded in agreement; even Burke, who typically always bitched about every order he was assigned.

"Okay, then. Make sure your radios are on, though. The last thing I wanna be doing is running around here chasing everyone, alright? Let's get this over with."

Camera C1
5:36

"All I'm saying is sometimes; you need to beat the shit out of some people to keep them in line, you know?" Burke said to Auclair as they walked down the long metal corridor. "It doesn't make me a bad person. I'm actually a really nice guy."

Since he was the newest on the team, Auclair had spent much time training with Catalano and Johan, but this was his first time on his own with Burke. And from everything he heard, he wasn't looking forward to it at all.

'What a piece of shit!' Auclair said to himself. 'Of all the people I have to work with, I get stuck with this asshole.'

Being a survivor of abuse himself, Auclair did his best to keep his emotions and the urge to knock out Burke with one punch to the face at bay. He kept his posture and focused on the approaching double doors they were heading toward while Burke went on about his—clearly flawed—out of work habits.

"You don't talk much, do you?" Burke asked once he realized Auclair didn't seem to be paying much attention to him.

'Not with you, I don't!' he wanted to shout at Burke instead of saying, "No, just trying to take in everything."

"Yeah, well, don't take it all in," Burke's tone changed.

"What do you mean?"

"What have you heard about this place?"

Unsure of what Burke was getting at, Auclair shrugged. "Just that this place is off the books. Why?"

Burke scoffed. "That's all they told you?"

"Yeah...were they supposed to tell me something else?"

Burke and he stopped at the entrance of the double doors; the square windows within the door were dark, indicating whatever was waiting for them on the other side had the element of surprise.

"This is a research lab," Burke began.

"Yeah, I know that," Auclair replied.

"But there's more than research done here...supposedly."

The tone of Burke had drastically changed from when he was bragging about domestic abuse. The transition of tones was so dramatic; it put Auclair on edge as he started to wonder what was behind the doors in front of them.

"So, what else do they do here?"

"Experiments."

"What, like on animals?"

Burke didn't reply, leaving innuendo and uncertainty in the air. Typically, if it as anyone else, Auclair would've dismissed the idea. He passed the age of believing in rumors long ago, but, even though he was still new on the job, he learned early on that Burke wasn't known for his humor.

"Humans?" Auclair whispered as if knowing the cameras were not only watching, but listening.

Burke shrugged then pushed the doors open and walked into the darkness.

Camera C2: Lab
5:41

Following his co-worker into the pitch black on the other side of the door, Auclair kept close, staying right at Burke's side.

"How do you know this?" Auclair asked.

"I don't, and neither do you," Burke said quickly.

With each step, the dim light coming in through the double doors faded, leaving them in a darkness so still and heavy, neither could see their noses in front of their faces. Burke stayed calm and annoyed while Auclair grew worried, feeling as if he was seconds away from something horrible happening, possibly his own death—

Two bangs emerged from the darkness. Auclair jumped. "Christ, what the hell was that?"

Lights blasted on.

White neon lights so bright, it disintegrated the shadows instantly, illuminating the large room in a brilliant white. The incredible light forced Auclair to look away as his eyes adjusted to the light—almost as if he had just woken up from a deep sleep.

Despite the horrible feeling, his eyes adjusted quicker than he thought, allowing him to look back up, only to realize, not just the size of the room, but also what type of room he was in. "Whoa."

He and Burke were in a science lab.

A massive lab so large, it looked like it could've been the back room of a loading dock—it was even tall enough to be a comparable idea. He started walking into the room, his head bobbing all around.

The all-white room was spotless. The smell of sanitizer mixed with other potent cleaning products thickened the air, looming large in the magnificent room. While it did smell fresh—like the cleaning isle did at the Shop An Save the next town over Auclair thought—it was on the verge of overpowering; for he knew if he stayed in the room for an extended period, he would develop a migraine.

"You coming?" Burke's voice bounced off the walls.

Realizing Burke had already made it to the other side of the room; Auclair sprinted over to catch up with him.

The deeper he got into the room, the more he started to notice his surroundings. In the center of the room was a long black marble countertop with multiple microscopes, state of the art computer screens with hologram keyboards, large vials with a green substance in it and surgical instruments neatly organized next to smalls sinks at each of the work stations. The sight reminded him of his old high school science lab, only much more efficient.

"I can't believe this," Auclair said once he caught up with Burke.

"Yeah, it's something alright, but it's nothing compared to what I'm about to show you," Burke grinned.

'Oh, shit,' Auclair thought. 'What is this prick going to do now?'

Burked pulled open a large glass door just in front of them. "Follow me."

"Where we going?"

Burke smiled. "You'll see."

Like before, darkness encased the other side of the door, leaving room for the imagination to run wild. The eerie silence that surrounded the two guards only added to the speculation of what may lie ahead. Everything in Anclair's gut was telling him not to proceed, but before he even got a word out, he found himself already walking into the dark and following Burke's lead.

Camera A5
5:48

Like every other night, Joe Catalano found nothing on his patrol of Section A.

"What a surprise," he muttered in the same flat tone voice he always used no matter what the situation was.

While not the most exciting part of the facility, Catalano was content with patrolling the section because it was always the quietest area and close to the entrance in case the need arose for him to have get out. The need had never come up, but he always felt like the day it would be wasn't far off.

The facility was divided into multiple areas; Section A held the offices of nearly all the staff, including Jess Sowa's office, located at the far end of the hall. Except for her office, all the others had glass doors, allowing those who walked by to get a look inside. But, because of how late in the day it was, much of the sunlight *was faded into the horizon, slowly filling up the offices with dim shadows. The later it got, the harder it was to see in, but Catalano would use the flashlight on his hip as the night grew darker.*

Section B—the smaller of the sections—held the school-like cafeteria. There was a large kitchen in the back and a massive seating area just before it. The manager of the kitchen—Robin Wright—had a bit of a crush on Catalano and when she found out he typically worked the night shift, she would always leave him a little snack by the register. Some nights it would be a piece of fruit like an apple or a banana. Other nights it would be something a little unhealthier. Catalano loved those nights. While he was determined to staying fit—his ropes of muscle beneath his gear were clear proof of his discipline—he also had a sweet spot and wouldn't pass up a chance to 'cheat.' Whether Robin knew he was gay was a mystery to him, but, regardless, he stayed under the assumption that she didn't, which was fine by him.

On many days, the cafeteria was filled to capacity with staff members and visitors alike. Dozens of different voices bounced off the walls. Sometimes, just before he left for the day, Catalano would pop in to grab a snack for his ride home and would be surprised by how full the room was. The night shifts made him forget just how many people worked in the building.

Section C was where the real work began. Nearly all of the science labs were located in that area. Access was restricted to the bare minimum. If you had no business or couldn't prove why you were there, you would not get in; that was the rule from the first day. At first, all the security guards had access to section C, but over time, as the work became more and more classified, the number started to shrink to the point where only Catalano and the others working the night shift had access.

Then there was Section D.

The most classified and restricted part of the base. With the acceptation of the research workers, Jess and the night crew, no one else had access.

It was so classified that Jess decided that only Catalano should have access to the area at night. Without telling him, she put in a request to take away everyone else's access. But, because of how long the process was, the order hadn't gone through yet—frustrating Jess to the point of no return, which meant they still had access to get through the three steel doors that lead into the forbidden area of the facility.

Feeling like he may have patrolled to quick, even though he was sure he didn't miss anything, Catalano decided he would take one last look around Section A before heading to the locker room and showers.

Camera B5

5:53

Like his ex, Jonah Manning finished his patrol a lot faster than he felt like he should've. Even though the area was smaller than the others, he still felt obligated to go back and double-check everything. Manning started with the cafeteria and ended with the kitchen. He got a chuckle when he spotted the piece of banana bread Robin had left Catalano next to the register. He and Catalano may have ended on a bit of a sour note, but he wasn't one to hold a grudge. Plus, a part of him felt like at some point down the road, they would try and rekindle. Although he wasn't holding his breath.

His second look around came up empty—nothing was out of the ordinary. It was reassuring to him because, in his mind, the night was on track to be just like every other: long and quiet. He was content with that. But he dreaded what came next.

Since he had finished the patrol, that meant he was going to have to head back and regroup with Catalano and the others. Meeting back up wasn't a big deal—in fact, he liked regrouping, mostly because it meant the night was moving along—but he knew for sure that Burke and Auclair wouldn't be finished with their patrol, which meant he and Catalano would be by themselves until they did so.

He decided he would take his time. He needed to use the bathroom and was parched beyond belief because of his new thyroid medication. He glanced down at his watch. Disappointment fell over him. A long night was still ahead. The thought of the shift dragging—especially around one o'clock in the morning when it would feel like time came to a standstill—didn't sit well with him. It started to piss him off.

All he could do was hope that, unlike other nights, this one would go by a little faster.

Camera C9

6:01

"Wait, wait, wait!" *Garrett Auclair said in a loud whisper as he walked behind Tom Burke.*

"What?" *Burke grumbled as they stepped up to the metal security door that would lead them into the first half of Section D.*

"You heard Catalano; we're not supposed to be in here."

Annoyed by Auclair's good boy act, Burke blew raspberries at him. But, rather than turning around and calling him names, Burke chose another route. One he was sure would get on Auclair's nerve. "What're you scared?"

"No, I'm not scared," Auclair replied quickly as he followed in Burke's footsteps and approached the door. "I just don't wanna get fired before my ninety-day review."

"You'll be fine. We'll be in and out before anyone knows we were here."

Burke reached down for his security badge and prepared to swipe it through the keycard. Auclair grabbed him by the wrist before he was able to do so.

"What about the security cameras?" Auclair pointed.

Burke looked at them and shrugged. "What about them?"

Auclair, dumbstruck by Burke's answer, took a minute to find the right words. "Um, we're going to be on them?"

Burke chuckled, amused by Auclair's righteousness personality. A part of him even wanted to commend him for trying so hard to resist the temptation, but, for time purposes, he replied, "So we'll just go back and erase the files. No big deal."

"What, have you done that before?" Auclair scoffed in a sarcastic tone.

"Yeah, I have," Burke firmly said. The seriousness of his tone forced Auclair's expression of sarcasm and dismissal to vanish completely. Before he was able to say anything, Burke looked down at his garb. "Would you mind letting go of my fuckin arm, now?"

Hesitant, yet aware he was going to have to at some point, Auclair let go.

As soon as his hand let go, Burke reached down, grabbed his badge, and scanned it across the security sensor. The small light on the bottom of the sensor transitioned from blood red to lime green. The metal door unlocked and opened with ease.

Burke grabbed the metal handle of the door and looked at Auclair, who had the same expression as he had before.

"I still don't think this is a good idea," Auclair reaffirmed.

"Noted," Burke replied before stepping through the doorway.

A part of Auclair wanted to stand his ground; the voice inside him kept wanting to say 'No! I'm not going to do this, Burke. You won't make me! You ca—'

He stepped inside.

Camera 2: Lobby
6:04

The eerie silence of the lobby kept the hair on Joe Catalano's arms raised toward the roof. The stillness was no surprise, given the guys were the only ones left in the facility, but something felt a little off to him. He couldn't place it or even figure out if he should question why he felt the way he did for that matter, but, nevertheless, something was off.

The same feeling overtaking Catalano was starting to infect Jonah as he approached the end of Section B and entered the lobby on the opposite end. "Joe!"

His familiar voice spun Catalano around like a bullet, almost as if he was taken off guard. All night he had been dreading the moment when he and Jonah would be alone—fearing that the scabs that had formed over the wounds of the past would be picked off as soon as they started speaking, but no such feeling came to him.

His mind was lost in thought.

Something was wrong.

The look of unknown tension on Catalano's face came into focus the closer Jonah got. He picked up on it right away. "Joe...Joe?"

It took Jonah nearly yelling his name before Catalano acknowledged him.

They met each other's eyes as Jonah took a small step closer, focusing on his ex's blank stare.

Silence returned to the large lobby.

Jonah swallowed the tension. "Joe...what's wrong?"

To his surprise, Catalano answered much quicker than he thought. "I don't know..."

The answer was like nails on a chalkboard despite only being as loud as a whisper. Jonah and Catalano had known each other long enough to be able to read one another, and in all that time, Jonah had never seen his ex-boyfriend look so on edge; borderline dumbstruck—

Catalano jumped into action and started for the security office on the opposite side of the lobby, jetting past Jonah as if he wasn't there. Concerned himself, Jonah followed him into the office.

Camera 3: Security
6:07

Catalano didn't slow his pace until he pushed open the door and stepped inside. Despite the size of the building, the office was small. Nothing more than a few desks and a table full of monitors occupied the room. Catalano raced for the monitors. Jonah—fearing something awful was happening—closed the office door. "Joe? What the hell is going on?"

Ignoring his question again, Catalano sat down in the metal chair resting in front of the desk and started scanning the dozens of computer monitors. Jonah kept his distance at first but closed the space when Catalano called him over.

"What?" he asked.

Catalano quickly started searching the screens, moving his finger up and down each monitor. "Can you find Burke?"

Jonah started looking.

The room grew still, yet the tension was high.

With each screen he went by, Jonah could hear Catalano's breathing amplify with trepidation. It made it difficult for him to concentrate—to the point where he was about to give up looking when suddenly movement on the far right monitor caught—

"There!"

Catalano looked up. "Where?"

Jonah pointed. "Right there."

Catalano nearly pushed him out of the way and leaned into the monitor. The feed was incredibly dark and grainy. Not much could be made out, frustrating him. He leaned in more—almost to the point his nose touching the screen.

There was movement.

A sudden yet soft movement.

Because he had been there the longest, he knew the place—and security cameras—like the back of his hand and the more he looked, the more he realized that one of the outlines just below the camera was Burke.

His heart pounded into his ear like a lingering drum just as his eyes trickled down to the label at the bottom of the monitor:

Camera D1

"Oh, shit!"

Catalano darted for the exit.

Jonah followed.

Camera D1

6:09

Just like the security camera had shown, the first hall of Section D was extremely dark compared to the rest. As soon as Auclair closed the door, he reached down for his flashlight. "Goddamn is it dark in here!"

"That's eerie, I was thinking the same thing," Burke's sarcasm was front and center.

Rather than engaging in Burke's childish response, Auclair dismissed the sarcasm and focused on what was before them.

The hall they were in was small, made of all gray colored metal, like the inside of a prison cell with a cold metal floor keeping it company. Had Auclair been forced to stay in there any longer, his Closter phobia would've gotten the better of him, but luckily enough, Burke moved quickly. Just as Auclair closed the door they walked through; Burke opened the next one.

He stepped through the door and held it open long enough for Auclair to reach it. "Stay close to me."

Camera C2
6:10

With fire under their feet, Catalano and Jonah sprinted, side by side, down the last hall, rushing past the first few science labs; each just as dark as the next.

Nothing but the sound of their feet stomping of the cold glossy floor filled the air, echoing throughout the hall. Knowing the dangers of where they were heading, Catalano used every bit of energy he had and pushed himself down the hall, causing Jonah to start trailing behind.

"Come on, hurry!" Catalano shouted. "Hurry!"

Camera D2
6:10

What poor light Burke and Auclair had in the previous hall was nothing compared to the entrance of D2. While the first hall provided enough light for shadows to peer amidst the corners, no such light illuminated in the second corridor. When Auclair stepped inside and closed the door behind him, darkness surrounded them.

It took time for their eyes to adjust to what they were—and weren't seeing. Once they did though, Auclair noticed the hall seemed wider with large rusted pipes hissing in the dark, creating an eerie, almost foreboding sound. Steam was trickling out many of them, especially at the opposite end of the hall which appeared to be a dead end. While the sight did little to cut the razor-sharp tension, it blunted his rising fear of small spaces enough for him to take a few steps forward.

The first thing he noticed, aside from the lack of light, was the smell in the air. A rotten, yet sticky, smell ineffectively masked by a dash of harsh disinfectants;

73

like a cross between a recently cleaned operating room and a damp basement. It wasn't enough to make him gag, but it was enough to force him to breathe through his mouth. He tried not to focus on the odor, but he was sure he'd smelt something similar before—or something close to it, at the very least.

Unlike the previous hall, the hall of D2 had something the first hall didn't: noise.

A loud noise.

Like an alarm.

"What the hell is that?" Auclair was able to muster through the vile smell.

Burke didn't answer; he waited until his eyes adjusted to be sure of what he was seeing. When Anclair realized no answer was coming from Burke, he looked forward, waiting for more shapes to appear in the blackness.

Slowly, they started to. And slowly, absolute horror began trickling into the two men.

A tint of red had adjusted into their vision. At first, neither were sure what it is. The light would get brighter, and then it would get darker. Over and over, like a band in synch with one another—it got to the point where Auclair started to think it was nothing more than his eyes playing tricks on him. But Burke, unlike his new co-worker, knew better.

Much better.

It wasn't a trick; far from it.

It was a warning light.

A warning light that was hanging above one of the doors of what appeared to a cell that occupied the hall.

Without thinking, Burke started walking deeper into the forbidden area. Feeling it would be safer to stay together, Auclair did the same, following Burke as they headed toward the light and the cell door below it.

Camera C2: Lab
6:12

Body slamming the doors to the lab open with his shoulder, Catalano entered the large room and sprinted across the way with Jonah, who was almost out of breath, but only a couple of feet behind.

Panicking the more he thought about the dangers of Section D, Catalano decided as soon as he got Burke out, he would fire him on the spot, without question. Possibly Auclair, too. But, first, he had to get to them.

Catalano ran toward the door that would lead him to Section D.

Camera D3
6:13

The closer Burke and Auclair got, the brighter and more detailed their surroundings became. When they were at the beginning of the hall, not much could be seen, but as they closed in on the light, they started to realize something was wrong. Gravely wrong.

Unbeknownst to Auclair, the dark hall was much narrower than he assumed. It also held many more secrets than he would ever know. The flashing light kept his attention focused on what lied straight ahead, allowing the details of the hall to remain in the dark. By the time he reached the strobing red light, he was still unaware that the corridor housed—not just cells, but many cells.

Since he'd never been in the hall before, but heard the rumors about Section D, Burk made out what he was seeing a lot faster than Auclair, which allowed the deepest forms of fear to strike him first. But, Auclair wasn't far behind. They both stopped when they were close enough to see what was before them.

The spinning light had indeed been one of the warning lights that hung above every cell—Burke had expected that but what neither of them expected to see was the cell door that was below the light lying face down on the metal floor.

Without thinking, Burke rush toward it. "Oh, shit!"

Auclair followed, keeping close as he'd be doing all night. When he reached the door, he pulled out his flashlight and shined the beam onto the metal door. Auclair did the same thing, hoping he could be of some help.

The hinges of the door had been snapped clean off. Large deep dents covered the inside of the door, too, creating confusion among the two guards. But, what struck them the most was what was happening inside the cell.

A large amount of steam was blasting into the cell, creating a fog-like atmosphere inside so thick not even Auclair's flashlight beam could penetrate. When Burke realized how much was coming out of the doorway, he got back to his feet and joined in on shining light into the cell.

Nothing was in sight.

The two men, frozen in fear, looked at each with blank stares.

"Wh—what was in there?" Auclair whispered loud enough over the hissing of the pipes.

Burke softy shook his head. "It's not what…it's more like who."

A chill ran down Auclair's muscular spine; a chill so deep, he could feel it in his feet. In his young life, there had been many times where he felt nervous—even scared, most of those times happening when he served over in Iraq, but those moments were nothing compared to what he was feeling in—there was a bang inside the cell.

Burke suddenly pulled out his pistol, taking Auclair entirely off guard, forcing him to step back.

"Get behind me," Burke ordered.

Auclair did as he was told, taking several steps back while keeping his flashlight pointed inside the steam-filled cell.

The steam had gotten thicker and was starting to overtake the outline of the door frame in the hall. The sight was intimidating—even to Burke, who had built a reputation of being fearless or at least bragging about being so. Even from behind, Auclair could see Burke was hesitant about going into the cell. He didn't judge though, for he knew had the shoe been on the other foot, he would be doing the same thing.

"Keep the light steady," Burke demanded as the hissing of the pipes amplified. Auclair didn't answer.

Burke turned back to the cell; keeping his gun drawn out in front of him. He started taking steps forward. A glass window was embedded into the metal door, but from what Burke could see, it didn't appear that the glass was broken. Nevertheless, he oversaw his steps, trying to avoid anything that could make a sound from beneath his feet.

Auclair started to panic silently—to the point where he could feel his knees starting to buckle. He was able to keep on his feet, but he was unable to keep the flashlight beam completely steady. Burke noticed right away. "Keep it steady, for Christ sakes."

Auclair attempted, but his trepidation was starting to become too much to withstand. The shaking intensified.

"I said keep it steady, goddamn it!"

Burke stepped up to the door.

Auclair trembled.

A loud bang bounced off the walls. Light emerged at the far end of the hall.

Auclair twisted his wrist and shined the flashlight down the opposite end of the corridor.

A door had opened—the very door they had entered from.

Burke snapped his head in the direction of the noise while the figure in the cell in front of him remained undetected.

A shadow emerged from the light trickling in from the doorframe.

"Burke!" Catalano shouted.

His eyes widening, Burke pulse picked up as he looked in the direction of his boss. Catalano through his hands in the air. His voice was distant and muted, but anger was palpable. "What the fuck are you doing?"

He didn't answer because he didn't have an answer. He knew anything he said would be useless. He chose not to say nothing even as Catalano shouted his name again in a much fiercer voice.

Burke's mind raced back and forth as he tried to come up with an excuse—any excuse—of why he was in the forbidden area. The early stages of a lie started forming—much faster than he thought it would've, but just as he was on the final stages, he halted.

Everything inside him stopped as a sense of violation rolled through him. He instantly grew uncomfortable, almost as if someone or something was invading his personal space. The feeling forced him to take his attention off Catalano.

He looked forward into the thick steam that clouded nearly all of his vision. But, unlike before, where he couldn't see anything, an extensive black outline had formed in front of him, surprising him by the closeness.

His mouth opened, ready to shout out a profanity-laced question at the fig—
A hand emerged from the steam and snatched him by the neck.

The gun slipped through his fingers and plummeted into the foggy cement floor.

Auclair turned the flashlight away from Catalano when he heard the gun land on the floor and pointed the bright beam toward Burke, lighting his body up as the arm started to lift him. Catalano and Jonah watched, distilled.

Burke—horrified as he felt the pressure on his neck tighten and his feet lift from the floor, started gagging, fighting to escape, but unable too. Saliva started oozing out of his mouth and trickled down the giant veiny fist crushing his windpipe.

Cracking noises started forming through the hissing of the steam. Burke's face turned beet red as his gagging intensified; the sight causing Auclair to take a few steps back rather than engage. There was a loud snap—so loud it made the hissing of the steam seem like background noise. The guys jumped.

Silence returned, but ended when Burke's lifeless body dropped on the floor. Auclair gasped.

"Run!" Catalano shouted.

Auclair did so, dropping the flashlight on the ground and started sprinting as fast as he could.

The figure emerged from the cell and joined in on the run. Catalano, still in shock from Burke's crushed windpipe being lit up by the flashlight beam, focused on Auclair and extended his hand, planning to grab him and pull him to safety, but turned his attention toward the looming figure charging straight toward them from behind Auclair.

"Auclair, come on," Catalano panicked. "Come on!"

The figure started closing the gap between him and Auclair.

"Come on!" Catalano screamed.

Painting from the speed he was going at, Auclair pushed himself, almost to the point where he would surely give himself a heart attack if he kept up the pace for an extended period; he had reached his maximum speed. He started groaning out loud as fear infected the rest of his body.

The footsteps behind him started getting loud. And fast.

His groans got louder.

The footsteps grew closer.

His groans turned to screams.

The footsteps closed within striking distance.

He extended his hand.

Catalano grabbed it, successfully pulled Auclair toward him and the exit.

Camera D1
6:21

"Close it!" Catalano shouted to Jonah once he and Auclair cleared the doorway.

Using all his might, Jonah grabbed hold of the steel door and slammed it shut only seconds before the figure made it to them. The echo of the door slamming shut bounced off the walls of the small hall. Once it dissipated, nothing but the sound everyone's heavy breathing occupied the area. Everything became still.

Catalano's heart was pounding in his ears like a marching drum—the same for Auclair and Jonah. Even though he was panicking, he spun to Auclair and snatched him by the shirt collar. "You son of a bitch, what the hell were you doing in there? I told you not to go in there!"

"I know, I know! But, Burke made me. I had no choice."

Fighting the urge to strike Auclair in the face because of his stupidity, Catalano pushed Auclair out of his grip and looked back at Jonah, standing next to the door with a look of worry covering his youthful face.

Auclair straightened out his collar while the sight of Burke's neck crushed kept playing in his mind front and center. He opened his mouth to speak—even though he knew Catalano was probably going to interrupt him the moment his mouth opened—but Jonah beat him to it.

"What do we do now?"

Catalano straightened himself up and took in a deep breath of damp basement smelling air. The look on his face was of downright uncertainty; it was apparent he had no clue what he was going to do—or at least that's what Jonah assumed.

"And what the hell was that thing?"

Catalano turned to Auclair. "No, you don't get to ask me shit! We're heading back to the lobby; you're gonna pack your shit and get the fuck out. You are so fucking fired!"

Jonah walked over to him. "No, seriously Joe, what was that?"

Catalano still didn't answer. So much was processing in his mind; he barely heard Jonah's voice. Jonah asked again, only this time much louder to get Catalano's attention. They looked at each other.

"Joe, what was that?"

It is evident that he could no longer try and save face about the situation—he was already sure he would most likely get fired, too once Jess Sowa and the rest found out about Burke's death. He prepared himself as he struggled to find the right words to say—a massive bang on the metal door stopped what would've been a hostile argument before it had the chance to start.

All three of them jumped before turning to the door. Catalano's eyes widened.

"Holy shit," Jonah whispered under his breath.

The thick door, made with state of the art metal and a sheet of steel barricaded in the center, was indented straight in the middle—the metal bulging out as if something came crashing into it. The three guards took a couple of steps back.

"What the hell is this?" Auclair whispered to himself.

"Joe…" Jonah whispered. "What are we gonna do?"

There was another bang on the door, the impact pushing out the bulging metal even more. Catalano turned as another bang—even louder than the others struck the door. "Run!"

The door bent in half, the hinges snapping off from the weight as it plummeted to the ground. The floor shook hard beneath the guy's feet when it landed. Catalano looked over his shoulder. The figure stepped out of the dark hall and started toward them.

"Run!"

Camera C9
6:22

They ran.
And the figure followed. Close behind.

Camera A1
6:26

"Close, close it, close it!" *Jonah shouted at Catalano as they appeared in the final security camera feed.*

With loud footsteps merely feet away, Catalano pushed Auclair into the hall, past the door entrance, creating a space for him to come rushing in and slam the door shut behind him.

A smash rocked the door as Catalano and Auclair leaned back against it. His eyes widened. "Jesus Christ!"

Another smash pounded into the door, violently vibrating it with ease. Jonah watched in horror as each hit on the door bounced Catalano off of it.

"Jonah!" *Catalano shouted through another loud bang.* "Get to the security desk and lock this place down! Hurry, goddamn it!"

Without thinking, Jonah rushed to the security desk on the opposite side of the lobby as quick as he could. Auclair, feeling useless as he put all his might into keeping pressure on the door looked at Catalano. "This is not good!"

The top door hinge snapped.

"No, it's not," *Catalano screeched.* "Jonah, goddamn it!"

Because he only logged into the security network once or twice, Jonah was unable to remember his login right away, but the letters and numbers came back when he glanced down at the keyboard. "Come on, come on."

The second hinge snapped.

"Jonah!" *Catalano screamed for dear life.*

Focusing on the screen, rather than Catalano's desperate plea, Jonah got to the emergency activation screen and typed the four-digit password.

1-0-7-8.

The lights to the entire facility went dark.

The pounding stopped, and everything turned still for a brief moment. Nothing but the sound of Catalano and Auclair's heavy breathing was audible. Total darkness surrounded all of them—even the lights in the lobby had gone dark.

Now unable to see, Jonah kept his eyes in the direction of Catalano, hoping, praying that he was going to appear in front of him at any moment. He was still painting as his heart continued racing inside his chest.

The deafening silence overtook—not just the lobby and hallway, but the entire facility. Borderline panicking, Catalano kept his body weight on the door; preparing himself for the next hit the ill-fated door would take.

A horrifically loud siren suddenly rattled the silence from overhead, turning the metal hall into an echoing dome as a blood red alarm light began flashing. The surprise and the overwhelming screech of the horn forced Catalano and Auclair to take their hands off the door and cover their ears. Even Jonah was forced to do so as he tried his best to keep his eye on Catalano through the strobing red lights all around.

The hall went dark, then went red.

Over and over. With no sign of stopping.

Jonah watched Catalano and Auclair for as long as he could until he spotted the shotgun leaning against the desk in front of him. He went for it.

The final hit on the door came—the force so strong, it snapped the last hinge off and sent Catalano and Auclair plummeting on the ground. The strike to the door was loud; the blaring alarm was not enough to offset it enough for Jonah to be unaware of what was happening. The siren muffled the sound of the door crashing to the floor and on top of Auclair, but Auclair's horrific scream was loud enough to overtake everything.

Jonah looked up.

The alarm suddenly shut off. Followed soon after by the red alarm lights.

By the time the alarm was off, Auclair's screams were inaudible, symbolizing what his fate was amidst the darkness that encapsulated the room. Jonah was able to get a hold of the shotgun before everything went dark. The cold heavy weapon in his hand provided some reassurance, but it wasn't enough to shake off the distress he'd felt for most of the night.

"Joe?" he shouted into the darkness.

No answer.

No noises, either. Everything came to a standstill.

The silence ran chills down his bones, and they only grew worse when he called out for Catalano, and there was no response. He called again. No answer.

Jonah cocked the shotgun, keeping it aimed in the direction of the hall. 'Oh, shit,' he thought. 'Oh shit, oh shit, oh shit.'

His heart thumped in his ears, but Jonah knew what he needed to do next despite everything inside warning him to do the exact opposite. He needed to head down the hall and find Catalano and Auclair to make sure they were okay and help them if they weren't. But he knew what would happen if he did.

As an avid horror movie fan, he was keenly aware of what typically happens when something goes wrong, or a strange noise is heard and needs to be investigated; which is one of the reasons he hesitated for so long. But, because the gun gave him a sense of security and power—which he desperately needed—, he felt embolden to ignore the warning and try to be the hero of the evening.

He took a step forward toward the dark hall—a voice called out to him. "Jonah…"

He aimed the weapon in the direction of the raspy—almost inhuman voice. It was coming from in front of him. The quiet, yet deep, voice called for him again, only closer this time. Jonah put his finger on the trigger.

"Don't move! Stay right where you are!" The words slipped out of Jonah's voice even though the voice sounded familiar.

"Jo—Jonah…" the voice said again.

Jonah suddenly recognized the voice. "Joe!" Relief swept through him. "You okay?"

The darkness made it impossible to see so much as a foot in front of his nose, but Jonah started walking toward the direction of Catalano's voice—

The lights to the facility blasted back on, lighting up the lobby and hall in a neon light, forcing Jonah to block his face with his hand so his eyes could adjust to the harsh LED light. "Jesus Christ!" he shouted.

Opening and closing his eyes back and forth, his pupils finally adjusted and he looked up and see Catalano standing in front of him. Jonah's eyes adjusted to his face and suddenly widened. A large piece of metal was sticking out of his chest.

"Joe," he squeaked out.

Blood gushed out of the massive wound and drizzled along the sharp tip of the piece of metal and into Catalano's hands. A horrific gagging sound started coming out of his mouth before blood began spewing down his rosy red lips.

Jonah rush toward him.

The figure grabbed Jonah from behind and pushed him into Catalano, sending him crashing into his ex-boyfriend and the sharp metal tip sticking out of his chest.

The lobby filled with Jonah's horrific screams as the piece of metal penetrated his flesh and sliced through every organ in its wake. Blood sprayed out across Catalano's nearly lifeless face as Jonah started gagging himself.

Footsteps approached from behind, and before either Jonah or Catalano knew it, large hands came crashing down on the back of their heads and started *squashing their faces together. At first, it hurt. Then, it was painful. Then it became agonizing as their faces pushed up against each other like a kiss gone bad. The piece of steel had taken all of Catalano's energy, leaving him mute, but Jonah used the last bit of air in his lungs to let out another horrific plea for mercy.*

A terrible cracking noise from the back of their skulls penetrated both of their eardrums to the point where it became the only thing they could hear. And in a final scream, as his vision started to blur, Jonah closed his eyes and started sobbing as his and Catalano's skulls buckled, crushing their faces and heads together, killing both of them instantly.

Camera 2: Lobby
End of Tape
6:31

CHAPTER 6

Snow took over the computer screen as the camera feed came to an abrupt end. Remembering that grainy picture and noise used to scare Tyler when he was younger, Sam made sure he shut it off the moment the camera footage ended, leaving the military trailer with nothing more than mute voices from outside as the only noise.

Tyler Benton remained still, unsure of what to say and still trying to process the horrific violence he had just witnessed. Sam, able to see that the video struck a nerve with his old school mate, gave Tyler some time to process what he'd just seen.

"You've never seen a murder before?" Sam said once Tyler's posture appeared to ease.

Tyler—still shaken—cleared his throat. "I—ah—not on camera, no."

Sam sympathized. "Yeah, me either."

Before responding, Tyler looked up at the large digital clock hanging on the wall above the computer desk. With everything that had happened so far in the night, Tyler was under the impression that dawn was close. Thoughts of a new day approaching brought him a bit of comfort at the start; he figured daylight would be an advantage to them. He rolled his eyes when he read the clock. The night was still young. Daylight was anything but close.

"I'm still confused, though…" Tyler finally said before a soft tapping on his left shoulder brought his eyes down from the clock. A black folder was being held in front of his face. "What's this?"

Sam didn't answer. Instead, he let the information in the file speak for itself. Unlike many of his colleges, Dr. Sam Rainey didn't believe in long drawn out paperwork filled with scientific terminology that one would only be able to comprehend with a certain degree—Sam liked to get to the point. And that's precisely what the file did.

The further Tyler got into the paper; the more his eyes started to widen. The security camera footage had chilled him to the bone, but the file arguably was what pushed him to the point of no return—Sam could see that in his eyes.

When he read the last word, Tyler rose from the computer chair. "No... no. That's impossible. I *know* that's impossible."

Sam picked up the file after Tyler placed it on the desk. An unintended sarcastic grin grew on Sam's face—clearly, he admired Tyler's innocence; innocence Sam had lost many science experiments ago.

"Is it, Tyler? Is it really impossible?" Sam followed up.

Tyler stood his ground. "Yes. It may have been twenty-years-ago, but I remember it like it was yesterday. I saw it with my own eyes, and so did you."

"I thought so, too, Tyler. I really did. But we were wrong. *I* was wrong."

The look of seriousness on Sam's face was striking. The determination glistening in his eyes proved that nothing was going to change his mind. And for a brief moment, Tyler started to question his memory of what happened twenty-years ago in the very woods they found themselves in.

"We watched him die though, Sam," Tyler finally found the words. "We watched Russel Fritz die. It was our fault."

Sam nodded his head, doing everything in his power to try and convince Tyler. "No, it wasn't. Russel Fritz isn't dead. Look!"

In what was a last ditch effort to change Tyler's thinking, Sam reached down to the desk, woke the computer screen and double tapped a file on the desktop. The file opened instantly, revealing a young child being held in a cell—the very same cell from the security camera.

Tyler stepped up to the screen to get a better look. Like the security feed, the picture was grainy, but it was clear just enough for him to get a good look at the child in the cell. The child looked scared. Judging from the facial expression on the boy, it was apparent he had been crying when the photo was taken.

His stomach started turning the more he looked at the camera as the overwhelming sense of panic rushed through his body. A shot of the chills blasted through him from head to toe. The boy he was looking at *was* Russel Fritz—the boy he and Sam left in the woods for dead all those years ago.

"But...how?" Tyler whispered to himself, but loud enough for Sam to hear and assume he was requesting a response.

"Remember when we were kids? You'd always come over, and my father would never be there?" Sam began.

Tyler looked up from the screen. He didn't reply, but the look on his face made it so he didn't need too.

"You would always ask, and my mum would say he was working?"

The questions about their younger days took Tyler back to—not just the days when he and Sam would spend nearly every second with each other, but it also brought back memories of how the town of Hunting used to be; when it was filled with life, unlike today where it compressed with urban blight. He focused on the memories Sam was referring too. "Yeah."

Sam pointed to the computer screen. "He worked here at Quimby Research—he worked in the facility we found in the woods."

The revelation resonated in Tyler's mind instantly, but the stress of the night was slowing him down as far as reacting. Sam's tone was smooth and firm and made it impossible to think he was bullshitting. Plus, it all seemed to make sense the more Tyler thought about it.

"That night was the same night your father said we weren't allowed to see each other anymore...because we were in the wood," Tyler said out loud as the puzzle pieces started getting put together in his mind. "We spent the next few years trying to figure out how the hell he knew we were out there. Jesus Christ."

"Well, now we know."

Knowing it was a lot of information to take in all at once, Sam stepped away from the computer, giving Tyler some space to process everything just as his father did many years ago when he revealed the same thing to him.

Tyler didn't respond right away—in fact, it appeared he wasn't going to respond at all. It got to the point where Sam thought Tyler was going to exit the trailer without saying a word. He opened his mouth to speak.

"He's really alive..." Tyler finally said, fixating on the photo of Russel Fritz in the cell.

"Yes, he's really alive," Sam said as he sat down on the small couch directly across from the entrance to the trailer.

The realization of learning that the boy Tyler thought him and Sam witnessed being killed all those summers ago was still alive, slowly started nesting in his hectic mind, but it wasn't easy—all these years of believing he played a role in Russel Fritz 'death' had eaten away at him. There was so much he wanted to say—so much he needed to say, but he was unsure of how to say it. Sam could sense it, too.

Tyler's phone started to vibrate before he was able to get another question out. He answered it quickly without looking at the screen to see who it was. "Benton."

A voice came through but was so overwhelmed with static, he couldn't understand a single word. The only thing he was able to make out was that the voice sounded familiar. "Hello? Hello?"

Two beeps alerted him in his ear; the call had been lost.

He looked at the screen. It wasn't a number he recognized; no name was on the top of the screen either, which meant the number wasn't in his contacts list. He entered his recent call app and pressed down on the phone number, but stopped shy of hitting 'send' when he looked at the top left corner of the phone.

No Service.

"Shit, we must be too far out to get a signal," Tyler assumed.

The door to the trailer flung open not a moment after Tyler finished his sentence.

"My service just went out," Lois said—a bit of annoyance in her voice shining through.

The two looked at each other, confused by why their phones suddenly stopped working. Footsteps approaching the trailer caught Lois' attention, spinning her around; her hand resting on her service pistol.

"Phones are out, Rainey," Sargent Dylan L'Heureux shouted from the doorway of the opened trailer door. "Working on the power now."

"Not good enough, L'Heureux," Sam replied quickly. "Power needs to be out first *then* the phones. Get them back online until we're ready to shut the power off."

Tyler and Lois turned from each other and focused on Sam, both showing signs of increasing frustration. Despite Jessica Sowa's demand to keep the details at a bare minimum, Sam knew he was going to have to explain.

"Why would the phones suddenly go out?" Tyler asked.

"And what the hell does he mean by 'working on the power?'" Lois followed up.

Turning to shut down the computer so he could exit the trailer, Sam pushed in the chair and stepped out into the cool air of the night, squeezing in between the two officers. "We need to keep this contained."

Following Sam out the trailer, Tyler and Lois caught up to him, walking on either side of his shoulders. The activity had gotten more intense since they all went inside the trailer. More Humvees had shown up, and more lights had been set up, lighting the surrounding woods to the point where no shadows could be seen as far as the eye could see.

"Wait, what does contain mean?" Tyler asked loud enough for his voice to be heard over all the activity that surrounded them.

"It means we need to keep this as isolated as possible. The more people that know about this, the more people will be in danger. Plus, we don't need what's going on here to be broadcasted over the entire country," Sam explained.

A low flying helicopter passed by overhead, the force of the spinning blades so grand it sent a rush of cold September wind through the thick branches of the trees. The extreme noise from the engine forced Tyler and Lois—both of whom who've never been that close to a helicopter before—to cover their ears until it passed overhead.

"Well, how long will the power be out?" Tyler shouted.

Sam turned. "Until we catch him."

"Catch who?" Lois shouted even though she'd only been able to hear half of the conversation.

"I'll brief you in the car," Tyler reassured her while keeping his attention on Sam. "What do we do now, then?"

Stopping short of Jess' van, he replied, "Why don't you head out to the main road and assist with the search—you two know the area better than anyone. Keep your phone on, and I'll call you so we can meet up."

Sam's brief—almost dismissive answer—left Tyler and Lois feeling useless, almost as if they were just in the way. Neither of them were used to that feeling, and neither of them liked it—especially Lois, who was already having a hard time keeping temper contained.

All those feelings shifted when Sargent Dylan L'Heureux and a few privets walked over to them with their rifles out and pointed to the ground.

"Can we help you, gentlemen?" Lois asked.

"Yeah, I'm Sargent L'Heureux, and this is my squad."

The trio shook hands.

"Sorry to be meeting you like this," L'Heureux civilly said.

"Its fine," Tyler said, trying to shake off any unnecessary tension. "Is there something you need from us?"

"As a matter of fact, there is," L'Heureux responded immediately. "My guys are going to start searching around so I was wondering since you know the area if you wouldn't mind tagging along with us…"

The two partners—partners of crime as Lois would say every time they worked a shift together—looked at one another, both surprised by the offer from such a high ranking Military Officer. Lois was borderline giddy.

"Yeah, happy too," Tyler said.

L'Heureux, relieved by their decision, turned to his fellow soldiers, ordering them to obey and listen to Tyler and Lois in the same way they do to him. Because of the seriousness of the situation, none of the privets objected.

Turning away from the soldiers, Lois spotted L'Heureux looking at her with icy interests.

"You still have that shotgun?" L'Heureux asked.

Lois shrugged. "Yeah."

"You should probably go get it…you're gonna need it."

Checking her phone for the third time, in hopes of seeing Tyler's number light up the cellphone screen, Kimberly took a deep breath before putting the phone on the glass coffee table before her and leaned back into the puffy cushion of the couch.

She was tired.

The overpowering adrenaline she'd felt earlier on was now gone, leaving behind a young woman who desperately craved rest—any type of rest. With Mike in the shower, hoping the warm water would calm his nerves, Kimberly had the Eaten house to herself. While she never really warmed up to the house—thinking that it was much too large for her taste—she appreciated the silence the home provided since she didn't get much at her own.

The house was closed up tight—sealed like the anticipation of a herd of flesh-eating zombies getting ready to charge from all sides. Except for the sliding glass door in the kitchen, no type of light from outside was able to get through. The house sealed to withstand such a herd.

Like always, Mike shower was long and drawn out, which left even more time for Kimberly to be alone with her thoughts. Typically, when they had the house to themselves, she would join him in the glass encapsulated stand up, but she couldn't find the mood—or even energy—to engage in such an activity. Instead, she chose to keep to herself until the quiet became so overwhelming, she'd have to put on the T.V. to prevent herself from going insane.

She reached for the T.V. remote ten minutes into Mike's shower.

"Oh, come on," she muttered to herself in her typical pissed off voice.

The writing on the T.V. said it all

No Service, please contact your cable provider.

Frustrated, Kimberly tossed the clicker onto the glass table, missing her cell phone by mere inches. It was apparent she was looking for something to keep herself occupied while Mike finished up. He would always get pissed when she tried to rush him, and since she was a guest at his house, it seemed inappropriate for her to do so.

She picked up her phone again and unlocked it. The first thing she noticed—aside from the scratches that were across the bottom of the screen from when she dropped it in gym class—was the battery percentage.

57%

To anyone else, 57 percent is a good amount left for a cell phone, but because hers was such an older model—she refused to get a new one to protest the outrageous one-thousand-dollar price tag on it—the 'life' in her phone didn't stretch as far as the newer models.

She and Mike also had different models, which meant they needed two separate chargers. And she just so happened to leave her charger at home, which is what kept her activity on the phone brief. The last thing she wanted to worry about was not having a phone in case the night required it.

No missed calls.

No missed messages, either.

Tyler still hadn't gotten back to her.

She had been bitching about Tyler's lack of response since before Mike stepped foot in the bathroom and he defended Tyler, saying he probably got busy. He was also against Kimberly calling him and told her it would be best to wait for him to call. She agreed.

But the more she thought of the attacker reaching in the truck to strangle her, the more she started questioning if she could sit and wait. It felt strangely out of character for her; she didn't like the feeling at all. She knew Mike always had good intentions, but she decided he was wrong on this.

With the cell phone gripped tight in her hand, Kimberly stood and carefully tiptoed to the bathroom door.

The water was still running.

She knew it was now or never.

Slowing backing away from the bathroom door and stepping into the kitchen, she decided to make the call.

It went straight to voicemail.

Hesitant about leaving one, Kimberly took the phone away from her ear and went to pressed 'End,' but the beep indicating a voicemail was recording forced her to bring the phone right back to her ear.

"Hi…Officer Benton, it's Kimberly Wilson. I was just trying to get in touch with you…uh…on our way home, Mike and I were attacked by some guy with some creepy mask on, and so we were wondering if you wouldn't mind stopping by tonight so we can file a report. Uh…no rush—we made it back home—so we'll be here whenever you get here. Thanks. Bye."

The shower water shut off.

Quickly, she ended the call and sprinted back to the couch and make believe she was searching around online as Mike wrapped a towel around his waist and exited the bathroom. Steam sped out of the bathroom door, grabbing Kimberly's attention right away.

"Jesus, how hot did you…" she trailed off, losing her train of thought to Mike's ropes of muscle.

"What?" Mike asked as he shut the light off to the bathroom.

She shook her head, trying to get her mind out of the gutter. "Uh… nothing."

Mike stepped into the living room as water slowly ran down his washboard abs. "Did Tyler call back?"

Kimberly's heart rate spiked, unsure how to answer, wondering if it was a trick question, even though she was somewhat confident it wasn't. "…No, not yet."

Mike rolled his eyes. *Jesus Christ, Tyler. You're killing me over here. You should've called back by now. Kimberly's getting pissed—yep I can see it.*

At first, he wrote it off as he and Lois were probably busy—maybe Old Man Claire again—, but then, he started to wonder if the no response meant that he and Lois were in trouble. The thought left him unsettled.

But, instead of replying, Mike acknowledged with a nod and headed to his bedroom on the opposite side of the house, leaving Kimberly, once again, alone with her thoughts.

She rechecked her phone.

Nothing.

With the blue police cruiser lights flashing as the patrol car turned onto Lancaster Street, Tyler slowed down. The half a dozen Humvees tailgating him followed his lead. As soon as he straightened out the wheel, Tyler reached for the radio, ignoring a couple of beeps and vibration coming from his cellphone resting peacefully in his pocket.

"L'Heureux?" Tyler spoke.

"Yeah, go ahead, Benton."

"This is Lancaster Street."

L'Heureux, looking up from the GPS on his cell phone, started looking around the depleted street. Every decaying house he could see was dark, leading the newly appointed Sargent to the assumption that the road was empty. With nothing more than an orange colored street light flicking off in the distance, L'Heureux knew the lack of lighting was going to be a problem.

"Every goddamn house is fucking empty, Sar," Privet C.J. Mears said as he pressed down on the breaks to the Humvee.

"Yeah, that's what deindustrialization will do to a small town," L'Heureux replied before pressing down on the radio. "Is this street empty, Benton?"

"Yeah, there's only one person on this street; everything else is abandoned," Tyler said.

"Jesus Christ," Mears muttered to himself; astonished by the sight of all the once beautiful houses now nothing more than a relic of the past.

"Alright, we'll start here and make our way down," L'Heureux responded over the radio.

"Copy," Tyler replied before putting down the radio.

Just like earlier in the night, nothing but the lights in the squad car provided light as he drove down the street, bringing back all the eerie feelings he had the first time he drove through the road.

"Where we starting?" Lois asked.

The cruiser bounced over a large pothole, Tyler unable to swerve in time.

"Shit…we'll start at Old Man Claire's house and work our way back," he signed.

Reluctant to think stopping at Old Man Claire's house was a good idea, Lois looked down at the clock radio. The night was moving along slowly but steadily, but much was yet to come. It was late enough, however, to assume many people in town had already turned in for the night.

"You think he'll still be up at this time?" she asked, keep the shotgun in between her legs.

Tyler shrugged. "Only one way to find out."

The blinding headlights from the Humvees started dimming as the space between them and the cruiser expanded. By the time they pulled up to the front of Old Man Claire's house, darkness had taken most of the light to the point where it was nearly impossible to make out what type of vehicle they were.

Rather than pulling into the driveway, like he typically would, Tyler kept the cruiser on the street, directly in front of the old house as he slowly came to a complete stop. The two leaned closer to the driver side window and started looking around; Lois squeezing the shotgun between her legs tighter.

The house was dark.

Unusually dark.

Old Man Clair may have been the only person on the forgotten street, but he typically had at least one light on in the house—hoping it would deter anyone with bad intentions away, but all the windows were dark. Lois came to the assumption Old Man Claire was sleeping.

"No, I don't think so," Tyler mumbled. "He always turns the outside light on before he goes to sleep to 'ward off the black.'"

"Hmm," Lois thought. "Maybe you should put on the lights; I bet they'll get his attention."

Despite it being a good idea to do so, Tyler hesitated, for he knew the shit storm they would face once Old Man Claire awoke—he was bad enough when he got up on his own Tyler thought. He had already had his share of the old man for one night, but the incredible depth of darkness that surrounded him pushed him in the direction of getting some well-needed light.

He turned to his partner. "Here goes nothing."

With the car in park and the engine still running, Tyler reached down and flipped the switch for the emergency lights to on.

A strobe of blue lit up the area almost instantly, cutting into the shadows of the night and providing enough light to brighten up the front of the house in a strobe-light fashion. Lois picked up the shotgun as Tyler pulled out his flashlight.

"Let's get this over with."

In synch with each other, they opened their respective doors to the cruiser and exited the cruiser, keeping their eyes on the front of the house. Tyler had only really searched the house once, right after Old Man Claire was arrested, but he remembered the setup of the house like it was yesterday.

Tyler pointed to the far left side of the house once Lois reached his side of the cruiser. "The bedroom windows are right there."

She cocked her head in that direction. The flashing blue lights bounced off the house, and no doubt could be seen from the window. Keeping calm, Tyler anticipated for that loud screech that was Old man Claire's voice to come yelling at him through the window…but it never came.

The windows—all of them—remained dark. When enough time had passed to the point where something started to feel wrong, the two looked at each other.

"Maybe's he's sleeping good?" Lois shrugged under a nervous chuckle.

Tyler pulled out his service revolver. Old Man Claire was known for a lot of things—racist being at the top of the list, but being a heavy sleeper wasn't one of them; Old Man Claire was a light sleeper. *Very* light.

Once his gun was out, Tyler turned on the flashlight in his opposite hand and shined it on the bedroom windows.

Nothing.

Tyler kept his attention on the windows, looking into the terrible darkness within them, hoping to catch a glimpse of anything. Lois did the same. But before she knew it, she found her head slowly turning back toward the front of the house, focusing on the opened front door. Curiosity—along with a bit of confusion—struck her like a two by four.

The emergency lights were flashing a mile a minute, making it incredibly difficult to make out much detail of anything and Tyler's flashlight was in the opposite direction, but she could see clear as day the unwelcoming entrance the house offered.

"Tyler..."

He spun around, unintentionally shining his flashlight into her face. "What?"

She answered by raising the shotgun toward the door. Knowing how she worked, Tyler picked up on the response right away and turned back to the house. He shined his flashlight at the entrance. A rush of confusion—much like the one Lois had just experienced—shot through him.

Tires screeched from another Humvee pulling onto Lancaster Street from the opposite end of the street, adding even more tension to an already tense situation. Sam was in it; Tyler could sense it. He knew he needed to get to him.

"Tyler...?" Lois finally said

Her firm authoritarian voice brought him back to reality.

"What do you wanna do?"

Keeping his flashlight aimed at the door, Tyler took a glance down the street. More Humvees were pulling up, creating a false sense of security for both of them, but Tyler wasn't going for it—he knew the consequences of letting his guard down.

Without thinking twice, Tyler stuck his flashlight under his armpit and pulled the radio from his hip. "L'Heureux? Sam?"

To his surprise, a response came through almost immediately. It was Sam, just like he knew it would be.

"Tyler, I just got here. Where are you?"

"Down at Old Man Claire's house."

Sam looked down the road, spotting the emergency lights from the cruiser. "Alright, I see you. I'm heading down now."

"Bring a few of your military friends with you," Tyler ordered.

Sam kept his eyes on the flashing lights. "What's wrong?"

Tyler turned his attention back to the front of the house. "I think something is going on here."

Picking up on the uneasiness in Tyler's voice, Sam wasted no time. "We're on our way."

Once Sam's response came through, Tyler holstered the radio, took his flashlight out of his armpit and shined it back onto the entrance of the house followed soon after by his service revolver. Lois took a few toward him, effectively keeping her fears at bay.

"You want the front or the back?"

"We'll both go in the back. I'll lead, you follow," Tyler replied almost instantly.

Taking one last glance at the entrance, Tyler turned and headed toward the right side of the house, pointing his flashlight on the dead yellow grass. Lois—keeping the shotgun pointed at the house—stayed close behind, leaving no room between the two of them. When Tyler got to the edge of the house, he straightened himself up and pushed his back up against the wood siding. He took the safety off his gun.

"Stay right behind me," Tyler whispered.

Lois acknowledged.

Tyler took in a big breath, held it, and broke from cover and started down the side of the house. Lois kept her word, not taking her eyes off him for anything. When he began to pick up his speed, so did she.

Unlike the front of the house, that was lit up in a strobe effect blue, the side of the house was in total blackness. Old Man Claire didn't have an outside light on this side of the house—something he pointed out to Tyler every time he was forced to go over. All the two had to make their way through the dark was the flashlight beam pointed out in front of them.

With the sound of Lois' footsteps right at his heel, Tyler didn't slow down; he pushed through the darkness until he reached the back of the house, keeping his thoughts—and frankly his fears of what he might find—tampered. The truth was that he *didn't* know what to expect; for all he knew, he may end up finding Lois was right and that Old Man Claire was sleeping in and maybe forgot to close the front door—after all he was old.

He focused on those positive thoughts as he raced down the side of the house.

The thoughts ended abruptly when he saw the broken window directly in the middle of his flashlight beam.

He stopped, forcing Lois to stop too.

A light breeze started to form.

Feeling his heart thumping hard, Tyler kept still as that feeling of being watched returned. The feeling—mixed with the slight September breeze—sent a chill down his spine. The atmosphere also reminded him about the dead deer rotting away off to his right in dense dark woods.

When Lois stepped up beside him, she spotting the blow out window for herself. The bright beam of the flashlight, lit up, not just the entire window and surrounding rotting wood frame of the house, but also the shards of glass scattered about the grass below—light reflecting off of them as if they were stolen diamonds.

"Shit," Lois whispered. "Shit, shit, shit."

Thinking the same thing, Tyler kept his gun pointed at the window, ready to blast anything that may pop out of it. Thoughts ran through his mind at a hundred miles an hour, almost to the point where he couldn't keep up with them; in fact, towards the end, he couldn't. But one of those thoughts was how Sam was on his way with back-up, so even if he and Lois found something, they wouldn't be alone for too long. But, the oath and the responsibility of being an officer of the law weighed heavily on his conscious, forcing him to question his next move.

Unlike every other time, he chose not to get Lois' opinion—mostly because he already knew it, and choosing to ignore the overwhelming feeling in the deepest part of his gut telling him to wait for Sam, he stepped forward and headed over to the shattered window.

"Tyler…" Lois whispered. "Tyler."

He ignored her concerns and focused all his attention to the window and glass scattered throughout. The pieces started off small and grew larger with each step he took. And when Lois finally realized Tyler wasn't going to listen, she joined him and started walking to the window, hoping that backup was closer than she thought.

Because the brightness the flashlight put off, Tyler was able to see everything from the glass in front of him to the entire wooden frame of the window dangling by a sliver against the house. He tightened his grip on his nine-millimeter as his pulse ticked up. The closer he got, the more surprised he was from all the damage to the entire window; it was obvious something happened. Something bad.

Blood came into his sight.

He stopped.

So did Lois.

Keeping his gun drawn, Tyler lowered the flashlight down. *Oh, don't tell that's what I think it is. Please don't be—*

Tyler swallowed hard, preparing him. Any doubt of it not being blood vanished.

It was blood, alright and not just a few drops, either. It was thick dark red blood splattered all around the inside of the window frame and up on the nearby wall.

The thought of the dead deer and the strange noises he and Old Man Claire heard earlier in the night rushed back into Tyler's wild imagination. He couldn't control them, either. They added fuel to that warning in his gut.

It's an animal—some type of wild animal. Something big, too! But, what in the hell type of animal could kill a deer like it did and get through a glass window?

The conclusion made perfect sense to him; he even started coming up with ideas as to which animal it could've been. He was leaning toward a bear—preferably a black bear—until he stepped up to the window.

He jumped back. "Jesus Christ!"

Lois—spooked by Tyler's reaction—also jumped, taking a few steps back.

A figure emerged from behind, silent and stealthy. Lois stepped back a few more times before the sound of heavy breathing closed in—she stumbled into the man standing behind her. She let out a horrifying screech of terror, deafening to the ear and spinning Tyler around.

Spotting the outline of a figure right away, he lifted his pistol and shined the flashlight to whoever—or whatever was behind her. A voice spoke out. "Hey, hey, hey! It's me!"

The blinding beam of light revealed Sam, holding his hands up, at the mercy of his once best friend. Breathing heavily, Tyler lowered his gun, but kept the flashlight in Sam's face, forcing Sam to cover his face with his hand.

"Goddamn it, Sam!" Tyler shouted. "Don't do that."

Lois backed away. "Jesus Christ, you nearly gave me a fricken heart attack. You're lucky I didn't shoot you!"

"Sorry! I thought you heard me," Sam replied, realizing he assumed incorrectly.

Keeping his weapon at his side, Tyler looked behind Sam, spotting no one around. "Where are the military guys I told you to get?"

Sam pointed over his shoulder. "Out front, they saw the door to the house wide open, so they're going in through the front."

Tyler wiped his forehead which was drenched in sweat. At this point, all he could think about was his anxiety medication he forgot to take resting peacefully on his kitchen counter, back at his apartment on the other side of town.

"Why?" Sam followed up. "What's wrong?"

Tyler finally lowered the flashlight off his face and spun it in the direction of the window. "Look for yourself."

Taking his friends advice, he moved his eyes into the direction of the blow out window, spotting the blood right away. "Shit."

As a scientist, Dr. Sam Rainey had seen a lot, and he knew the difference between bright red blood like you'd get from a papercut or a bloody nose, and deep red—almost black looking blood. He stepped forward and realized his worst fears.

Leaning to the right side, in the direction of the window was the body of Old Man Claire, sitting still in his rocking chair.

"Good God," he mumbled beneath the soft breeze coming from the nearby woods.

The entire top of Old Man Claire's head was gone, leaving only his lower jaw attached to his body. Sam had a hard time making out what happened at first. "Oh, shit."

Blood saturated the entire area around the rocking chair and window sill with white pieces mixed in. At first glance, it looked like nothing more than pieces of glass, but further examining revealed it wasn't glass. It was teeth.

Lois stepped up to the window and got a glance for herself, focusing on the skin hanging from the back of the old man's head. She started gaging before vomiting up what little of her dinner that hadn't digested yet. Tyler had a weak stomach himself and had to look away with the sound of Lois vomiting turning his own stomach.

A voice came over the radio. "Rainey?"

Tyler grabbed the radio as if his life depended on it and handed it to Sam. "Yeah, go ahead L'Heureux."

"We got about a third of the street searched and so far nothing," L'Heureux said.

"I need everyone down to the Claire residence."

Confused since he didn't know the area, L'Heureux turned to Humvee driver C.J. Meyers who was equally confused. "Which house is that?" he asked

"The one in front of the cruiser down the street."

L'Heureux, who was standing in the doorway of a once magnificent living room that was now rundown and uninhabitable, poked his head out and looked down the street. He spotted the flashing blue lights right away.

"Copy we're coming to you now." L'Heureux lowered the radio and let out a loud whistle that echoed through the house loud enough for his entire team to hear; even the ones upstairs. "Let's move out people, let's go!"

Meyers stepped up to his Sargent as soon as the order came down. "You sure it's a good idea to just skip over the rest of the street?"

Had anyone else questioned his decision, L'Heureux would've lost his shit, but since it was Meyers—the man who saved him from an IED back in Iraq—he let it slide. "Nope, but then again, nothing about tonight has been a good idea."

Myers, amused by L'Heureux dry sense of humor, chuckled before a bright set of lights pulled up to the front of the house. It was another Humvee, but not just any Humvee; it was Jess Sowa's Humvee. Unhappy by her presence because of her personality—or lack of—he let out a deep sigh. "Great. Just what I need."

Getting out before the Humvee was even in park, Jess closed the door shut and stepped up to the crack-filled sidewalk, spotting L'Heureux as he walked out of the rundown house. "Dylan."

"Miss. Sowa."

"Where is Sam?"

L'Heureux pointed at Tyler's cruiser down the street.

She started down the street right away, her hips swinging back and forth. L'Heureux watched her until he felt comfortable enough she was far enough away so she wouldn't see his middle finger lift in her direction. Myers stepped up to him. "Should I go with her?"

"Naw, wait a bit. Maybe with any luck, she'll get lost," L'Heureux grabbed his radio and up it up to his scruffy beard. "Rainey, you got company, but not the one type you want."

"Great," Sam sarcastically replied, knowing full well what that meant. "Thanks for the warning."

"Anytime, brother. Good luck."

Sam holstered his radio again and walked back over to Tyler, who was still at the window. He was about to warn him of Jess' impending arrival, but Tyler spoke before he got a word out. "I can't even imagine dying like this. Yeah, the old man was a prick, but still…"

Sam agreed.

Sweat started collecting in the small age lines forming on Tyler's forehead, sending a trickle down his face. He wiped it off with his forearm. "Christ, between this and the cemetery, this is one fucked up situation we got going on…not to mention that fucking deer over there."

Sam looked up quickly. "What deer?"

Tyler pointed his flashlight to the far end of the backyard. "There's a dead deer down there; looks like its fricken face was pulled off."

"Show me."

As Lois finished vomiting and began cleaning herself up, Tyler lead Sam to the end of the yard where Old Man Claire had brought him to only hours ago. With the severed head of the old man burning into his mind, Tyler felt like he was having an out of body experience, as if he was in a bad dream he couldn't wake up from.

The outline of the bloody animal lit up the closer Tyler got as he cast light on the still carcass. When Sam reached it, rather than staying a reasonable distance away, he reached into his pocket and pulled out white surgical gloves. "Keep the light on it."

"Why, what're you doing?" Tyler asked.

Sam didn't answer; he started for the animal and ignored everything else. The sound of Lois dry heaving caused Tyler to take his eyes off Sam—who quickly reached the animal to examine it. He called out to her, making sure she was okay. She replied with a thumbs up as thick saliva dripped from her lower lip.

Because the attacked happened so recently, the animal had no time to start the process of decomposing, which left the earthly sent of the woods the only smell in the air. Once he reached the animal and dropped to his knee, Sam started looking at the body. Except for its bloody skinless face, no other wounds were visible.

"What?" Tyler asked.

Again ignoring the question, Sam kept his eyes on the animal, watching as blood dripped down its skinless head. Realizing he wasn't going to get an answer, Tyler walked over himself and dropped down to his knee.

The look on Sam's face revealed he was deep in thought, but Tyler, on the other head, wasn't so deep. He was downright confused, even though he'd been for most of the evening. He was about to ask Sam for the third time, but Lois' vomiting returned with a vengeance.

A sudden breeze emerged through the heart of the woods, passing the trees and into the direction of Old Man Claire's backyard, sending a case of the chills through the two best friends. The temperature was starting to drop; Sam could feel it. It was brief, but enough to remind them winter was just on the horizon. When the wind finally died down, Sam and Tyler finally made eye contact; each looking into a pair of eyes heavy with guilt.

"We used to make fun of him for wearing a mask every day," Sam finally spoke.

The sentence was short of facts, but Tyler knew very well what Sam was referencing. Time had changed a lot of things, but it didn't change how much of bully both of them were, particularly to one individual— an individual that they chased into the woods all those years ago and presumed died—blood splashed up from the ground, spraying Sam's face and white jacket, followed by a horrific screech, deafening to both of them.

Sam jumped back as blood dripped down his face. *Holy shit!*

Screaming in agony from the overwhelming pain that crippled its body, the presumed dead deer jerked helplessly as it raised its skinless head and made eye contact—or what was left of its eyes—with Sam.

Sam's eyes widened with panic.

Tyler drew his pistol.

The animal leaned to its side and let out one final scream into the dark star-filled sky before a bullet blasted through its brainstem and out the other side of its exposed skull, ending what little life the animal had left in it. The animal flopped to the ground with a horrendous thump as the gunshot echoed throughout the empty street before the night engulfed the sound and nothing but the wind retook the yard and surrounding area.

Drenched in blood, Sam turned and glanced up at his friend, watching the bit of smoke drizzling out of the tip of Tyler's service revolver. Breathing profusely from the shock of the animal awakening from its dirt nap, Sam started to wipe the blood from his face but a loud bang from behind force him to stop short of finishing.

Tyler drew his pistol. Then, he slowly lowered it when he realized it was three of the military privets rushing out of the back door, ready to be at the rescue should they need to be. Once the trio spotted Tyler's police uniform, they lowered their automatic rifles.

A voice called out. "Everything good?"

Tyler holstered his gun again. "Yeah, everything's fine."

Another voice also called out; a voice that got Sam's attention immediately.

"Sam! Sam!" Jess Sowa emerged from the side of the house and shouted with an extra four military soldiers behind her—one of them being C.J. Meyers.

Rolling his eyes while wiping the rest of the blood off his face, Sam rose to his feet as Sowa's heavy footsteps approached.

"Jesus, what the hell is going on here?" she demanded with her condescending voice loud and clear.

Tyler, coming to the conclusion he wasn't a fan of Sowa, was about to speak to remind her this was no longer her jurisdiction—

"He's been here," Sam said, taking his blood-covered jacket off and tossing it over his shoulder.

As soon as the answer resonated, which didn't take long at all, she started searching around, turning in every which way direction. "Goddamn it. And you're sure about that?"

Sam pointed toward the house—specifically the destroyed window. "You look in there and see for yourself."

Footsteps approached from behind them as Sowa covered her face with her hands, the stress was getting to her, along with worry. She didn't anticipate the night to be going as it was; even the thoughts of it being an early night were long gone.

Tyler stepped up to them, followed by L'Heureux, forming a circle.

"That's quite a carcass in there," L'Heureux joked in his flat-toned voice. "My guys finished their search; there's no one else in the house. Doesn't look like anything was taken, either."

"I didn't expect him to linger," Sam mumbled, loud enough for all of them to hear.

After popping in a breath mint, hoping to mask the foul smell that had overtaken her mouth, Lois picked the shotgun up off the ground and headed over to the circle. As she walked up, she could see a serious conversation was taking place.

"Well, where the hell would he go?" she heard Jess ask.

Sam—trying to figure out what to do next—only managed to shrug. "Maybe someone found something else down the street?"

"Negative," L'Heureux replied quickly. "Something would've come over the radio by now."

"Goddamn it," Jess grunted as she turned to the woods directly in front of them. "You don't think he would've headed back in the woods, do you?"

"You really want more of my guys searching the woods?" L'Heureux said before Sam responded.

Annoyed by his condescending tone, Jess turned to the Sargent. "I'm throwing out ideas, which is more than what you're doing."

L'Heureux stepped toward her and leaned in, violating her personal space with his angry eyes and a scruffy beard. "You really wanna go down this road again, Jess?"

"I will if I have to, Dylan. So, don't push me."

Their voices—not to mention tension—grew louder; almost to the point where Sam and Tyler thought about taking a few steps back. Lois, on the other hand, was much more about dealing with a problem head-on and she decided if Tyler, or Sam for that matter, weren't going to step up, she would; not in defense of Sowa, but so the argument could wrap up.

She stopped short when a large black area on the ground caught her attention from the corner of her eye. Her eyes went swooping down and fixated on it almost instantly while Sowa and L'Heureux continued on with their argument; both voices growing brassier with each response.

Clawing down at her deputy belt for her flashlight, Lois kept her eyes on the spot, fearing she'd lose it if she looked away.

"Oh, fuck you!" Sowa shouted to L'Heureux, finally reaching her breaking point.

Reaching the point himself, L'Heureux took another step closer to her, ready to call her out—after all these years of wanting too, but stopped short once Sam raised his voice and injected himself into the conversation. "Stop! Jesus Christ, both of you, stop!"

Lois grabbed her flashlight and turned it on.

"You two bitching isn't helping anyone!" Sam continued. "Besides, he didn't go back in the woods. He wouldn't."

Sowa—having a hard time getting over Sam raising his voice to her—scoffed. "And what makes you think that?"

Lois interrupted. "Um…guys."

The trio spun around in Lois' direction to find her down on her knees with her flashlight tilted to the ground, lighting up the dying grass and surrounding dirt. "You might wanna take a look at this."

Without hesitation, Tyler, Sowa, Sam, and L'Heureux rushed to Lois. Because they didn't know her that well—at all, in fact, Sam, Sowa, and

L'Heureux didn't pick up on the nervousness in Lois' voice, but Tyler did almost instantly. He knew whatever she found was something serious.

"Wh—" Sam stopped short, spotting it right away.

So did everyone else.

Sam, being the one piecing everything together a bit faster than everyone else got down on one knee to get a better look. As soon as he did, he knew exactly what it was and where it came from.

It was blood. A large amount of blood, but, unlike anything else, it wasn't just in one spot; there was more blood next to it and more blood after that, followed by a trail of drops leading to the opposite side of the house.

"I told you he didn't head in the woods," Sam said before stepping away from the group and following the trail.

"Where are you going?" Sowa shouted.

"Where do you think?" Lois sarcastically asked before she started following Sam.

Tyler left also, leaving Sowa and L'Heureux the only remaining ones. They looked at each other, Sowa rolling her eyes, clearly not a supporter of the idea. She nodded her head. "Goddamn it, go with them."

Springing into action—he would've even without Sowa's blessing, L'Heureux turned to Meyers exiting Old Man Claire's house. "Meyers! You're with me."

Teaming up together—like they would every other time they were out on the field—L'Heureux and Meyers clung onto their rifles and started in the direction of Sam, Tyler, and Lois, quickly disappearing in the darkness that occupied the right side of the house, leaving Sowa alone to her thoughts and the dead deer only feet away.

The trail of gas went on longer than the test subject thought it would. It wasn't tired or in need of a rest—it had no need for rest, but the darkness from the lack of street lights and the sour smell of flesh surrounding its face made it difficult to stay with the scent. It needed to come up with a better idea.

It did.

The subject turned to its right side. Nothing more than a rundown house with shattered windows and a front door wide open was there —clearly, nothing of value.

It turned to its left. A large white house with a single light on at the end of the driveway—the only light on near the house —clearly, some potential.

A flash came from behind, grabbing the subject's attention.

It turned in time to see the last street light it walked past start flickering and abruptly shut off, followed soon after by the light at the end of the white house's driveway. Darkness returned.

It took one last look around, realizing no other opportunity was around.

Closing its bloodthirsty fists, it focused on the house and marched to the front.

Being one of the last remaining livable houses on Lake Street, thirty-nine-year-old Dave Manson and his wife Cherry had been heading to bed early, unable to sleep because of the stress going on at work and, most importantly, because of the miscarriage that Cherry suffered only weeks before. While she was only a few weeks into the pregnancy, it was their second one in less than a year.

The loss of a child and the hospital visits—not to mention hospital bills, had caused a lot of tension between the couple of three years, to the point where Cherry, late at night starring at the ceiling, started contemplating about separating until she was able to clear her mind and get over the loss of her unborn children.

But, on that fateful night in September, she was, in fact, able to drift into the world of sleep; so much so, that she was unaware of the power going out. But, Dave, on the other hand, woke as soon as the alarm clock on his nightstand shut off. He let out slight yawn once his eyes opened and adjusted to the darkness in the room.

Because of his early stages of Kidney Disease, Dave was always forced to get up—especially in the middle of the night—to relieve himself. And, sure enough, once his mind started up, the pressure of a full bladder forced him out of bed and into the small bathroom that was in their bedroom.

Doing his best to stay quiet and not bump into anything, he carefully closed the door to the bathroom and headed to the toilet. Relief rushed through his body once the draining of his bladder started, allowing him to let out a breath of satisfaction as a trickle of skylight from the window beside him lit the bathroom up in a hazy blue tint.

Knowing he was going to be there for a while, he turned to the window and looked down below to the backyard. Many of the more giant trees in the back casted shadows on the outskirts of the yard, but the night lit up everything else in the yard, including the shed, along with its door, which was wide open.

Taken aback, Dave wiped his eyes, trying to get the crust out of the corners. Then, he looked back out the window, leaning in as far as he could without urinating out of the toilet. His eyes weren't playing tricks on him; the shed door was open.

What the hell…why in God's name is that goddamn thing open? he thought to himself as he finished up. *I locked it, though. I swear to Christ, I did.*

Once he was done, he stepped away from the toilet, deciding not to flush to avoid waking Cherry. Trying to remain quiet, he stepped out of the bathroom and walked over to the window on his side of the bed, which also looked over the yard.

The shed was still open.

To anyone else, they wouldn't have cared and left it until the next morning, but Dave's OCD refused to let him fall back asleep until that door was closed; he knew he was going to have to go out and shut it if he was to get any more sleep.

Keeping his eyes on the shed, he reached for his brown slippers with his feet and slid them on as he tightened the knot on his blue bathrobe. Then, with his eyes now wide awake, he walked over to his nightstand and slowly opened the drawer. He reached in and grabbed hold of the flashlight and his six-shooter revolver resting on top of the folded clothes inside. He closed the drawer as stealthy as he opened it and headed out of the bedroom and into the hall, keeping the gun aimed toward the wooden floor.

When he made it out, he reached for the doorknob and closed the door shut, successfully not waking up Cherry, who was still deep in sleep. As soon as he got it closed, he turned on his flashlight and started for the staircase at the end of the hall.

The hall and staircase were pitch black, but the flashlight impressively lit up every nook and cranny for Dave, allowing him to make it downstairs without the fear of tripping. When he reached the ground level living space, he stopped tiptoeing and headed straight for the side door that was adjacent to the living room. Once there, he pulled open the door and stepped outside, closing the door behind him to avoid it swinging open.

Cool air rushed up his bathrobe, giving him goosebumps and forcing him down the outside staircase and into the back yard with the hope of getting back in the house as soon as he could. *Jesus Christ, it's cold out here! Goddamn!*

With one hand holding the flashlight out in front of him and the other clinging onto the gun and pushed up against his bathrobe, trying to prevent it from opening, he darted across the yard but slowed down considerable the closer he got to the shed. He finally came to a dead stop when he was within feet of it.

The approaching wind picked up in intensity and started shaking the door, causing it to slam against the plastic doorframe. Keeping the flashlight shined on the door, Dave casually stepped closer. From the distance he was at, nothing was out of the ordinary until he stepped into the pitch black shed and spotted the lock to the door resting at his feet.

Without thinking, he bent down and picked it up right away. A chill ripped down him—a much different type of chill than the one he obtained from the wind. The lock was not just pulled off the door but snapped completely in half. *What the fuck? How the—*

A figure stepped up in front of him.

Dave whipped the flashlight beam up to it, revealing a figure dressed in dark clothing with its face hidden by a deer mask. Dave screamed and lifted the revolver in its direction and fired two shots— the figure swung an ax down and smashed it against the front of his face, the force of the impact splitting Dave's head in two, sending him into eternal darkness.

The flashlight dropped to the ground, the blob inside shattering from the impact.

Picking up the flashlight as the body twitched before its feet, the test subject lifted the red ax and brought it into the flickering beam of light. Blood dripped off the razor sharp edges where it had made contact with its victims face. Then the subject began lifting it up and down, coming to the conclusion the object was too heavy. Something smaller was needed.

Tossing the object to the side, the subject searched around, using what remaining light the flashlight beam provided in the shed. Before it, was an entire wall, covered with tools of all shapes, colors, and sizes. Much more potential than the test subject thought there would be.

A tool resting on the floor caught its attention first. The subject grabbed the long yellow handle and lifted the object.

A sledgehammer. Far, too heavy.

It looked up, searching the tools hanging from the higher shelves across the shed wall, trying to find that perfect one.

Hanging were lawn clippers, screwdrivers, a crowbar, a machete, a small shovel, and a chainsaw—all none the test subject was interested in. But, on the far right side at the end of the wall, on the outskirts of the flashlight beam, sat one of interest.

The subject focused on the object through the eye holes of its raw smelling mask. It reached and clutched the object and then brought it into the light, allowing the light of the beam to glisten across its metal surface.

A steal handled hammer. Perfect.

Satisfied with its choice, the subject stepped out of the shed but stopped short when it tripped over something. It quickly looked down, raising its newfound weapon up, ready to use. Then, it lowered the weapon before extending its free hand and reached down.

It cradled the object in its hand, turning it back and forth so its eyes could exam it on each side. A smile grew from behind the deer flesh; it was intrigued. Then, it placed the revolver into the pocket of its jacket and started for the house, squeezing onto the handle of the metal hammer, refusing to let go for anything.

What pain it had received from the gunshot wound in its shoulder was now gone. In fact, it felt like it had never even been wounded. Confused by this, the subject briefly looked down at its shoulder. A bit of blood was on its jacket, but no bullet wound could be seen. No other bullet wound could be felt, either—the subject assumed the second gunshot had missed.

When it reached the side door of the home, the subject lifted his boot and sent it soaring into the door, breaking the door frame and sending the door crashing into the wall it was attached to. Then it stepped inside, looking for the entrance of the home.

Noise from upstairs forced the subject into the shadows as it made its way around the first level of the home to find the exit. The footsteps from above grew louder as it walked through the living room and found the entrance. Keeping the hammer at its side, it focused on the door as it drew closer, but shifted its attention to the staircase directly in front of the door.

A woman emerged, holding a bat and began shouting out a name—her husband's name: Dave.

Using the shadows as long as it could, the subject walked up to the woman, ignoring the heaviness of its footsteps, which gave away any element of surprise it had left. The woman suddenly turned to its direction and swung the bat. The subject grabbed the metal bat and ripped it out of the woman's grip before swinging the claw of the hammer into the center of her skull, splitting her face in two.

The subject struck her again once she landed on the hardwood floor. Then again. And again and again. Finally, once it was sure the woman was dead, it lifted the weapon up and down, trying to shake as much blood off the hammer as it could, before it unlocked the front door, flung it open and started back for the road.

CHAPTER 7

Even before the power went out, Tyler and Lois had lost the trail of blood, but that still didn't stop Tyler from stumping his foot on the cracked curb beneath his feet and shout obscenities into the night air. Lois felt the same way; only she was able to mask her disappointment so nobody could tell. Sargent L'Heureux and Privet Myers just rolled their eyes when they noticed for themselves that the trail had gone cold; both, not the least bit surprised.

Down on his knee, Sam Rainey started looking around where the last drop of blood was, hoping to find something they might've overlooked. Nothing was in sight. "Goddamn it."

Walking back from the middle of the abandoned street, Tyler shined his flashlight down on the ground to the last bit of blood as Sam got to his feet. "Nothing in the street."

Lois, after examining more of the sidewalk further down the road, walked back over. "Nothing down there, either. Of course, having no power doesn't help the situation."

Static came over the radio, sending a horrific screech into the air. L'Heureux answered it right away. "Yeah, go ahead."

"Sarg, the power is out to the town," Privet Jason Vaughan said.

"Never would've guessed that," Myers mumbled to himself as he looked up at the dark streetlight across the road.

"Copy, how much longer until the phones are out?" L'Heureux followed up.

"Half hour or so. Give or take."

"Let me know when it's done. Over and out."

Once they realized L'Heureux's conversation had ended, Tyler, Sam, and Lois stopped eavesdropping and re-focused their attention to the final drops of blood at their feet. The dumbfounded look on both Sam and Tyler's face proved neither of them was going to break the silence first, so Lois decided she would be the one to do it. "Any idea where we go from here?"

Not having the answer, Tyler looked to his best friend, hoping he could come up with something. Sam, disappointed himself, forced out a shrug just as L'Heureux and Meyers walked back over to them, keeping their rifles pointed toward the ground.

"Trail ends here," Sam said to the both of them.

"Does anyone live on this street?" Myers asked as his head bobbed back and forth to the darkness on either side of them.

"No, this street is empty," Tyler answered.

Once he got the answer, he followed up with another question, specifically for L'Heureux. "What should we do now?"

Instead of answering right away, as he always did with just about everything, L'Heureux took a moment to think, allowing Tyler and Sam to try and figure out where to go next.

"We'll head back and finish the search on Lancaster Street, and then we'll start on this street," L'Heureux finally said as he looked at Tyler and Sam. "That okay with you?"

Sam nodded, agreeing it was best if they helped assist in the search. Much of Lancaster Street still needed to be covered, mostly the back yards of some of the once populated houses. Tyler, also agreed while reminding them to be careful because of the lack of stability of the decaying houses.

Thanking Tyler for the advice, L'Heureux and Meyers started back to Lancaster Street, but stopped short and turned back to the trio. "Oh, and the powers out all across town, next is the phones, so keep your radios with you."

"Copy that," Tyler shouted back. Then, as the two military soldiers started back for Lancaster Street, more specifically, Old Man Claire's house, he re-focused on Sam. "I don't like this whole no power and now no phones idea."

Lois raised concern about that too, making sure her disapproval was also known. But Sam, despite understanding why they would disapprove, tried explaining the reasoning behind the choice to shut the town off from the rest of the world. "The army focuses on containment, first—that's the way it's always been. The last thing we need is to start a statewide panic."

"Well I still don't like it; it's my job to protect the people in this town, not to be a part of some 'containment' shit," Tyler fired back.

As the two bickered back and forth, just like they used to when they were young boys, Lois re-focused her attention to the blood that they had been following, trying to figure out why it stopped so abruptly. A part of her felt like the answer was staring at her in the face, while another part felt like she wasn't looking at the situation the right way.

Despite being so engrossed in the situation before them, she was able to keep up with Sam and Tyler argument from afar, when suddenly, she remembered the noise that came from Tyler's pocket before they reached Old Man Claire's house. "Tyler."

"What?"

"Your phone went off in the car, right?"

Her question—even though she already had the answer—refreshed his memory instantly, causing him to grab his front pocket and slide his hand into it. "Oh, shit! That's right!"

Taking a step back to give him a bit of privacy, Sam joined Lois in resuming the examination of blood on the ground, quickly realizing he stepped in a small puddle. He jumped back as Tyler put the phone to his ear and began listening to the message.

"So what's the cure for cancer?" Lois asked, taking Sam off guard by the sudden randomness of the question.

"What?" Sam replied, making sure he heard the question correctly.

"Back at the cemetery, said we were on the 'cusp' of the cure of cancer… so what's the cure?"

The pessimistic tone in her voice was impossible for Sam to ignore; it was obvious she wanted a real answer and not just some hopeful yet factionless answer. Before he responded, he remembered what Lois said about her father and what a horrible time it must've been for her. Sam had been fortunate enough to never have anyone close to him die from the terrible disease—his father succumbed to complications of Alzheimer's disease, another terrible illness he intended to find a cure for, but many people around him had friends and family members die from cancer, including Jess Sowa's own mother.

Even though much of what goes on at Quimby Research is classified at the highest level, Sam felt, almost as if, he needed to provide her with *some* type of answer, hoping to give some form of closure, if nothing else. Echoes of Sowa's warning about keeping the research lab under wraps, swirled through his mind like a bad omen, reminding him of what was at stake. But, instead of listening to her harsh warning, like he always did even when he didn't agree, Sam decided to ignore them and proceed.

He stopped short of the answer when he saw the look on Tyler's face. Picking up on Sam's sudden and drastic facial change, Lois turned to Tyler in time to watch him lower the cellphone from his ear.

"What?"

Instead of spending the time to try and put a sentence together, Tyler answered by turning on the speakerphone and playing the message, loud enough for Sam and Lois to hear from the distance they were standing.

Hi Officer Benton, it's Kimberly Wilson. I was just trying to get in touch with you…uh…on our way home, Mike and I were attacked by some guy with some creepy mask on…

Lois and Sam looked at each other as the message played and finally ended, leaving a strange stillness unlike anything either had felt so far in the night. Tyler—taking in the trepidation in Kimberly's voice—placed his finger on the cellphone screen over the message and kept replaying Kimberly's haunting words.

Some creepy mask on…

some creepy mask on…

some creepy mask on…

"Oh, fuck," Lois said out loud.

"Come on!" Tyler shouted.

After giving up trying to find the lights—*any* lights with his telescope, James Nelson remained in his room, unable to sleep because of the speed his mind was going. Typically, when it was racing back and forth, he was able to control it to an extent and slow it down, allowing him a slight window to fall asleep. But, he was unable to do so on this night. It was rampant beyond comprehension.

Unlike many kids his age—that still lived in town—James was able to keep himself content, mostly with reading and occasionally even trying to write something on his own, all with the company of music. If there was one thing young James couldn't get enough of, aside from every UFO book he could get his hands on, it was music. Everything from eighties rock to today's music was loaded into his old fashioned iPod Classic, which he made sure received a fresh charge almost every night. So, even with the power out, he was still able to listen and let his mind wander.

The world around him may have been silent and still, but the earbuds tightly pushed into his eardrums brought noise into his. First, he started with a little rock, a couple of ballads, to get the emotions going and finally settled on ambient space music, which took him to a place that even he couldn't describe. He had seven days' worth of music on that old iPod but replayed the same synthesized space song over and over, taking into relaxation and an out of body experience.

The song was called *Eternity*. At an astonishing running time of twelve minutes, the song was about a ship lost in space, trying to find its way back home but gets lost in a void of light near the planet Saturn. It had everything from a light piano, meaningful bass and mysterious synths so grand in scale, that if you closed your eyes, it would—just for a moment—make you feel as if you were lost in that void and floating through space.

While many of his classmates blasted hip hop music and bass-driven songs to the point where your ears hurt, James, being the drifter that he ultimately is, found comfort in a class of music he assumed only a select few in his age group would appreciate. And once the song was over, he would press down on the playback button and listen to the full twelve minutes again without a care or worry in the world, holding onto the hope that one day it would be him out there in space.

When the song finally ended after the second—or third—time playing, James popped the headphones out of his ears, bounced onto his feet and away from the wall beneath the bedroom window and headed to his bookshelf tucked in the corner. Despite being on the verge of OCD, the books were not in alphabetical order, but they were categorized by their genes, with the sci-fi and UFO books placed in the front, which is where he went first.

Altogether, he had thirteen books on unidentified flying objects, with the latest one—*USA-UFO*—being the latest he bought during the Hunting Universal Library book sale just days before it closed its doors forever this past summer. Usually, he would've found a way to control himself long enough to sit and read the book cover to cover in one—possibly two sittings, but the constant traveling he'd been doing with his parents and his obsession with the lights in the woods got in the way of him doing so. But, since the power was out, and he couldn't find it in him to sleep, he figured it was the perfect time to try and blast through as much as he could.

Being the first one on the top row, James was able to find the book with ease, despite the darkness that loomed across his bedroom. But, because of the shadows; which only seemed to be getting darker, the only spot James could hope he'd have enough light to see the words on the pages was right back where was; underneath the window where the blueish tint of moonlight was shining through. And that's right where he went.

USA-UFO was a six by nine softcover that contained one-hundred-ninety-two pages with nothing more than a small alien spacecraft like object directly in the center of the cover; a very unappealing looking book. But, when James spotted it, scanned through the pages and saw the book also consisted of pictures, he knew he had to have it. Clutching the book close to his chest as his fingers slid up and down the matte finish, he sat back down by the window, opened the book and started reading.

We are not alone, the first sentence in the book bluntly stated. *UFO conspiracy theories argue that varies governments throughout the world, most notably officials in Washington D.C. are suggesting evidence extra-terrestrial unidentified objects—most likely alien visitors—are on the nerve of being revealed. Such revelations could include communication and/or cooperation with said extra-terrestrials beings.*

In pop culture today, claims or stories have circulated linking the first types of contact taking place during World War II in Nazi Germany. The German UFO theories describe supposedly successful attempts to develop advanced aircraft or spacecraft prior to the war, however. While these early speculations and reports were limited primarily to military personnel, the earliest assertion of German flying saucers appeared in newspapers as far back as the early 50s.

Despite being engrossed with the amount of information the book contained in its first few pages, James was more interested in events around the modern day era. Specifically, within the past twenty years. Once he finished the page he was on, he prepared to flip to another when he spotted a name—a familiar name at the bottom of the page. *Pennsylvania.*

Hey…what is Pennsylvania doing in the middle of a story that takes places during World War II, James asked himself, nearly saying it out loud. *Is it some type of typo? Yeah! That's what it is; it has to be…right?*

He double checked again, lifting the book within inches of his face to make sure he was positive he was reading it correctly. And once he realized the book, indeed, did say, Pennsylvania, a rush of coldness ran down his skinny body. He started trembling.

But, instead of flipping to the chapter titled *Area 51 Science Experiments,* he turned the page and started reading, both excited and yet fearful by what he was about to learn.

Pennsylvania Roswell-1957

On the late evening of December 9, 1957, a massive, brilliant fireball was seen by thousands in at least six U.S. states—many of them across the Industrial Midwest (a.k.a. The Rust Belt). Reports of hot metal debris over South-East Michigan and northern Ohio, combined with Sonic booms in the Pittsburg metropolitan area was attributed to the fireball. Many people in the area of Kecksburg, just about 30 miles southeast of Pittsburg, reported something substantial crashing in the woods with what appeared to be blue smoke after a massive thump and vibrations were felt across the area.

Authorities discounted proposed explanations such as a possible plane crash, errant missile test, or reentering satellite debris while some even believed it to be a meteor. A spokeswoman for the Defense Department in D.C. said the initial first reports indicated the fireball was merely a natural phenomenon. But, further analysis decades later, determined the metallic fragments from the area were a type of metal that was only produced from Russia during that period of the war.

The story went on for many more pages, but James stopped short of reading it in its entirety; he unable to control his emotions.

Ah ha! I knew it! It IS a spacecraft! James concluded. *This whole time, I was right! Now, I finally have proof, and everyone will have to apologize to me!*

The Roswell story—while still contested even to this day—provided enough justification for James to start fantasizing about certain people having to apologize to him; his arch-rival Zach Dempsey being the main focus.

'I'm sorry, James. I'm sorry I doubted you,' Zach's voice said as it returned to James' mind. *'I was wrong; you were right. And for that I—'*

A loud bang from outside broke his train of thought, pulling him out of his fantasy as fast as he entered it. Without thinking, James slammed the book shut, tossed it out of his hands and cowered close to the wall just beneath the window and staying out of the moonlight. He started shivering.

The echo of the bang lingered before drifting off into the night, staying long enough for James to replay the sound over and over in his mind. The more he thought about it, the more he realized it sounded like a massive bang. Almost like a thud.

He reached for the tinfoil hat he took off, scoffing at the idea he didn't need any longer. Without thinking, he squeezed it down on his head before keeping an ear out for any other noises that might follow. He remained still, struggling with the fear of an invasion and the thrill of seeing an extra torrential once and for all.

He listened.

Nothing. Nothing but the silence of the night and the foreboding breeze was audible.

The words he just read circled his mind, most notably the *massive thump with vibrations across the area.* He kept still and waited, bracing for the fluctuations. But, to his surprise, they never came. And another loud bang—or thump; he wasn't sure which one to call it, never came, either. All there was now was silence.

James remained crouched down, keeping his right hand firmly on the tinfoil hat. Whatever the sound was, it was too loud, and too real, to be something from his wild imagination, but he was surprised by the lack of noise, specifically from just below him in his parent's room. *Why aren't Mum and Dad up? They must've heard the sound. I know they're heavy sleepers, but they can't be THAT heavy sleepers.*

A light appeared around the frame of his bedroom window. James didn't spot it right away, but once it started to flicker, he noticed it from the corner of his eye. His head instantly looked up. The light was dim but bright enough to pierce the moonlight in the window and bright enough for James to see it had a yellowish—almost orange—tint to it; like a mix between headlights and the brilliant glow of a summer sunset. Curious, he pushed the tin foiled hat down, making sure it was secure and then lifted his head enough so he could look out the window.

Confusion set in.

The light was coming from fire, but, not just your ordinary type like that of a campfire. This fire was one long line that started as far down the street as he could see and ended underneath a truck—Mike's truck.

Getting to his feet as fast as he could, James rushed to the telescope and stuck his eye into the eye scope, fixating on the flames, starting at Mike's truck and following it until something caught his attention. Something that appeared to be coming closer, almost in the direction of his house.

His breathing intensified, but he managed to lift the telescope away from the flames and focused on what he saw just off to the side of the fire, hoping his parents were right when they said the telescope made him see things that weren't there.

With nothing but a couple of candles flickering around them as they sat in the living room, Kimberly and Mike remained quiet, deeply engaged in the game of Go Fish they were about half-way into. Since both were very competitive people, to put it lightly, they treated the game as if their life depended on it. And at the point they were at, neither of them knew who had the advantage. The entire house was silent when the sudden bang was made.

"What was that?" Kimberly asked, looking up from her handful of cards seconds after the sound.

Mike—also with a pair of cards in his hand—looked up right after her. "It almost sounded like a firecracker."

Kimberly dismissed the idea quickly, concluding there was no way in hell someone would be shooting off any type of fireworks this late at night with no power, despite it actually sounding like a firecracker in a sense. Because the Eaten house was closer to the sound than James' house was, Kimberly and Mike heard the noise much brighter and were able to figure out right away the sound had come from down the street.

As they—like James—waiting for a follow-up sound, the dark living room remained still with shadows flicking back and forth due to the constant movement of the candles resting on the coffee table. The game of Goldfish, with the combination of Mike's presence, clamed Kimberly's nerves, almost to the point where she started feeling comfortable, but the sound brought back those earlier fears she had right away.

"Maybe it came from the Kramer's house," Mike hoped.

Kimberly shrugged, not convinced the noise came from that direction, even though the Kramer's were a bit of an odd couple. "You think?"

"Maybe...they're always out in the garage working on some type of contraception," Mike reminded her.

Deep in his gut, Mike didn't believe what he was saying, either, but he wanted to make Kimberly feel secure. But, he knew it was a long shot; the only person who could calm Kimberly down when she was wired was herself.

"Yeah..." she muttered.

"Hey, it could've always been James Nelson. After all, he's literally right up the road," Mike joked.

The idea got a smile out of Kimberly, enough so that Mike felt somewhat relieved—movement outside the front living room windows caught his attention. His smile faded, never to reemerge for the rest of the night.

The drastic change to Mike's face mirrored the same look he had back in the truck when they were being chased.

Kimberly halted her movement like a deer in headlights. "What?"

Insurmountable fear filled Mike's body, he pointed to the front of the room. Kimberly looked over her shoulder the moment his arm was extended fully and focused on the front windows of the Eaten house, spotting the light right away.

The same type of fear that was paralyzing Mike started creeping up her body, but she pushed through it, got to her feet and headed over to the window, ducking down as she approached the front of the room.

"Kim! Kim!" Mike whispered before her lack of response forced him up and followed her over.

The closer she got to the window, the brighter the light appeared to be. By the time she was within inches of it, she was able to realize the movement they had seen was coming from the light. When she finally reached the window sill, she stepped to the side and straightened her posture as she pushed her back against the wall of the far left side of the room. Mike did the same; only he went to the right side.

The blinds to the window were closed, but the paper thin curtains that ran down to the floor allowed light to trickle in from both sides; the gap between the curtain and the blinds being large enough for both of them to see through without having to open, or even touch, the shades.

They glanced at each other before taking a look outside, both with the same expression of nervousness visible on their youthful faces. Mike spoke first. "Think its Tyler?"

"No, I don't," Kimberly said with confidence. "Headlights don't flicker. Besides, knowing Tyler, he would pull into the driveway with the police lights on...it's gotta be something else."

As they looked away from each other and back to the sides of the window, they prepared themselves for what they were about to see.

"Ready?" Kimberly asked.

"Yeah," Mike sighed.

Like always, when they would do something together, they both counted to three, and once they did, the two of them moved the curtain out of the way and peered out the window and missing the man in the deer mask glaring at them through the sliding door in the kitchen.

Because of how deep into the night they were—combined with the lack of power—it was difficult for either of them to make out what they were looking at. But, the more their eyes adjusted to the eternal blackness the window provided, the more they realized what they were looking at.

The flickering yellow and orange light was coming from a trail of fire—a trail of fire that appeared to be coming from up the road and ending in Mike's driveway, directly beneath the undercarriage of his truck. Kimberly was the first to realize it, but Mike wasn't far behind.

"Oh, shit!" Mike said out loud. "You gotta be kidding me!"

Kimberly thought the same thing. *'Great! This is exactly what we need. More drama on this shitty ass night. What's next?'*

Unable to do anything more than shake her head, she pulled away from the window and leaned back against the wall as the stress built up, forcing her to close her eyes, hoping that when she opened them, she'd discover her eyes were playing tricks on her; even though she knew it was a long shot. She took in a few deep breaths, effectively calming herself enough to get a sense of released tension and opened her eyes—they filled with absolute horror.

Her heart started pounding in a way like it never had before. A cold sensation shot through her body, giving her goosebumps as her mouth dangled open, unable to speak or even scream. Her legs then started to buckle as a gasp emerged from her.

Mike turned to her. "What?" he asked before looking for himself.

Everything grew still, allowing a haunting quietness to take over the room. Mike joined Kimberly in the feeling of sheer terror as his body started giving off a heaviness to it as if he would need to put all his effort into moving.

Remaining still, they kept their backs to the wall as they looked at the stranger with the deer mask glaring back. Mike blinked his eyes over and over, hoping what he was seeing was maybe a creepy shadow the moon had cast down onto the deck, but it was ineffective; he knew for sure it was anything but a shadow. In fact, the outline looked vaguely familiar—especially the mask.

The room was dark, but the multiple candles flickering gave off more than enough radiance for the masked stranger to spot the two teenagers looking back at him. The stranger knew due to the darkness inside his fleshy mask that they were unable to see his eyes, which was true. For a moment the two love birds gave hope to the idea they'd be able to blend in with the darkness enough so they could avoid detection from the uninvited guest.

Clinging to that thought while her legs stiffened like concrete, Kimberly tried to keep calm. *Oh, my God. Oh, my God. No, this can't be happening! But, Tyler is on his way—I know he is. Tyler is on his way and plus this person's outside, and we're inside so that me—*

The stranger slammed his shoulder into the door, shattering the glass.

Kimberly screamed.

Mike grabbed her shoulder and pushed her to the front door. "Go! Go!"

The intruder entered the home and charged at them, stepping on the large chunks of glass scattered across the floor.

Kimberly grabbed the doorknob. "Oh, my God!"

Mike, panicking as his breath heightened in volume, slapped his hand down on top of Kimberly's, grabbed the doorknob and pulled it open.

Footsteps from behind approached fast.

Kimberly flung the front door open and ran outside with Mike only a step or two behind. "Go, Kim!"

Stepping into the blue moonlight, Kimberly raced down the small walkway from the front of the house and approached the line of fire that ran down the middle of the driveway, screaming at the top of her lungs. "Help! Help us!"

Her screeches into the night felt useless, considering the time of night it was, but they were loud enough for many to hear, including James Nelson who moved the telescope away from Mike's truck and focused on her running out of the house. He looked at her first, then lifted the scope to see Mike, who had an equally horrified look on his face. But, then, from the top of the lens through the telescope, a shadow among shadows moved from the front of the house, taking James' attention off them.

The intruder, drenched in dark clothing with the deer mask losing wobbling with each step, exited the house and started in their direction, clinging onto an object in its right hand—a blood-drenched hammer. The young—borderline autistic boy, started quivering as Kimberly's screams continued. *Help!*

The fear was substantial and persistent but felt somewhat expected—almost as if he'd been training for this day—this night. The more James watched, the more he noticed the thing with the strange mask over its head didn't look like a human at all. *It's here! It's finally here! Now's my chance.*

He sprinted into action, racing over to his closet on the opposite side of the room and flung the wooden door open, its hinges squeaking until it banged against the wall. Initially, all his UFO books were on the bottom shelf in his closet, but he moved them once his obsession with extra-terrestrial life lead to him creating what he called his "alien hunting gear", which consisted of a Taser, a paintball gun, a hunting knife, a pair of toy handcuffs and a flashlight with a strobe effect setting—all of what he figured he would need. And as Kimberly's screams continued to howl through the window, he concluded, it was time to gear up.

Kimberly and Mike raced across the street and headed to their closest neighbors, the Kramer's. Without looking back, Kimberly charged at full speed, jumping over the trail of fire that ran up the entire road and sprinted onto the Kramer's yard, despite the number of signs placed around the front warning to stay off the property.

Because she's been around the neighborhood so much after all these years of dating Mike, she knew the Kramer's had motion sensor lights that lit up the moment someone even approached their two-story home, but the lack of power dissipated that level of security, leaving the two freighted teenagers in the dark as they raced to the farmers porch.

"Mr. Kramer!" Kimberly pounded on the front door.

The masked intruder jumped over the line of flames and headed toward the Kramer's house, sprinting, which quickly turned to running.

Mike, watching as the stranger closing the space between them, moved from the door and started pounding on the front windows of the house, screaming over Kimberly's voice. "Mr. Kramer!"

Like the rest of the houses on the street, it was pitch black, not even a piece of furniture could be made out through the window. Regardless of the lack of light from inside, Kimberly persisted with her assault on the door, hoping, praying they would be loud enough for *anyone* to hear.

A light emerged from the staircase directly in front of the door. "Oh, thank God!"

Mike stepped away from the window and turned. The intruder had made it onto the Kramer's front lawn, close enough for his footsteps to be audible. He turned around and rejoined Kimberly at the front door.

The light inside amplified into a brilliant glow, evaporating the darkness in front of the stairs and around the door. Emerging from the illumination was an old man in a bathrobe, carrying a lantern in his right hand and a twelve gauge in his left hand. It was Mr. Kramer.

"Mr. Kramer! Help us!" Kimberly pleaded through the stained glass window in the door.

The masked man assailant drew closer, picking up speed as he closed in.

Using the energy his fifty-two-year-old body could muster at this time of night, Mr. Kramer unlocked the door flung it open. "What the hell is going on?"

The masked stranger reached the steps to the farmer's porch.

Mike, knowing they needed to keep moving, grabbed Kimberly by the shoulders and pushed her into the house, Kimberly bumping heads with Mr. Kramer and she fell forward. Mr. Kramer shouted, dropping the lantern on the floor, cracking the bulb and plummeted onto the wooden floor. Darkness retook the room.

Mike rushed inside and slammed the door behind him as the person chasing them got so close; Mike got a whiff of the sour smell from the mask over the persons face. Mike locked the door—the intruder smashed into it with force so great, the door collapsed forward, sending thick wood and stained glass raining down on Mr. Kramer.

The intruder stepped into the house.

Mike grabbed Kimberly's hand and sprinted into the dark house.

Shouting from the large piece of glass sticking out of his left thigh, Mr. Kramer began feeling around for the twelve gauge as the shadow of the stranger loomed over him. He quickly found it and lifted it up.

The intruder's large hand seized the tip of the gun, stopping Mr. Kramer from aiming it directly in his face. Mr. Kramer tried resisting, using all the might to pull the gun out of the stranger's intense grip.

The gun started leaning back. He fought back, trying to push it back in the direction of the stranger, but the hand overpowered him with little effort. Mr. Kramer started screaming, crying—the intruder's large foot swung down, landing on the piece of glass sticking out of Mr. Kramer's leg. A terrible crushing sound and the surprising rush of pain made Mr. Kramer jump and pull the trigger of the shotgun, blasting his own face off instantly.

Blood splashed across the floor with a mist spraying across the deer mask as Mr. Kramer dropped dead onto the floor as the roar of the shotgun blast bounced off the walls within the entire house. The intruder then turned his attention to the direction Kimberly and Mike went in.

Despite never being inside The Kramer's house, for good reason, Kimberly and Mike sprinted deeper into the house, searching desperately for anything that resembled a way out. Mike led the way, his head bobbing in every direction. Kimberly did the same, only faster until footsteps coming from behind brought a terror upon her so horrific, she lost any sense of direction. The only thing that kept her from freezing in fear was Mike's firm grip on her hand, pulling her through the dark house.

They stepped into a long narrow hall that went straight across the entire first floor with a door at the end. Unsure of where it might lead, Mike rushed toward it, squeezing Kimberly's right hand harder with each step. The footsteps got louder the further they went into the dark hall. Mike began to panic. *Oh my, God! This is it! We're not going to make it out of this house alive! Oh, God! Oh, G—*

He pushed open the door and rushed through it without knowing—or even looking, what was behind it. A blast of cold air crash into his face, with Kimberly not far behind. Once she was past the doorway, she reached out, trying to grab the door and slam it shut, but her arms weren't long enough; only the tips of her fingertips were able to make contact with the metal door.

They were back outside, looking at the backyard of the Kramer home. The tallness of the house cast a shadow, so large, nearly half of the yard was covered in darkness, creating plenty of spots to hide, but also plenty of places to get snuck up on. They only had seconds to think, but both decided the best way to lose their attacker, now just feet away, was to run through the back yard and into the woods—the very woods they had just ran out of early in the night.

They jumped off the deck and down onto the wet grass. The fall wasn't far at all, which allowed both to remain on their feet. But, it also allowed the masked assailant chasing them to stay on his feet, too.

"Come on!" Mike shouted as Kimberly's hand slid out of his grip.

Out of breath, but knew she couldn't slow down, she grabbed his extended right hand, squeezed tight and headed straight into the forest, hoping the area they left, only hours before because they feared for their lives, would end up saving them.

Despite already being in the woods before the first person stepped out, Kimberly's screams into the night, hoping to alert the nearby neighbors had worked. Not long after the shotgun blast incinerated Mr. Kramer's face, his next-door neighbor, Alfred Bates, stepped out onto his front porch and headed to the front of his lawn, tying his bathrobe while keeping his eye on the orange flames in the middle of the street.

"Be careful, honey!" his wife, of twenty-five years, Janet shouted to him as she stood at the front door, cowering from inside.

The outline of a lantern emerging from the house directly across the street caught Mr. Bates attention before he could reply to his worried wife. Then, the voice of longtime Hunting Resident and neighbor of Mr. Bates, Charlie Ray, cried out into the night. "Al?"

"Yeah, Charlie, it's me!" Bates shouted back.

"You alright? Did that gunshot come from your place?"

"No, I thought it came from yours!"

The two men met in the middle of the street, on opposite sides of the trail of fire. Ray curiously lowered the lantern to the burning pavement. The two men, growing more frightened by the moment, focused on the small blaze.

"What the hell is this?" Bates finally asked.

"Looks like its heading up to the Eaten house," Ray thought out loud.

"But I don't think that's where the gunshot came from," Bates replied.

The old man has a point, Charlie Ray thought. *But it must've come from—*

"Look," he pointed, forcing Bates to look over his shoulder.

The two men remained silent, taking in what their eyes spotted. Finally, before Bates had the chance to ask, Ray pointed the lantern to the front of the house next to Bates', the beam bright enough to reveal the front porch and broken front door of the Kramer's home.

"Kramer leave his door open?" Ray asked.

"No, look at the frame," Bates pointed. "It's broken to shit."

Ray took another look at it, fixating on the frame only to realize his neighbor was right. He swallowed. "Should we go over to look?"

Bates sighed. "I guess—"

A loud bang behind spooked both of them, followed by a voice both neighbors recognized.

"What's going on out here?"

"Something strange, Stephen," Ray shouted out.

Overlooking Ray's ominous response, Stephen Queen, also a life-long Hunting resident ran into Bates yard and met up with his neighbors. He focused on the line of fire first, following it with his eyes as the flames reflected from his thick glasses. "The fire stops at Eaten's place."

"Yeah, and look at Kramer's door," Ray followed up.

Wide awake because he was unable to sleep when there was no power, Stephen turned to the Kramer home and spotted the broken door right away. "Jesus. Either of you check on him yet?"

They both shook their heads. Stephen, shivering from the night wind drifting through his air, suggested they should check and make sure everything was okay. Because they've all been friends for years, their hearts told them they should while their guts told them to stay away.

Picking up speed with every road he turned on, Tyler Benton ignored the rusted speed limit signs scattered throughout the deserted streets and focused on the road ahead, swerving left and right, doing what he could to avoid as many potholes as he could. For the most part, he missed nearly all of them, but the ones he didn't, drew criticism from the passenger seat.

"Easy, Tyler!" Lois said, keeping the shotgun safely between her legs with the barrel pointed to the roof. "The last thing we need is a flat tire way the hell out here."

The bright headlights lit up the street well while the blue emergency lights flashing overhead flickered all around the patrol car, flashing off the woods and decaying houses on each side of the road. No doubt, the lights could be seen from a distance, but the lack of the loud siren wailing into the night allowed an eerie silence to overtake the inside of the cruiser.

"Why not put the siren on?" Lois asked from the backseat.

"What good would that do? Nobodies out here anyway," Tyler responded. "Plus, the last thing we need is to wake up any more people."

The tires screeched as Tyler made a hard turn, knocking Sam to the left and nearly making him strike his head on the back of Tyler's leather seat. "How much further?" he asked.

"Not much, why?" Lois asked.

"I want to make sure we're not too far away in case we need backup," Sam replied as he looked through the windows of the backseat.

"Why didn't we just bring some with us?" Lois asked, a bit of sarcasm lacked in her question.

"Because we don't want everyone scattered too thin. We're going to need as many people as we can to apprehend Fritz," Sam said. "Besides, I doubt he'd make it out this far."

"Why do you say that?" Tyler asked.

"He's been locked up for years; one would assume he doesn't remember his way around."

Tyler looked in the rearview mirror, his eyes meeting Sam's the moment he did. "You sure about that?"

"No," Sam said rather abruptly. "I'm not sure of anything anymore."

The cruiser got quiet again briefly before Lois, as she had all through the ride, interrupted the stillness. "So all these years of putting up missing poster signs and people searching for Russel Fritz were for nothing?"

Neither of them answered her, which, in turn, she considered a response anyway. She turned to Sam in the backseat. "And why exactly was he there?"

The straightforwardness of Lois' question and the classified warning from Jess replayed over and over in his mind, like a record player off its rail.

He had the answer; Lois knew that for sure, but the answer he could give was going to be so cryptic, it would raise more questions than anything else. He looked at her—

"Whoa!" Tyler stomped on the break, sending Lois and Sam flying forward.

Lois' seatbelt prevented her from striking her head on the dashboard, which would've happened had she not been wearing it, but Sam wasn't wearing his, which allowed him to fly forward and hit his head on the back of Tyler's seat. "Ow, goddamn it!"

The breaks had just been replaced on the cruiser, and it showed, it came to a screeching halt much sooner than it did when the brake pads were down to nothing. Once the car came to a dead stop, nothing more than heavy breathing from each of them filled the cabin. Lois reached down to the shotgun and felt it still between her legs; it hadn't move at all. *Oh, thank God.*

She turned to Tyler as Sam pushed the palm of his head down on his forehead, groaning as he applied pressure. "What the hell you stopping for?"

Tyler pointed. "Look."

Lois and Sam turned and focused their attention to the windshield, looking past the LED headlights and into the darkness at the far end of the road. They spotted it instantly despite the distance they were at.

"Is that fire?" Sam asked.

"It can't be," Lois thought out loud. "That's in the middle of the street. Why would a fire be in the middle of the street?"

Tyler examined the light a few more seconds and then slowly relieved pressure from the break. "Keep that shotgun ready," he ordered Lois.

They picked up speed the more Tyler lifted his foot from the break until it was entirely off and the cruiser was rolling down the street. Tyler glanced down at the speedometer every few seconds, keeping an eye on the speed. Sam and Lois maintained their focus on the trail of fire as they got closer.

With the interior of the cruiser lit up by nothing more than the green tint from the speedometer and the mounted laptop, an unsettling feeling of isolation came over them, leaving the tension at a razor-sharp level; even worse than what it was at Old Man Claire's house. The more the feeling loomed, the more Lois squeezed the barrel of the shotgun.

Tyler pressed on the breaks again as they drove past the Mansur residence, unaware of the horror that lay inside the house, and banked the cruiser left, allowing Lois to roll down the passenger window and stick her head out to get a better look at the flickering orange and light blue flames. The first thing she noticed was how small the flames were compared to what they looked like from afar. The second thing she noticed was the distinct scent of gasoline, lingering around the fire.

"Should we stop?" Tyler asked.

Lois pulled her head back in the cruiser and refocused her attention to the windshield, nodding her head. "No, keep following the trail."

"You sure?"

"Yeah, I'm sure."

We should really stop, Lois. There could be a clue or something that we might miss just driving by, but okay. Listening to her, Tyler applied some pressure to the gas and started driving beside the trail, following it down the rest of the street until he noticed the straight line of fire didn't stop at the end of the street. It went to the right and seemed to be going straight up Merrin Street—the street Mike and the Eaten family lived on. Once, he connected the two, he pressed down on the accelerator and flipped the siren on, which allowed a horrific screech to roar into the night air as they drove up to the hill.

"What're you doing?" Lois asked as soon as the siren started blaring. "We don't wanna wake these people up!"

"They're already up," Sam replied as the outline of Stephen Queen, Alfred Bates, and Charlie Ray emerged in the headlights.

Lifting their hands as the cruiser's lights revealed their faces, Mr. Queen, Mr. Bates, and Mr. Ray stepped away from the flames and onto the sidewalk, allowing space for Tyler to pull the cruiser up and stop right in front of them.

"Saved by the cleverly," Mr. Ray joked.

"I wouldn't place any bets on that, Mr. Ray," Mr. Queen replied.

When the cruiser came to a halt, Tyler switched off the siren and stepped out of the car, keeping the blue lights flashing. The lights were a candle in the dark compared to the blackness of space lingering from above, but they were enough to light the area up as more and more neighbors emerged from their houses. Sam and Lois got out of the car and followed Tyler over to the three neighbors.

"Benton," Mr. Bates spoke first.

"Mr. Bates, what the hell is going on, here?" Tyler asked.

"I was hoping you could tell us," Mr. Queen said.

Tyler stepped up to the three of them while Lois and Sam distanced themselves. Because this was the part of town Tyler patrolled; he had grown a strong relationship with the remaining townsfolk who lived up here, Lois kept her distance, allowing Tyler to speak with them in private.

The night air started growing colder as the wind began to pick up from the north, giving all those who were outside goosebumps, but the chill didn't stop the memories of the past from flooding into Sam's mind. Many of his childhood memories—and Tyler's, for that matter—were made on this street nearly twenty years back, creating an almost sixth sense feeling that lingered.

"You guys see anything weird? Anything out of the ordinary?" Tyler interrogated the three men.

"Nothing until I looked out the window and saw the flames leading up to the Eaten's place," Mr. Bates replied.

As soon as the name slipped out of Mr. Bates' mouth, Tyler spun around and focused on the flames, following them with his tired eyes until they stopped under a vehicle; Mike's truck. Mr. Bates was right; it was the Eaten house.

"Lois," he shouted.

"What?"

"The fire stops at Mike's place,"

Snapping her head back, she looked, gasping when she saw it. "Oh, shit!"

She broke away from everyone and started rushing to the house, clinging onto the shotgun with both hands.

"Lois! Lois!" Tyler shouted, hoping to stop her, even though he knew his attempts were useless. "Goddamn it."

Sam turned to him. "I'll go with her."

"No, Sam. Wait!"

Preparing to run after his partner and best friend, Tyler reverted his attention to the neighbors when Mr. Ray said, "There was also a gunshot."

Tyler glanced at him briefly before he looked at Mr. Bates—the one he felt most comfortable with since Mr. Bates used to be a town selectman a decade or so back. "Where?"

Mr. Bates nodded his head to the left. "Kramer's place."

Taking in a deep breath, Tyler directed his eyes to the Kramer residence off to his right, spotting the opened front door right around the same time Lois and Sam spotted the front door opened at the Eaten residence, too. He did what he could to control his breathing, but between the cool night air and the flashing blue lights bouncing off everything in sight, it seemed impossible for him to do so. But, the gold badge hanging on his chest reminded him what he needed to do.

He drew his pistol with one hand and took out his flashlight with the other and started toward Kramer's place. *Maybe I should wait for Lois and Sam,* he thought. *Yeah, that would be a good idea!* He kept marching forward—closing in on the old Kramer's house; almost as if he had no control over his own legs.

The sight of the reasonably young officer took the three neighbors by surprise, especially Mr. Queen, who had extreme feelings—mostly negative—about the youth of America. It felt strange for him to just stand there and watch. "Hold up!" he cried. "I'll go with you."

"No, it's okay. I got this under control," Tyler replied without looking away from the opened door.

His response fell on deaf ears; before he knew it, footsteps from behind started approaching him. Tyler rolled his eyes when he felt Mr. Queen's presence on his left side. "I told you I'll be fine."

"Better safe than sorry," Mr. Bates' voice spoke suddenly on his right side, spooking him. "Besides, God only knows what's in there."

While the three crept closer to the house, Mr. Ray's presence was nowhere to be found; he was heading in the opposite direction, running to his house. The echoes of his footsteps were noticeable to each of them, but it was Mr. Bates who focused on them.

"Where are you going?" he shouted.

"I'm gonna grab my revolver, and I'll be right there!"

Mr. Ray's answer got a reaction out of Tyler, enough so that he stopped and turned around to say he didn't want him to do that, but—just like Mr. Queen—Mr. Ray ignored him. *Goddamn old bastard! This is just going to make—*

"Hey, what's going on out here?" a voice called out.

"Yeah, what's going on?" another said in the opposite direction.

Taking his eyes off Mr. Ray, who dashed across the street to his dark, powerless home, he turned and looked up, only to see multiple other neighbors walking up to them, many dressed in nothing more than the clothes they went to bed in hours before.

"What the hell is all this?" a man's voice called out. "Do you have any idea what time it is?"

The size of the crowd grew as many neighbors—including younger children emerged from the darkness and approached the police cruiser from all sides. Because of his patrolling the street, Tyler knew nearly all of the people who lived on Merrin Street, so the large crowd wasn't as intimidating as it would've been to any other officer, but the overlapping conversations that started to amplify and overtake the street caused him to take a few steps back, along with Mr. Queen and Mr. Bates, who remained at his side.

"Does this have something to do with the power being out?" a woman cried out.

"Mommy, I wanna go to bed," a toddler's voice squeaked.

Tyler, lowering his flashlight to the ground interrupted the voices call out and demanding answers. "Everything is fine, but everyone needs to get back in their homes; this is not a request! I need everyone off the street now, please."

"Why?" the voice of an elderly woman cried out in fear. "What's happened?"

Trying not to start a panic, Tyler remained calm, hoping that Lois would finish up at the Eaten house to provide backup and help assist with the growing crowd; he figured having her would reassure some of the woman mixed in the crowd. While, he did his best to deescalate the situation, Mr. Queen, curious himself, stepped away and started to the front porch of the Kramer home, unbeknownst to Tyler.

Despite the Kramer's being private people, they had become friendly to Mr. Queen the longer they lived together, to the point where they would offer him a cup of coffee whenever they spotted him out and about. It was that sense of unacknowledged friendship that allowed him to feel comfortable enough to step onto the porch and eventually to the front door to figure out what was going on. "John? John?"

The sound of glass crackling beneath the rubber sole of his blue slippers chipped into the air as he approached the destroyed entrance of the home. With nothing more than the flashing blue lights from the patrol car illuminated the opening, it was hard for Mr. Queen to make out many of the details inside the—

"Oh, my God. Benton!" Mr. Queen shouted.

Mr. Queen's cry pulled Tyler's attention away from the crowd of neighbors—who were just starting to settle down, and sprinted over, detecting the horror in Queen's voice instantly. Mr. Bates and a number of other neighbors followed, each just as curious as the other.

Had it not been for the sound of distress in Mr. Queen's voice, Tyler would've told—and even warned—people to stay back, but the ideas of keeping the crowd back ceased the more Mr. Queen continued calling out his name, rushing him to the front door so he could see with his own eyes what Mr. Queen's eyes would never allow him to stop seeing.

Like Mr. Queen, glass started cracking beneath his service boots the closer Tyler got. But, unlike the old resident; who had the advantage of darkness to hide much of the graphic detail, Tyler lifted his flashlight, keeping the beam one step ahead, until the light shined down on a large piece of flesh that was once part of the face that made up Mr. Kramer resting peacefully next to the shotgun that made the brutal wound. Tyler gaged, unable to control the urge due to the grisly bloody sight. *His face! H—his face is fucking gone!*

In spite of the taste of vomit building in the back of his throat, Tyler shook the feeling off, reached down for the radio and called for immediate assistance, all while not taking his eyes off Mr. Kramer's faceless head. Sargent Dylan L'Heureux's responded first.

Many of the other neighbors, along with Mr. Bates, who charged to the front entrance were only able to see a fraction of what Tyler's flashlight revealed, but it was more than enough.

"Oh, my God! He's dead! Someone killed him!" a woman's voice shouted out.

"Holy shit, Kramer's dead!" said another.

"There's a killer on the loose!"

Screams and panic erupted, spreading beyond the front of the Kramer's home and reaching all the way to the Nelson residence in a matter of seconds. The large gathering of neighbors started scattering.

Panicking himself, as he came to the realization that they were only minutes behind the killer—a loud explosion from behind rocked the street, creating a massive fireball that hurtled into the air. Everyone on the street ducked, including L'Heureux and Meyers as they turned and watched Mike Eaten's truck burst into flames.

The screams on the street became deafening.

Tyler bolted out of the house, sprinted onto the front lawn and placed his hands across his cheeks in an attempt to amplify his voice.

"Everyone get out of here! Go! Get inside, now! Everyone get inside!!"

CHAPTER 8

With hands locked together, Mike and Kimberly ran, passing trees, broken branches, uneven ground, and slippery autumn leaves as they pushed deeper into the heart of the woods. The leafless branches stuck out like sharp obstacles, casting down shadows that resembled large fish hooks through the blue tint the moon above provided, reached out as if to grab the young couple the first chance they got.

The further they went in, the more unsettled the earth floor became; rocks and tree branches that snapped off during the ice storm the previous year made the path ahead trichinous. Mike nearly fell from tripping on a bolder sticking out of the ground while Kimberly struggled to avoid slipping on the piles of wet sticky leaves beneath her.

"Come on, come on!" Mike said, completely out of breath.

I'm trying, Mike. Goddamnit, I'm trying!

Both were exhausted. Both were out of breath, but the two teenagers kept pushing forward, using what little energy they could muster to keep up their speed; both fearing what may happen if they slowed down.

Because all the tree branches were naked, the cloudless sky allowed the moonlight to keep the entire forest lit up in a baby blue tint, lighting the path ahead as they pushed deeper, hoping the direction they were going would lead to something. *Anything.*

We're too loud. Kimberly thought. *Our footsteps are going to give us away. We need to find a place to hide! We nee—*

Mike shouted as a terribly loud thud came from his forehead, stopping him in his tracks. He suddenly shook his hand out of Kimberly's grip and pressed it to his forehead. Blood oozed out between the cracks of his fingers as the tree branch he'd struck bounced back and forth.

"Mike," she squeaked out.

He pressed his hand down on his forehead and pushed Kimberly on the shoulder with the other. "I'm okay; I'm okay! Just go! Go!"

They resumed running, refusing to look back no matter what noise—or noises—came from behind. They continued into the forbidden forest, trying to dodge every tree that was in front of them. Kimberly, while maintaining the same speed, was still concerned about the lack of quietness they were making; their footsteps were so heavy and loud, neither of them could hear any noise coming from behind. That only made the anxiety rushing through their teenage bodies even heavier to bear.

They had no sense of direction, and no landmarks or visible light could be seen, they were lucky they could see even six feet in front of them, so they choose to run in the direction of the moon shining down on their faces with each step. Nothing provided hope and the light of the moon was all they had to go with.

With Kimberly's phone in her pocket and Mike's phone resting peacefully on his kitchen counter, neither of them were able to know for sure how long they'd been running, but both silently agreed they hadn't run far enough. They wanted as much distance as they could get.

Mike started to slow down first, but Kimberly wasn't long after. She didn't want to, but the farther she had to extend her arm to keep her hand holding his, the faster she slowed down. A large bolder approaching from their left seemed to be the best—and really only spot for them to rest and not be out in the open.

They stopped, leaping behind and leaning their backs onto the cold balder. Both were utterly out of breath, so much so that Kimberly felt as if she didn't have enough strength in her body to breathe in or out while Mike struggled with the weak feeling lodged in the middle of his left knee—a warning sign that it hadn't fully healed from the trauma it received last football season.

Inhaling deep with her nostrils—trying to avoid using her mouth for the purpose of remaining quiet, Kimberly calmed herself faster than she thought it would take her to do so. Once she and Mike had their breaths back, they turned to each other, both shivering with fear as the night air blew against their rosy cheeks.

They listened.

Soft—almost ambient—noises surrounded them.

Leaves. Kimberly whispered. *That's coming from leaves…right?*

The two lovers stared blankly into each other's eyes, fearful to so much as move a muscle. But, they knew they, at some point were—*Snap!*

They turned, preparing to run.

Another snap. Only this time closer.

Kimberly placed her hand over her mouth, hoping to stifle any sound that may come out. Keeping themselves pressed firmly against the rock, Mike turned to the direction of the sound.

Another snap cried out into the forest; a snap so close, it generated a vocal gasp out of Mike as he looked up, preparing for a face to jump out in front of them. A face of a deer. Kimberly, also looking in the same direction, focused on the forest floor, preparing for that rush of fear to go racing through her body the moment a large shadow emerged. It did—a shadow just as tall and bulky looking as she imagined it would be.

It drew closer, providing a more definite outline with each step it took.

Large ears emerged.

Mike closed his fist and prepared to attack.

Kimberly's heart thumped against her chest.

Another snap.

Mike prepared himself.

Another step.

Mike jumped out and swung.

The face of a deer emerged.

Then, it suddenly jumped back, turned and darted away; its four hoofs thumping onto the ground as the spooked animal ran off and eventually disappeared back into the forest. Dropping his fist after watching the frightened animal run, Mike hid back behind the rock and grabbed Kimberly's cold clammy hand. "It's okay. It's okay."

His soothing voice surprisingly brought her panic down to bearable, allowing her to lower her hand from her face. She trembled as she looked into his eyes. It was apparent they both felt the same way; scared, isolated, and cold as the night air brushing against their faces with fear overtaking everything else. Once the deer was out of sight and its footsteps scamper away, it became quiet again. A few crickets chirped somewhere in the darkness, and a couple leaves crackled against the ground, but no other noises were audible.

They had lost their purser; at least for the time being, but both knew the longer they remained motionless behind that rock, the higher the chance that would change. They needed to move quickly. Kimberly emphasized that as she dug into her pocket and pulled out her cell phone. The battery was down to *51%*.

50%

The cellphone screen lit up her face in a bright white as she tapped on her location app, hoping to get a sense of where they were. Because they were in the middle of the woods, Kimberly didn't have much hope for the app, but she figured it was better than nothing. *Please, please, please, give me something to go on…come on load. Load!*

"The signal is too weak out here," Mike concluded.

An hourglass appeared on the screen. "Hold on."

Mike leaned in closer, nearly bumping against Kimberly's head.

49%

The map loaded, revealing nothing more than their location in the shape of a blue dot with a pulse beating every few seconds. Nothing but a white canvas surrounded them on the map, an indication there was nothing around. It was proof they were alone. The sight forced an eye roll out of Mike. *Of course.*

Kimberly felt the same way, but, in one last attempt of hope, she placed her fingers on the large screen and pushed them away, which allowed the map to expand, revealing what appeared to be a trail not that far ahead. "What's that?"

Mike took the phone from her and looked carefully. The more he looked, the more he started to question whether or not it was, indeed a just a trail. Kimberly thought the same and asked before he was able to speak.

"Maybe it's a road?" he suggested.

Dismissive at first, but the more she thought about it, the more she thought it could be plausible; after all the entire town was filled with vacant and unused road, so the idea wasn't as farfetched as it sounded—

A snapping noise off in the distance forced both of them to their feet. Instead of trying to figure out what the sound was, they grabbed hold of each-others hand and resumed running, pressing deeper into the woods with each passing second.

48%

Dozens of Humvees pulled onto Merrin Street and followed the dying trail of flames until the lead vehicle drove up to Tyler Benton's police cruiser and stopped mere inches from the bumper. The horrific screech of the breaks coming to a hard stop rattled into the ears of everyone remaining on the street as the military convoys arrived.

Despite Tyler's harsh warnings for everyone to get off the street, some neighbors still remained, curiously looking on, trying to figure out what was going on, including Scott and Ellen Nelson—parents of James Nelson—who were far enough away from the scene to see the vehicles pulling up, but unable to hear Tyler's pleas for everyone to get inside.

"There's something you don't see every day," Ellen joked.

While they looked on as the Humvee's blocked the street and military soldiers came rushing out from each vehicle, James—once sure his parents were outside—raced across the living room and into the kitchen, using the darkness as cover. With his aluminum foil hat stretched across his head combined with the semi-automatic paintball gun in his hand, a sense of adventure and even excitement filled the young boy. What fear he had back when he first saw the figure through the telescope was now gone as he pushed open the backdoor and went darting outside.

Which way? Which way, James? He mumbled. *Maybe I can go down the street and meet up with the military men and help—no. No, they wouldn't let me. They won't let me at all.*

For the first time, a sense of hesitation came over James. He started questioning himself and what his true intentions were for heading out into the night when there was clearly something wrong. The feeling of second-guessing his decision took him off guard because, in his short life, he'd never reconsidered *anything* once his mind was made up. But, on that crisp September evening, he found himself doing so.

Lost in thought, he tightened his grip on the loaded paintball gun, staring at the ground as he contemplated what his next move would be. Should he stay or should he go? He weighed both options and consequence of both before he made his decision.

Staying close to the house, James walked to the end of the house and turned the corner, crouching down to keep his movement a secret. By the time he was halfway to the front of the house, the decision to proceed felt like the right one despite the momentous backlash he would receive from his parents the moment they discovered what he was up to. Watching where he stepped, James nearly tiptoed up to the front and slowly lifted his head above the railing to the front steps to get a better view of—

He ducked back down.

His heart started pounding.

He closed his eyes and started shaking as he fearfully anticipated for the sound of his mother's voice to emerge in front of him and demand to know what he was doing with a paintball gun and his backpack on. He started brainstorming his mind; trying to come up with some logical excuse that his folks might believe, but nothing came to mind. Instead, he kept still and hoped that the reaming he anticipated wouldn't be as bad as some of the others he's received before.

Her voice never came. Neither did any footsteps.

Confused as to what was taking her so long, James opened his eyes and slowly lifted his head back up over the railing to get another look. His parents were still in the front yard; standing in the same position they were when he spotted them. The sight brought a sense of relief to him; he hadn't been spotted.

In the distance, he could see more vehicles approaching from the end of the street, but all his attention was focused on his parents as he crouched down, waiting for the perfect moment to leap from cover and jet across the street without being spotted. He stayed patient, anxiously waiting until he had the confidence to move.

The bright headlights to the approaching Humvee's were blinding, casting a bright beam across the entire lower half of the street. The illumination revealed much, including neighbors running to their houses as quick as they could along with multiple military soldiers exiting the Humvees and starting to spread throughout the street. *Oh, shit. I gotta get going before they come up here. They'll spot me for sure if I stay here! I gotta—*

He ran; darting across the street as fast as he could while clinging onto his paintball gun as if his young life depended on it. His mind raced faster with each step, but regardless, he pushed through and made it across the street. The moment he cleared the street and felt grass beneath his feet, he ducked down and leaped behind the large pine tree directly across from the house. Again, he waited for his mother's voice to cry out his name.

She never did. He still hadn't been spotted.

He kept behind the tree, deciding to remain there until his parents went back inside, thinking it would lower the chances of being spotted. The idea faded when sounds of approaching boots and military orders being shouted out started getting closer. He turned quickly to the direction of the noise. Soldiers were approaching straight toward him. They were still a reasonable distance away, but the footsteps grew louder with each one. He needed to move if he was going to avoid being seen.

He turned—taking once last glance at his parents, making sure they still weren't looking over, while indirectly casting a muffled goodbye, in a sense. He gave a quick glance at his father, but focused on his mother, hoping deep down their close relationship wouldn't be affected by his choice to head off into the night.

James could see the look of nervousness smeared across her face and began feeling guilty; he knew it would be the feeling she would end up struggling with for the rest of the night. But, his imagination and sense of inner vigilantly was calling louder than anything else, and he chose to take the more unclear path, intending to prove all his doubters wrong and be hailed a hero!

Using the shadows of the night, he stepped away from the towering pine and ran off, past the Koontz home and into the woods behind.

Being one of the first military personnel at the scene, Dylan L'Heureux took charge right away, joining Tyler Benton in ordering people to get back into their houses and behind locked doors. As his voice screeched and his men began spreading across the once quiet neighborhood, Lois Tangley and Sam Rainey rushed out of the Eaten home, charged past Mike Eaten's burning vehicle and darted across the street, spotting Tyler standing with L'Heureux in front of the Kramer house. Lois spotted the military soldiers entering the house as she approached.

"—we're searching the area now," L'Heureux answered Tyler. "How many houses on this street are vacant?"

"None, this is one of the only streets that's still at 100% capacity," Tyler replied.

The conversation paused when they spotted Lois and Sam running up to them. Sam snapped his head back and forth between his best friend and his military advisor. "What?"

"He's been here," Tyler said.

"How do you know?" Sam asked.

"Because someone smashed through John Kramer's door and killed him with a shotgun."

Lois gasped, lifting her hands to cover her mouth.

"Jesus Christ," Sam sighed, trying to take in how bad the situation was deteriorating. "He must've been over at the house across the street, too. Their doors all smashed in."

Tyler turned to Lois. "Did you find Mike and Kimberly?"

The blank expression across her face answered before the words came out of her mouth. Tyler, holstering his pistol as military soldiers started scattering around him, wiped his hand across his face and began contemplating how to proceed.

"Neighbors say the saw the flames first before they heard any screams," C.J. Meyers explained as he walked over to L'Heureux. "Nobody heard a gunshot, though. At least, no one we've talked too. Everyone heard the explosion, though."

With his voice loud enough to be heard over the constant noise that surrounded them, Tyler, Lois, and Sam were able to hear most of what Meyer's said. Tyler opened his mouth to speak, but Lois beat him to it. "What do you mean screams?"

Myers turned to her. "Neighbors heard a woman screaming after they spotted the flames."

"Whose house does the flames go to, anyway?" L'Heureux followed up.

"The Eaten house," Tyler answered.

"Any idea why?" Meyers shrugged.

Tyler—feeling like the answer was staring him straight in the face—unnoticeably squeezed his cellphone through his pants pocket, making sure it was there, despite already knowing that it was. "Not, yet, but I'm working on it."

Taking in Tyler's answer—along with his look of unfathomable confusing—L'Heureux turned to Sam, his unofficial boss, and asked what the next course of action should be.

"Search the area, get statements from everyone, and we'll see where we are from there; that's all we can do for now," Sam answered.

L'Heureux and Myers took the orders in strive and sped away, but slowed down when Tyler's voice cried out, asking for them to insist on keeping all the neighbors and civilians off the street. L'Heureux replied with a simple thumbs up. Once he got his reply, he turned to Lois, who was blankly staring at him. "What?"

"I should probably go help them?" she suggested.

Responding quickly, Sam agreed, adding, "It might make the interview process go a little smoother with someone familiar to the people here— might make them more comfortable."

Clearly not for the idea, preferring Lois stayed close by, Tyler hesitated, but only briefly as he could see it was something Lois wanted to do. *Always the fixer,* Tyler thought. *Where would I be without you?*

He didn't want to tell her no, for fear of making her think that he didn't trust her, but he also didn't want to say yes off the cuff, given the dire situation they all were in. It was a tough choice for him to make. "Alright, but radio me if you need anything."

She smiled, sensing the worry in his masculine voice. Rather than making a humorous joke, she chose the more sensitive way, promising him she would as she patted him on the shoulder.

"Lois?" Sam spoke suddenly, forcing her to look back. "Feel free to stick with L'Heureux. He doesn't make for the warmest company, but he's got good intentions."

Taken by the thoughtfulness of the advice, given their butting heads earlier in the night, she answered with a quick, "Thanks."

Sam even forced out a smile, keeping it long enough for Lois to not be able to see it disappear until she started running after L'Heureux, shouting his name to get his attention. Fearing he made the wrong choice, Tyler kept his eyes on her until she caught up with L'Heureux and Myers just in front of the Castillo home.

"She'll be fine," Sam broke the silence. "Those guys know how to take care of themselves. It's everyone else in this dying town I'm worried about."

Sam's blunt—yet truthful—words, that were clearly an attempt to make Tyler feel at ease with the decision he made, brought him out of his train of thought and back into the disaster they were currently in the middle of. Sam watched from the corner of his eye as Tyler's attention shifted away from his partner and onto himself.

"What?" Sam shrugged.

Tyler stepped closer to him as military soldiers passed by on all sides, heading in L'Heureux's direction. "I need answers."

The blunt, yet forceful demand from his once best friend drew a chuckle out of Sam, a chuckle he desperately needed on a night that seemed endless. The action drew the utterly opposite reaction from Tyler. "What?"

Sam—nervous as he was—brushed his hand through his sweaty hair. "You make it seem like I have all the answers when I don't."

Assuming incorrectly that Sam was trying to pivot, Tyler stood his ground. "You know a hell of a lot more than the rest of us."

"Not as much as you'd think," Sam mumbled, wishing for the first time in years that he had a cigarette.

The activity surrounding them forced Tyler to look up, spotting military personnel expanding their presence across the entire street with a large group surrounding the Kramer home. He was a bit taken back by what he was witnessing; the only time he saw such a large military force together was typically in the movies. Never in real life. The sight felt a little overwhelming, but thoughts of Lois and even Sam with him, helped that feeling stay somewhat dormant. But, he still wanted answers. "We both saw how Old Man Claire was killed. No man is strong enough to rip someone's head in half; let alone pull an entire window out of its frame. There's something you're not telling me, and I wanna know what it is."

Being friends for over two decades, Sam could tell very easily when Tyler was confident, and when he was serious; the look in his eyes revealed it to be the latter. *Goddamn it, Tyler. Don't put me in this situation. Not again...*

"Jess and I have been working together for years; trying to find the cure for cancer," Sam began. "It took years for us to get the funding—everyone said it was a waste of resources. 'Why use the money for science when there are towns like this on the verge of collapse?' That's what nearly every person in Congress said. It got to the point where we thought about just calling it a day and moving on."

"What changed?" Tyler quickly asked, hoping to get the answer he was searching. "Money doesn't move until something changes."

"The right person in the right place got affected by the disease, and all of a sudden, we found ourselves swimming in cash. Long story short, we concluded that the cure—or at least the foundation—of cancer isn't going to be found in some off the grid research lab. It's in us. Each of us."

The normalized scientific explanation was enough for Tyler to follow, but he got confused by the last three words to come out of Sam's mouth.

Tyler stepped closer as more military Humvee's pulled onto the street, the engines roaring throughout the neighborhood. "What?"

Growing a bit impatient due to the activity rattling his anxiety, Sam tried to find the words to dumb down what he was explaining. "It's like when you get cut—it bleeds, then it stops, then it scabs over and finally, after a few weeks, it heals, right?"

Tyler, no stranger to cuts, bruises—or even fractures, because of his football days in high school, agreed. "So?"

"Well, Jess and I thought if we could speed up that process, it would bring us one step closer, but we needed to build up the body's metabolism and muscles, first. So, we tested that theory, and apparently, it works," Sam shrugged, knowing full well Tyler would react negatively. "At least the metabolism part, anyway."

*

Watching as the vile of green liquid, they both called XXC sat peacefully on the lab table, Jess Sowa and Sam admired their latest achievement. Unlike previous attempts, this newest, and what was possibly the last batch, the two brilliant—and at times purposely braggadocios scientist, decided that, instead of rushing to try and get results in order to persuade the top leaders at the Center for Disease Control to keep the cash flow going, they would take their time to make sure the experiment—or "cock tail" as Jess would call it, was in line with what their beliefs were. It was a risky idea, though, as the deadline to provide a result had come and gone weeks ago. And money was drying up fast.

"You think this is it?" Jess finally asked, keeping her eye on the vile.

God, I hope so, Sam thought, for he knew that if this last attempt failed, everything was over. It left him uneasy.

Despite the lab having no windows to the outside world and because the only clock in the entire room was on the far back wall, out of his view, Sam knew it was late into the evening; possibly close to midnight or perhaps even later. He could feel the urge—and need—of sleep starting to build up. Jess, on the other hand, was the total opposite. The night was young as far as she was concerned,

"So how do you—"

A groan from across the room spooked Jess, and she was unable to finish her sentence. In a panic, both scientists looked in the direction of the noise. Another groan rumbled into the lab, deep enough to bounce off the white walls.

"Oh, shit," Jess said. "He's starting to wake up."

Sprinting into action before Jess made the analysis, Sam spun around to the lab bench behind him. The metal slab on the top of the table, that reeked of disinfectants, was neatly covered with blades, clamps, and many other necessary tools required for a research lap, all made of pure tempered steel for surgical quality and accuracy. He reached past all of them and grasped onto a large syringe filled with a clear thick liquid.

The groans intensified, panicking the both of them even more. Jess, keeping her eyes in the direction of the noises, began taking several steps back. "Sam, hurry. Hurry!" she pleaded.

"I am, I am!"

Knowing the danger of what would happen to their patient—Russel Fritz—and the agonizing pain he would be in, Sam rushed over to the opposite side of the lab, his heart beating like a drum inside his chest cavity.

The closer he got to his patient of ten years, the more detailed the burns on Fritz's hands and arms were. It may have been years prior, but Sam still felt guilty for not paying more attention to the potential side effects of the first round of XXC, despite the results seeming positive on, Charlie, the mouse used for the experimentation. But, by the time Charlie started showing side effects of disastrous proportions, the first round was already in Frtiz's body. Charlie died less than a week after receiving the first round; Fritz was placed into a medically induced coma.

Sam gave him a week to live. It turned out not to be the case.

Fritz's skin burned from the inside out, charring most of his hands, all of his stomach, chest, penis and much of his face, but, he clung on against it all—

The shackles that held down the burnt subject clanked back and forth as Fritz woke up and began attempting to break free. Assuming Fritz's hearing had diminished as his ears had also received substantial damage from the first round of XXC—so much so that the right one had nearly melted into his head, Sam shouted, "I'm coming, I'm coming! It's okay; it's okay!"

Watching with a sense of dread, Jess felt as if she was unable to move. Thoughts of Fritz breaking free to seek revenge after years of scientific torture—typically at her order—shook her like a traumatized victim.

The groans turned into grunts as Fritz began his assault on the chains wrapped around his wrists and ankles. With the white sheet over his face, he was unable to see anything, which only added to his built up anger. He started pounding on the table, slamming the bottoms of his fist onto the metal slab he was strapped to. Then, he did the same with his feet, using every bit of energy he had to break free. The pounds were so fierce; he didn't even know Sam was next to him until a sharp sting entered his right arm.

Fritz grunted as he reached out, attempting to grab anything within reach. A rush of an ice cold substance entered him and slithered up his right arm, numbing the veins it flowed up in before spreading into the rest of his body in lightning speed. His arms suddenly became heavy, almost as if they were caved in cement. Darkness then entered his vision, forcing his chard eyelids to close, until that sudden cold rush reached his brain and drifted him off to sleep.

Once the last drop of IV was out of the syringe, Sam stepped away. He sighed with relief when Fritz's hand tumbled down onto the metal slab, and his movement stopped. The strength of the IV was impeccable—strong enough to knock out a horse, but Sam didn't want to take any chances.

Silence returned to the large lab, a calm so deafening, Jess thought for a brief moment she'd gone deaf. Slowly overcoming his fear, Sam controlled his breathing—and emotions—with minimal effort; he knew Fritz was immobilized for the foreseeable future. He tossed the empty syringe into the trash beside him.

"Are we good?" Jess asked.

Sam, desperately in need for sleep, acknowledged with the bare minimum.

A smile grew on her face as she picked up a syringe beside her.

Excellent, she concluded, now is as perfect time as any. We'll get this done tonight and by tomorrow; we'll have it! After all these years, we'll finally—

"What are you doing?" Sam frantically asked her.

She looked up from the syringe that was nearly full of the latest—and possibly last—batch of XXC. Her lack of a response was muted, but her action spoke louder than anything she could've said. In a swift swoop, she pulled the large needle out and began taking steps toward the now comatose Russel Fritz. Sam grabbed her arm after the fourth step. "No, Jess."

"Let go of me, Sam." She ordered.

"No, this is not how we do it! It needs to be tested before we can try it on him. We have no idea what will happen if we don't test it first!"

Jess began shaking her arm, trying to get it out of Sam's grip. "We don't have time to wait; this needs to happen now."

"That's a lie, Jess! That's a goddamn lie—we both know why you're willing to do this," Sam rumbled as he squeezed her arm tighter.

She resisted harder. "Get the fuck off me, Sam! Get off me!"

Her shout echoed throughout the large white room. From the look in her eyes, it was clear she was a word or two away from swinging a fist in his direction.

She was angry; angrier than he'd ever seen her before. There was no reasoning with her—there was barely any on a good day. So, instead of trying to keep her still, he loosened his grip, allowing her to shimmy her arm out of his hand and resumed heading over to Fritz.

"Goddamn it, Jess! This isn't how it's supposed to be!" Sam shouted, trying to get in the last word.

"Losing everything we've been working on for years just to follow protocol isn't how it's supposed to be, either."

"We'll find another way Je—"

"No, we won't. CDC will be here Monday, and if we don't have something concrete to show, then this gets shut down. For good this time."

Sam halted his response, allowing the revelation of Jess' answer to sink in. It didn't take long for it to do so, and once it did, a bit of understanding fell upon him—he was able to see where Jess was coming from. His silence allowed Jess to refocus on Fritz; the syringe grasped tightly in her hand.

The white sheet placed over Russel Fritz covered him from head to toe; not even his hands were sticking out anymore. Despite paying little attention, the sheet was so still, it appeared that Fritz wasn't even breathing. It almost looked as if he was dead. She reached for the corner of the sheet closest to his burnt hand and slowly lifted it—

"What if something happens?" Sam said, suddenly. "Something we can't control?"

The hesitation in his voice was enough to slow Jess down for her to give it some thought, but not enough to change her mind. Nor was his warning that should she proceed, the consequences—no matter what they were—would fall directly to her. She responded by inserting the needle deep into Fritz' inner forearm; deeper than necessary, almost as if to purposely harm him. Sam spotted the cruel gesture but chose to remain quiet about it.

As soon as the last drops of XXC were pushed out of the syringe, Jess yanked out the needle and took a few steps back, almost as if anticipating some response from the comatose experiment. But, to her surprise, nothing came to pass. There was no sudden jerking of the body or horrible screech from the subject. Just silence.

When enough time passed, to the point where Jess felt foolish just standing there, she looked over her shoulder to Sam, who was also waiting on some reaction from the still body of Russel Fritz. The look on his exhausted face revealed he was as dumbfounded as she was. He responded with a simple shrug.

She crossed her arms over her breasts, annoyed. What the fuck, she thought, why isn't anything happening? Something should've happened by now.

She stepped back and finally turned to Sam. "So, now what?"

Responding with the same shrug as he did before, he took in a deep breath of disinfectant air, concluding that this batch of XXC—just like the rest—was nothing more than a dud. Ineffective.

"Let's just get him back to his room and see if anything changes in the morning; nothing we can do now."

Sam's answer—while being the right one—frustrated Jess. Her body language and face made that quite obvious. "Fine."

Rather than trying to reassure her that tomorrow could—and would—provide them with answers, Sam let Jess stew with her annoyance for fear of getting into yet another argument with her; he was too tired to fight and just wanted to get home and pass out the moment his head hit the pillow.

Without speaking, the two co-workers walked back over to the motionless patient, preparing to take him back to his 'room' in Section D, all the while overlooking that the hole where the needle was pushed into his arm was no longer bleeding, or even visible—almost as if the wound was never there.

*

"Great, a serial killer hocked up on steroids and running around Hunting at night—just what we need," Tyler sighed.

"Call it what you want, but he needs to be found," Sam bluntly said.

Tyler sighed as he watched the activity throughout the street. With the power out, nothing more than the Humvee headlights provided light for the surrounding area. The HID's were blinding, but since they only lit up half the street, they were going to have to move them further up the road. Tyler shifted his attention again to directly across the street, spotting Mr. Ray talking with L'Heureux and Meyers; his hands flopping in the air as he told the two of them what he'd seen.

"Dead or alive?" Tyler asked, suddenly.

The blunt—yet quick question, forced Sam's attention away from the darkness that loomed in front of the headlights where the range of the HID blubs stopped. "What?"

"Do we keep him alive, or do we kill him?" Tyler asked again.

Sam took his time answer. It was evident by the expression on his face he'd never given the idea any thought; he always assumed he knew what the unspoken answer was. Tyler waited—longer than he thought he would—for a response.

"He's U.S. government property; he technically doesn't belong to us."

"Well, technically he's killed two civilians. So, in my book, that makes him ours," Tyler followed up.

Sam sympathized, but it was of no use. Tyler was set in his way, and nothing was going to change his mind, ending the discussion with a simple, "If I get the chance to take him out, I will."

What! You let him get killed? HOW STUPID ARE YOU? All the time and research we put into this, now pissed away. All because you couldn't obey one goddamn thing I said! Jess' voice echoed in Sam's ear. In the years he's known her, Jess has always had a short fuse, but he knew damn well that should something happen that resulted in any type of setback, he would see a side of her that he's never seen before. The thought gave him goosebumps as the wind started picking up.

As he brought himself back into the moment, he started to observe the full picture and came to the realization that the situation had passed the point of no return a few murders back. He was confident that Jess wouldn't see it that way—she would lobby for the exact opposite. He made his decision about how to proc—

"So, if you were psychopathic serial killer, running around in the middle of the night, where would you be?" Tyler interrupted.

The wind picked up in intensity, sending a deep shiver down his spine as Sam began thinking, trying to determine where his mass murdering test subject would head next. At first, nothing came to mind. Like the rest of the once lively town of Hunting, this part was also riddled with pockets of urban decay and loss of population. Everything pointed to a dead end—shouts emerged at the far end of the street, forcing everyone to look up. Tyler and L'Heureux made eye contact on either side of the street, both with a look of surprise.

The first noise was a scream, but the next was unmistakably a cry for help. "Please, someone help! Help!"

Drawing his pistol, Tyler and Sam charged toward the cries for help. L'Heureux and Meyers followed suit, shouting to the surrounding soldiers, "Up the hill! Move, move!"

The deafening pleas for help were impossible to ignore as they amplified and caught the attention of the neighbors, who had obeyed orders and got themselves behind locked doors, to the point where many, including Mr. Queen and Mr. Ray, peered through their windows to get a glimpse at what was happening.

When first running up the road, Tyler was unsure where the screams were coming from; it wasn't until he was nearly at the top before he found out. "Mrs. Nelson!"

Sobbing in her light pink bathrobe with her hands covering her face, Ellen Nelson stumbled around in her front yard. Her legs were so weak, Tyler nearly lost his footing once he reached her and she collapsed in his arms. He placed his pistol down on the cracked sidewalk and wrapped his arms around her, allowing her face to bury in his shoulder. She swept.

"Hey, hey, hey. It's okay."

Lois and Sam caught up quickly, but stopped short of the sidewalk, allowing enough space in between them and Tyler so Mrs. Nelson wouldn't be bombarded with military personnel standing over her during her moment of hysteria. L'Heureux and Myers were the first army officers to reach the house; their footsteps echoed the closer they approached.

"What the hell is going on?" L'Heureux asked.

The front door to the Nelson house swung open. A flashlight beam emerged. Meyers drew his rifle. Lois raised her arm and pushed the barrel of the gun down, not a second after Meyers raised it. "Wait," she ordered.

Tyler looked up at the approaching figure. "Scott."

"Benton! Benton, he's gone," Scott Nelson said in distress.

"Who?" Sam asked.

"James!"

The answer immediately drew Lois to the same level of panic. "What? Are you sure?"

"Of course I am!" Mr. Nelson shouted as he bent down and took his wife out of Tyler's arms. "I checked the whole damn house, and he's not here!"

Tyler stood the second she was out of his grip and turned to Lois, knowing the news of James missing would be tough for her to hear, given her past history with the Nelson family.

"Somebody took him!" Ellen sniffled out. "Someone came into our house and took him!"

No, Tyler thought. *That's impossible. This psycho skinned a deer alive and pulled the head off Old Man Claire, but he wouldn't break into a house and kidnap a child, right? I mean, what would he want with a borderline autistic kid, anyway?*

"No," Sam replied. "No, he wouldn't do that. There's no reason for him to do so."

"There was no reason for him to rip off Old Man Claire's skull either, but here we are," Lois replied.

"Old Claire is dead?" Scott Nelson asked from the ground, clearly listening to everything the trio said to each other.

The panic in Scott Nelson's voice grew, nearly reaching the same level as his muted wife. A rush of adrenaline ran down Tyler's spine, fearing that Mr. Nelson would start demanding answers—answers that he didn't have. He started calmly asking the worried father to get his wife back inside and promised he would get a search of the area underway to find James.

"The hell I will!" Mr. Nelson rose to his feet as he tightened the knot to his bathrobe. "You expect me to do nothing while my son is out here running around with all this going on? No, I wanna know what the fuck is going on, Tyler! I wanna—"

"Scott," Lois calmingly interrupted as she raised her arms and walked over to them. "Scott, just relax, okay? Just relax."

"No, Lois!" his voice cracked. "Don't tell me to relax. James is missing! He's out here all by himself!"

Having known Scott for many years and getting to know him every time she was called over to the house because James was being picked on at school, Lois knew how devastated Scott must've been, because she felt the same way, too. The thought of James out there, somewhere in the night with a killer on the loose, created a sense of unrest so astounding, it was hard for her to try and calm Mr. Nelson when she felt the same way. But, regardless of what she was feeling, she knew allowing Mr. Nelson to head out on his own and put himself in danger would solve nothing.

"I'll find him," Lois said loud enough over all the noise throughout the street. "I'll find him. We're gonna go look right now, okay?"

Watching as Lois remarkably calmed Mr. Nelson down, Tyler turned to Sam as L'Heureux and Meyers stormed toward them.

"What the hell is going on?" L'Heureux shouted.

"Some kid ran off, and they don't know where he is," Sam answered.

"Not just some kid, Sam. He's autistic and probably scared out of his mind," Tyler barked.

"You sure he ran off or was he taken?" Meyers asked.

Jesus Christ! Sam thought. *Does anyone ever listen to a goddamn thing I say?*

"We need to find him," Tyler borderline ordered.

L'Heureux—offended by the demanding tone—scoffed. "This is a military operation, and in case you forgot, we have bigger problems going on here. You expect me to drop everything and start searching for a kid?"

Tyler stepped forward. "Let me tell you—"

"Sarg!" a voice shouted from behind them before Tyler finished his sentence, which was about to persist of a reminder about jurisdiction and who was technically in charge.

"What?" L'Heureux growled.

The soldier, Private James Curtis, ran over to them, out of breath. "Neighbors next to the Kramer house said, they heard screaming and then heard noises from the back of the house. We checked the back yard, and there's footprints that lead into the woods."

"What size footprints?" Tyler asked, fearing the prints might be the same size as James'.

The soldier replied quickly. "Size twelve; same size as Joe Catalano."

L'Heureux and Meyer's heads sprang up and looked in Sam's direction. "Show me," L'Heureux ordered.

Following the order, Private Curtis lead L'Heureux and Meyers down the street toward the Kramer house. Their footsteps echoed in their heaviness, but paled in comparison to L'Heureux's deep voice, shouting out for as many soldiers as he could get to follow him.

Sam, despite fighting the urge to follow, remained with Lois and Tyler as the crowd of soldiers grew in size the closer L'Heureux and Meyers got to the Kramer house. Thoughts raced throughout his mind, questioning why Patient 37—Russell Fritz—would be in this part of town. *Why here? Why on this street? Why Old Man Claire? Wh*—

"Who's Catalano?" Lois asked.

"A security guard back at the lab," Sam finally answered after Lois asked again. "Fritz killed him and took some of his clothing just before he escaped."

"Great," Lois sighed, trying to fight off the lightheadedness she could feel creeping up on her. She focused her thoughts on James, effectively adding to the feeling. She turned to Tyler, figuring he would have an idea of where the trio would go from here. "Now what?"

Lois was right, Tyler did have an idea, but it was far from finished or even promising. It was basically just a hunch. "The abandon steel mill is about a mile and a half into the woods. If he did head through the backyard and into the woods, that's exactly the direction he would be heading."

Lois, after taking the idea in, was impressed. Sam was not. "What makes you think he would head there?"

Sam's question gave Tyler a considerable pause. That was the part of his hunch that he couldn't figure out. *There's something—something I'm missing. What the hell is it, though. Come on, Tyler. Think, goddamn it, thi—*

His face fixated onto the far end of the street toward the Kramer house, long enough to see L'Heureux and Meyers reach the front yard, but they slowly started to drift to the Eaten house.

"He's after them," he thought out loud.

"He's after who?" Lois asked. "I'm confused."

"Kimberly Wilson left me a message earlier saying her and her boyfriend Mike Eaten hit someone on their way home. Then, the person attacked them…it must've been Fritz they hit," he theorized.

Slowly realizing that the idea was credible, Sam turned to the Eaten house. Despite the vehicle still in flames, the fire that lead to the house was now completely out; nothing more than a bit of light smoke rising from the cracked pavement was visible. *Son of a bitch,* Sam thought. *That's exactly what happened.*

Lois nodded, agreeing with Tyler's theory. "Yeah, the front of Sam's truck is all dented to shit—I spotted that the second I saw it."

"That doesn't explain how he found them, though," Sam said, crossing his arms as the wind started to pick up.

Shit, it doesn't, Tyler thought to himself. *But, something must've happened during or after the accident. What the hell could've—the fire!* "What road were we on when we first saw the fire?"

Lois, unprepared for such a random question, turned to Sam, hoping he might remember. The look on his face proved he didn't know the answer off the top of his head; it was up to her. "Um…"

"Lake Street, wasn't it?" Sam asked with a lack of confidence in his voice.

"Yes!" Lois shouted. "Lake Street. It was Lake Street."

"Why?" Sam asked.

"I'm trying to think of which streets you have to drive down to get here…" Tyler explained. "It's been so long since I've had to remember any of these street names."

It was true, so many streets on this side of town were completely abandoned, which meant many of the employees of the Hunting Police

Department—Tyler and Lois included—very rarely patrolled the area because nobody was there. It was a struggle for both of their memories.

Lois' attention, however, drifted away and onto James when the sobs from Ellen Nelson started up again. "I have to go find James."

Against the idea, Tyler hesitated to respond but knew a missing person—most importantly, a missing child, was a priority that needed immediate attention, especially a child such as James. Plus, Tyler knew the relationship between Lois and the Nelsons was something she kept close to her heart. He allowed it, adding, "Sam and I will head to the abandon steel mill. Maybe, with any luck, we'll be able to find something there."

"Okay," Lois sighed. "But be careful!"

"Always," Tyler assured. "Keep your radio with you. I'll call you if we find something."

The adrenaline in Lois was at full throttle, she could feel the energy building up in her legs to get going and join L'Heureux and Meyers, but she paused. The night was going along at a pretty fast rate, but in that brief moment, time felt as if it slowed down. She kept her eyes locked onto Tyler's, gazing deep into his dreamy brown eyes—eyes she'd secretly fallen in love with years ago. She couldn't explain it, but an emotional feeling started building inside her; a feeling she thought would remain dormant for her entire life. It was a feeling of distress and sadness, a feeling that resembled the same characteristics as an unwelcomed goodbye.

Her mouth opened, ready to reinforce her order to be careful, and possibly even reveal a sign of her true feelings for her partner, but by the time she found the words to say, Tyler and Sam were already back to the patrol car.

That feeling of sadness only grew as she re-focused her attention on James.

The sour smell had essentially faded to the test subject—the scent had blended in with the night air that blew into the nose holes of its fleshly disguise. The lack of peripheral vision had become accustomed, too. The eye holes it peered out of

were plentiful, but the loose chunks of flesh that dangled on the sides limited its 20/20 vision. But, both were ineffective in stopping the rabid patient from its one and only goal: finding the people it was chasing.

The light breeze that had made brief entries into the night was starting to pick up in intensity. Gusts were quick, but strong enough to push the dead leaves that scattered the floor of the woods back and forth, creating small moving shadows in every direction, making it harder for the test subject to find his intended targets. Shadows from the large trees, also make it difficult to make out anything.

The test subject stopped.

Standing, almost lifeless, it turned its head in either direction, trying to get a sense of where its targets would've headed. It held its breath and started listening into the night air, hoping to pick up any noise loud enough to be heard over the crackling of leaves at his feet.

The noise came.

Snapping its neck in the direction, the patient remained still as it processed the sudden noise and replayed it over and over in its mind, trying to figure out what the noise originated from. It was the sound of metal clanking, the thing behind the moist flesh concluded; a familiar sound that resembled the sound the metal fence made back at the facility when it escaped.

Squeezing the metal handle of the blood-stained hammer, the test subject resumed its pursuit, keeping its attention forward as each step brought it closer to the abandoned steel mill that loomed on the far, but not too distant horizon.

CHAPTER 9

Leaping over the five-foot fence, Kimberly grabbed ahold of Mike's extended hand and dropped, landing on the firm, unleveled pavement with a loud thump and a terrible ripping sound as a sharp pain struck her lower back and sliced straight up to the center. A rush of night air hit her exposed flesh with a loud squeak emerging under her breath; loud enough to overpower the sound of the wind and get Mike's attention.

He quickly turned to his girlfriend, noticing the look of pain across her face as her left arm swirled around her back. "What?"

"I got stuck on the fence," she whimpered in agony.

Spotting drops of blood landing on the pavement behind Kimberly, he ran over to her, placing his hands on her shoulder and slowly applied pressure. "Let me see how bad."

Sniffling in the cold breeze, Kimberly wiped her eyes with her free hand, then turned around, revealing a large gash straight up from her lower back to just below the center. Blood oozed out of the wound like an opening on a doomed vessel, sinking into the fabric of her once white shirt. He winced at the sight. *Oh, my God! That looks deep!*

Carefully pushing the shirt to the side to get a better look at the wound in the moonlight, he kneeled, hoping it wasn't as bad as it looked. The thick red blood that had fallen to the pavement now appeared to be black under the bluish tint of moonlight—the same thing for the blood that saturated into Kimberly's shirt, making it difficult for Mike to get a sense of how serious the wound was. He could only guestimate. "It's big, but it doesn't look that deep. I'll try to get a better look when we're inside."

Kimberly's head shot up. *What! We're going inside, Mike? You can't be serio—*

A large flock of black crows blasted out from the tree line in the distance, screeching as they lifted into the night sky. Kimberly's eyes widened in disarray. *He's coming.*

Mike's heart began racing. *Shit, we gotta go. We gotta move. Now!*

Wasting no time, he snatched Kimberly's hand and started running toward the abandoned mill, praying—hoping it would provide a place to hide from whoever—or whatever was under the horrific mask pursuing them. "Come on, hurry!"

Kimberly squeezed Mike's hand and picked up her speed, using all the energy she had regained from their shallow moments of rest. It wasn't much; she slowed down quickly, but enough to get her and Mike to the entrance with ease. "Hurry!"

The once majestic mill that provided nearly fifty percent of all the steel used for the skyline of New York was now covered with rusted siding and worn painting from the many harsh Pennsylvania winters it endured since its closing back in the late seventies. The large chimneys sticking out of the unstable metal roof were on the verge of collapse, much like the rest of the vacant building. Rust also expanded across the side door Mike and Kimberly made their way to. So much rot overtook the entrance, the handle snapped off the second Mike applied pressure to it.

"Goddamn it," Mike grunted as the worn gold handle crashed to the ground.

He turned, looking for another way in, completely unaware that despite the old knob breaking off, the side door that many of the blue collar workers that occupied the mill used as the main entrance, had indeed opened.

"Look," Kimberly pointed.

Turning back to the now opened door, Mike squeezed Kimberly's hand as another sound from the woods emerged behind them. Without turning to see what the noise was, he pushed the door open and rushed inside, slamming it as soon as they cleared the opening.

A rush of old musty air surrounded them as the echo of the door slamming bounced off the old walls before dissipating into the far end of the mill, allowing the silence that engulf the mill to return in force. The thick foul air wasn't enough to turn their stomachs, but it was sufficient enough for both of them to cover their noses as soon as they took in their first breath.

The shadows throughout the large, nearly empty building loomed over much of the building, hiding the decaying siding and large cement chunks missing from the floor. On any other night, darkness kept the mill's company, but on this night, because the moon was nearly full, beams of light were able to creep through the metal meshes that protected the long windows near the top of the building that ran the length of the mill. It was far from good, but enough to guide the two teenagers and help them avoid crashing into any of the debris left behind years ago.

Picking up the pace as their eyes adjusted to the poor lighting, Mike and Kimberly stayed close, refusing to let go of each other's hand. About halfway through the large empty room, they stopped and started looking around, trying to find someplace—*anyplace* to hide.

Kimberly started shaking. *Where, where, where? Where can we hide? Oh, God, there's no place to go! Everything's out in the ope—wait...what's that? Goddamnit, I can't see it, but it looks like...a staircase! It is! That's where we can go, that's where we can—*

"No," Mike replied to her quickly. "You know how unstable those stairs must be?"

"But they could be fine."

"No,"

Groaning as the pain from the gash across her back starting to sting, Kimberly cried. "Well, there's no place down here."

Mike kept looking around, hoping to spot something. "There's gotta at least—look!"

Kimberly snapped her hand in the direction Mike was pointing. At first, it looked as though he was pointing at nothing but darkness, but the longer she looked, the more her eye began making out details of the area.

"We'll go in there. Maybe the door locks! Come on!" Mike said with as much enthusiasm as he could on a night that was sure to haunt him for the rest of his days.

They ran, resuming the speed they were going back when they first entered the woods. Kimberly still had her doubts and was confident they would be safer upstairs, but she knew there was no time to waste; they needed to get to cover as fast as they could.

There fast moving footsteps echoed loudly, jeopardizing their location in the hollow building. But, by the time that thought came into fruition, they were charging toward the door. Mike reached it first. From what he could see, the handle was nowhere near in as terrible shape as the one to the entrance was, but a thick layer of dust stuck to his hand when he reached down and twisted the knob. It was unlocked. He pushed the door open, revealing what must've been an office at one point when the mill was at its prime. The moment Kimberly was out of the doorway, he slammed it closed, sealing them in.

Inside the old office was a rundown desk, a cracked window in the middle of the wall that overlooked the shop, and scattered papers on the floor covered with years of dust, all accompanied by the same musty odor that occupied the rest of the building. The only difference between the office and shop floor was the small window on the back wall that overlooked the nearby woods; the window also protected by a metal mesh nailed to the outside wall.

There was no lock on the door, but the surrounding walls of the room—however thin they were—provided the teenagers with enough sense of secureness to take in a few deep breaths. "I think we're safe for now," Mike determined.

Light from the moon filtered into the small office, creating enough of a glow for Kimberly to walk over to the mesh covered window and lift her shirt for Mike to get a better look at the wound running down her spine. The stinging feeling was now transitioning back to a horrible burning sensation. She could feel trickles of blood running down before disappearing beneath the waist of her pants. Biting her bottom lip in an attempt to fight back the tears, she turned when Mike got down on his knees. *God, it hurts so bad! It must be deep. Goddamn you, Mike! Why the Christ did you decide to go in here? Why the—*

"It doesn't look as deep as I thought it would be. And the blood looks like it's starting to clot, too."

"Are you sure?" Kimberly replied in a skeptical tone. "It fucking hurts."

Mike reached to try and carefully pull the waist of her pants down a little farther so he could get a better idea as to how far down the wound went, hoping it didn't go as deep—

The entrance door flung open.

Mike and Kimberly froze in place.

There was a brief bout of silence, long enough for both of them to question if what they heard was, indeed, the central door opening.

The door slammed shut.

Panic reemerged in the two teenagers. Unable to move, they stood frozen, their eyes fixated on the dusty broken glass window in the wall before them.

Footsteps began. They were hard, loud, and echoed with each one made. A chill raced through Kimberly once she realized not only were they footsteps, but they were getting louder. And closer. *Much* closer.

They dropped to their knees and took cover behind the rusted desk that rested in front of the outside window. Trying to remain as quiet as they could, but also move as swift as they could, Kimberly got to the floor first with Mike not long behind. Another footstep echoed, closer than the previous one. Another one followed.

Then another.

And another...and another.

They're right outside the door, Kimberly panicked. *Oh, God! Oh, shit!*

She bit down hard on her bottom lip, hoping to stop an audible gasp from slipping out of her. The bite was so hard, her teeth broke flesh, as she prepared for another footstep that would be so close, one could only assume it was right outside the doorway.

Mike, while in a state of panic on his own, looked around, hoping to find something to use as a weapon, should it come down to that. Because of the dusty papers that covered the floor, any objects that could've been down there were hidden and the light coming in from the moon wasn't strong enough to make out anything that could be lurking in the shadows.

There was nothing; nothing but his fists.

If I can get close enough, the young athlete thought, *maybe I can get him in a headlock and choke him out. I'll kill the son of a bitch if I have too.*

Another footstep struck the concrete floor, so close the vibration of the step was felt by the both of them, just as Kimberly knew it would be. She closed her eyes.

Mike clenched his fist and prepared for the sound of the office door handle to giggle before finally squeaking open. *Oh, Christ. This is it. This is...*

The sound never came.

Neither did another footstep.

All that came was silence—the same silence that had welcomed them into the decayed mill the moment they stepped inside. Petrified, to so much as move a muscle, Kimberly remained still, listening to her pulse thump in her ear. The feeling of hopelessness only grew when her eyes turned to Mike and saw the same terrified expression on his face.

Seconds felt like minutes and minutes felt like hours for the two teenagers as they hid in the office from whoever loomed on the other side of the door. The wait was agonizing as more—a footstep ended the silence. Kimberly gasped.

The footstep was loud, oppressive, and close, like the previous ones before it. However, there was one difference. Mike didn't pick up on it right away, but Kimberly did. The footsteps were loud and heavy, but not as heavy as the previous ones. Then, the steps that followed were also lacking that heaviness. *They're walking away—that's what it sounds like. We're in the clear. We're—*

A loud slam broke Kimberly's train of thought. The slam—like every other noise, was loud and unmistakable, but it was apparent the sound came from further down the large building. Kimberly and Mike slowly turned to each other, each thinking the same thing. *That was the side entrance door; they must've left.*

The stillness and lifeless silence returned, allowing nothing more than flutters of wind to come in through the rusty holes along the roof. But, despite the feeling of isolation reemerging, Mike and Kimberly remained crouched behind the desk, too scared to even take in breaths of damp, moldy air, let alone get up and attempt to leave. The stinging sensation from the large slice across Kimberly's back slowly started to reappear as the silence went on.

Minutes went by and still nothing. No sounds, no strange noises, no footsteps. Finally, knowing full well they couldn't remain in that small office forever, Mike made the first move. As quietly as he could, he rose to his feet. Moonlight trickling in through the metal mesh over the window cast an outline of his shadow upon the opposite wall. Once he spotted the shadow, he rushed to the side of the window and pressed his back against the wall, blending in perfectly with the surrounding darkness.

Keeping his back against the cold wall, he extended his hand out. "Come on."

Kimberly, struggling to keep focus from the pain returning in her back, reached for his hand, anxiously waiting to regain the sense of comfort from the warmth of his hand. Mike kept his eyes fixated on the office door, preparing himself physically and mentally for when it flung open and—a fist smashed through the window and latched onto Mike's neck.

Kimberly jumped as she let out a horrific scream.

Large shards of dusty glass sprayed into office, raining across the paper covered floor. Kimberly covered her face, trying to avoid any shards aiming for her face.

The bloody fist wrapped around Mike's neck started to squeeze, creating pressure so great, it blocked any path for air to get into his lungs. Not even a gasp could come out of him. He grabbed the hand and started to resist, using every muscle in his arms. Then, he began pulling on the hand, trying to get it off.

For his age, Mike was strong, but the overwhelming force of the bloody hand wrapped around his neck took its toll fast as the grip tightened, and the fingers dug into his skin. The violent act took Kimberly by surprise, the viciousness violence stunned her.

Mike started gagging as he jerked around, doing everything he could to get out of the death grip, but his resistance was doing very little, the pressure was crippling. His face started turning red as the vein in the middle of his forehead started bulging.

His legs jerked around the floor, shooting up dust and papers on the office floor. Raising to her feet, Kimberly grabbed onto the hand and started pulling, hoping to provide Mike with any relief he could get. She looked into his eyes, only to see they were slowly fading away with each second that passed by. He was in trouble.

Mike's leg lifted again, slamming hard onto the floor. *Snap!*

Kimberly gasped, fearing the noise came from Mike's neck, but when she realized the noise came from the floor, she looked down. Shared of glass covered where they were standing. While many pieces were small—to small to even pick up, a blue reflection coming from the moon bounced off one shared, getting Kimberly's attention right away. The piece was dust ridden and flimsy but was the largest piece she could see. She reached down.

Incredible darkness started invading the corners of Mike's eyes. The blunting pulse he could feel in his face only grew louder. He could feel the warmth from his forehead reaching a boiling point. Panic saturated his mind. He started gaging—a scream cried out.

Kimberly swung her hand down and stabbed the large piece of glass into the blood-stained hand that covered Mike's neck. The hand released instantly and pulled back. Air flushed into Mike's throat as he fell to the ground.

Kimberly yanked out the piece of glass and drew it back when the hand let go. Blood dripped onto the dirty floor, a few drips even landing on her running shoes. Mike coughed and gagged at her feet, but she kept focus on the window, ready to attack again.

The wounded hand drew back and disappeared out of sight. It was a welcoming gesture, but Kimberly was smart enough to know it wasn't over. *Come on, mother fucker! Stick your hand in here again. I dare you!*

The idea of getting Mike to his feet and rushing out of the office was there, but Kimberly, while distraught by the attack, wasn't ready to follow up on that idea. She stepped to the side of the window and leaned against the wall, in the exact position Mike was in when the hand slammed through both the metal mesh and the window.

A shadow stepped into the light of the window. She squeezed down on the glass, the piece cutting the wrinkles in her fingers. And with a war cry coming from the heart, she stepped in front of the window and raised the piece of glass—she screamed in horror. Glaring at her were two dark eyes covered beneath a foul smelling mask of a deer.

The masked figured clawed at her, trying to latch onto anything—she swung the bloody glass into the eye hole of the mask. A loud grunt came from behind the mask, and the thing inside stepped away from the window frame.

Kimberly grabbed Mike's arm and helped him the rest of the way up. She wasn't sure where or if the person attacking them was wounded, and she didn't care to find out; the only thing on her mind was getting out of that office.

"Come on, Mike!"

Locking their hands together, the two got to their feet and darted for the office door as the sound of glass smashing echoed from behind. Neither of them looked back, but they knew what was happening. *Oh shit! He's coming in from behind us! He's coming through the window!*

Kimberly pulled open the office door. She exited first.

Mike followed with a loud thump not far behind; the attacker was through the window and inside the office. Once Mike cleared the path of the door, Kimberly elbowed the door and slammed it shut, the old hinges squealing like a wild animal before slamming shut.

The two started to run, sprinting to the shadows near the side of the warehouse, hoping they would be able to blend in. Kimberly raced for the side door, clutching Mike's hand with her firm grip. Her breath picked up.

The office door flung open.

"Come on!" Kimberly shouted. She could feel Mike slowing down. "Mike!"

His lungs were empty of air, and his body was hollow with energy, but the loud footsteps approaching from behind alerted the two teenagers of the danger if they stopped. Mike started running faster when the footsteps from behind turned into sprints.

Charging after them from behind, blood drizzled out of the stab wound from Kimberly, but that by no means stopped or even slowed down Russel Fritz. Kimberly aimed for his left eye, but missed, only nicking the bottom half of his eyebrow. To any other person, that would've been enough to slow down, but the attack only fueled the rage inside the horrific monster behind the mask. With his eyes peering out through the eye holes, Fritz clutched the bloody hammer in his hand and continued to charge after them.

Kimberly reached the door, grabbed the rusted knob, and twisted it, only to find out it was locked. "Shit!"

"What?"

"It's locked!"

Mike pushed Kimberly out of the way, grabbed hold of the weathered doorknob and pulled harder than Kimberly did, hoping by some bit of luck it was just stuck. The door didn't budge. The footsteps drew closer.

Mike grabbed the doorknob with both hands, stretched his feet apart and used all his football might on the door, grunting the more he pulled.

The echoes of the footsteps amplified.

Kimberly, unknowingly, turned around. Her eyes widened with absolute horror as the sight of the hanging flesh over the attacker's head sent chills down her. The skin was so loose; it was nearly impossible to realize the flesh had originated from a deer.

She grabbed Mike by the shoulder. "Mike, hurry. Hurry!"

The masked attacker picked up his speed.

Kimberly squeezed Mike's shoulders and started pulling with him. "Hurry!"

The steps got louder.

Mike's grunts intensified.

"Come on, goddamn it!"

Fritz closed in, now only feet away from his intended targets.

The door wasn't going to open in time. Mike spared the last bit of energy. *Closer...closer...*

Kimberly turned her head.

The masked man raised the blood-stained hammer.

She screamed.

Now!

Mike suddenly spun around, sending Kimberly plummeting into the door and away from Fritz. Then, he charged, slamming into Fritz's chest, using all his upper body strength to stop the attacker from swinging the hammer in their direction.

Taking in the thunderous impact, Fritz—surprised by Mike's strength—fell back and nearly lost his footing as the young teenager dug his head into Fritz's chest and continued to push back as if they were playing their own game of contact sport. Fritz swung the hammer down but stopped midway when Mike's large, firm grip latched onto his wrist.

Mike's ability to push the killer away, created enough space for Kimberly to try getting the door open on her own. She grabbed the knob with both hands, spread her feet and started yanking, hoping by some miracle, the rust that weakened the entire building had weakened the door during the process. "Come on!"

Keeping his head buried in Fritz's chest, Mike pushed harder, unwilling to budge for anything. With each step he was able to take, the more of a window he provided Kimberly to get the door open. Years on the Hunting football team paid off, but Mike wasn't in the clear. He was able to move him, but the amount of muscle it required to get Fritz to budge was enormous.

Mike's dwindling energy became more glaring with each passing moment. His face returned to a beat red stage, and sweat started forming across his cheeks and forehead. The sound of the door raddling from behind warned him Kimberly had yet been able to get it open. "Kim, hurry!"

"I'm trying!"

Panic set in as Mike's words circled in her mind—she knew she was running out of time to get it open.

"Kim!" Mike shouted again.

Jesus Christ! She let go of the doorknob and slammed her shoulder against the door. Nothing. She hit it again, only harder. *Open, goddamn it! Op—*

A grunt deep from within Mike's gut squeaked out when his ability to push Fritz suddenly stopped; almost as if he struck into a brick wall. The sudden halt caught the young football player by surprise, but not as much as the sudden grip that came crashing down on his shoulder. Mike looked up, allowing fear to rush in and overtake any form of resistance.

Glaring at him through the deerskin were two deep menacing eyes, so full of hate, it rivaled anything Mike feared was hiding beneath his bed when he was a boy. The pressure from Fritz's hand was crushing, but Mike shifted his attention to his other arm when he started to feel it retracting, and the hand with the bloody hammer started descending in his direction.

Kimberly body slammed the door again, striking it so hard, it left a significant dent in the middle. *Come on!*

Mike resisted Fritz's descending hand and the murder weapon, grunting louder the more he did so, but it was ineffective. The hammer picked up speed in its fall. "Shit."

Kimberly slammed into the door again.

Mike grinded his teeth.

Kimberly crashed into the door again, snapping one of the old rusty hinges off.

A terrible snap noise came from Mike's shoulder. He screamed.

The monster behind the mask smiled—

Mike thrusted his head forward, smashing his face directly in the center of the deer mask. A crack noise came from beneath the mask, followed soon after by a slight grunt. The hand that cracked the bone in his shoulder let go.

Kimberly backed up, closed her eyes, and charged for the door, hoping the running start would be enough to get the door open.

Mike head-butted the mask again, his forehead striking the broken nose just beneath the flesh. Another grunt creaked out.

Kimberly slammed into the door, effectively snapping off the last hinge and sending it plummeting to the ground. A rush of freezing night air hurtled over her as she landed face down on top of the cold rusty door. The sharp pain from the wound on her back shivered with tenderness as the cold breeze hit the open flesh.

She rolled onto her back and started to get to her feet, keeping her eyes in Mike's direction, watching as he struggled with the person in the mask.

Mike head-butted the attacker one more time.

The pressure on Mike's shoulder suddenly dissipated and the attacker stumbled back. *He's hurt*, Mike thought. *Here's my chance!*

Spinning around to spot Kimberly on top of the fallen door, struggling to get to her feet, Mike yelled out her name, hoping to get her attention and reassure her he was on his way to help. The sound of his voice provided much need relief. "Mi—

A stomach-turning scream shot out of Mike. Kimberly's eyes widened, unable to see why Mike's voice came to an abrupt halt. Then, her eyes adjusted, revealing the horror.

Mike collapsed to his knees, dumbfounded, confused, and pain-ridden as pressure increased from the center of his back. His mouth hung open, like an animal in the jungle freshly caught by a predator after a long chase. The jarring impact of the metal hammer plunged in the center of his back muted his ability to scream—or even think—the more seconds ticked by.

Not able to turn around, even after hearing the heavy footsteps creeping up behind him, Mike remained on his knees, glancing—almost lifelessly at Kimberly. Her jaw—much like Mike's hung wide, inhaling the cool air that surrounded her. Her eyes began to water as blood started to flow out of Mike's mouth.

A painful grunt escaped Mike as the claw of the hammer was ripped out of his back, the yank being so hard, it sprayed blood all across the cement floor behind him.

Mike joined Kimberly in weeping, unable to remain strong because of how much pain he was in. But, he slowly raised his blood riddled left hand and extended it; almost as if he was trying to reach for her. Blood collected below his tongue, but with his mouth open, he looked into her eyes and told her to ru—the hammer swung down and crashed into the center of his head.

She screamed.

Gagging from the biting edge of the claw cracking his skull, Mike's vision blurred along the corners of his eyes before another forceful yank thrust his head up, taking his eyes off Kimberly and refocusing them to the rusted roof above. Blood oozed down the back of his neck and his shirt but was unable to distract him from the deer mask looming over him.

A terrible blackness started overtaking his eyes, but not fast enough to prevent him from witnessing his attacker raise the hammer again and swing it into his forehead, shattering the bones beneath the skin.

Kimberly cried out in horror as the life exited Mike's body. Her body shook, her heart cracked, and tears soaked her eyes. For a moment, she felt paralyzed, almost as if her body weighed so much, she couldn't get back to her feet.

Once the body stopped twitching, Fritz slammed his hand down on Mike's lifeless face, his thumb entering Mike's right cornea, and pulled the claw of the hammer back out. A massive crater-like hole in the teenager's head appeared, deep enough for the old musky air within the mill to slither into the cracks of Mike's brain.

The release of the hammer allowed Mike's body to collapse to the floor of the mill. A pool of dark blood surrounded his head almost instantly as it quickly expanded and reached his murderer's boots in seconds. Because of the distance, Kimberly couldn't make out many details, allowing her mind to add them on its own.

She wept profusely, but the overwhelming sense of heartache turned to absolute horror when she looked up from Mike and saw the deer mask lift in her position. Her tear-filled eyes widened, and her breathing was no longer controllable. Then, in horror, she watched as the man in the mask stepped over Mike's lifeless body and start in her direction.

Agonizing pain from both her heart and the wound across her back blunted much of her thinking, but not enough for her to overlook the realization she was in danger—the man behind the deer mask, the man who had just killed what she was sure would be her future husband was now focused on her.

Realizing the imminent danger, she was now in, she sprung to her feet, using every last ounce of energy she had and started running away, screaming as she did so, while her pursuer, followed, clutching tightly onto the blood riddled hammer.

A gust of wind hurtled through the trees of the forest, rocking the giant pines and swirling the leaves in a tornadic fashion. The lifeless brown leaves crinkled and crackled from every direction, creating an eerily lonely feeling, but no such noise or wind affected young James Nelson on his quest to find the lights. To any other child his age—or even one a little older—they would've been terrified—running and screaming for help, hoping that their voice would be able to penetrate the wall of howling wind, but James was doing no such worrying. In fact, he couldn't have been more content.

Blood was still trickling out of the gash on his left arm from where he fell, and the tear in his sweatshirt created an opening for the wind to sneak in, yet the coldness and a decent amount of blood dripping onto the floor of the forest didn't slow him down for a moment. Neither did the sting of the gash.

If I was an alien, trying to take over the world, why would I hide in the woods? He thought. *Why would I hide at all? That's what I'll ask them first! If I can find them, that is.*

With nothing more than the moon illuminating his way through the forbidden forest, James halted his pursuit, removed the straps from his backpack off his shoulders and pulled down the large zipper to grab his flashlight. Despite debating whether to take it out or wait, James decided it was best to have out, only do to the thickening of the trees up ahead that blocked out much of the moonlight he'd been using as a guide. He dug deep into the large pocket, and even started questioning if he left it at home—the tips of his fingers found it resting sideways at the way bottom of the backpack.

Whipping it out with force, young James clutched the metal handle tightly in his hands and pushed down on the rubber button. Suddenly, the surrounding darkness winced and pushed back behind the surrounding trees as the white neon beam of light ignited, lighting up the earthy ground beneath him and the tops of the pines that hung over.

The flashlight had been a gift he received from his father last Christmas and he typically only used it when they lost power, usually during a massive snowstorm, which gave him the opportunity to see how bright it was, but it wasn't until that moment in the forest, did he realize just how much light the flashlight possessed.

He grinned as he stared up at the trees. The child in him felt like being silly and was eager to start pretending the beam of light was a lazar-sword; he had always dreamt about having one, but the mature, more rational part of him, the part that was slowly starting to become his standard, thanks to his classes at school, reminded him of the task at hand.

And with his, more rational thoughts prevailing, he zipped the backpack up, flung the straps back over his shoulders, lowered the flashlight beam to ground level and picked up walking where he initially left off, keeping his eyes forward, hoping to find anything that resembled a clue that hinted he was heading in the right direction.

Weeping as she sprinted onto the unused street the mill was just off—Barker Street—Kimberly ran down the pothole infested street, refusing to look over her shoulder for anything. Her once perfectly done makeup now ran down her rosy red cheeks and the cheap mascara she bought at Stine Pharmacy was no match for the tears of agonizing sorrow and horror she'd cried.

Her hair flung in the rapid energizing wind, pushing the long strands into her face with a few making it into her eyes. But, even when she was forced to push the hair out of her face, she didn't slow down, for she knew what awaited for her if she did. Her lungs were empty, her legs were buckling, and her mind was racing, but yet, somehow, she was able to maintain her speed.

The neglected street was empty, mostly due to it being a dead end. Because of budget cuts, many of the street lights throughout the town, especially in the abandon sections, were forced to get shut off, including the five streetlights that ran down the half a mile-long street of Baker. Nothing but moonlight lit the way for her. She staggered, hoping—by some miracle, she'd be found.

Pleading for help at the top of her lungs, Kimberly's voice cracked as it rose up into the black autumn sky. Her screams for help evaporated into pleas before transitioning to gentle coos. Goosebumps covered her from head to toe as a gust of wind emerged within the woods, causing the looming trees to snap from all sides.

Her sobs intensified as the last bits of energy depleted from her body, and she was forced to slow down. The urge to look behind her intensified with each second that passed, but she was unwilling to do so. Although she made a reduction in speed, she kept up her screams, thinking maybe they'd help even though she knew the road was completely deserted. The effort was nothing more than false hope, but that's all she—

Lights emerged at the far end of the road. They started fairly dim but quickly grew brighter with each second. At first, because of her traumatized state of mind, she didn't spot them. Tears blurred her eyes; the wind swooshed her hair with a sudden gust so strong, it nearly knocked her over. But finally, when she looked up, her watery eyes locked onto the approaching lights. "Hey! Help!! Help, please!"

Jumping up and down, she begged for mercy, hoping that whoever was approaching, would help her. Typically, the skeptical type, the notion of the lights being just as or possibly even more dangerous than the person chasing her, never crossed her mind. At that point, she was willing to take the trust of a questionable stranger—like her neighbor Mr. Straub, the town drunk who'd been suspected of a hit and run—just to get away from the impending danger she was sure loomed closer than her imagination thought. "Help!"

A sudden screech roared into the air, echoing throughout the road, but the sound didn't come from Kimberly, even though she kept screaming at the top of her lungs—the shriek had come from the lights in front of her. Raising her hands to cover her face as they approached, Kimberly remained in the center of the decaying road, hoping it would help her be spotted. Red and blue lights suddenly illuminated above the suspected headlights.

Thrusting the gear shift into Park, Officer Tyler Benton flung open the driver door to the cruiser. A sheer look of panic took over the expression of nervousness that made up his face for most of the evening. Dr. Sam Eaten, taken aback by both the girl in the middle of the street pleading for help and the sudden movement by his best friend, followed close behind. "Who is it?"

"It's Kimberly Wilson," he said before lifting his hands to either side of his mouth and shouting out her name.

Her mind was lost in appalling grief, which was shifting her thoughts in all different directions, especially with the sudden sight in front of her. It didn't take her long to realize the lights were coming from a police cruiser, but her skepticism refused to budge. Tyler's voice, however, was able to break through, allowing a sudden rush of relief to come crashing over her. She sprinted into his arms at full speed.

"Kimberly?!"

Dust, runny makeup and fear saturated the young teenagers face Tyler spotted from the dark before her head buried into his chest and arms wrapped around his shoulders. He returned the gesture, trying to comfort her.

"Oh, my God, thank you! Thank you!" Kimberly pleaded.

Her arms tightened around Tyler's shoulders, almost to the point where he had a bit of a struggle to take in air, but he returned the gesture, hoping the comfort and warmness of his body would calm her down. From the other side of the cruiser, Sam watched as the teenager trembled in Tyler's arms.

"It's okay; you're okay, Kimberly," Tyler softly said.

Quickly rejecting his conclusion, she lifted her head off his chest. "No, we're not! He's here. He's here, and he kill—he killed—"

She started sobbing. Her head returned to his chest, allowing warm tears, mixed with eyeliner to drip onto his uniform. Unsure of how to react, Tyler looked at Sam, who equally had the same blank expression on his face.

"—Mike!" Kimberly suddenly shouted as her knees buckled.

A sudden rush of wind blasted between the trees, forcing Sam to look away. Unable to move his body away from the wind due to Kimberly leaning on him, Tyler lifted his head and closed his eyes, trying to keep Kimberly's long blowing hair out of his line of sight. The wind howled, but it wasn't loud enough to offset the sobs Kimberly cried out. "Mike's dead! He killed Mike!"

Disbelief filled Tyler's mind first, followed soon after by a paralyzing shock from Kimberly's revelation. He held onto her tighter, squeezing his hands firmly on her shoulders.

The wind dissipated as fast as it emerged, leaving nothing but a haunting stillness behind that overtook—not just the street, but the entire area. Kimberly continued to weep in Tyler's chest and didn't raise her head until she felt some resistance coming from him.

"Come on, let's get you in the car," Tyler suggested.

Unable to process much of anything else, Kimberly kept her hands around Tyler's waist and applied much of her weight onto him as they walked to the back door of the cruiser. The opening and closing of the cruiser door was loud and broke the stillness that surrounded the road, but it was unable to pull Sam's attention off the end of the street. Tyler opened the driver door when Kimberly was safely in. "We'll take her to the station; she'll be safe there. Once we do that, we'll get some people out here to—Sam?"

Ignoring every word, Sam remained still as he kept his eyes toward the end of the street. Not even the sound of Tyler's footsteps approaching him was enough to get his attention. Curious why Sam seemed to be fixated in place for no reason, Tyler tapped him on the shoulder and asked. Sam replied by lifting his hand and pointing. "Look."

Following Sam's finger, Tyler skeptically turned to the far end of the street. A notable gasp trickled out of his mouth. "Oh, Christ."

In horror, they both watched as the masked figure—Russel Fritz—stepped out of the tree line and into the middle of the street; his fingers tightly wrapped around the metal handle of his blood riddled hammer.

Like Sam and Tyler, Fritz remained stationary while facing forward. Between the darkness and distance they were at, it was impossible for either Sam or Tyler to see what exactly Fritz was looking at, but judging by the angle of the large ears sticking up, it appeared as though he was focusing in their direction.

Weeping in the backseat of the cruiser, Kimberly didn't give much attention to what was happening outside; the loss of Mike grew more overwhelming with each passing second. But coincidently, she happened to raise her head to wipe a few tears out of her eyes, hoping to take control of her hysteria and looked through the metal bars in front of her and out the windshield. *No! No, no, no! It's him! He's coming for us—he's coming for me!*

A horrified scream blasted out of her. The screech was muffled from being enclosed in the cruiser, but Sam and Tyler heard it with ease. Wanting to do the same thing, Tyler carefully took one step back as Sam took one step forward, keeping his eyes on his patient. "That's him. It's him."

Tyler, unsure of what to do next, slowly lowered his hand, trying to rest it on the butt of his service revolver discreetly. He gently leaned over to Sam. "What do we do?"

He needs to be captured! Jess' voice returned to Sam's mind. In fact, not only did it return, he could picture Jess shouting those exact words in her firm and passive aggressive manner. And to be honest, a part of Sam felt the same way. He had put years of time and effort into his work at Quimby Research and capturing Fritz was the best way to ensure all that effort wasn't wasted.

But, as he stood there, watching his test subject clutching onto the murder weapon in his hand, an eerie feeling that resembled a warning, grew in his gut. While he made many mistakes over his years of work—trusting

Jess to be rational just to name one—he learned over time to not only believe but listen to that feeling.

Fritz started toward them.

Kimberly screamed louder from the backseat.

Sam took a step back of his own. "Shoot him."

Fritz started walking faster.

Then started sprinting.

Then started running.

"Shoot him!" Sam shouted.

Tyler drew his pistol.

"Fucking shoot him!"

"Where?"

"Anywhere. Anywhere, just shoot him!" Sam reaffirmed.

Fritz's grew closer as the sound of his feet striking the pavement overtook the road. Kimberly's screamed louder with each step Fritz took.

"Shoot him!" Sam shouted again as he prepared to yank the gun out of Tyler's hand and pull the trigger himself.

Closing his right eye and looking down the sight with his left eye, Tyler steadied his aim and fired one shot, but to no effect; the bullet missed a mere six inches off Fritz right side. Fritz picked up in speed, closing the gap significantly between them.

Tyler fired again, the roar of the gunshot blasting through the silence of the night, but still missing its intended target.

Kimberly's scream amplified to the point of deafening.

Sam took another step back, preparing to get back in the cruiser to—

Tyler fired a third shot; striking Fritz. Because the light of the moon was behind him, it was impossible for Tyler to see where the bullet struck him, but wherever it did, the impact was enough to reduce Fritz's speed drastically. But, it didn't stop him completely.

Tyler fired another shot, aiming at Fritz's chest, but striking him in the right shoulder. A pink mist of blood sprayed out as the bullet entered Fritz's flesh, forcing him to stop his pursuit and adjust to the terrible burning and numbing sensation that quickly overtook his entire arm.

Realizing Fritz was wounded and coming to a stop, Tyler took a second or two longer to steady his aim, hoping it would help his shot be more accurate. The loudness of the gunshots blasted its way through the cruiser, forcing Kimberly to scream even more as she ducked down behind the passenger seat and covered her hand with her quivering hands.

Standing motionless as blood oozed out of the bullet wound in his shoulder, Fritz lifted his head to Tyler, grinding his teeth inside the mask. The pain was insurmountable, but, instead of letting it overpower him, he squeezed the handle of the hammer and took another step forwa—Tyler fired again, striking him in the center of the chest, the force knocking him onto the pavement with a loud smash. Fritz's head bounced after the back of his skull violently landed on the tar, followed soon after by his hands.

Tyler and Sam kept their eyes on Fritz the entire time, refusing to so much as blink.

When the clattering of the hammer bouncing out of Fritz's hand stopped, stillness returned to the street. The echoes of the gunshots vanished into the woods as Kimberly's scream muted before finally coming to a much-wanted halt, with nothing but the flashing blue lights on top of the patrol car keeping them company.

Noticing that Fritz didn't appear to be breathing, Tyler lowered his service revolver and turned to Sam, who spotted the same thing. A look of shock had overtaken Tyler's face while a look of disappointment made up Sam's face. *It's over,* Sam concluded. *It's fucking over. Twenty years of work, experiments—hope, now lies in the middle of the street. And all for nothing.*

Unable to dwell that his hopes and dreams of the better part of a decade would remain just that, Sam looked away from his patient, trying to remind himself why he made the decision to take out Fritz. In the aftermath of the shooting, it was difficult for him to do so. Tears and anger were building up and desperately wanted to be released.

Out of the corner of his eye, he spotted Tyler's head turn in his direction, forcing him to look up. Tyler holstered his revolver and began taking several steps back to the cruiser. Sam did the same, at first, but only at a much slower pace, until he stopped altogether.

"Sam, come on," Tyler shouted as the driver door squeaked open.

The wind started to pick up in intensity again, sending shivers down Sam's spine, creating a hopeless feeling like the which he's never felt before. Tyler's voice was persistent, but it wasn't enough to pull Sam out of his train of thought right away, it took Tyler walking over and shaking his shoulder to do so. "Sam! We gotta go."

"No."

The sudden—yet lifeless—response took Tyler by surprise. "What?"

"You go and get backup…I'll stay here with him," Sam answered.

Tyler scoffed. "You just expect me to leave you out here all by yourself?"

"It's not like there's any danger, anymore Tyler," Sam's voice amplified as he pointed to Fritz lying on the pavem—

The wind howled, forcing both of them to cover their faces with their hands. The air temperature was getting colder; the early warning signs of a long winter had arrived. The flashing lights on the patrol car were blinding as Sam covered his face from the wind, but he was persistent with his choice to remain behind.

"I don't feel comfortable leaving you out here!" Tyler reinforced.

The wind came to a drastic halt.

From inside the patrol car, Kimberly's eyes widened.

"Just go, I'll be—"

Sam froze.

Tyler, spotting Sam was suddenly looking behind him, turned around. "What're you..."

A haunting feeling came over the street, condensing their emotions. A night of horror had shaken all three of them—particularly Kimberly, but the hellish moments of the evening failed in comparison to what they were looking at.

Standing in front of them was Fritz, very much alive. The moonlight was still behind him, leaving much of his front side to the imagination, but without thinking, Tyler reached for his flashlight and turned it on. Then, he shined it directly in Fritz's face. His heartrate joined Kimberly's as astonishment overtook Sam's thoughts.

The bright flashlight—bright enough to rival James Nelsons—lit up the entire front of Fritz, revealing that horrifying deerskin that covered his face. The grisly skin sagged, due to its large size unable to fit proportionately on the man beneath it, allowing hunks of flesh to dangle around the neckline. But, despite the stomach-turning mask, Tyler and, Sam primarily, focused on the bullet hole in Fritz's chest, slowly diminishing in size.

The dark-colored jacket Fritz had taken from Old Man Claire's home hid many details of all the wounds, but the bright beam of light was strong enough to reveal much of what the darkness hid. A massive amount of blood had poured out of the gunshot and absorbed into the jacket, creating a damp tint along the front that glistened in the light, proving Tyler's gunshots were accurate.

Tyler panicked. *I shot him; I shot him! He couldn't surviv—he should be dead!*

Tyler took several steps back.

Sam took several steps forward, astonished by what he was seeing.

With his eyes peering through the foul-smelling flesh, Fritz remained still, watching the two men before him as the sensation of pain from where the bullets entered him slowly diminished to the point where no pain existed as all—almost as if the wounds never happened.

"It works," Sam mumbled to himself. "It works."

In spite of where they found themselves, on that dark, cold night in September, a rush of joy flooded through Sam; a slight grin even made a brief appearance as the realization of his work, all the years of testing, researching and experimenting finally meant something after all. The cure had been found. *Holy shit! It works! It actually works! Wait until Jess sees this—the look on her face—*

Fritz reached down and grabbed the handle of the bloody hammer resting at his feet.

The feeling of joy that flooded Sam disappeared abruptly, leaving behind a void for an overwhelming sense of fear to take its place. *Oh, shit, it works!*

He started taking a few steps back toward the car as he raised his left arm. "Tyler..."

"What?"

Fritz began toward the car.

Sam sprinted to the door. "Get us out of here. Now!"

They darted for the cruiser, both hoping inside at the same time. Sam whipped around and put on his seatbelt. "Let's go!"

Tyler started the car.

Kimberly started panicking.

Tyler looked at her through the rear view mirror. "It's okay, Kim."

Fritz started walking faster.

"Now, Tyler!"

"I'm going; I'm going!"

Because he needed to turn the car around, he briefly hesitated about whether he should try and turn around or—"Come on, Tyler!"

Succumbing to Sam's pressure—and Fritz approaching—Tyler yanked the leather-wrapped gearshift into reverse and stomped his foot on the accelerator. The exhaust of the cruiser howled, followed soon after by a screech of the same nature coming from the rear tires. Then, they suddenly jerked forward as the powerful V-8 engine sent them flying backward down the road and created a large space between them and Fritz.

Tyler kept his attention out the back window. Sam focused on Fritz as he grasped the armrest of the passenger door. His eyes widened when Fritz started picking up his speed. "Faster, Tyler. Faster!"

"My foot's all the way down!" Tyler shouted back.

Kimberly's soft coos transitioned back to gasps as the bright headlights of the cruiser lit up Fritz directly in the middle street, running as fast as he could.

Focusing on the back window, Tyler spotted the sharp corner approaching fast; he needed to turn around. He grasped the emergency brake and turned to the windshield. Fritz was picking up speed, but Tyler felt comfortable enough with the space between him and the cruiser. "Hold on."

Sam looked at him. "What're you—"

Tyler yanked the emergency brake and spun the steering wheel as far to the left as it would go. The terrible screech from beneath the car returned, this time coming from the front, as smoke billowed out from the rear tires.

Sam grasped the door.

Kimberly violently slammed against the backseat, her back cracking as sudden pain shot up her spinal cord from striking the giant slash. She screamed.

Taking his foot off the gas as the cruiser started to spin, Tyler held onto the steering wheel firmly. The reduction in speed allowed Fritz to close the gap at a frightening pace. Sam's eyes widened with each step his patient took. Panic set in. "We're not gonna make it. Jesus Christ, we're not—"

The roar of the engine blasted its way through the cabin of the car as the RPMs skyrocketed to the red line, indicating Tyler's foot was back on the gas pedal. The cruiser jerked forward, veering off the road and onto a patch of dead grass. A mist of dirt and small rocks blew into the air from the rear wheels spinning with dread.

Fritz reached the trunk of the car.

Tyler released the emergency brake and steered the cruiser back on the road, sending it soaring down the empty street, leaving Fritz standing in a fog of dust; his eyes focusing on the cruiser until the taillights disappeared into the darkness.

CHAPTER 10

The police station of Hunting, Pennsylvania sat in the center of Crystal Street, directly in the center of town. While most of the area had seen a staggering population decline, Crystal Street and the surrounding streets and neighborhoods had been able to weather the storm of de-industrialization that had swept through much of the state—and Rust Belt itself.

Every building on the street was occupied, many places being small restaurants and a local bank that had been operating since the early fifties. The next road over—Krueger Street—occupied the Hunting Fire Station along with the last remaining grocery store in town. The area of Crystal and Krueger Street was typically full of movement and even had a decent amount of traffic flowing through the area on a typical day, but on that September night, the area resembled the rest of the town—empty.

The lack of people wasn't that out of the ordinary—Tyler Benton started seeing a decline in traffic every evening around six-thirty, but no matter how quiet the street was, he always had the company of street lights to the keep the darkness of the night at bay. But, because the power was out to the entire town, those street lights loomed in the dark, unable to be seen.

The street had been empty most of the night; nothing more than a handful of cars had passed by, one of them only pulling on the street to make an illegal U-turn. The night had a firm grip on the street, but bright LED headlights turning onto the road and speeding toward the equally dark police station loosened that grip, if just for the time being.

Racing up to the entrance of the building, Tyler jammed on the breaks hard, bringing the cruiser to a rough stop before unbuckling himself and getting out. The first thing he spotted—aside from the darkness—was that they were the only ones of the street. *Goddamnit, where the hell is everybody? It doesn't take that fucking long to get here from Merrin Street!*

The sight of seclusion brought Tyler to a boiling point. His request for immediate backup over the radio couldn't have been more straightforward. "This is Officer Benton; I need assistance at the station now!"

Sam Rainey's request—borderline order—was just as forceful. "L'Heureux, Meyers, Jess, all of you to the Hunting police station now! Now!"

Sam mirrored Tyler in unbuckling himself and stepping out of the car. He looked down the street, hoping to spot headlights, but saw nothing more than blackness. He grunted. "Jesus Christ, where the hell are they?"

Tyler slammed his door shut and opened the back to assist Kimberly. "Come on; we'll figure out what to do next once we get inside."

Coping with both the physical and mental pain she was in, Kimberly grabbed Tyler's extended hand and carefully got to her feet. Nearly all of her eye shadow had bled down her rosy red cheeks; she was clearly in pain. The sight crushed Tyler. *God, I hope Lois gets here. She can help Kimberly— she's much better with words than I am.*

Headlights turning onto the street forced all three of them to look up. Tyler took his left hand off Kimberly's shoulder and placed it on the butt of his service revolver. Sam remained still, trying to figure out what type of vehicle was heading toward them.

Another set of headlights pulled onto the street.

Followed by another one.

And another one.

With the wind dying down again, it was quiet enough for the engines in the approaching vehicles to be audible, even from the distance they were at. Kimberly kept her grip on Tyler, refusing to let go. Another set of lights turned onto Crystal Street. Suddenly, a humming noise appeared on the horizon. It started soft but amplified with great intensity as each second passed. Blinking green and red lights flashed through the darkness. Sam sighed with relief. "About goddamn time."

Pulling up to the station first, L'Heureux shut the engine to the Humvee off and exited the vehicle as fast as he could. Meyer's did the same, only getting out of the passenger side. Once he saw the two, Sam waved his hand. "L'Heureux! Over here!"

The sight of them provided much-needed relief for both Sam and Tyler, even though they were still very much strangers to—the back door to the Humvee opened, taken Tyler's attention away from L'Heureux and Meyers. Life reemerged in his eyes. "Lois!"

Sirens blared, and the sensation of the approaching helicopter was enough to keep the area full of noise, and it grew worse by the moment, but not enough to stop Lois from hearing his voice. And, once their eyes locked, she slammed the door to the Humvee closed and sprinted up to the front steps of the station.

Lois, spotting the boyish look across Tyler's face even from the distance made her heart melt like every other time she saw it. They were only half a dozen yards apart at most, but because she purposely kept eye contact with him—in a muted attempt to show him how much she cared about him, it felt longer. So much so, that, despite the activity surrounding them, the thought of walking up to him, grabbing his shoulders and finally passionately kissing him in the way she's alw—"Oh, my God! What happened?"

Pivoting her attention to the overwhelmed looking Kimberly, she wrapped her arm around the distort teenager in an attempt to make her feel safe. Once Tyler felt Lois' arm clench around Kimberly, he carefully lifted his arm off her.

"Her and Mike were attacked," Tyler said.

"Oh, God!" Lois gasped. "Where's Mike?"

Kimberly started sobbing again, burying her head in her dirt covered hands. Her reaction, combined with the petrified look on Tyler's face, answered Lois' question for her. She held onto Kimberly tighter, hoping to provide as much comfort as she could. "I'll take her inside and clean her up."

Agreeing it was best to do so and get the young teenager to an area where she'd have some privacy, Tyler handed Lois the keys to the lobby so she could unlock the glass doors to be first ones inside. Not a moment after Lois stepped away, L'Heureux and Meyers stepped forward. A look of curiosity glistened their faces, both eagerly waiting to hear why Tyler and Sam ordered them to the station.

"We found him," Sam started.

"Where?" L'Heureux replied quickly.

"Out by the old steel mill," Tyler answered.

Meyers—assuming Sam and Tyler were able to overpower the killer and get him in a jail cell—asked why Fritz was nowhere to be found. The answer wasn't surprising.

"No, he's not dead. We picked up the girl and left," Sam said.

Meyers stepped forward. "What? You had the chance to take the son of a bitch out, and you didn't?"

The bluntness of Meyer's tone took Tyler off guard, leaving him unable to think or even react. Sam attempted to intervene and start explaining with as little detail as he could as to why they didn't engage, but Meyers refused to accept the explanation. "You had your gun with you, right?"

Another Humvee pulled up along the side of the department, coming to a screeching halt before the driver door flung open. The expression on Sam's face changed drastically. He stepped away from the trio. "Excuse me for a second."

L'Heureux and Meyers nodded, knowing full-well who exited the Humvee and decided to stay with Tyler to give the illusion they were busy.

"Come on," Tyler said. "I'll explain inside."

Following close behind, the two commanders kept their usual tone, which consisted of sarcasm and offensive jokes, to themselves—nothing about the situation came off as inspiration for humor. From the corner of his eye, Sam watched as Tyler brought the two of them inside, but his attention shifted back to the Humvee that had pulled up after hearing the front doors to the station close.

"Well?" Jess Sowa threw her hands up in the air. "What's going on?"

Exhausted by how much he'd been through over the past few hours, Sam's patience was nullified at best. He was tired, stressed, and wanted nothing more than to head to the nearest bar and order every drink on the menu so he could forget everything and pass out. The look on Jess's face was unflattering; it couldn't have been more apparent how angry she was. His lack of acknowledgment only added to her annoyance. "Hello? Are you going to answer me, Sam, or stand there like a goddamn idiot? I asked what is going on here!"

Her words hounded over and over, to the point where they became numb. It wasn't the first time she had spoken to him in such a tone, and he was sure it wouldn't be the last, either. The louder her voice grew, the more his frustration grew to the point where he couldn't take it any longer. "Jesus Christ, will you shut the fuck up for a second, Jess?"

She paused, allowing Sam's voice to echo around them before vanishing into the outskirts of the street. Her demeaning tone and demanding voice came to an abrupt halt; she was unsure of what to say next. And once it was obvious his demand was effective, Sam decided to start the conversation off.

"We have a problem, Jess," he said in a much softer tone. "A big one."

Jess had been working with Sam for years, and in all that time, she'd never seen him as angry and flustered as he looked on that night—it frightened her. Still, she kept her posture and hid those feelings well, just as she'd done all her life. She didn't answer him, but she made sure he noticed that her attention remained solely on him.

A look of astonishment with a blend of utter shock waved over Sam's face as his eyes drifted off into nothing, almost like he was dreaming with his eyes open. There was sadness in them, but also a sense of joy—a sort of happy medium that left Jess unsure how to feel.

After what felt like a lifetime of silence, Sam finally spoke. "It works," he whispered, echoing the only words he could mutter back at the abandoned mill.

Just like with Tyler, Sam's cryptic words confused his brilliant—yet cocky—boss. Jess shrugged her shoulders. "What works?"

"The XXC," Sam remade eye contact with her.

Unable, and even unsure, how to react, she stepped closer as several military soldiers came rushing pasted them and made their way into the station; a common routine she's been doing ever since she was hired at the top-secret lab when they had top secret discussions. "What do you mean 'it works'?"

More soldiers came rushing passed them, their boots clambering in synch with one another, forcing Sam to close the gap between the two of them, hoping to keep their endangered secret hidden for as long as they could. "You know what I mean, Jess."

It works

It works

It works

Sam's voice kept replaying over and over in Jess' stressed, yet determined mind. While most times—nearly every time, actually, Sam was upfront and direct, always answering her questions with great detail. The lack of such an explanation forced Jess to process it for herself. Without knowing, her face changed suddenly, mirroring Sam's.

"How do you know?" she flatly—almost lifelessly—asked.

"Because I saw it with my own eyes. I saw him take a gunshot to the chest and get right back up with no bullet wound anywhere in sight. Plus, he was also stabbed in the face, and that didn't seem to bother him, either."

The overwhelming answer forced Jess to let go of her frustration and take in the moment—the moment she'd been waiting for her entire adult life. Suddenly, she found herself lost in thought. Rushes of emotions, ranging from joy and excitement, swept through her body. The night wind picked up in intensity, but it wasn't strong enough to dampen the warmth that filled her up inside. *We did it! We did—I mean, I did it. All on my own; I found the cure! Mom would be so proud if she were here, but I know somewhere she's—*

"We have to kill him."

Sam's voice brought Jess back to reality and, unlike the coldness of the wind, his blunt sentence halted the joy. She snapped her head in his direction. "What?"

He repeated it, only in a much forceful tone. Just as the news of their experimental treatment XXC working took Jess by surprise, Sam's blunt and undebatable decision did the same. She scoffed. "What the fuck are you talking about?"

"He's killed almost a dozen people; he literally ripped someone's head off! Do you have any idea how much strength that takes?"

The details rattled Jess' stomach, the thought of blood, much less blood coming from an attack such as that left her unsettled, but, unlike other times where Sam would poke holes of reason into her cold, many times heartless front, this time she stood her ground, refusing to cave. "So restrain him, tranquilize him, knock him in the back of the head with a frying pan, do whatever you want, but don't kill the thing!"

"We can't restrain him!" Sam shouted. "Don't you understand? The amount of strength we have is nothing compared to what he has! Think about it, Jess!"

Biting her lip, Jess refused to concede.

"We wanted the white blood cells to reproduce at a rapid pace so, even the worst trauma the body would receive can heal in minutes, and that's not even mentioning the muscle strength the cells are providing him, either."

"That doesn't mean he needs to be killed, Sam!" Jess shouted over the rumbling from the helicopter flying by. "We can find another way!"

The space between the two of them closed the louder their conversation progressed, but, clearly not getting anywhere with Jess, Sam threw his hands up in the air and prepared to head back inside. "I'm giving them the order to shoot on site. End of story."

Wanting those to be the last words of the conversation, Sam started for the front entrance of the station, which was now guarded by several military privets dressed in army uniforms and carrying assault rifles in their hands. His mind was made up, and nothing was—Jess' hand plummeted onto his right shoulder, stopping him before he could reach the front steps.

"No, I'm not going to let you give that order!" she said as she forcefully turned him around to face her.

"It's too late, Jess. My mind is already made up," Sam reaffirmed.

"I don't give a shit what your mind is!" Jess screamed. "He's my patient, it's my experiment, and I am your boss! You do not have the right the determine what happens to him by yourself!"

A plush of red seeped into the middle of Jess' cheeks, matching the same redness in her eyes; she was angry, more than Sam ever thought she could be. The longer he gazed into her hazel eyes, the more he realized it wasn't just rage staring back at him, but also passion. A deep passion that was coming from the heart. He'd only seen that passion once, and he remembered the moment as clear as day despite never seeing it since.

"I know how you feel, but—"

"No, you don't!" Jess interrupted him. "You have no idea how I feel! You have no idea what it's like to watch someone you love waste away to nothing, and all you can do is watch and hope the pain can somehow be managed."

Sam's mouth opened for a rebuttal, but Jess's voice—and the point she was making—prevailed.

"For seven months, I watched my Mom go from this beautiful angel to nothing but skin and bones to the point I couldn't even recognize her. Her own daughter couldn't even recognize her, Sam! And when she died, I vowed to stop at nothing until I found a cure because I wanted to make sure no daughter ever went through what I went through with her. And now that we found something—something realistic that could wipe out this fucking disease, you're saying we have to stop!"

Sam sighed, crossing his arms and trying to respond without adding any more emotion into the conversation. "That's not what I'm saying, and you know that."

"Yes, it is! That's exactly what you're saying. Instead of trying to fight for what we have you just wanna throw it up in the air and piss it away!"

"Jesus Christ, listen to yourself. You're obsessed!"

She lashed out, slamming the palms of her hands onto his chest. Sam stumbled, nearly losing his footing. "Well, at least I fight for what I want!"

"I'm fighting right now!"

"No, you're not! You're a coward, trying to take the easy way out!"

Sam flung his hands up.

"The hell with you, I'll deal with it myself." Jess turned and started walking away, heading back to the Humvee to—Sam grabbed her hand and forcefully turned her around.

"How many rules do you need to break to get what you want, huh? Do you think you're the only ones who knows what it's like to have someone close to you die? I've lost people, too! But that's the way life is! You can't explain it; you can't predict it! Putting yourself and everyone else in danger won't bring your mom back. I'm sorry she died, but that's what happens in life, Jess. You can't bargain with God; you'll lose every time."

The humming of the helicopter faded into the far horizon and with many of the military soldiers already inside the station, the two of them found themselves alone, gazing into each other's eyes, allowing the words they spoke to sink in. Sam half expected some type of response from Jess; she always had something else to say, but this time, she didn't. Jess had always been a tough one to read, but the expression she had was misty and unsure, hinting that, for the first time, she didn't have anything else to say.

Sam lowered his head as regret started to seep in. He knew the tone he used was harsh, and letting that be the end of their conversation didn't sit well with him. He wan—Headlights emerged at the far end of the road.

Snapping their heads in the direction of the lights, Sam and Jess watched as the approaching vehicle sped up the road at an alarming rate of speed, the squeal of a supercharged engine echoed as the vehicle approached. With the headlights distinctly set to high, the blinding white light hid the exterior of the car, making it impossible for either of them to see what make and model it was.

It's a car, Sam thought. *Yeah, it must be a car judging by the outline of the headlights—goddamn are those things bright!*

Lifting their hands to cover their eyes from the harsh lights, Sam and Jess took a few steps back but stopped moving when the front tires of the car suddenly shifted in their direction. The engine revved as the automobile barrel straight at them. Sam started moving his legs, preparing to jump out of the way should the car not slow—

The car picked up in speed, sending chills down Sam as the headlamps brightened his face to the point they became so blinding, he was forced to look away. The sound of the engine roared so loud it overpowered the nearby Humvees. Panic started to set in as thoughts roamed throughout Sam's mind. *Shit, it's him. He's in that car. It's gotta be—* the car came to an abrupt halt. It was followed by the engine shutting off after a dramatic pause.

Despite the engine off, the headlights were still on, aiming directly at the two scientists, but the lack of sound coming from under the hood allowed a sense of reassurance to sweep across the two. About ten seconds after the engine shut off, the headlights finally went dark, sending shadows swarming back and surrounding them from all sides like a hungry pack of hyenas closing in on their worn out prey. Jess and Sam lowered their hands when the lights powered off.

The eerie silence that had made minor appearances throughout the night returned, but only briefly. Like every other time, the lack of noise was penetrating, creating an atmosphere rattled with a foreboding warning. The driver and passenger doors swung open simultaneously, followed swiftly by figures getting out of the car and slamming the doors shut.

With their backs to the moon, it was impossible for Jess and Sam to make out any facial features on the mysterious couple, leaving them drenched in gloom. The outlines the moon made from the cloudless sky was enough to reveal that the two people in front of them were men, but they weren't positive until the two figures started walking toward them. The sound of professional dress shoes clattering on the pavement echoed from all sides. By the time Jess and Sam made out any facial expressions, the two men were only feet away.

Confusion remained intact with Sam; he had no idea who he was looking at. Jess, on the other hand, knew very well who was in front of her. She chose not to say anything and instead wait for a response from the two men.

Tailored suits? Sunglasses? Who the hell are these guys, the Men in Black? Sam thought. While he was intrigued by the presence of the two strangers, he'd had enough mysteries for one night. "Can we help you?" he grunted.

"Jess Sowa and Sam Rainey?" a flat toned voice that came from the driver.

Sam shrugged. "Who wants to know?"

While the man next to him remained motionless, the driver pushed his black tie off to the side, reached into the breast pocket of his suit, and pulled out a gold object with a black leather frame surrounding it. "I'm Agent Vitukevich, and this is Agent McCann."

The bravado and forcefulness in the agent's voice was unmistakable, borderline obnoxious; he clearly wanted his presence known. The hollow answer provided still left Sam unsure as to who the mysterious men were. "Are you with the F.B.I. or something?"

"C.I.A." Agent McCann replied in just as flat-toned as his partner.

Sam stood immobile, stunned by the response Agent McCann provided. He turned to Jess, assuming she felt the same, but the assumption faded when he spotted the look across her face. Wanting to avoid looking at Sam, Jess engaged. "Why is the C.I.A. here?"

A smile—almost evil grin—emerged on Vitukevich's face as he placed his badge back into the pocket of his jacket. "You seemed surprised to see us, Jess. I figured by now you'd be used to us dropping by."

The cryptic reply left Sam in limbo, forcing him to confront Jess, hoping to get an answer—*any* answer from her. The lighting surrounding them was still nothing short of dim, but enough for Vitukevich to see the blank expression on Sam's face. His smile grew even more sinister. "I take it you haven't told your partner about our little visits, have you?"

"What visits?" Sam broke his silence.

Jess, despite seeing Sam looking at her from the corner of her eye, remained focused on Vitukevich. He shrugged his shoulders. "Would you like the honors of telling him, or would you like me to?"

"Tell me what?" Sam's shouted in frustration from the lack of answers he was getting.

Jess opened her mouth to speak, but nothing more than a muted squeak came out; she was unsure of how to word what she wanted—what she needed to say. It took a few moments, nearly pushing Vitukevich to the point where he was about to answer himself—

"They're here for him," she finally said with a distilled look of defeat on her face.

"Here for who?" Sam blurted out without thinking.

"Your patient," Agent McCann said.

The revelation drew pushback from Sam, demanding to know why.

Sam's voice was powerful and forceful, but Jess resisted the urge to tell him. "Go inside, Sam," she mumbled loud enough for him to hear.

Sam scoffed, dismissing the idea.

"Go inside," she repeated. "I'll deal with this."

An overwhelming look of disgust lathered Sam's face; Jess could see it as clear as day, but she kept her focus on the well-dressed agents that loomed in front of her. She knew full well she would be getting an earful the next time she and Sam were alone, but the threat Agent Vitukevich and Agent McCann posed was much more significant than anything Sam could threaten her with. When Sam realized he wasn't going to get the answer—any answer from Jess, he walked away, leaving her in the dark with the two mysterious men.

When the door to the station slammed shut behind Sam, Jess confrontationally stepped up to the two agents. "What in the hell are you two doing here?"

The smile on Agents Vitukevich's face all but disappeared. "You know goddamn well why we're here! To clean up the shit show you and your partner created."

Reviled by Vitukevich's tone, although not out of the ordinary, Jess attempted to put up a front to match his, but it dwindled when Agent McCann knocked on the hood of the undercover cruiser and the back door behind the passenger seat opened.

Jess refocused her attention to the back of the car as a figure stood up. *Another one? Great, who the hell is it this*—"Shit."

A paralyzing horror gripped over her body, leaving her unable to react as the person emerged from the backseat, closed the door to the cruiser and walked over. The slight limp in the steps gave the identity away before Jess could even make out the face.

"Mrs. Quimby."

Emerging from the darkness, Mrs. Betty Quimby, a short, medium built women with matching short hair stepped up to the front of the car, pushing past the two agents. Her face was well applied with makeup, making her look a lot younger than sixty-five, but no amount of powder could cover how angry she appeared to be. "Miss. Sowa, we have things to talk about."

Jess swallowed hard, preparing for what the president of her Research Lab was going to say. The presence of Mrs. Quimby alone was enough to cover Jess with goosebumps—much of the time, Mrs. Quimby was always behind the scenes, so for her to make an appearance herself only capitalized the moment and possible peril Jess found herself in.

"You let me down, Jess," Mrs. Quimby began as she stepped toward her employee and began circling her like a swimmer trapped in shark-infested waters. "You promised me everything would be alright and I had nothing to worry about. But, then I get a phone call in the middle of the night saying I actually *do* have something to worry about. So either, I received that phone call by mistake...or you fucking lied to me."

The thumping in Jess' ear from her pulse reached the point where it made hearing Mrs. Quimby a challenge. Still, she remained calm and kept eye contact each time Mrs. Quimby circle around to her front side.

"It's either one or the other," Mrs. Quimby continued. "It can't be both, so I'm hoping you can clarify which one it is for me."

Oh, she's pissed already, Jess thought. *And I haven't even told her what happened.*

Jess paused briefly, trying to figure out the best way to word the nightmare the evening had turned into, but no matter which way she thought about spinning it, nothing about the night was positive. She started with the news of the experimental treatment working, hoping it would change Mrs. Quimby's attitude—

"Well congratulations, but that still doesn't help the situation we find ourselves in, does it?" Mrs. Quimby growled.

The nighttime hid many details of Mrs. Quimby's face, unintentionally providing her with much more intimidation than she typically would on any other day, though that's not saying much; many people feared the wrath of Betty Quimby just as they did the legend of Russel Fritz being slaughtered by something that haunted the woods.

Jess did what she could to reassure Mrs. Quimby. "The town's communication has been shut off, and we have dozens of people searching for him. He won't make it out of the town, I assure you."

With lightning force, Mrs. Quimby spun around. "Oh, he won't, huh?"

The abrupt answer took Jess entirely off guard. "I'm sorry?"

Mrs. Quimby walked back over to her. "I didn't spend years of my life and millions of dollars to have my experiment shot and killed somewhere in the woods like an animal...no. I won't let that happen and neither will you, Miss. Sowa."

Mrs. Quimby stepped up to her top scientist, looming over her and violating her personal space in a way that only a head CEO could do to a nervous employee. The two made eye contact, both not fans of each other.

Jess did her best to remain civil while standing firm. "What would you like me to do, Mrs. Quimby?"

"You're going to make sure nothing happens to him while he's running loose. Then, once he's captured, you are going to bring him back to me in one piece."

Jess nodded, quickly acknowledging. Most times—nearly every time, actually, Mrs. Quimby would be breathing down Jess' neck and forcing her to do the opposite of what she wanted to do. And since she was the one with the money, Jess always had to obliged, but this time, much to Jess' surprise, their interests matched up—probably for the first time.

"I can do that," Jess said with confidence, hoping to try and get herself on anything that resembled Mrs. Quimby's good graces.

A draft of cold night air fluttered between the two of them strong enough to send a slight breeze through Jess' blonde hair and obstruct her vision. But, she was still able to see a dark, sinister smile grow on Mrs. Quimby's face, followed by a witch-like hand lift from the darkness below and forcefully land on her shoulder. "Good…good."

The evil smile on her face kept Jess' guard up as high as it possibly could go, but for the briefest of moments, it felt like they would remain civil due to the seriousness of the situation—

"I'm glad we have an understanding," Mrs. Quimby concluded as she slid her hand off Jess and started back to the cruiser, her dress shoes clacking away on the worn out pavement of the station parking lot. "It would be a shame if people were to find out all this grief started in your lab…under your supervision."

As she had for most of the conversation, Jess remained stoic, watching as her boss limped to the backseat of the cruiser, taking in the unspoken warning Mrs. Quimby hinted out. Jess' mouth hung open, trying to find a way to respond, but nothing was able to come out; the threat was effective.

But, despite knowing Jess was brilliant enough to understand what she was implying, a part of Mrs. Quimby felt the need to add a brief follow up to make sure her point came across as intended. She sat back into the car and yelled out, "Surviving is a binary choice, Miss. Sowa; you either do or don't. There is no in between."

The sadistic tone in Mrs. Quimby's voice was haunting and left no room for any mischaracterization. Part of Jess was hesitant to take on such a powerful woman—or "poke the bear" as Sam would call it, but another part felt encouraged to make a stand and forcefully confront Mrs. Quimby about her borderline blackmailing threat.

By the time Jess decided she would speak up, Mrs. Quimby and the cruiser had vanished into the night, leaving Jess alone in silence, contemplating what her next move would be.

Unlike the parking lot, that was utterly still and muted, inside the police station was the exact opposite. Throughout the rather small station, soldiers and military commanders were scattered once the generator kicked on. While many were in the large conference room, some had snuck into the kitchen, hoping to get a drink, and possibly find something to eat while a large concentration stood outside the bathroom door—many had not been able to go since they were called out to the facility.

Noises all around accompanied the constant movement in the building; everything from voices shouting to boots stomping filled the room in a way like the small aging station had never experienced before. On a day considered 'busy,' a state police trooper dropping off paperwork or even Old Man Claire popping in to file another complaint was a busy day. The sight was overwhelming, to say the least, but instead of focusing on the noise outside his office, Tyler focused on Commander Dylan L'Heureux and his partner C.J. Meyers standing at his desk, overlooking a large map of the town, both asking questions about everything from the most abandon streets, to the busiest ones. Tyler answered all of them, but not before circling a part of the map with a red sharpie.

"This is the mill we found him at," he said.

"So at least we have a sense of where he is," Meyers nodded, looking on the bright side.

"Unless he gets a method of transportation," L'Heureux brought up.

"No," Sam said, pulling himself away from the large bulletin board on the opposite side of the office covered in paperwork. "He's been in isolation since he was in middle school; he wouldn't even know what to do with a car, much less drive one."

Refocusing on the yellowish map spanning nearly the entire top of Tyler's metal framed desk, L'Heureux started scanning around the area where Tyler had circled. From the side, Meyers was only able to see very little of L'Heureux's face, but he could see his left eye bouncing all around; clearly, he was thinking up a storm.

"What else is out that way? Is there anything that's not on this map?" L'Heureux followed up, hoping for an answer that was anything other than "forest."

Because Tyler had lived in Hunting his entire life, he knew the place like the back of his hand—even the areas that were completely abandoned. It had been a while since he'd spent much time on that side of town; the fact that it was a dead end street and every single house nearby had been condemned or bulldozed to the ground made it a wasted effort to patrol. Nothing stuck out that he could think of—

"The school!" Sam said.

Everyone looked up.

"What school?" Meyers asked the question before anyone else in the room could.

Knowing full well L'Heureux and Meyers wouldn't know what he meant because they weren't from the area, Sam looked at Tyler, curious by what his reaction would be. At first, Tyler gave off nothing but a blank stare, confused by the sudden answer himself. But, once the words finally resonated, he sprang up. In one swift move, Tyler dropped his head to the map and started anxiously looking around the area within the red circle. The lack of response by him prompted L'Heureux to ask the question again.

"The old middle school down on Mimic Road—it's been closed for over a decade," Tyler replied with his eyes still fixated on the map.

L'Heureux, clearly confused, asked, "What makes you think this guy would go to an abandoned school? Why wouldn't he just make a run for Pittsburgh?"

"Because this isn't about escaping for him," Sam said. "It's about something else."

"What the hell does that mean?" Meyers shot back, the tone in his voice unimpressed by the answer.

Tyler interrupted Sam before he had the chance to reply. "That was the school Fritz went to before he disappeared. It makes sense that he would go there."

Neither Meyers or L'Heureux had any idea about the background of the person—or thing—they were hunting, but Tyler's confidence was enough for the two of them to take him at his word. Out of the two, it was Meyers who acknowledged what he was saying made sense, but L'Heureux was still pandering about something, his hand caressing the peach fuzz that made up his facial hair on the bottom of his chin.

"Where did he live at the time he disappeared?" he finally asked.

Tyler paused, lifting his eyes up off the map and spun around to Sam. The look on Sam's face was completely blank, indicating he was unsure of the answer. Tyler felt the same way, but only for a moment. "Over on Prescott Street, wasn't it?"

"Yeah!" Sam snapped his fingers. "That's right; it was on Prescott Street."

"How far away is Prescott Street from where you saw him?" Meyers asked as the door to the office opened.

The noise barreled through the small office the moment the door opened but became mute once Jess and closed it. Making eye contact with Sam briefly, she forced out a fake smile before shifting her attention to Tyler looming over the large yellow map. Tyler answered Myer's before Jess could ask what was going on.

"About three miles Northwest."

L'Heureux and Meyers turned to each other, both thinking the same thing. *He could get there*, Meyers concluded. *It would be a long ass walk, but he could get there. Hell, he could be there now for all we know.*

The volume of noise coming from all the movement outside the office was picking up with intensity; the soldiers were eager to get going.

"What're you thinking?" Sam asked the two commanders in charge.

L'Heureux slowly stopped stroking his facial hair and refocused on the map, specifically the part of the map where Tyler had drawn the circle. "Meyers and I can head to Prescott Street and search the house—"

"What's going on," Jess interrupted.

Her sudden voiced carried throughout the small room, taking nearly everyone, with the exception of Sam, off guard.

Rolling his eyes, L'Heureux turned back to Tyler and Sam. "If we find anything, we'll radio you…"

Tyler nodded, very much in favor of the idea. "Alright, Sam and I will head to the school. We'll head to you if we don't find anything, either."

"Question," L'Heureux said.

"Answer," Tyler replied.

"Prescott Street...is it—"

"Abandon? Yes. Every house on that street is vacant; you'll be alone out there, so prepare yourself for that," Tyler said, his voice firm and steady.

Meyers smiled as he gently elbowed L'Heureux in the stomach. "Well, looks like we might have a little quiet time tonight, after all."

L'Heureux turned to Jess. "When we make contact, how do we engage?"

"Shoot to kill," Sam answered for her.

Jess snapped her head in his direction with a questionable look across her parched face; Sam assumed her reaction was a response to the mysterious people who showed up outside. But, whatever the reason was, Sam reaffirmed his order.

"Alright, I'm gonna need that in writing when this is done," L'Heureux said.

"You'll get it," Sam replied.

"So it's settled; you'll take Prescott Street; Sam and I will take the school," Tyler said.

Anxiety grew inside Jess as the words of Mrs. Quimby rattled like a bad memory she couldn't shake. The thought of losing her job, her hard work, her freedom, consumed her to the point where she needed to act if she was going to get out of the situation unscathed. Thoughts of her mother also flooded in, mixing in with Mrs. Quimby's harsh warnings.

Thinking quick on her feet, like the master planner she was, Jess stepped to the desk, and with a worried tone, she said, "What about the woods?"

Everyone in the room turned to her, shifting their attention to her. No one spoke up, so she continued. "What if he's not in either place and he's somewhere in the woods? Not to mention that kid out there..."

Tyler, stressed to the max, dropped his head in defeat and sighed. "Shit, that's right. L'Heureux, did you or your guys find anything?"

L'Heureux and Meyers anxiously glanced at each other, like a group of friends about to tell their parents something terrible they did. Tyler hadn't known L'Heureux—or Meyers for that matter—longer than a few hours, but he picked up that there was something both of them knew.

"About a mile out, the guys found blood and a piece of torn cloth, most likely from a T-shirt—"

Tyler slid his arm across the desk, sending the piles of paperwork showering onto the floor. "Goddamn it!"

There was more to say, but L'Heureux remained silent, allowing time for Tyler to let out his frustration. Feeling the same way, Sam thought about joining, but kept those feeling suppressed, hiding them behind a blank stare so lifeless, it matched the lifelessness that compensated his rampant patient Russell Fritz.

Tyler looked back up, his cheeks rosy red with annoyance. "Was it a lot of blood?"

"Not a whole hell of a lot," Meyers shrugged.

"Could the kid could still be alive, then?" Sam asked.

"Yeah, it's possible," L'Heureux said with a fair amount of confidence.

Enjoying what she was hearing, Jess laid down the final pawn on her vicious chessboard. "We can't just leave him in the woods if he is! That kid must be so scared out there all alone."

Passion was in her voice as tears glossed her eyes. L'Heureux and Meyers were surprised by the emotion her voice carried; even Sam felt reflex by such an out of character tone. It was a side of her that he'd never seen before. Tears continued to fill her eyes the more she spoke. "We need to keep searching for him!"

While being as sympathetic as he could, or at least trying to be, Meyers dismissed the idea. "We'd be way to scattered. We're better staying together in numbers—"

"She's right," L'Heureux interrupted his partner. "If the kids still out there, we should have people looking for him."

"That's a lot of ground for us to cover, boss," Meyers said, reinforcing his idea it was wiser to stay in numbers.

"You and I can head to Prescott Street by ourselves," L'Heureux patted Meyers on the shoulder, reassuring him they could easily fend for themselves should the need arise.

"I'm going with you!" Jess abruptly shouted.

"That's not necessary, Miss. Sowa," L'Heureux replied as politely as he could.

Jess pushed back. "It's not up for discussion, L'Heureux."

Not surprised by Jess' forceful, yet unofficial order, L'Heureux knew it was pointless to argue. *Annoying ass woman.*

"Fine, but when we're out there, you listen to me."

"Fine," she conceded. "But I want a gun."

L'Heureux sighed, hoping to ease his frustration as he turned to Meyers who replied with a simple shrug.

"There's one in the car."

Now that L'Heureux and Meyers had their game plan, Tyler turned to his best friend to come up with there's. "We'll head to the school on our own, too. If we find anything, we can radio the guys."

Russell Fritz rising after getting shot still left Sam feeling uneasy. In part he agreed with Meyers about staying together, but the point Jess made, and the real possibility that Fritz might not be in either location forced him to accept Tyler's idea and ignore the feeling in his gut advising him against it.

"Yeah, that's fine."

Once he got an answer from Sam, Tyler reached down, pulled open the top drawer on the left-hand side of his desk and took out a broad set of keys. Then, he walked over to the large green cabinet on the back wall of his office. Fidgeting with the keys, Tyler shifted through them until he got to a gold one with a red top. Everyone in the office watched as he reached the cabinet, pushed the key into the bottom of the silver lock, unlocked it and pulled open both doors to the cabinet simultaneously, revealing multiple rifles, shotguns, and handguns neatly displayed on either side.

"Take what you need," Tyler turned to everyone in the office. "We're going to need it."

CHAPTER 11

Keeping the beam of his flashlight pointed straight ahead, James Nelson continued on with his pursuit to find the lights. His pace wasn't fast or slow, but steady, having only stopped twice to relieve himself. He wasn't sure how far out he was, but the young boy knew he was in deep. Nothing but the sound of the wind and leaves crackling beneath his feet accompanied him.

The LED beam lit up dozens of trees that were ahead, guiding him toward his mysterious destination. At this point, James assumed he would've found *something* by now, but that was not the case. He was very much alone with nothing but denser patches of forest coming straight at him.

The night had gotten colder, much faster than he anticipated; he could feel the tip of his nose losing its warmth, and it was only a matter of time before the first signs of condensation from his breath appeared. But, despite the drastic change in weather, the wind had died down significantly, almost to the point where there was none at all.

Brr, it's cold! I should've packed my hat—no, that's right I couldn't because I left them in the living room and mum would've seen me. Dammit. I guess I'll just have to suffer—my mittens!

Coming to a sudden halt, James whipped the straps of the backpack off his shoulders and unzipped the small pouch in the front compartment. He reached in and felt a soft, warm fabric—the same fabric his mittens were made out of. He snatched the gloves out and slid them onto both hands in one swift move. The warmth of the fabric coating his cold palms brought a bit of joy to the young child. He placed his arms back through the straps of the backpack and carried on into the forest, unsure of what lied ahead, but excited for the possibilities.

Keeping the light aimed at his feet, he resumed the same pace he was walking before he stopped to find his mittens. He even found himself humming and joyfully whispering lyrics from one of his favorite songs as he eagerly awaited what he would end up finding once he made it out of the forest.

The forest remained hauntingly silent, and the shadows of the trees towered overhead, casting devilish shapes across the forest floor, but none of it impacted James in the slightest; he wasn't scared at all.

He kept his focus straight ahead, watching as the beam of light lit up the way like headlights down an empty countryside road; guiding him through the thick, dense woods. *I've gotta be close by now! I think I am—I can't wait to see the look on their faces—especially Zach Sweeney—when they find out it was me who discovered the aliens. Ha-ha, Zach will be begging to be my friend after this. The look on his dumb face will—whoa!*

He stopped.

His pulse picked up.

A rush of adrenaline blasted through him from head to toe, warming his body in a matter of seconds.

Without blinking, or really thinking, James moved his right thumb around the top of the flashlight head and shut it off, leaving him in the blue moonlight. Because of the brightness the flashlight had, it took his eyes a few moments to adjust to the natural light in front of him, even forcing him to open and close his eyes, hoping to speed up the process. Once they did, curiosity came over the young adult and before he knew, his feet were already marching straight ahead.

There was a light a couple hundred feet in front of him—a natural glow that almost mimicked the same color as the light of the moon. *That's strange*, the young boy thought. *Why would there be light up ahead? It should be all trees...unless it's a ship! Yes, it's a ship! I found it!*

Excitement flushed through his borderline autistic body, so much so that he was unable to control himself—he sprinted to the light. Using all the might his body held, he charged forward, only slowing down to jump over a few rocks that stuck out from the leaf-covered ground. The cold air hitting his face, stiffened his cheeks and chilled his ears, but he kept his pace, racing faster and faster to the illumination up ahead.

The speck of light grew larger with each step James took. His heart started to beat; then it started to pound. Taking in a deep breath, the young boy pushed himself to the limit as he sprinted for the finish and leaped out from the thick brush. *The lights, the lights, the light—wait. It's not lights. It's a light. Moonlight. But, how could—*

James stopped moving, allowing time for him to catch his breath.

It's a field. Why would a field be out here?

Grabbing the straps of the backpack with both hands, James stood motionless, confused by the random clearing that was before him. He looked around, trying to find any markers or signs that might explain why the clearing was there. Nothing stood out—everything seemed reasonably normal. It was just a large empty field with no trees for at least half a mile.

Because the town of Hunting, Pennsylvania had already gotten close to the first frost of the year—with their second well on the way—nearly all of the grass on the field was dead. Nothing more than a lifeless yellow covered the ground. Hesitant to move, James looked around, realizing he was still very much alone. His impatient head bobbed back and forth, holding out hope he might've missed something. Nothing was there.

Thoughts of turning around and heading home crept upon him. It lasted briefly, but it was present enough to make him stop and really debate it and question what he was doing. The voice of his arch-nemesis and school bully Zachary Sweeney echoed somewhere deep in his mind, not as loud as previous times, but enough for James to hear the soft echo if he listened carefully. *No, no, Zach. You're not telling me what to do! I'm gonna keep going, and nothing you say will stop me!*

James twisted the ropes of his backpack with either fist, bit down on his bottom lip and marched forward, squashing doubts he allowed to flutter in. The chill of nighttime air tickled through the hole in his shirt from where he fell, but it didn't faze him. In fact, it didn't even seem to get his attention at all. He kept his eyes forward, focusing on each step until they started to lift and fixate on the towering object dead ahead. *Wow! Look at the size of that rock! Ah, I wonder if I can jump to the top...I think I can!*

The childish idea nested like hooks in his mind, leaving him unable to think about anything else—he tightened his grip on the backpack straps and ran to the large bolder, concentrating to make sure he leaped at the right time so he wouldn't go hurtling into it.

You can do it, James. Almost...almost...and...now!

He let out a loud yell and jumped as if he were swinging from a vine in the Brazilian rainforest. His legs flung out and his arms tightened. *Oh, crap…oh, shit—*

He landed on his feet, keeping his balance despite missing the edge by only inches.

He extended both arms, hoping to maintain his balance as he wobbled back and forth. Everything got silent again as his swaying diminished. James kept his hands out until his body came to a complete stop. He looked around before a large smile appeared. *Yes! I knew I could do it! I knew it!*

Pumping his fists in the air, like a racer would do after getting first place, James jumped up and down, relishing in the symbolic victory of overcoming the obstacle in his way. The rush of confidence mimicked a high that he'd never felt before in his young life and he took in the moment while gazing up at the starry sky with a flutter of hope keeping him company.

Spinning around as he jumped up and down, he shouted with childish glee. *Go, James! Go, James! You did it; you did—whoa!*

He stopped jumping. Not a moment after, the excitement vanished as he kept still and focused out on the horizon. Out in the—not too far— distance was what appeared to be light. He rubbed his eyes, making sure the night wasn't playing tricks on him like they had so many had before. *It's them…holy shit, I found them—I found the lights! They're right there!*

Keeping his eyes on the neon light off in the horizon, James kept still. Unlike how many of his other classmates would feel, he wasn't scared—not in the least. He was, however, hesitant as the idea of finally discovering what the lights were became intimidating the more he thought about it.

But, the idea of retreating never crossed his mind. Instead, he jumped off the large boulder, landed on both feet and started running across the vast flat field into the direction of the woods that would lead him to the answer he'd been chasing all night.

With all the military soldiers gone and heading to their assigned destinations, deep quietness returned into the Hunting police station. Except for a few food wrappers scattered across the kitchen floor and muddy boot prints near the front entrance, the station looked just like it did every other day of the year: empty. But, there was one thing that stood out in the station that was very different from every other day. It was the sound of sniffles coming from the back office.

Taking her fourth tissue, Kimberly put the soft tissue to her eyes. Her screams of pain that morphed into cries were now turning into sniffles of disbelief. But, whenever a memory of Mike came across her mind, she broke down in tears.

Standing on the other side of her office, Lois went back and forth from Kimberly to the walkie-talkie on her desk, waiting to respond the moment she heard Tyler's voice. At times, she questioned if she should let Kimberly have some time alone. She nearly acted on those thoughts may times, but if Kimberly was anything like her, being alone was the last thing she would've wanted.

Neither woman spoke, but even in deafening silence, Kimberly knew Lois was ready to be there the moment she asked her. While her presence did little to blunt the pain that racked her, it was comforting to the young traumatized teenager now forever changed. Lois kept her eyes out the window but paid close attention to the sound of Kimberly's sniffles. When they began growing further and farther apart, she slowly approached her.

"I'm sorry, Kim. I truly am."

Remaining quiet, Kimberly blotted her eyes with the mascara covered tissue. Her mouth opened to say 'thank you,' but the words never came. The overwhelming pain Lois could see she was in was enough to bring her to tears as memories of her own tragic loss many years ago found their way in—her eyes looked down when she spotted drops of blood underneath Kimberly's chair. She sprinted into action.

"You're hurt."

Kimberly, remembering she was wounded, dismissed it, saying she was okay. The response didn't faze Lois. "No, it's not."

Racing over to a green cabinet that matched the one Tyler had in his office, she pulled open the double-wide doors and reached to the top shelf and pulled down a red first-aid kit resting beside her additional service revolver. Kimberly had shot down the idea of going to the hospital to before they even reached the station.

Placing the red box on her organized desk, unlike the disaster that scattered Tyler's desk, Lois lifted the top, revealing multiple band-aids, gauze, anti-inch crème, a brown bottle of hydrogen peroxide and shaving crème, of all things. She grabbed the bottle of peroxide and one of the last remaining tissues in the box beside Kimberly.

Cautiously, Lois approached the teenager, hoping she'd let her help. Rather than asking if she could, Lois walked around her and dropped to her knees. Kimberly didn't say anything, but she leaned forward and lifted her shirt to reveal that gash, indicating it was okay for Lois to proceed.

Crusty blood had dried on the outline of the wound while glossy blood engulfed the open skin. Lois, being the weak stomach that she was, winced at the sight, but kept herself together. Placing the tissue over the top of the peroxide bottle, she tipped it enough, so the tissue absorbed it.

"This is gonna sting for a second," Lois warned.

Kimberly remained silent, preparing for that god awful pain.

"Ow," she mumbled, squeezing her eyes closed.

The twitch Kimberly's body gave off forced Lois to withdraw some of the pressure she was applying, but she made sure the peroxide touched every part of the wound. Kimberly kept twitching each time the tissue made contact with her open wound.

"Sorry," Lois said. "I just wanna make sure I get it all."

The pain intensified the more pressure was applied, forcing Kimberly to bite her lip harder to avoid screaming out in pain. She came close to doing it, but she stopped short when she felt the pressure lift. An awkward silence fell upon the two women, both unsure—especially Lois—of what to say. Not wanting to come off as a typical person preaching false sympathy, Lois tried to stay away from telling Kimberly that 'she understands what she's going through' even though she really *did* understand, but the unsettled atmosphere cried out for something to be said, and at that moment, that's all Lois could come up with.

"I'm sorry, I know this must be hard for you."

An unexpected scoff came from the rebellious now damaged teenager. "I just watched my boyfriend get slaughtered in front of my eyes. How could you possibly know what I'm going through?"

"Because I watched mine get hit by a drunk driver and die in front of me," Lois replied sharply as she rose to her feet.

The anger and disdain Kimberly had, thinking Lois was only saying she understood to make her feel better, vanished. Her facial expression lowered like that of a child after being reprimanded by their parent; Lois' answer was not what she expected. The office became silent again; only this time, *she* felt uncomfortable by it. Lois walked over to her desk, throwing the bloodstained tissue in the metal trash barrel and started digging through the first-aid kit.

"I—I'm sorry," Kimberly mumbled, her voice weak, but sincere.

Lois didn't say anything at first, and in all honesty, she didn't want to. For years, she's struggled to keep the memories of that fateful day dormant—and most days she was adequate, but just that sentence alone brought the memories and suppressed feeling back to the surface. The feeling brought back the anger she'd hung onto for years, but the anger wasn't intended to be aimed and Kimberly; Lois understood she was lashing out because of what happened to Mike.

Lois continued searching through the kit, hoping to find anything large enough that would cover the wound. "It's fine."

Sadness reemerged on Kimberly's face—not for the situation she found herself in, but for Lois. The look of defeat frightened her for fears that years down the road, she would be and feel the same. But, as uncomfortable as it was, curiosity overtook Kimberly. "What happened to the driver?"

"He was never found," Lois answered immediately, hoping the faster she explained, the faster the conversation would be "I provided a description of the car—a dark-colored Pontiac Grand AM with tinted windows—and a description of the driver, but nothing. No such match came up in the system the officers said."

Finding herself in the same situation as Lois was in moments before, Kimberly repeated her apology, hoping it would help.

"Just like that, it was over. All our plans, all our dreams—our future. All of it over, just like that. In the blink of an eye. You see, that's the hardest part, especially in the beginning. Just hours ago, you had your whole life ahead of you and now…"

Lois trailed off. Tears returned to her eyes, proving her words carried meaning. But, unlike the broken-hearted teenager in her office, Lois remained, almost lifeless as the words flatly came out. There was no emotion, nor was there any sense of lingering pain for her; it was almost as if she was talking about a stranger—a stranger from a different life.

Lois closed the lid to the first-aid kit, the loud crash of the lid bringing the two women back to the present. "I don't have enough gauze in here; I'm gonna go see if Tyler has any in his. I'll be right back."

Assuming the conversation was over, Lois headed for the door, spotting the muddy boot prints scattered across the floor right away. *Men...always messy! Can't they atlea—*

"Lois?"

She halted hallway to the door. "Yeah?"

Kimberly sniffled. "If you could find the driver of the Pontiac, what would you do?"

Lois paused as her face unintentionally changed with emotion. The question was offsetting; she'd spent so much time trying to find the driver of the car that she never bothered to think about what would happen *when* she finally did. The pause lasted longer than Kimberly thought it—

"The same thing you would do to the person who took Mike away from you...sit tight, I'll be back."

Lois walked away, leaving Kimberly with her head slumped down. She closed her eyes and took in several deep breaths until Lois' footsteps were no longer audible. The time alone allowed her emotions to run rampant. Everything from incredible sadness to overwhelming rage drifted in and out of her mind. All the thoughts combined with the stunning silence of the station felt surreal, almost as if time had come to a standstill—static emerged from the walkie-talkie resting on top of Lois' desk. Followed soon after by a familiar voice.

"Radio check," Tyler said. "Come in, L'Heureux."

The static ceased.

Then it returned. "Copy, Benton. We hear you. Did you make it to the school yet?"

Kimberly rose her head.

"Yeah, we're just a few streets away from Mimic Street. You make it to Prescott Street?" Tyler asked.

"Just about," L'Heureux confirmed.

"Okay, radio if you need anything," Tyler responded.

"10-4."

As the static faded, Kimberly kept her eyes fixed onto the walkie-talkie, but they slowly began to drift as Lois' answer whispered back and forth in her mind. Before she knew it, she was looking at the set of car keys hanging up on the wall beside her, next to the green cabinet Lois left open. She refocused her attention to the walkie-talkie.

Mimic Street...

While waiting inside the undercover cruiser she pulled up in at the police station to confront Jess Sowa, Mrs. Quimby remained quiet as she reached for her cellphone, hoping to make a call. *Oh, that's right, there's no service. Goddamn it!*

Following her order, Agent Anthony Vitukevich had backed the cruiser onto a small dirt opening off the main road, getting the car in deep enough so it wouldn't be spotted by anyone driving by. The dark-colored vehicle blended in well with the equally dark forest that surrounded, which meant Vitukevich didn't have to back in too far, but he didn't stop until Mrs. Quimby ordered him to. "That's enough, Vitukevich! Jesus Christ, we don't need to back into the middle of the goddamn forest!"

Using the darkness to hide is eye-rolling, Vitukevich pushed on the breaks, put the car in park and shut the engine off, leaving them with no type of sound. An unwelcoming silence—much like the one Lois and Kimberly found themselves in—overtook the car. Waiting for their next orders, Agent Eric McCann looked at Vitukevich with a questionable look.

With nothing to do but wait for the anticipated voices of Tyler Benton or Sargent Dylan L'Heureux to come screeching through the radio, the two agents grew impatient as their fear intensified. From outside, shadows of leaves crumpling on the ground surrounded the entire vehicle, spiking their paranoia—particularly Vitukevich's as his eyes danced all around. Because the car was off, nobody was able to keep an eye on the time, forcing McCann to take his cellphone out of his pocket and keep checking it.

Three minutes went by.

Then five.

Then ten.

Fearing he would see something from his worst nightmares, McCann kept his head low and away from the window so he wouldn't be tempted to lookout. Vitukevich, while feeling a bit unsettled himself, kept his eyes out the window, moving them from the driver side window to the windshield. Unlike his partner, Vitukevich had a much harder time hiding his true feelings, specifically with his facial expressions. The car was dark, but Mrs. Quimby was able to spot the appearance once her eyes adjusted when she looked away from her cellphone screen.

"Is there something you wanna say, Anthony?"

"Yeah, what the hell are we waiting for? I thought you said we were going to let Jess handle this," he forcefully said.

An evil yet amused chuckle emerged from the backseat. "Oh, please. Do you really think I'm going to just leave and put all my faith in her? I don't trust that bitch as far as I can throw her. We're going to handle this ourselves."

McCann's eyebrows slowly rose. "We?"

Mrs. Quimby started looking out the back window, trying to get a sense of the surrounding environment. "What, you weren't expecting to just sit on your asses and do nothing, were you?"

"What about everyone we saw at the station?" McCann whined.

Mrs. Quimby snapped her head in his direction. "What about them?"

"You just expect them to just roll out the red carpet and let us take over the scene?"

Mrs. Quimby nodded. "Yep. That's exactly what I expect."

"And if they don't?" Vitukevich asked.

"You're a smart guy, Anthony. I'm sure you can figure that out for yourself," Mrs. Quimby growled. "Right now, we focus on capturing this thing; we'll cross the other bridges when we get there."

Not one for questioning his boss, McCann didn't replay, but even if he wanted to—

"Chasing a psychotic science experiment wasn't in the job description," Vitukevich interrupted his train of thought.

"Your job description is to follow orders from your boss, which is me. But, if you don't like it, then feel free to get the hell out of the car and make your way home," Mrs. Quimby replied, menacingly leaning forward. "Otherwise, sit there and shut the fuck up until I tell you otherwise."

Vitukevich scoffed, unamused by his boss's tone, but chose to remain silent, keeping all the horrible things and names he wanted to call Mrs. Quimby to himself. *Jess isn't the only bitch around here you nasty-ass hog. Well, fine, if you don't want me to talk, then I won't talk, bitch.*

He obeyed the order—Vitukevich bit his lip, allowing the car to re-fill with ambient sounds coming from the surrounding forest. Because of how deep Vitukevich backed in, the tall trees looming over the car blocked much of the moonlight from filtering in through the car windows, encapsulating them in darkness. Not knowing what to do, Agent McCann took out his cellphone and rechecked the time.

Another five minutes had passed by.

Choosing not to check his messages, fearing the movement would draw criticism from Mrs. Quimby, he shut the screen off and began putting the phone—static screamed through the radio, spooking all three of them.

"Jesus Christ!" Vitukevich shouted.

Mrs. Quimby used the seat to help her lean forward, pushing passed McCann and extending her arm to the dashboard. "Quick, give me the radio!"

Abruptly doing as she said, McCann grabbed the radio off the center of the dashboard and handed it to her. Once she had it, he felt a sudden relief of pressure come off his seat as Mrs. Quimby flopped back down into the backseat.

Cranking the volume knob to the max, Mrs. Quimby lifted the radio to her ear, impatiently waiting to hear a voice emerge. *Come on, you sons of bitches, talk. Talk!*

No such voices came to be.

The radio was dead silent; not even static came through, angering Mrs. Quimby even more. She exhaled with a low grunt audible toward the end before tapping McCann on the shoulder with the tip of the antenna on the walkie-talkie and handing it to him. He grabbed it and placed it back on the dashboard.

"God, I'm getting too old for this shit," she whined as she reached down, picked up an opened bottle of orange soda and finished the last mouthful.

McCann and Vitukevich didn't say anything, assuming Mrs. Quimby was talking to herself. Tension felt high to McCann while the pissed off look on Vitukevich's face remained. Both had been on stakeouts with their boss before, but this was, by far, the most awkward—a loud burp came from the backseat. Followed soon after by the backdoor behind McCann opening.

"I gotta take a piss. If that radio so much as squeaks, let me know," Mrs. Quimby ordered as she stepped out of the car and slammed the door shut, rocking the entire vehicle.

Piles of dead leaves crackled beneath her feet as shadows of long tree branches surrounded her from all directions. But Mrs. Quimby—not being afraid of the dark at all—continued her walk without hesitation. At first, the sounds of the leaves snapping at her feet was deafening to the two agents in the car, but the further she walked away, the quieter they became. And once she was out of sight, Vitukevich slammed his hand on the wheel.

"God, I hate that bitch! I hate her, hate her, hate her!"

McCann watched Mrs. Quimby until she disappeared into the shadows. "Oh, come on, Vitukevich! There's goodness in everyone, you just gotta care enough to look for it."

Also facing forward after Mrs. Quimby vanished into the dark, Vitukevich elbowed McCann to get his attention. "What do you say we leave her? Huh?"

McCann chuckled, amused by the idea despite not taking it seriously.

"Come on, you know you want to," Vitukevich pressured.

McCann kept smiling but dismissed the idea. "As much as I'd like to, I can't. I kind of need the job to pay for the wedding."

Vitukevich sighed, not surprised by his partner's decision. "How's that going by the way?"

McCann shook his head immediately. "Oh, my God. I just want it to be over! I didn't realize how much shit goes along with a wedding. Finding a place, getting a dress, catering, getting all the invitations out. At this point, we should've just went to Vegas."

McCann's bluntness drew a chuckle from the typically serious Vitukevich. "I can understand—"

Static squealed from the walkie-talkie, preventing Vitukevich from finishing. Simultaneously, both agents looked at each other and straightened their posture and leaned directly in front of the radio.

The rough static wasn't as loud as the previous bolt that sent both them and Mrs. Quimby jumping, but it was enough to raise the hairs on the back of their necks. Then, a voice spoke through the grainy ear-numbing static—a voice they'd been waiting for.

"Radio check," Tyler said. "Come in, L'Heureux."

"Copy, Benton. We hear you. Did you make it to the school yet?" L'Heureux asked as the two agents, along with Kimberly, listened.

Footsteps approached the hidden cruiser.

"Yeah, we're just a few streets away from Mimic Street. You make it to Prescott Street?" Tyler asked.

"Just about," L'Heureux confirmed.

"Okay, radio if you need anything," Tyler responded.

"10-4."

The back door behind McCann opened.

Vitukevich looked in the rearview mirror in time to see Mrs. Quimby's face enter the mirror followed by the loud bang of the door slamming shut. The emotionless look she was known for was very much present, indicating to Vitukevich she was still flustered by their conversation.

"Benton and Rainey are heading to the abandoned school on Mimic Street, Mrs. Quimby. Do you wanna head there, first?" McCann asked.

"Um-Hmm."

Not a second after they got the answer, Vitukevich started the car, shifted it into gear and sped forward, the back tires screeching and throwing up dirt as they pulled onto the main pothole-filled road and started for Mimic Street.

With the moon off in the far horizon and the massive trees covering its presence, darkness had overpowered the entire street of Mimic. Like the rest of the dilapidated town, the neighborhood was abandon not long after the school closed its doors permanently. Now, the once prosperous street that occupied the hopes and dreams of the children of Hunting, Pennsylvania was now a ghost town with surrounding houses riddled with decay and blight.

When the cruiser pulled onto the street, Tyler Benton reached down to the lock button on the driver side door and pressed it, the locks clicking into the place, trapping him and Sam Rainey inside. Despite the sudden noise, Sam kept his attention out the passenger window, looking at each abandoned house they drove by.

Despite only being in Pittsburg, this was the first time Sam had been back on the street since he graduated from the school, over twenty-years-ago. Because of how dark it was, many details of the street were hidden, but the headlights provided just enough light for memories of his childhood to come flooding back. It felt surreal to both of them. The street of Mimic wasn't long, but at the slow pace Tyler was driving—in order to avoid potholes, the street seemed to stretch into eternity.

The inside of the cruiser was just as dark as it was outside with the only light providing them company being the digital clock in the center of the radio. Tyler kept his eyes on the road, but he was able to make up the outline of the pistol resting in between Sam's hand when he glanced over.

"Almost there," Tyler finally said.

"Yeah, I can't remember the last time I was here," Sam mumbled.

"Same here. Nobody lives out this was—not one person. Every house here is empty," Tyler flatly said.

"Yeah, it looks like a ghost town out here."

Tyler smiled. "It *is* a ghost town out here. Hell, horny teenagers don't even bother coming out this way anymore. It's like all the history in this town has been forgotten. But, time takes it all, I guess."

"Yeah..." Sam turned back to the windshield. *Yeah, time takes everything alright, everything out here is gone! Even*—"Hey!"

"What?"

Sam pointed out the windshield. "That was Miss. Machnik's place, wasn't it?"

Following Sam's finger, Tyler turned to spot an old rundown house passing by on the left side. Just like every other home on the block, it was completely decimated and deserted. But, Sam's question got Tyler thinking about their days in school all those years ago.

"Yeah, it was. I remember that," Tyler answered with not much enthusiasm in his voice. "She taught math."

"Yeah, we had her our final year here."

Tyler smiled as thoughts came racing back about the more youthful days the two friends shared together that they thought would last forever like most kids do. "Seems like a long time ago."

"Yeah, and not many people are still here from those days, either," Sam added.

Tyler agreed, and before he knew it, he found himself naming out some of their former classmates in an attempt to take him and Sam away from the horror that lied ahead.

"Let's see...uh...Tyler Chagnon is still here."

Blankly staring into the darkness outside the cruiser, Sam shrugged. "Don't remember him. I remember Ricky West, though."

Tyler smiled. "Ah Big Rick. Of course you remember him; it's kinda hard not to forget a personality as unique as his."

"Exactly. The big guy with an even bigger heart. Is he still around?"

Tyler's smile faded as Sam's question pulled him out of those forgotten memories and brought him back to reality. "He died this past February."

Sam rocked back in his seat, taken aback by the news he didn't see coming. "Oh, shit. Really?"

"Yeah," Tyler acknowledged as he refocused his attention to the windshield.

Sam joined him in doing so as the news set in. "Wow. Wasn't expecting that."

"None of us were."

It had been years since Sam and Tyler ever had a real conversation and decades since he thought about his early days in school, but Sam learned early on some memories are impossible to forget. "I'm sorry, Tyler. I know you guys were close way back when."

Tyler forced out a smile. "Yeah. The brightest lights leave the darkest shadows. I never understood that until I found out he was gone."

"Huh..." Sam sighed. "I always liked him. Him and that other kid we had in math class; you know, the one who wanted to open some sort of nutrition store?"

"Oh, Dalton Criswell?"

"Yeah, he was pretty cool, too."

"He actually did open at store," Tyler revealed, with a note of satisfaction in his voice. "Several of them, too."

"No, shit," Sam exclaimed.

Tyler tapped the accelerator as they closed in on the school. "Yeah, he works out of Michigan; Royal Oak, I think."

The news brought a rare smile to Sam—the first and only one of the night. He and Dalton were friends—even good friends—when they were kids, and Sam always had a fond respect for him. Despite the friendship, he was unable to remember precisely when the last time he saw Dalton, reminding him how much time had passed. Memories that typically felt close now felt far and out of reach.

"Well, least someone from this town is living the dream," he concluded.

"While we're all trapped in a nightmare," Tyler scoffed. "But, now that I think about it, it's just you and me left...and Old Man Claire. But, I don't think he counts anymore."

The tone of Tyler's voice hinted that he wanted to end a conversation, and that's just what happened. He re-focused his attention to the windshield and kept his eyes on the right side, waiting to see the outline of the old decaying school—

"Hey," Sam started. "That girl we picked up in at the mill...Kimberly?"

Tyler spotted the school. "Yeah, what about her?"

"You said she left a message for you early tonight?"

"Yeah, why?"

"What did she say on the message?"

Trying to remain engaged in the conversation while keeping an eye on the school coming up at the end of the street, Tyler hesitated before answering. "Uh...she said that her and Mike Eaten hit someone on their way home—someone in a mask. Why?"

A look of fear mixed with an unreadable emotion slowly overtook Sam's face, followed soon after with his eyes transitioning into a blank stare. Out of the corner of his eye, Tyler spotted the change. "Why do you ask?"

"And that neighbor that was killed, he had a weapon with him, right?" Sam shot back, blatantly ignoring the question.

Tyler's eyes squinted with uncertainty, unsure of why Sam was asking such random questions. "Yeah, a shotgun. Why?"

Biting his lip, Sam focused on the scenario forming in his mind, so much so, he didn't even hear Tyler ask the question. It took Tyler nudging him on the shoulder before he responded. And, even then, it wasn't much of an answer.

"Him, Kimberly, Mike, Catalano, Burke, Manning, Auclair...and Old Man Claire. Son of a bitch!"

"What?" Tyler nearly shouted, just as he would do when they were younger and Sam wouldn't answer.

Finally, Sam's pale face turned and made eye contact with his friend of over a few decades.

"Middle school...1997. On that day—the day we went in the woods."

The sun shined high and bright in June of 1997, the last day of school for the students of Hunting, Pennsylvania. The crowded halls of the school on Mimic Street were filled with the future generation smiling and gleeful by how fast the school year had come and gone. Everyone from Travis Soterion—the future congressman—to the principle of the school Miss. McGorry struggled to hide their excitement to leave.

The students and teachers had been cursed with a ruthless winter, which lead to constant snow days. At the height of the season—early January in particular, the weather forced nearly one snow day a week with a delay to follow the next. By the middle of February, the school district was already on its fifth snow day with the expectation of more to come. At the rate they were going, school wouldn't have been over until June 30th, the longest the district had even been in session by two days.

Because of the lack of funding, and the acceleration of people moving out of town, the district was already facing financial hardships. For years' prior, Principle McGorry had been lobbying hard to get air conditioning for the school, but the budget left no room for such accessories. Every year, during town meeting, Miss. MvGorry would be called on and say the same thing. "We need air conditioning, at least for the fourth floor, if nothing else. It's unfathomable to expect our students to learn in ninety plus degree classrooms."

Her plea came from the heart, but fell on deaf ears; the town selectman always gave the same politically driven answer. "They're only in school for the first half of June! There's no reason whatsoever to spend thousands of dollars on central air conditioning if it's only going to be used three weeks out of the entire year."

Miss. McGorry became frustrated along with some of the teachers that attended the meeting, but nothing they said was able to persuade the selectman; the students and overworked teachers would have to deal with the uncomfortable conditions. The lack of central air and the unbearable accommodation of the fourth floor played heavy in Miss. McGorry's decision to cancel February vacation, but was ultimately the driving force which lead her to do so. The students weren't pleased in the least.

But, on that 25th day of June, the official last day of school was hazy, hot and humid. The overnight temperatures only dropped into the mid-seventies. By late morning, it was already close to eighty-five. And like always, the school was scolding. Everyone was fighting to stay cool, especially Sam and Tyler, who were in History class on the top floor.

"Could it get any damn hotter in this place?" Jorge Castillo shouted out as sweat dripped down his cheeks.

"Language, Mr. Castillo!" Mr. Van Uden said even though he was thinking the same thing.

"Sorry, Mr. Van Udan, but it's hot in here!"

Jorge's profanity and unapologetic tone got a few giggles in the medium size class, but in the second row, Sam and Tyler—sitting across from each other, laughed the hardest until Mr. Van Udan told them to simmer down. But, undenounced to Mr. Van Udan, the two weren't laughing at Jorge. They were laughing at the number of spitballs they were able to shoot into the open backpack of Russel Fritz, who was sitting directly in front of them. Once Mr. Van Udan went back to reading his magazine while the rest of the class finished up their last assignment of the year, Tyler carefully took out the saliva riddled piece of paper he had folded into a ball with his tongue and pushed it into the end of the straw he stuck in his pocket during lunch.

Glancing at Sam, Tyler spotted the evil grin on his face right away. He had seen that look before. It was the same look Sam always had when he and Tyler would pick on young Fritz back in pre-school, which was early every day. And the last day of school on that afternoon in 1997 was no exception.

Once the spit covered piece of paper was securely in the end of the all-white straw, Tyler glanced up briefly, making sure Mr. Van Udan was reading his Hunting Town Newspaper, before he lifted the straw and took aim at Russel's bag again. He took in a deep breath of thick air, concentrating on the open compartment of the bag.

The sound of Mr. Van Udan turning the page of the newspaper filled the air and Tyler fired. Using all the breath he had in his little lungs, he blew into the straw with such force; the sticky spitball blasted out like a cannon. Sam couldn't even follow it with his eyes. Tyler, on the other hand, was able to follow it and watched as it spun in circles before disappearing into the darkness of the backpack. Tyler pumped his fist in the air.

"That's eight," Tyler whispered to his partner in crime.

Covering his mouth to mute his childish giggles, Sam bent down and reached inside the small opening of the desk and began feeling around. Inside the nearly twenty-year-old desk was nothing more than a few pencil shavings, lose staples scattered about and a giant mountain of dried gum that had been there for months—nothing he could use for a spitball. Preparing to give up on the idea, Sam pulled his hand out but stopped short when his pinky finger slid across something as he pulled it out. He stopped and reached back inside.

The history class of Mr. Van Udan consisted of ten students. With the exception of Tyler, Sam and Russel the rest of the guys all were on the Hunting

Football team and, as always, all of them demanded respect and felt like they owned the school. The team caption Cormack Fitzpatrick was the one all of them looked up to and listened to—everything Cormack did, the team followed. Including the personal pleasure of traumatizing and harassing the quiet and strangely awkward Russel Fritz.

Every time any of the players spotted Fritz in the hall, they went out of their way to make sure young Fritz was aware that they had seen him. Most times, the players—everyone from Cormack Fitzpatrick to Tommy Dole—would step into the path Fritz was walking down and violently slam their muscular shoulders into his below the average-sized shoulder. The force of the hits were enough to cause Fritz to stumble backward and nearly lose his footing; a few times he even dropped the folders he carried for his classes, sending papers loosely tucked in the pockets to come flying out and scattered about the busy halls.

That was only the beginning.

As the years went on, the bullying got worse. It was now at the point where the team began to started to hit the awkwardly tall and skinny boy, the first time being in the locker room right before gym class. Cormack started it, but it was Tommy Dole and Johnathan Wright that finished it. Tommy, unimpressed that Fritz would never respond to his harsh rhetoric struck Fritz in the stomach, taking the breath out of his body before Tommy decided to punch Fritz in the face, knocking him onto the cold tiled locker room floor. Once that bridge had been crossed, and Tommy received no punishment due to Fritz's fear of being labeled a narc, the behavior kept up and got worse with each—the door to the classroom opened.

Mr. Van Udan glanced up from his paper, and a smile came rushing over his face like a child seeing a new pet for the first time. "Mrs. Curtis! How may I be of help to you?"

Returning her own flirtatious smile, Mrs. Curtis, dressed in her red skirt with shoulder-length hair in a ponytail, remained at the doorway. "Would you mind giving me a hand, I can't get the T.V. to work."

Nearly jumping out of his seat, Mrs. Van Udan threw the rather dull paper on top of his messy desk, and started for the door. "I'd be happy to help!" It wasn't until he was one foot out the door until he thought about saying something to the class so they wouldn't run amuck while he was gone especially since he had every intention of dragging out his visit to Mrs. Curtis' classroom. "I'll be right back, so no funny business."

Smiling with his boyish charm that nearly every girl in school had a secret crush on, Cormack lifted his thumb up in the air, confirming he would keep himself and the other guys in check. Satisfied with the responce, even though part of him didn't believe it, Mr. Van Udan stepped out of the classroom, closing the door behind him.

Not a second after the door closed, Cormack's face changed back to its evil ways as the classroom started filling up with conversations. Cormack leaned back in his chair, picked up his legs and crossed them over the top of the desk, turned to Tommy Dole, who was on his left side and started talking about a box of magazines he'd found in his basement, hidden behind a bunch of crates. Briefly, Sam and Tyler spoke amongst themselves, but began eavesdropping on Tommy's story when they heard him say the word 'boobs.'

"Bullshit, I don't believe you," Cormack scoffed.

"It's true! There's gotta be like thirty magazines. And some even have pull out posters!" Tommy added.

"Pullout posters?" Johnathan Wright asked, joining Cormack with skepticism. "Sure..."

"I'm telling you! Come to my place after school—I'll show you myself."

Despite having severe doubts, considering Tommy was known at school for being one of the most dramatic players on the team, the thought of a box filled with naked pictures of woman was an idea Cormack decided was worth the risk of being let down.

"Okay, deal."

"Alright," Tommy smiled. "You'll be glad you did."

Chuckling as the thought of boobs infested Cormack's hormonal mind, he spotted Sam and Tyler staring at him. A look of curiosity on Sam's and Tyler's faces nearly matched that of his own. While he never did—and never would—consider the two of them friends, the oddball chemistry between Sam and Tyler cracked Cormack up just enough to take them off his bully radar. But, he could tell the two of them were itching for him to allow them into the 'cool kids club' and he thought this was as good a time as any.

"You two wanna join?" Cormack finally asked them.

Confused by the sudden invite, Sam and Tyler looked at each, checking to see if both heard Cormack—the unnamed king of the school—correctly.

"U-Us?" Tyler stuttered out.

"Yeah, both of you," Cormack replied, ending any doubt that remained in their minds that he was talking to them.

The two boys thought about it for a moment, even though they didn't need too—the only plans they had was to head down to Hackett River and walk along the railroad when school let out; the idea of hanging out with the cool kids never crossed their minds. The thought brought a joyful flutter to their bellies, almost like a sense of recognition they'd be craving ever since school started. Plus, the idea of pictures with boobs fazed them just as much as it did Cormack.

Simultaneously, they both shrugged and answered seconds before Cormack followed up. "Sure."

Cormack chuckled and clapped his hands together with excitement. "Alright! We'll show you two something that'll be the highlight of your summer."

Sam nodded. "Cool. Can't go wrong with boobs."

The entire class broke into laughter.

With the exception of one.

The one at the front of the classroom with his head buried in a book and his head down.

Russel Fritz.

Spotting the lack of response from the outcast, Cormack's smile vanished, and disgust befell on his face. "Hey! Jerk off in the front!"

The laughter halted as Cormack's deep voice penetrated through the giggles like nails on a chalkboard. Slowly, one by one, the students in the class turned their attention to the front. The quietness that was in the room when Mr. Van Udan was reading his paper reemerged. The look of disgust on Cormack's face morphed into anger when he didn't get a response. "Hey, dipshit up front! I'm talking to you!"

At the front of the classroom, with the hood of his black sweatshirt covering his head, Russel Fritz paid no attention to the name-calling and continued to read 'Lights in the Sky: A UFO Story', a worn out yellow-stained book which marked the last remnants of items his father left behind nearly a decade prior. Hoping the book would be strong enough for Cormack to see nothing was going to get his attention, Fritz turned the page even though he hadn't finished the bottom paragraph. The attempt to look busy, however, was not successful in keeping the bullies at bay. It got them angrier.

The sound of a chair sliding across the tiled floor of the classroom broke the silence and before Sam and Tyler even knew it, Cormack stood from his desk and walked over to Fritz with Tommy and Johnathan right behind him. A chill ran down Tyler, forcing the small hairs on his arms to stand at attention. The same type of feeling came over Sam, only not as heavy. But, unlike other times—especially when they walked through the halls, the feeling vanished as quick as it came once Cormack and his gang of friends—or goons as some would say privately—stormed passed their row and stepped up to the desk in front of them.

Looming over Fritz, the look of utter distaste returned to Cormack's face. Typically, the type of bully that regularly got in your face, Cormack kept somewhat of a distance from Fritz due to the heavy scent of body order that rose from his clothing—particularly his sweatshirt. Everyone in the school—from teachers to students that didn't even know his name—knew that the young, strange-looking student Russel Fritz was one of the most impoverished students that attended the school—possibly even the poorest. And it wasn't just his serious struggle with body odor that gave it away; it was also his house.

The home of the Fritz family, which rested at the end of Prescott Street was known to everyone as an "eye-catcher", but for all the wrong reasons. While many of the houses on the street were far from perfect, the Fritz house was by far the worst. Everything from its puke green color exterior and cracked front windows to the yellow grass that surrounded the house cried poverty. It was an unspoken fact that Fritz came from no money; not even Cormack said it out loud. He did, however, start a rumor that the house had all dirt floors, which ended up circling the halls, but not nearly as long as Cormack and his group of friends thought and hoped it would.

Looming over the quiet student, Cormack glared at him, waiting for an answer he was determined to get…no matter what. Fritz turned another page, this time not even reading half of it. Cormack finally looked up at Johnathan, who had made it up to the front of the classroom and gave him a slight nod. Johnathan returned the gesture and stepped up to the classroom door, peering through the glass window that overlooked the hall.

"You're good," he said.

With sweat trickling down his face, Fritz continued to keep his eyes in the book, hoping the bell would ring sooner rather than—a fist slammed onto his left shoulder, pushing his entire body forward. The sudden impact took Fritz by surprise, even though it really shouldn't have, and sent his small shoulder jerking forward. A burning pain shot through the area of impact and started racing down his left arm. A soft groan unintentionally slipped out from his lower lip as he squeezed the loose spine of the book firmly.

"Hey, asshole! Can you hear me, or are you shit deaf?" Cormack's voice rose.

Numbing pain warmed the back of Fritz's shoulder, but he remained quiet, still clinging to the idea that his silence would get them to stop. Another punch to his shoulder in the same spot proved that was ineffective. Cormack looked up at Tommy and smiled. "I think the kid is on the fritz again."

Tommy laughed. "Awe, is Russel on the fritz again? Yeah, I think he is!"

The well-named insult—that Tommy came up with himself—drew laughter from the students. Even teachers, including Principle McGorry, found the name humorous, though none ever publicly acknowledged it.

"Russel's on the fritz again! Russel's on the fritz again!" Tommy sang off-key.

Laughter inside the classroom grew, allowing an all too familiar sense of humiliation to come sweeping through Russell's paper-thin persona, but still, he remained silent and focused on the book.

Growing tired of waiting for a response, Cormack shook his head and looked back up at Johnathan. His eyes were met with a thumbs-up as Johnathan continued to guard the door. Once he got the all-clear, Cormack looked over his shoulder to Tommy. And without having to say anything, Tommy reached into his pocket, pull out a black, shiny object and handed it to Cormack.

Unsure of what Tommy had handed him, Sam and Tyler watched with great curiosity, trying to figure out—Snap! The two of them jerked back in their seats, their eyes widening as a blade snapped out from the handle of the knife.

Cormack stepped closer to Fritz, keeping the black switchblade firm in his left hand, the same hand he used to hit Fritz in the shoulder. His shadow overcast the fluorescent light overhead as he towered over Fritz. Then, once his patients reached the end of the road, Cormack engaged.

In one swift move, Cormack grabbed the black book, violent yanked it out of Fritz's hand and threw it across the room. The harsh yank was too much for the fragile binding to overcome and it split in two. Tommy joined in. Sam and Tyler jumped out of their chairs and stepped away. Dozens of yellow pages broke off the ill faded book and rained down across the front of the classroom like confetti.

Johnathan kept his attention on the window that overlooked the hall, watching for anything that resembled an adult. He even kept an eye out for Mr. Van Udan despite being confident he wouldn't be coming back before class ended.

The force of Cormack's abnormally large fist knocking the delicate book out of his hands terrified Fritz, forcing him to jump. A sudden crushing force wrapped around his neck and lifted him out of his seat before he had the chance to react.

Using his strength, which rivaled that of his football caption, Tommy hoisted Fritz up and body-slammed him into the nearby wall. The force of Fritz's thin body smashing into the wall shook the room as the sounds of papers and markers Mr. Van Udan had on a long wooden shelf fell to the floor.

The violent sight forced Tyler and Sam to take a few more steps backs. The sound also forced every student in the classroom—those who ignored the original bullying—to look up, including one girl who sat in the corner like the lone—yet respected outcast she was.

"Hey, cut the shit!" she said without giving much thought to what the consequences of taking on Cormack and his friends would be.

"Shut up, Lois!" Cormack forcefully shouted before lifting the knife to Fritz's face. "I'm about to give this piece of shit a lesson he'll never forget."

Cormack lowered the knife, aiming for Fritz's leg. An evil smile returned to his face as he prepared for the resistance of the tip of the blade when it reached Fritz's flesh followed by that final push to penetrate the skin—the bell rang.

Cormack looked up, spooked by the sudden alarm—smash!

"Oh, fuck!" Cormack dropped the knife and brought his hands to his nose as blood started to gush from the nostrils. "What the—"

Fritz lunged his head forward again, striking Cormack in the face with his forehead.

The knife clattered as it landed on the tiled floor.

Cormack stumbled back, pressing his hands harder onto his nose in a failed attempt to stop the blood. "Ah, shit!"

Lois brought her hands to her mouth and gasped.

Blood from Cormack's nose began dripping onto the floor.

Fritz picked up the knife, and without thinking, he wrapped his fingers around the cold handle and swung it upright. A horrific scream blasted out of Cormack. Followed soon after by a line of blood appearing across his right cheek where the blade had made contact and split open the skin. Cormack stumbled back again, providing enough space for Fritz to get to his feet and start for the door.

With the knife still in his hand as he got closer to the door, Johnathan Wright, who was still guarding the entrance, folded like a deuce before a royal flush and stepped away from the door.

"Hey, hey, hey," John begged moments after putting his hands up like he was under arrest. "I don't want any trouble."

The groans of Cormack Fitzpatrick lingered behind him, but Fritz kept his eyes on Johnathan, the knife held upward in a defensive position, warning him of the counter offensive he was prepared to do. Johnathan, still in awe of what Fritz had just done, stepped away and provided enough room for Fritz to open the door and run out of the classroom.

Tommy, just as surprised as the rest of the class by the violent retaliation, helped Cormack to his feet.

Cormack screamed. "Get that motherfucker. Now!"

Despite being in the hall that was filled with excited students heading for the nearest exit to start summer vacation, Fritz heard Cormack's command and proceeded to push through the large group of his peers as quick as he could.

Cormack plowed into the hall, crashing into the fellow classmates marching passed the classroom door. Blood continued to seep from his nose and the slice across his face, but it didn't stop him from darting his head left and right to figure out which way Fritz went—

"There!" Tommy pointed. "I see him; he went that way!"

Cormack took Tommy at his word and ran in the direction he was pointing too. Rage fueled his ability to charge through the students in his way with such force, he slammed Mr. Van Udan out of the way and into the lockers on the side of the hall. Gasps from his fellow classmates echoed in the hall, but Cormack ignored both those and Mr. Van Udan's orders to stop and instead focused on Fritz.

Being the last students to get out of the classroom, Tyler and Sam looked down the hall in the direction where Cormack had gone. Neither of them could spot him, but Tyler was able to spot Tommy moments before vanishing into the immense rush of students approaching.

"Let's follow them," he suggested.

"What, why?" Sam nearly shouted because of all the noise and movement that filled the hall.

"To make it look like we want to help," Tyler answered in the same amplified voice.

Sam was hesitant; he knew full well that when Cormack caught up with Fritz, it wouldn't be good, and Sam didn't want to be a part of that. He made his concerns known, but Tyler kept up the pressure. "Come on! This may be our only chance to prove we're tough enough to join their group. Besides, what if he takes back his offer because we didn't help?"

Still unwilling to concede to Tyler, Sam was, however, unable to deny that Tyler did bring up a good point—if it looked like they chickened out, Cormack could easily take back his offer, which he knew would effectively ruin the summer before it began.

"Fine! Let's go if we're going!"

Tyler smiled, happy with Sam's decision. "Alright, follow me!"

Listening, Sam did his best to stay right behind, trying to avoid hitting as many of his fellow classmates as he could. Tyler, on the other hand, did everything he could to keep his eyes on Tommy, and for the most part, he was successful.

The front doors of the school flung open with a herd of students, and some faculty members mixed in, rushing the streets in apocalyptic fashion. On the far right hand side of the street were a row of long yellow school buses for the students who lived farther out in town, but on that summer day—the first start to summer vacation—Russel Fritz stormed out of the school and sprinted across the busy street, hoping to get lost in the group of students and head straight toward the large pine tree his bike was resting behind.

Typically, it would only take him seconds to reach it, but due to the large volume of people on the street, it took more time than he expected. But, by the time Cormack charged out of the doors, Fritz was already more than halfway to his bike, but his plan of blending in with the crowd proved to be ineffective, thanks to him being the only one in a hoodie.

"There! He's going that way!" Cormack shouted.

The top of the stairs gave Cormack a better view of the street, while Sam and Tyler raced to catch up. Tommy and Johnathan stormed down the steps and raced across the street to where their own bicycles were. Unlike Fritz, Cormack and his friends had the respect of the entire school—no one would dare try and steal his bike; therefore, he was able to park it much closer to the school. Since Fritz was already on his third bike of the year, he was more cautious of where he parked his.

Reaching his bike first, Cormack lifted the kickstand with his foot and jumped on the padded seat and started toward the large pine tree where Fritz was heading to, shouting at his fellow teammates to hurry the hell up. By the time Sam and Tyler got onto their bikes, Cormack was riding with lightning force.

Lifting his bike as his heart thump in his chest cavity, Fritz hopped on and began pushing the peddles as fast as he could, keeping his eyes straight ahead, ignoring Cormack's foul language and name-calling that wasn't far behind.

When he got to the end of the street, Fritz squeezed the brake handle in front of the left handle of his worn bike and pulled onto Wicker Street, a suburban street filled with well-maintained homes with microscopic cracks in the pavement. Only one house was vacant on the street, and it was the last house on the left—a small ranch type home with a fenced-in yard that wrapped around the entire house. Had it not been for that tall wooden fence, Fritz would've slid into the driveway and took cover behind the empty aboveground pool in the middle of the yard, but since that wasn't an option, he rode right passed the house and headed straight to a more isolated part of town—the street of Lancaster.

"He's getting away!" Cormack shouted. "Hurry up, faster! Faster!"

Pushing themselves, as they would on the football field, Tommy and Johnathan started peddling faster and effectively closed the gap between them and Cormack. Sam and Tyler did the same, only with much slower results. "Faster!"

The blood from Cormack's nose and the gash on his face had clotted, allowing the blood to stop, but the pain, especially from the cut, began to sting in the wind the faster he went. But, it didn't slow him down. It made his anger loom larger. The faster he went, the blunter the stinging became.

The end of Wicker Street came fast, forcing Fritz to squeeze hard on the brake lever, so much so that he nearly lost his balance and went tumbling to the ground. But, he was able to maintain his upright position enough to ride off Wicker Street and onto Stine Street, then Stoker, then Duncan Street before finally reaching Peacock Street—also known as 'hold onto your cock' street because of how steep of a downhill it was. The second he turned onto the road, Fritz could feel his bike picking up in speed. Unable to keep up with the peddles, he lifted his feet off them and let the bike roll while keeping his hand placed on the brake lever for when he needed it.

The summer afternoon wind blew into his face like a sauna. Sweat from the humid rays of the sunshine beating down on him began forming in the small creases that would become age lines on his forehead. The need for something to drink started entering his thoughts as he barreled down the hill at such speed; it felt like he could rival a car. The wind blasting across his face hit with such force, it blew the hood of his sweatshirt off his head, exposing the knife marks his father left that faded over time, but were still visible after all these years—

"I'm coming for you, you piece of shit!" Cormack shouted not far behind.

Fritz placed his feet on the metal bike peddles and started spinning them; pushing himself and the bike to its maximum peak. The end of Peacock Street was rapidly approaching and everyone in town—no one more so than Russell Fritz, knew the sharp corner at the end wasn't one to take lightly. It came up quick with very little time to react before you found yourself face first in the woods.

Fritz knew that going in, but chose not to slow down for the turn and instead chose to turn the front wheel hard to the left. His timing couldn't have been any better—he turned just as he wanted and remained on the street as he pulled onto the beginning of Lancaster Street. Once completely on the road, he pumped the breaks.

Because Lancaster was on the outskirts of town, it had suffered the most population loss since the closing of the mill. Because of the lack of residence, the massive potholes and cracked pavement from the frost heaves in the winter were left unfixed, forcing Russell Fritz to slow down drastically in order to avoid—a thunderous pop exploded from the front of his bike, followed by a sudden jerking sensation. Panicking, Fritz looked down, holding onto the handlebars.

The front tire was completely flat.

The bike started to vibrate harder as a more profound sense of panic overcame the frightened child.

"You can't run forever, jerk off!" Cormack's voice shouted from disturbingly close behind.

Taking his hand off the break handle, Fritz began pushing the peddles, trying to regain the speed he'd lost, but the resistance coming from the front of the bike was becoming overpowering, and his speed diminished. Dread overshadowed Fritz as he frantically did what he could to get his bike to go faster but to no avail. His breath got more cumbersome, to the point it felt like no amount of air in his lungs would be enough—a fist smashed across his left cheek.

A paralyzing pain crushed his thoughts and sent him into a state of disarray as he'd never experienced before. An agonizing ringing rattled in his ears as a pitch-black darkness formed in the corner of his eyes. The bike beneath him rattled, jerked, bounce and began tipping to the right side. Clinging onto the handles, Fritz pushed to the left, hoping to keep the bike stable—another fist crashed onto the left side of his face again, knocking Fritz entirely off his balance.

Fritz went crashing onto the hot pavement with a violent thump, landing on his right side. His decision to not wear any type of helmet or pads—to avoid getting made fun of at school—allowed the tip of his right elbow to slide across the pavement and rip open the fragile skin it was behind. Blood began dripping out of the wound instantly. The burning sting wasn't far behind.

Fritz's left hand had absorbed most of the fall, sparing his head from hitting the ground, but it didn't do much good; the fist he took in the face had the same effect as the pavement would've. For the first few seconds, all he could do was groan in agony as pain seeped along his right side.

The darkness that formed in the corner of his eyes from the first punch took over the rest of his sight when he was struck with the second one, leaving him unable to see two more than feet in front of him even when his eyes were wide open. But, slowly, the light from the afternoon sunshine burned through the darkness and brought life back into his eyes in time to see Cormack, Tommy and Johnathan throw their bikes in the middle of the street and come racing over.

The sunshine lit his face, but his sight was blurry. It took time for his eyes to readjust to his new perspective, and they did only to see Cormack's red and black basketball shoes come swinging down, heading straight for his face.

Blood splattered out of Fritz's mouth as his head swung up from the powerful kick to the face—the force was so great, it rolled him onto his back. A large piece of skin hung from his lower lip, hidden by the blood running from the wound. Had Fritz been able to scream, he would've, but his little lungs were as airless as the front tire to his rusty steel-framed bicycle, which laid in the middle of the street as motionless as he did. He was spent; the running out of school and long bike ride that forced him to use every ounce of energy he had, left him hollow, but the punches to the shoulder and the forceful kick to his face—hands suddenly clenched the collar of his hoodie, and before Fritz knew it, he was back on his feet.

Cormack stepped up to him and glared at his fellow classmate, getting within inches of his face. "Oh, you have no idea what I'm going to do to you now, Fritz."

The blood from the slice across Cormack's face had run down enough to drip onto his white t-shirt and become an eye-sore to anyone who noticed it. Cormack started squeezing his hands tighter on Fritz collar as another pair of hands wrapped around his neck and started to squeeze. Cormack looked up. "You got him?"

"Yeah, I got him," Tommy confirmed as Johnathan caught up with them.

"Good." Cormack looked back at Fritz with disgust as he pushed a mouthful of saliva around with his tongue before hawking it in Fritz's face. "Bring him over here."

Following the order, Tommy kept his right arm wrapped around Fritz's neck, squeezing tighter with each step they took. Johnathan wasn't far behind, clearly not objective by what Cormack intended to do, but at the beginning of the street—still, on their bikes, Sam and Tyler watched, both feeling the exact opposite.

"I don't like this, Tyler," Sam confessed. "Maybe we should just get out of here."

Despite not responding right away, Tyler was starting feeling the same way, but the thought of becoming part of 'the gang' was too potent for Tyler to entirely abandon, even though he felt like Cormack was going too far.

"Hey!" Cormack shouted. "You two coming or what?"

His voice echoed throughout the nearly empty street. The two finally looked at each other. Sam reaffirmed his hesitation, but Tyler replied by getting off his bike and propping up the kickstand with his foot. Tyler's decision was made; a decision that Sam couldn't agree with, but the notion of leaving Tyler behind never crossed his mind for fear Cormack would grow tired of beating up Fritz and redirect some of that anger toward his best friend. Sam got off his bike and started to follow.

When Cormack saw the two of them approaching, he smiled. "Good, I thought you two were about to chicken out for a second!"

"Naw, of course not!" Tyler replied in a poorly acted macho fashion.

Chuckling from Tyler's response, Cormack refocused his attention to Fritz. His face changed completely. Blood from the wound on Fritz's lip poured down to the tip of his chin as the throbbing of the open wound twitched his lower lip. His mind was still trying to recover from taking a kick to the face—much less the fall he took from the bike, but he was conscious enough for tears to fill his eyes from the terrible pain he was in.

Walking as fast as he could, Cormack brought Tommy and Johnathan to the opposite side of the street where a rusty guardrail was the only barricade between the town and the forbidden forest. Once, he realized where they were taking him, Russell Fritz started to resist as his fears of Cormack Fitzpatrick morphed into horrors about the forest. And what lied within it.

Fritz pulled on Tommy Dole's arm and flung his arms in the air while simultaneously purposely dragging his feet to slow Tommy down. When it started to work, Johnathan Wright ran to Tommy's aid by picking up Fritz's legs and lifting them up as if he and Tommy were carrying a lifeless corpse they were about to dispose of. While Fritz never uttered so much as a plea for help, his grunts and feet rattling in Johnathan's hand were enough to get Cormack's attention.

"Hold him, steady! Don't let him go!"

Even though they had closed the gap between them, Sam and Tyler were still trailing, but close enough to see everything. Sam continued with his offers to leave 'while they still could,' but neither of them slowed down. They never admitted to one another, but a part of them, deep down inside was an aroma of pleasure that resembled butterflies of excitement; much like the ones kids would get as the last day of school approached.

Cormack reached the rust-covered guardrail that extended the entire length of the dead-end road first. Tommy and Johnathan followed, and when they were in within reach, Cormack slammed his hands onto Russell Fritz neck and pulled him up. "Alright, you piece of dog shit. Time for a little payback!"

Cormack squeezed hard, blocking much of Fritz airway, causing him to gasp as a flush of pink overtook his face. Then, he started gagging. Cormack squeezed harder but looked up when he heard footsteps approaching.

"Nice of you to finally make it," Cormack growled at Sam and Tyler. "You guys wanna do the honors?"

Confused, the two boys looked at each other with the same blank stare as before. Sam shrugged. "Do what?"

Cormack re-focused to Fritz and smiled. "Beat the shit out of shit brains here. Then, maybe we'll ditch him in the woods so the monsters can get him."

Fritz gasped louder, his cheeks became redder, and Cormack's fists squeezed harder. The soul-crushing darkness returned to the lower corners of his eyes. Sweat dripped down from his forehead until it mixed in with the blood running down his lower lip.

Cormack's face also began to turn red, but for a much different reason; the anger was overwhelming and undeniable. The look of rage was so fierce; it frightened Fritz's—making him fear for his life. Silver specs of stars began populating the darkness in the corner of his eyes and began expanding to slowly overtake the rest of his sight—slam!

Cormack immediately released the pressure from Fritz's neck, allowing a gust of hot, humid air to go racing in Fritz's lungs as he began to cough up a storm. As soon as he loosened his grip, Cormack snapped his head over his shoulder toward the direction of where the loud noise had emerged. Tommy and Johnathan, being the followers they were, did the same. Fritz was forced to wait until the darkness in his eyes subsided again, but once enough of it was gone for him to see, he too looked up.

The sound had come from a house across the street—a house Cormack nor any of them had taken into consideration when they dragged Fritz to the end of the street and prepared to beat him silly; the road was a dead-end and, from what they heard, the street was abandoned. But, the noise was undeniably the sound of a door slamming shut and once everyone turned in the direction of the house, it was all but confirmed.

Standing on the front porch of the poorly maintained house was an older man at or near retirement age—a blue-collar worker that one would assume worked at the mill in town. The old man stared with disdain as he puffed on the large cigar tucked on the left side of his mouth. A low growl came him his crusty lips as he glared at the kids. "What the fuck is going on here?"

The loud and raspy voice echoed as it made its way across the street. The tone was deep and annoyed, which sent an adrenaline shot into Cormack, fearing he was about to be in trouble. But, the exact opposite feeling flooded through Fritz— the sense of relief like he had been rescued from an ill-fated situation overtook him.

The man puffed out a large cloud of smoke from the half used cigar. "Are you beating that poor son of a bitch?"

Cormack swallowed hard, knowing full well there was nothing he could say but the truth. Thoughts of being kicked off the football team for the next school year or worse—being kicked out of school indefinitely circled through his mind and effectively transitioned his bout of rage to a sense of dread and uncertainty, much like what Fritz was feeling only moments before.

The lack of a response from everyone left the street in dead silence. Had Fritz been able to muster up enough air in his lungs to scream and plead for help, he would've done so, but he had no energy in his body to do such a thing.

"Yeah," Tommy finally answered.

Cormack's eyes widened and turned to him. "Would you shut up, you idiot?"

Tommy, confused by why Cormack would be angry for answering, shrugged his shoulder. "What? We are."

As blood spewed out of the wound on his lip and Cormack's large hands wrapped around his neck started loosening, Fritz smiled and let out a sigh of relie—

"Well keep it the fuck down, will ya!"

The smile disappeared from Fritz instantly, and the look of overwhelming fear returned.

Sam and Tyler turned to each other, both stunned by the answer.

Realizing the old man posed no danger to him, Cormack glanced at the end of the driveway and spotted the rusty mailbox—specifically the name on the mailbox.

"Sorry, Mr. Claire," Cormack said in his typical innocent yet hidden sinister voice.

Dismissing the kids by throwing his hand in the air, Old Man Claire inhaled another puff of his cigar and wobbled back into his house, slamming the door behind him. Cormack, feeling emboldened, turned back to Fritz. The innocence is his voice vanished. "Well, it sucks to be you because it doesn't look like anyone's around to help—"

Fritz jerked his head forward; crashing his forehead into Cormack's face. A horrific groan came roaring out, forcing him to take his hands off Fritz's neck. "Ah! You stupid motherfu—"

Fritz swung his leg up and sent it soaring in between Cormack's legs. A terrible crunch sound came from his testicles. Pain flooded up from his groan instantly, causing his legs to buckle before his weight became too much and he fell to the ground. Had Fritz been alone with Cormack—the worse of all bullies—he would've continued, but when he saw Tommy and Johnathan closing in, he spun around and jumped over the rust-covered guardrail and started heading into the woods.

Running as fast as they could to grab Fritz before he did so, Tommy and Johnathan used all their might to reach him, but were unsuccessful. If they had followed him into the woods, they would've been able to catch up, and Fritz would've received the wrath of Cormack, but they stopped just before the *guardrail. Sam and Tyler watched on in astonishment, both unable to take their eyes off Fritz as he ran up the hill and vanished into the thick brush.*

Johnathan helped Cormack up. Despite the overwhelming pain he was in, a terrifying yell rumbled out of him. "That piece of shit! Where'd he go?"

Tommy pointed straight ahead, answering in a calm, fearful voice. "In the woods."

The answer brought pause to Cormack. He had come from one of the wealthiest families that lived in Hunting—an advantage that would get him far in life once he moved away for college, but not even money spared him from receiving the warnings about staying out of the woods. In fact, he received it the most, especially by his father.

Everyone remained still; almost as if they were quiet enough, it would give the illusion to Fritz he was safe and come back out. They kept still for a minute. Then two, but still nothing. Fritz was nowhere in sight. There was no noise coming from the woods, either.

Tommy and Johnathan finally broke the silence, with Tommy suggesting they go back and head to his house, reminding Cormack about the skin magazines, but the rage boiling in the bully was too much for that idea to breakthrough.

"I want the piece of shit dead! Johnathan?" Cormack shouted.

"What?"

"Go after him."

"Hell, no! I'm not going in there!" Johnathan replied with lighting speed. "Nobodies supposed to go in there, remember?"

Cormack scoffed. "You're such a baby."

"I don't see you go going in there," Johnathan replied.

Instead of replying, Cormack dismissed Johnathan and turned to Tommy. Knowing what the look on Cormack's face was implying, Tommy through his hands in the air. "Screw that! I'm not going in there, either."

"Babies!" Cormack growled. "None of you have any balls to do any—"

"We'll go!"

The street grew silent again with nothing more than a slight draft pushing the thick humid around. Finally, after what felt like a lifetime, Cormack looked over his shoulder and into the direction of where the voice had come from.

Standing motionless, Tyler focused on him, doing everything he could to keep his attention off Sam, who was without a doubt glaring at him with the highest form of contempt. Typically, when Sam was angry at him, Tyler would try and defend himself, but he could do no such thing in this case; the words slipped out of his mouth by accident.

That sinister smile Cormack lost moments ago reappeared—Tyler's offer brought joy to the school bully. "Alright!" Cormack shouted with enthusiasm. "I knew you two had it in you, unlike these other ball-less losers."

The offensive joked got a chuckle out of Tyler, for a moment even making him forget about the offer he'd just made. Sam, on the other hand, didn't forget. He could tell from Tyler's nervous grin he regretted the offer, but had no intention to backpedal for fear of looking like a coward; it was apparent Sam was going to have too—

"You hear?" Cormack shouted into the woods with his hands covering both sides of his mouth for amplification. "You heat that, you bastard? We're gonna fucking find you!"

Without acknowledging it to each other, all of them assumed Fritz was far in, assuming he kept the same speed, but, aside from being the biggest bully at school, Cormack was also known for his loud voice, and they were confident Fritz must've heard the warning.

Finally, once the roar of the threat dissipated, Cormack looked back at Tyler and Sam with that same eerie smile. It sent chills down their spins as they gazed into his beautiful yet harmful eyes. The smile suddenly faded, and frustration re-emerged. "Well, what're you waiting for? Go! Go get him!"

Everything inside was telling them—both of them not to go, but the pressure and fear of Cormack's anger overpowered whatever worry they had. Sam was still hesitant and contemplating to join Tommy and Johnathan in the "ball-less" group, but by the time he found the words, Tyler had already walked over to the guardrail.

"Hey, Rainey!" Cormack shouted after patting Tyler on the arm. "You coming or what?"

"Yeah, of course!" he conceded.

Cormack swung his fist into Tommy's arm. "That's how you do it, Tommy!"

The forceful hit drew a vocal reaction, but Cormack disregarded it. Instead, he focused on Tyler jumping over the rusted guardrail and help Sam when he reached it. Once they were over, the two looked at each other, fearful of the forest that lay ahead. And without saying anything, they took their first steps forward—

"Hey!" Cormack said from behind.

The two stopped and spun around with lightning force, hoping Cormack was about to say it was all a bluff and they proved they were cool enough to join the group. Walking up to the guardrail, but stopping short of hopping over it, Cormack pulled his hand out of his pocket and extended his arm. Since Sam was the closer of the two, he walked back over and reached for whatever Cormack was giving him.

The blonde hairs on Sam's arms shot straight up. Once he got a good look at what Cormack handed him, he swallowed hard. The evil grin on Cormack's face was accompanied with a menacing gaze that seemed to pierce through Sam's outer persona and glare at the nervousness that rattled within.

"What's this for?" Sam finally mustered.

"An eye for an eye, Rainey. I want you two to do the same thing to him that he did to me."

Sam hesitated before he responded, allowing the orders Cormack said to sink in. "So, you want us to drag him out here?"

A thunderous laugh blasted out of Cormack, the grin on his face growing even larger. "You really think I'm gonna stand around here waiting for you guys? No…"

Sam looked back down at the metal object Cormack had given him. "I don't understand."

A few more chuckles rumbled from Cormack's belly. "And here I thought you were the smart one…I'll tell you what you're going to do: you're gonna go in there, hunt that prick down and wreck his face while me and them leave."

The condescending tone flustered Sam, forcing him to bite his lower lip. He knew Cormack was stronger and faster than him, but at that moment, Sam had a difficult time fighting the urge to challenge that assumption. He closed his hand and started to squeeze.

"See, I knew you could read between the lines," Cormack said as he patted Sam on the cheek. "Tomorrow, I'll head off too Fritz's house, and once I see proof you did what I asked, you'll officially be in the group. So good luck, boys!"

Taking everything in, Sam stood behind the guardrail and remained still until Cormack, Tommy, and Johnathan got on their bikes and rode away. Once they were nothing more than little specs in the distance, Sam let out a low, yet forceful grunt before staggering away to meet back up with Tyler.

As he made his way closer, Sam kept his head to the ground, but Tyler knew with certainty how his best friend was feeling. Tyler opened his mouth but stopped short when Sam flung up the object Cormack had given him and sent it hurling his way. He reached out, hoping to catch it, but when he saw what it was, he pulled back instantly, allowing the object to land to the ground.

"Jesus!" Tyler shouted.

"Here, I figured I'd give it to you since you're the one who got us into this!" Sam shouted with frustration.

A sudden gust of thick humid wind picked up around them, sending dead leaves from years prior swirling at their feet in tornadic fashion. Bits of dirt lifted from the earthy forest floor and stuck to their exposed legs where their shorts stopped. The small specs of dirt—with the possibility of small chunks of pavement from the road that had broken off mixed in also—stung where it hit the skin, but Tyler ignored the irritating pricks in his attempt to try and save face with Sam. "I didn't think he was going to make us! I thought just offering would be enough."

Sam continued his walk up the small yet steep hill. "Well, good thinking. Now, look where we are."

"Hey, shut up, Sam! I didn't see you volunteering to back out of it!"

"How could I?" Sam waved his hands in the air. "You didn't give me the chance. Instead, you just threw me into it."

Reaching out for Sam's hand once he was close enough, Tyler helped him get to the top of the hill, and the two diverted their attention to the thick brush of woods that loomed before them. An eerie feeling overcame them moments after the wind calmed. The sense of fear that accompanied them for most of the afternoon returned. Tyler broke the silence and asked Sam what they should do now.

Sam didn't say anything at first; mostly because he was unsure himself. He would never admit it, or even show signs of willingness, but a part of him wanted to impress Cormack just as much as Tyler wanted too—not because he enjoyed bullying Russell Fritz, but because he knew how much easier life would be if they didn't need to worry about being on the wrong end of Cormack Fitzpatrick's wrath for the rest of the time they went to school together. Finally, after what left like a decade, Sam reluctantly reached down and picked up the metal object resting at his feet. A small metal latch stuck out at the top of the object. Despite never using one before, Sam placed his pointer finger on the latched and pulled down.

With a sudden snap, the latch came down, allowing a large silver blade to come racing out of the other side of the handle. Tyler jerked back with fright, but Sam didn't for he knew what it was the moment Cormack handed it to him. It was a switchblade—much like the one his father had.

Keeping his distance while focused on the sharp tip of the blade, Tyler asked, "Are we really going to do this?"

Sam lowered the blade, forcing Tyler to shift his attention to him. "What choice do we have? Maybe with any luck, we won't be able to find him."

The look of reluctance on Sam's face brought Tyler to the realization of his actions. At that moment, he felt just as hopeless as Fritz must've felt. It didn't take long for Tyler to admit Sam was right and suggest they don't go through with. Sam started for the forest.

With nothing else he could do, Tyler raced into the sharp sticks and thorn bushes of the dense woods to catch up with Sam and search for Fritz, both completely unaware of the consequences their decisions would bring.

The universal darkness of the night overpowered the entire cockpit of the police cruiser, hiding much—if not nearly all the details of the interior. But, it was unable to hide the look of unimaginable terror across Sam's face as he replayed the events of that summer over in his head. It was a look he'd only had once before; a look he'd only shared with Tyler; a look he vowed he'd never make again.

Tyler—still trying to figure out what Sam was getting at—leaned into Sam's eyesight, hoping the move would get Sam to answer. "Sam! What is it?"

"He's after us," Sam said in a panic, keeping his eyes fixated on the windshield.

The lack of explanation in the short and still confusing answer left Tyler baffled. "What?"

"You and me forced him into the woods and didn't help him when we found him, the security guards at the facility Catalano, Burke, Manning, Auclair tried to stop him from escaping, Kimberly and Mike hit him with their car and drove away, and Old Man Claire did nothing when he could've stopped Cormack Fitzpatrick back in 97. Don't you see it?"

Pieces of the mysterious puzzle Tyler had been trying to complete all night in his head began shifting. And just as he closed in on the answer, Sam said the answer out loud: "Everyone who's hurt him, he's killing!"

Shock overtook Tyler as the answer to what he'd been unable to figure out all night came to fruition. His jaw hung low, allowing fresh night air to enter his mouth and chill his chapped lips. "So, that means—"

"He's not doing this randomly. *We're* the ones he's after," Sam interrupted. Suddenly, he reached down to the floor and felt around for the pistol Tyler had provided him. Once his fingers touched the cold steel of the weapon, he wrapped his hands around the grip and lifted it from the darkness that surrounded his legs. "We have to kill him before he kills us."

Agreeing, Tyler took off his seatbelt, reached into the backseat and picked up his assault rifle—an M16A1 rifle. In one swoop, he brought it to his chest and pulled out the magazine from the bottom. Moonlight coming in from the windshield shimmered across the large golden bullets that were resting in the middle of the magazine. Once his eyes spotted the ammunition, he forcefully pushed the magazine back in.

"This is sure to stop him," Tyler confidently said as he spotted the pistol tucked in between Sam's legs. "You sure you don't want the shotgun in the trunk? It's a lot more powerful than that thing."

Caressing the grip of the pistol, Sam answered in a whispering voice, "This is all I need."

Spotting the confidence in his best friends eyes—a confidence he hadn't seen all night, Tyler reached for the handle of the driver side door but paused just short of opening it. "You ready?"

Sam opened the passenger door.

Tyler opened his a fraction of a second after and in sync with one another, they each stepped out, closed the doors and walked to the nose of the cruiser, both keeping their eyes on the looming, shadow-infested school before them.

The apocalyptic stillness that accompanied the interior of the car followed them out onto the street, creating a haunting atmosphere so chilling and silent, the two of them could hear their pulses thumping in their eardrums. Sweat started to build up across Sam's forehead. Sweat also built up under Tyler's armpits, but his uniform was able to hide it, unlike Sam.

Both of them were nervous.

The hesitation and looks of reluctance were so overpowering; it mimicked how they felt back in the summer of 1997. The feelings creeping inside were all too familiar as they were accompanied by the whispering voice lying deep in their guts, warning them about the dangers that lurked ahead. But, unlike when they were children, the chance to run away and try to forget wasn't an option. Like it always does, the past finally caught up with them, and all they could do was face it head-on.

Tyler raised his rifle. "Stay right behind me."

Annoyed she was unable to find any gaze for the gash on Kimberly Wilsons back, Lois Tanguay sprinted across the empty police station to her office. While she didn't find what she wanted, she was able to find a small tube of Neosporin and a larger Band-Aid. It wasn't much, but she figured it would be enough to get Kimberly through the rest of the night.

Just as it was when she exited her office, the station was dead calm. Not a single sound was discernible. Lois spotted a breeze when she glanced out the front windows, but paid no attention to it—her main concern was Kimberly. When she turned the corner and saw the light peering out through the doorframe of her office, a sudden—yet random feeling of joyfulness rushed through her; almost as if the night was already over. It was a silly feeling, but she embraced it as she approached her office. "I couldn't find any gaze, but I was able to fin—Kimberly?"

Her office was empty. Frantically, Lois turned to the floor of the police station. Darkness engulfed a large part of the room, making it so Lois couldn't even see the other side of the room that was behind Tyler's office. She began trembling as panic boiled inside, followed soon after by worry.

She called out Kimberly's name again.

There was no response.

She took a deep breath and held it in, hoping the lack of her breathing would allow her to hear something she may have missed. The room was still silent.

She held the breath for as long as she could until her lungs cringed and forced her to exhale. Adrenaline pumped through her veins—she ran into her office to the lowest drawer on the left-hand side of the desk and pulled it open to grab her flashlight, preparing to search the station to find Kimberly—she paused.

For some random reason, as she bent down to take out the large black flashlight, her eyes had drifted across the room and over to the wall where the cabinet rested against it. At first, she spotted nothing—nothing seemed to be out of the ordinary, until she looked at the key holder that was mounted off to the side of the cabinet. *Huh, that's odd. I swear to Christ I hung them up when we got bac—no! No, she couldn't; she wouldn't!*

Kicking the drawer closed with his foot, Lois sprinted to the keyless hanger but stopped short when a white paper in the middle of her desk caught her attention. Curious, she picked it up, spotting the small yet neatly cursive handwriting; handwriting that was too neat to be hers. But as bizarre as it was, the words on the note was even more unusual.

Mimic Street

Lois looked back at the keyless hanger.

Then back at the note.

Mimic Street…Mimic Stree—son of a bitch!

Dropping the white stickie note, Lois darted to the other side of her desk and this time opened the top drawer on the right-hand side and pulled out her service revolver. The cold dead weight of the handle struck her, chilling the palms for her hands. Despite carrying it every night, the idea of actually using it never crossed her mind. In fact, most time she forgot the weapon was even there. But, on that cold dark night, the idea was anything but forgotten. The idea nested deep and did not waver her from proceeding.

Keeping her mind focused, she cocked the pistol, placed it in the holster attached to her belt and raced toward the exit for the back parking lot where the spare cruiser was located, all the while unable to keep the pessimistic feelings at bay.

CHAPTER 12

Like the rest of the town of Hunting, the roads leading Sargent L'Heureux, C.J. Meyers and Jess Sowa to their deserted destination, were covered in pitch black as far as the eye could see. The headlights to the Humvee sliced through the darkness as it went down the road, but was no match for blackness that surrounded the vehicle. Large trees towered across the street on both sides, some so tall they blocked out nearly all of the light the moon provided.

Growing tired of looking at the dim outline of her face through the backseat window behind the passenger seat, Jess looked away and glanced at the clock in the middle of the radio. She rolled her eyes, annoyed by how much time the night still had felt.

Aside from Meyers pointing to certain turns, he thought L'Heureux would miss; the entire ride was mostly silent. Had it just been L'Heureux and Meyers, the drive would've had a much different atmosphere—one with crude and offensive jokes being tossed back and forth while the radio blared classic heavy metal, Black Sabbath being one of the most common. But, because Jess was technically a higher rank than they were—even though she was really not, they felt it best to keep any crude comments or jokes to themselves.

As they closed in on Prescott Street—yet another abandon neighborhood—Meyers straightened his posture and leaned forward, hoping he'd spot the turn before L'Heureux drove passed it. The gesture got L'Heureux to pump the breaks, but he was still well over the speed limit. "Fucking creepy out here," he said.

"This whole town is creepy," Meyers said, keeping his attention to the windshield. "Can't wait to get out of this shithole and get back to civilization. This whole abandon town thing is depressing as shit."

L'Heureux agreed, adding, "Doesn't look like anybody's out here, either."

"Nobody is," Jess' voice from the back emerged. "The last residents who lived out here died about five years ago—all these streets are abandoned."

"Great," Meyers said, rolling his eyes by the unwelcoming news.

L'Heureux thought the same thing; he—much like Myers, had grown tired of always being in such a rural area with no people around. Despite the tough-guy persona, they both maintained even outside of work; the two soldiers enjoyed being around people. All except for Jess.

"The next street over is Prescott Street," Meyers pointed, his voice amplified loud enough to spook Jess.

"You sure?" L'Heureux asked, not purposely questioning Meyer's direction, but double-checking.

Meyers flung his thumb up as he reached to his side and pulled out his pistol. L'Heureux spotted the movement and immediately did the same thing, but instead of checking the ammunition in it himself, he handed it over to Meyers.

From the back seat, Jess watched the pistol exchange hands, keeping an eye on the glossy black finish on the barrel of the gun. While her eyes fixated on the deadly object, her mind roamed elsewhere. *It would be a shame if people were to find out all this grief started in your lab under your supervision,* the raw and sinister threat of Mrs. Quimby replayed in her mind. Between Mrs. Quimby's voice and the final moments she spent with her mother before she passed, emotions swirled around Jess like a boat caught in a raging whirlpool. Anger mixed with fear that transitioned to regret followed by nervousness, all the while a sense of desperation rested at the foundation of her stomach.

L'Heureux stopped at the rusty, bent stop sign at the end of the street and looked both ways as if the road was a busy freeway despite being an abandoned stretch of pavement. Shadows engulfed both sides, leaving them nothing more than a spec of light in a world of darkness.

"Left or right?" L'Heureux asked.

"Left. It's the last house," Meyers guided.

L'Heureux turned the wheel and pulled onto the road. The once lively road—if you want to call a road with twelve houses lively—was in rough shape, but not one pothole lay bare on it. This allowed L'Heureux to continue down the road at a slow, but steady pace. Unable to see anything more than his reflection, Meyers pulled out the small flashlight in his pocket, flicked it on and rolled down the window to shine the beam out. "Let me know if you see anything, Jess."

She didn't reply, leaving Meyers to assume she would. L'Heureux, while keeping most of his attention to the road in front of him, started peering out through the driver side window, hoping to spot something himself. Nothing stood out; everything was dark. The cold night air came rushing into the interior of the car, sending goosebumps along Jess' arms. The chilling sense only added to the massive amount of anxiety that was reaching its peak.

L'Heureux tapped on the breaks. "I think I can see the house."

Meyers and Jess looked through the windshield simultaneously. At first, neither of them spotted anything, but slowly, as the vehicle crept forward, an outline of a white house emerged from the darkness. Meyers squeezed the pistol in his hand, keeping it in between his legs for safety, despite the safety being off.

From the angle they were approaching, only the left side of the house was visible, the rest of the home was entrenched in darkness, leaving much of the structure and its surroundings to the imagination. The closer the vehicle drew to the house, the more L'Heureux pumped the breaks. Because the Humvee had received a new set of brake pads—Meyers and L'Heureux did it themselves—the vehicle slowed down with a drastic tone, forcing the headlights to conquer the shadows that covered the house and surrounding area with razor-sharp precision. When L'Heureux reached the side of the house, Meyers shined his beam out the driver side window, hoping to shed more light on the childhood home of Russell Fritz. "Whoa."

About to say the same thing, L'Heureux brought the Humvee to a complete stop and put it in 'Park.' Mimicking his partners lead, he pulled out his flashlight and shined it to the left side.

Remaining quiet, the three of them kept still as they overlooked what the flashlight beams revealed; an old rundown house that was partially collapsed. From the street, the house was deceiving; the entire left wall was standing and even appeared to be in good shape, but the closer they got, the more they realized that was not the case. The sight of the rundown home brought a sense of skepticism to L'Heureux as he took his pistol from Meyers.

"Doesn't look like anyone's home," Meyers joked.

"I was kinda thinking the same thing," L'Heureux agreed.

"You think he could be in there?"

L'Heureux shrugged, keeping his attention on the blown-out windows and dilapidated farmer's porch that stretched across the entire length of the house. "I don't think so; look at the porch. This shithole is probably as stable as you when you're drunk."

"Hey! I'm a good drunk," Meyers replied instantly.

"Tell that to our last Humvee."

Fighting the urge to tell both of them to shut the hell up, Jess stayed silent. While her patience and sense of humor were nowhere in sight, her mind was focused somewhere else. Somewhere dark—somewhere desperate.

"You just wanna skip it and head to the school?" Meyers asked.

Unlike any other day where L'Heureux would castrate anyone—even Meyers for suggesting a shortcut, he thought about the idea before writing it off completely.

"I mean, look at that foundation. No sane person would risk going in there," Meyers followed up.

It was a well-made point—L'Heureux couldn't dispute that, but the feeling of self-righteousness and obligation pushed through. "No, we should probably check it out. Might as well since we're already here."

Meyers' face indicated he was unamused, but since L'Heureux never steered him in the wrong direction before, he didn't dispute the choice. "Alright, shotguns in the back, right?"

"Yeah. There's also a spare pistol in the glovebox; I'll get that out for Jess," L'Heureux said. His eyes lifted to the rearview mirror. A blank stare consumed Jess' face. "Is that alright, Jess?"

It would be a shame. Mrs. Quimby's voice replayed over like a vinyl disc. *It would be a shame.*

"Jess?"

It would be a shame. It would be—"What?"

Meyers stopped tapping her on the shoulder with the butt of the handgun once he got a response. "Here."

Jess dropped her head, spotting the gun being held in front of her chest.

"You think you can handle this?" Meyers asked.

Jess, trembling beneath the darkness, carefully took the gun from Meyer's hand. A sudden chill raced from her hands to her arms, casting goosebumps on her as the coolness of the metal took any sense of warmth she'd built up. Meyer's smiled. "All you have to do is pull the trigger."

As soon as the weight of the gun left his hands, Meyers turned back around and closed the glovebox. "What else is in the back?"

"A shotgun and two or three different rifles. Plus, a shitload of ammunition. I wanted to make sure we didn't run out."

"Alright," Meyers acknowledged. "I'll go grab—"

A bullet blasted out of Meyer's chest and through the windshield, sending a mist of blood across the dashboard. A pain emerged from Meyers, but the loudness of the gunshot continued to roar inside the vehicle and forced L'Heureux to cover his ears. Blood mixed with saliva as it covered Meyer's teeth and started spewing out of his mouth.

The overwhelming ringing rattled L'Heureux to the point, it was difficult for him to keep his eyes opened, but he was able to turn around and—a bullet blasted into his forehead, killing him instantly.

Like the first gunshot, the second one also created a horrendous roar inside the car, a rumble so great the echo could be heard from inside the forest. Finally, it dissipated, leaving nothing but the sound of the horn blaring from L'Heureux's head pressed down on it and a few muffled gags coming from Meyers.

Opening the door behind the driver's seat, Jess hopped down onto the cracked pavement and slammed the door shut. The night air hit her much like the bullet she just fired. The goosebumps on her arms expanded to the rest of her body as the misty spots of blood on her face chilled her cheeks. She wiped it off with her left arm and pulled the driver side door open with her right.

The blaring horn amplified when the door opened, creating a deafening tone that matched the gunshots. She placed the gun down on the dashboard in front of the steering wheel and lifted L'Heureux's head off the wheel, ending the ear-piercing noise once and for all. His muscular body—combined with all his military gear—was heavy and on any other occasion, Jess would've been unable to move such a weight. But, the burning desire reminding her that her past, present, and future was on the line, gave her the strength to get her small hands around his massive arm, pull him out of the seat and onto the pavement with a loud thump.

Blood had oozed onto the driver's seat, much of it absorbing into the cloth seats, leaving Jess no other choice but to sit in it. Typically, a germaphobe, the thought of wiping the seat didn't even occur to her. Once

L'Heureux's body was on the ground, she grabbed the safety handle above the door and hopped in, slamming the door behind her.

The green light from the digital display center lit up her blood-splattered face as her head bobbed up and down, trying to get the seat adjusted so she could reach the peddles. A gag came from her right side. Her head quickly turned. So did her gun.

The terrible gaging sound mustered out of Meyers, who was still alive, but barely. His breathing was inconsistent, and he'd lost nearly a third of his blood, but he had strength to lift his head and look Jess in the eyes. A look of dismay coated his face, but the expression was nowhere near as surprising as Jess thought it would be.

Another gag managed to come out of Meyer's along with a mouthful of blood. It was apparent he was trying to say something, but her sense of humanity and mercy was gone, which allowed her to reach across his body, pull the passenger door handle enough to get the door open and start to push him out. Groaning in agonizing pain as she began to do so, Meyers flung his bloody hands up in an attempt to stop her, but the bullet that struck his chest and exited through the windshield took every ounce of energy in his body, leaving him unable to defend himself from Jess' desperation.

Meyers weighed less than L'Heureux—by a good fifty pounds, but the position he was in made it difficult for Jess to get him out. She grunted, using everything she had to get him out, all the while, glancing at the digital clock on the radio. *Come on, come on! Get out! Get the fuck out!*

She raised the gun up to Meyers to pull the trigger, but pushed one last time before she did. Meyers let out another deep groan as his shoulder jerked forward from the shove, knocking him off balance and forcing his body out of the seat and onto the pavement with a forceful thump that mimicked L'Heureux's.

"Goddamn it!" she shouted, panting as if she'd just run a mile long marathon.

Because of how tall the Humvee was, she was unable to see Meyer's body but assumed there was no way he could've survived. But, instead of checking, she reached for the handle on the passenger side, grabbed a hold of it and slammed it shut. Then, grabbing the gearshift, she put the Humvee in reverse and turned the wheel as far to the left as it would go, allowing the right tire to run over Meyer's skull, effectively ending any hope that he could've survived.

Once there was enough room for the Humvee to turn around, Jess slammed the gearshift into 'Drive' and pressed hard on the gas and sped down the road to get to Mimic Street, leaving L'Heureux and Meyers on the street to be consumed in eternal darkness.

The old double-wide door squeaked open as Tyler Benton, and Sam Rainey took their first steps into the deserted school. Once Sam made it through the narrow opening, he held the metal knob and closed it carefully, hoping to keep the element of surprise.

Like the rest of the town—and the Rust Belt itself—the school had seen better days. A once thriving school that was home to hundreds of students now stood battered and hollowed out. Large cracks engulf the cement floor with even larger ones running up the sides of the walls. Many of the windows that stretched across the main entrance were blown out despite the metal bars that entrenched them. Layers of dust and cobwebs covered the last shards that were still intact, mirroring the dust that covered the floor.

Keeping the M16A1 rifle pointed straight ahead, Tyler pulled out his flashlight and turned it on. Trickles of dust rained down in the beam of light, resembling a light snowstorm like the ones they would typically get around late November. The borderline suffocating blanket of dust was accompanied with an overwhelming sense of dampness that resembled a basement after days of heavy rain. The thought—and sight of breathing in the dirty— potentially hazardous air, was enough to force anyone to turn back. But, with their weapons at the ready, Sam and Tyler proceeded onward.

The windows that ran across the length of the main entrance allowed light from outside to come filtering in, providing enough ambiance to reveal outlines of the floor and debris—which consisted of leaves and dusty paper. The multiple skylight windows that were a good two stories above the large room also provided light, creating sinister square shapes shining down. Preferring to stay in the dark, Tyler slipped passed them, hoping to avoid the pieces of glass that rained down years ago when the windows finally gave way.

About halfway into the vast space, Tyler shined his flashlight to the left, the beam of light, revealing a staircase that only went up to the third floor. Due to the east side of the school being built decades after the west side was built, initially due to the booming number of people moving into town, only one staircase in the middle of the school would lead up to the fourth floor. Because of Sam's trip down memory lane, the classroom they were in on that summer day, was primary on his mind.

"Where should we start?" Sam whispered.

Staying on guard, Tyler kept his eyes forward as he answered. "We'll head to the fourth-floor first. Then, we'll work our way back down."

Agreeing with the idea, Sam cupped the bottom of his pistol with both hands and continued to follow, staying no less than a step behind. Tyler glanced over his shoulder to his best friend. "Shoot to kill, right?"

"Shoot to kill."

Tyler stepped up to the first stair, keeping the flashlight aimed at his feet so he would be able to get a sense of where he was walking. Like the main entrance, the stairs were also covered in layers of dust so thick; the blue painted stairs appeared as a dirty brown. He was unable to see it because he kept the beam one step ahead, but each step Tyler took, his footprint was left behind in the dust, providing a blueprint for Sam. A terrible groan came from beneath the staircase as the stepped up, reflecting the failing structure of the staircase.

Keeping slow, but steady, Tyler reached the top step and spun the flashlight around for Sam to see where to step. Thankful for the gesture, Sam safely made it to the top level. "Thanks."

Standing motionlessly, they found themselves on the second floor, staring down a hall that ran the entire length of the school. Unlike the floor below, the second floor was riddled with papers and old classroom furniture scattered about. The length of the hall was far too long for Tyler's flashlight to make it all the way down, but the windows in the classrooms on the left-hand side of the hall allowed the light from the moon to peer in through the doorways. It had been years since they last stepped foot into that hall, but the passing of time couldn't erase the memories the hallway held. Flashbacks of their childhood loomed in the shadows, accompanied by the smell that had occupied the school for decades. The flashbacks became so overwhelming; both felt like if they were any deeper in thought, they could hear the echoes of the voices that once filled the hall.

Tyler began taking steps forward, remembering his way around the school like it was yesterday. "This way."

Sam followed, keeping his head moving as the hall grew darker the deeper they went.

Spotting the cruiser parked in the front of the abandoned school, Anthony Vitukevich shut the headlights to his undercover vehicle off and turned the wheel hard to the left before parking it along the sidewalk on the left-hand side. The car came to a sudden stop, bouncing Agent Eric McCann forward, causing him to almost hit his head on the dashboard.

"Jesus Christ, could you stop any harder?"

"Sorry," Vitukevich said as he raised his hand and pointed. "Looks like Rainey and that cop are already here."

McCann drew his pistol from its holster. "Shit. Do we still go in?"

"It's not like we can wait for them to leave," Vitukevich said as he took out his gun and looked into the rearview mirror. "What do you think, Mrs. Quimby?"

The backseat was dark due to the large trees off to the side of the road, but he was able to see the blank stare that still glistened his bosses face. He fought hard to resist the temptation of rolling his eyes—he was in no mood to deal with her attitude, and the lack of an answer didn't help. Attempting to get an answer as quick as he could, he placed his hand over McCann's seat and spun around. "I said—"

Mrs. Quimby's face turned.

Vitukevich words trailed off, leaving nothing but a muted gasp to slip out of his mouth. For three years, Vitukevich had been working under the thumb of Mrs. Quimby and knew nearly everything about her— everything from the smell of her awful perfume to the color of her eyes. But, a sudden confusion with a bolt of fear rushed in like a crowd stuck in a revolving door because he was looking at Mrs. Quimby's face—without question, but it wasn't her eyes looking back at him.

He gasped.

McCann looked up. "Wha—"

A hammer swung down from the backseat. A terrible crack came from McCann's left side, forcing him to turn and see the claw of the metal-tipped hammer lodged deep in Vitukevich's throat. A loud ear-piercing scream erupted from the back of his throat.

The back of Mrs. Quimby's head leaned forward. McCann pushed up against the passenger door, his back striking the door so forcefully, it rocked the cruiser. The face snapped in his direction. McCann screamed, spotting the eyes weren't Mrs. Quimby's.

He raised his pistol. He placed his finger on the trigger—the hammer ripped out of Vitukevich's throat and went soaring into his lower stomach.

A violent exhale shot out of McCann's mouth, breaking his steady aim and forced him to fire the gun out the driver side window. Glass shattered and crumbled inside and outside of the car as the bullet disappeared into the woods. The roar of the gunshot rang in McCann's ears, temporally deafening him. Pain began expanding in his stomach, forcing him to cry out in agony. The ringing wore off and was replaced by the sound of ripping flesh as the burning sensation in his gut deepened. "Fuck!"

Death had become Vitukevich; his head dangled like an animal in a meat factory. Knowing he was only moment's way from the same fate, McCann raised his pistol again, hoping to get another shot at his attacker. The move forced out a groan from him and the higher he raised his arm, the more the groan transitioned into a yell. The sound of his own flesh splitting amplified with each passing second—along with the overwhelming pain, but McCann took aim at Mrs. Quimby's face and fired one shot.

Slicing through the left side of Mrs. Quimby's face, the bullet entered through the left cheek and out the back. A gush of blood sprayed out like a fine mist across the driver's seat with some reaching the back passenger window. McCann aimed again, closing his left eye to get a better shot—a hand from the back seat grabbed him by the wrist and pushed his hand to the side.

Mrs. Quimby's face fixated on him and began leaning closer the more McCann's hand was pushed in the opposite direction. McCann resisted, hoping to overpower the firm grip—which was clearly not Mrs. Quimby's and get another, hopefully lethal shot. His face turned to red, but confidence emerged when he started to feel himself pushing the gun back to his attacker. *That's it, you bitch! I got you! You're not gonn—*

The hand let go of his wrist, sending McCann's arm into the direction of Mrs. Quimby's face, but the hand re-emerged and snatched the gun from his hand in a fraction of the second. The sensation of the handle being pulled out of his hand took McCann by storm, but before he could react, Mrs. Quimby's face leaned forward and suddenly the barrel of the gun pushed into the back of the seat and fired.

Blood splattered across the dashboard as the bullet ripped through the material of the passenger seat, along with McCann's flesh and organs. A haunting sound coughed up in his throat, followed by thick red blood. He started shaking as he began struggling for air. In shock, McCann lowered his head to look at his wound. A persistent flow of blood oozed out of his chest and started collecting on his lap.

His eyes started going in and out of focus as his breathing slowed down. The pain from the gunshot was unfathomable, only adding to the lightheadedness. But, a large shadow slowly emerged into his blurry vision. At first, it was out of focus, but as it drew closer, details started to form. As his head drew heavy, McCann watched as Mrs. Quimby's face came straight at him, stopping only an inch away from his.

The musk smell of Mrs. Quimby's potent perfume darted up to his nose, forcing him to cough; the coughing adding to his pain. But, he remained focused on the black eyes behind Mrs. Quimby's face glaring at him. His breaths started to decrease as his eyesight got burlier. As he began to lose consciousness, he was able to make out the eyes behind Mrs. Quimby's skin, moving back and forth between his right and left eye. A soft gag slipped out of him as his head jerked forward and slammed on the dashboard, cracking his skull.

Once its latest victim stopped twitching, the test subject ripped the hammer out of Agent Eric McCann gut and began shaking the murder weapon up and down, trying to get as much blood off it as possible. Then, it carefully placed the hammer on the seat and raised its other hand, looking curiously.

A glimmer of moonlight shined off the black nine-millimeter pistol it held. Thoughts of keeping the weapon and using it again brought hesitation to the test subject. A long hesitation—so long the headache it was getting from the perfume started dematerializing. The subject needed to choose how to proceed.

It did.

It concluded a gun was much too sudden. A personal weapon was needed—a weapon that required close range in order to be effective.

The gun fell out of its hand and landed on the carpeted floor in dramatic fashion. It then kicked the weapon under the passenger seat with its black steel toe boots before raising its hands to the face that covered its own and pulled it off carefully, attempting to keep the skin intact.

Cold air rushed onto its face as the mask came off. The scent of perfume— while still in the air, diminished as the flesh was removed completely. The test subject gently placed the skin down and reached to the opposite side of the seat, picking up another mask it had brought into the car. The deer mask.

With absolute delicacy, the subject placed both hands into the mangled opening at the bottom of the mask, stretched out the loose skin to widen the opening, raised it to its face and carefully pushed it down. The sour and fermenting smell of freshly peeled skin overpowered the scent of perfume as its face pushed into the moist interior.

It took in a deep breath, allowing the vile smell to fill its lungs like it had all night. A demented sense of satisfaction and incognito reclaimed the test subject's thoughts. It took in another breath. It was followed by another...and another.

When the mask was fully on, the test subject began sliding the loose skin to the right and left, adjusting the large eye opening holes to fit perfectly over its own.

Perfect.

It took another breath.

The test subject reached down and picked up the metal hammer, squeezing the handle in its murderous grip as it caressed the neck of the weapon gently. Beneath the skin, it smiled.

Finally, complete again.

The back door to the cruiser squeaked loudly as Fritz stepped out of the blood-filled police cruiser and into the cool—almost refreshing air.

With the exception of the breeze in the forest swirling at the far end of the street, the area was completely silent. Fritz marched steadily to the school, keeping his eyes on the main entrance, the sight bringing back his own memories from years ago. Any noise his footsteps made were unable to penetrate through the approaching breeze.

Blood dripped off the head of the metal hammer, leaving a trail alongside him. While it trailed off the closer he got to the school, the drops of blood stood out on the dry pavement because of the moonlight shimmering off them. Squeezing the metal handle harder the closer he got to the abandoned school, Fritz took a glance into the police cruiser parked near the front as he walked by. Spotting that no one was inside, he re-focused his attention to the front of the school and started up the concrete stairs that lead to the main lobby.

Stillness reclaimed the lobby as Fritz pushed through the double doors and stepped inside. He started looking around only to find that nothing appeared in sight. Had he taken the time to reflect, many of his childhood memories—some of them good, but many of them bad—would've entered his mind and brought him back to a part of his life that he'd closed off for many years. But, he gave no such time for those memories to do so. Instead, he focused on the rage and anger that was building—he looked down, spotting two pairs of footprints on the dusty floor that trailed across the large lobby.

Using the natural light coming in from the skylights, he followed the freshly made footprints with his eyes across the room until they stopped at the staircase. His eyes then pivoted up the steps and began remembering where the stairwell went too. A low growl came from beneath the mask followed by a rush of absolute anger; a wave of anger like the which he'd never felt before.

He stepped onto the stairs and began heading up, keeping the hammer tightly in his grip.

CHAPTER 13

Keeping his flashlight on the staircase, Tyler Benton cautiously continued his approach to the top floor with Sam Rainey following close behind. "Just a few more steps," he whispered.

Like the rest of the building, the old staircase was in poor condition at best; each step they applied weight on creaked and cracked as if the entire stairwell would collapse at any second. The creaking only got worse they further up they went. At one point—near the third floor, Sam even brought up the idea to abandon the stairwell and focus on some other part of the school, but Tyler dismissed it abruptly. "We're already more than halfway up. We mine as well finish."

"Fine."

Remaining right behind Tyler throughout the whole way up, Sam kept his attention shifting back and forth from the path ahead and the road behind. Knowing Tyler was right next to him the entire way brought some reassurance—so did the gun in his hand, but each time the staircase squeaked it sent adrenaline racing down his body. He took the safety off his weapon by the second floor and by the third floor, his finger was resting on top of the trigger.

The dampness in the air had only gotten thicker as they reached the top steps, forcing them to take only the shallowest of breaths. While the school was in far better condition the last time the two of them had been inside—nearly twenty-five years ago, the smell of the old building hadn't changed at all. Tyler thought the same thing as he approached the two dark-colored doors, but neither of them acknowledged it to one another.

Sam stepped up and moved to the right side of the doors. He lifted his pistol to his shoulder as he pressed his back against the yellow tiled wall—a sudden crack came from below them. Both of them spun around and aimed their weapons down the dark staircase.

Nothing.

Nothing but silence and an empty staircase was before them. Despite the sight, both kept their weapons draw, remaining as still as they could. But, the more Tyler thought about it, the more he started to conclude the noise didn't seem to come from the staircase; it came from the floor. He tilted his head down, along with the flashlight. Sam followed the light to the floor and let out a sigh of relief.

"Goddamn it," he whispered.

Glass covered the floor they were standing on, much of it small pieces, but when Sam lifted his foot, the light revealed he'd stepped on one of the larger chunks. He looked up to Tyler and forced out a small smile. Tyler responded by raising his pointer finger to his lips.

Sam broke a sweat. *Glass, it was just glass. But, glass from wha—oh!*

Shining the flashlight on the door, Tyler focused his attention to the small rectangular windows that ran vertically above the door handles; both windows completely glassless. Gently, he reached for the metal knob, keeping his gun aimed directly at the center of the door.

Sam raised his gun, preparing himself for what terrible thing could be beyond—

Tyler flung the door open and rushed in. Sam did too. The force of the door pulling open didn't give the rusty hinges a chance to make any noise, but as they closed, the terrible sound of the gears scrapping against each other filled the area until the door slammed shut, allowing an overwhelming echo to go racing down the stairwell.

Tyler rubbed his forehead, massaging the headache building up behind his right eye in an attempt, the action would somehow make it go away. *Well, there goes any element of surprise. Shit.*

Sam felt the same way but focused on remaining still as he waited for the echo to fade away. Knowing frustration would be plastered on his face, Sam chose to not look at Tyler even after spotting his head turn in his direction from the corner of his left eye.

Finally, after what felt like hours, the echo was absorbed by the walls and faded away. The haunting silence returned, allowing a distinct sense of dread to remerged inside the two best friends. They kept still and dramatically focused on the sound of nothing, hoping—and preparing—for anything or anyone to break that sound of silence.

"Alright," Tyler whispered. "Let's go."

Obeying, just as he had all night, Sam followed, keeping his guard as high as he could. "It's on the left…right?"

"Yeah. 413," Tyler replied over his shoulder as the number of the classroom centered in his overwhelmed mind.

Unlike the previous halls—specifically the second-floor—the fourth-floor hall had much less debris; a few papers and shards of glass were all there was, which made staying quiet somewhat more manageable for them to do. Accompanying the papers and shards of dusty glass were giant cobwebs, empty lockers on either side—many of them with their doors flung open and the overpowering smell of dampness was front and center. Because the fourth floor was one of the oldest parts of the building, the smell was stronger than the previous halls. It was so strong; it forced Sam to cover his mouth in his arm and cough a few times.

Tyler pivoted the beam of his flashlight to the first classroom door that approached on the left-hand side. Mimicking the second floor, the classroom had a large glass window in the center of the classroom door, allowing light from the moon to peer in from the doorway, giving off an unsettling isolated atmosphere. Taking a glance down the hall, Tyler spotted one classroom near the middle of the hall with its door open. *That's gotta be the fricken door we need to get in—yep, it is. Goddamn it! Why am I not surprised?*

He stepped up to the approaching doorframe of the first classroom and rather than waiting for Sam, Tyler rushed inside the room, keeping his gun steady as he scanned the entire room. Sam did the same, only at a much slower pace. Aside from eerie shadows, nothing else was in the room. They lowered their weapons.

Inside the room were multiple student desks—many of which remained in a row with a bulletin boards dangling from the back wall and a large black chalkboard that stretched across the entire front wall of the class, much like the rest of the classrooms across the floor. Time had not been kind to the school, but this classroom, in particular, seemed to withstand much of the harshness that the Rust Belt winters had; even the windows were intact. The condition of the room took both their attentions briefly, but it was suddenly overshadowed when they glanced at the chalkboard.

Brown thick dust covered the entire length of the chalkboard, making it difficult to see what appeared to be writing on it. Curious, Tyler lifted his flashlight and shined it on the board; the move taking Sam's curiosity, too. The light lit up the board, revealing the messy words written in white chalk. An unexpected sadness overcame the two men, forcing them to halt their attention and take in what was before them.

Both had been so frantic about the situation they were in, they forgot about the real-world consequences their actions had on the remaining people in town. And for the first time in quite a long time, memories of what the town used to be and what it turned into started overlapping each other.

Pennsylvania was my home, but I lost it

After reading it half a dozen times, Tyler finally lowered the flashlight and turned away, forcing Sam to reread the short, yet haunting words in the dark. Had Tyler not tapped Sam on the shoulder and reminded him they needed to move, he would've spent much of the night—or what remained of it, deep in thought about how hollowed out the town he once called home had become.

"I'll check the left side of the hall, you get the right, okay?" Tyler asked.

"Yeah…yeah, that's fine," Sam whispered as they stepped back into the hall.

"Alright, let's move fast."

Despite the words still sending chills down both their spins, they resumed their search, staying as quiet as they could. Just as planned, Tyler checked the classrooms on the left side, and Sam checked the ones on the right. Both were met with the same style and interior as the first classroom.

The classrooms were entrenched in darkness—especially Sam's side since he didn't have any moonlight to come shining in from the windows. It took him a bit longer to scan the rooms, but both were able to search without ease.

"Unreal," Sam said loud enough for Tyler to hear.

Tyler spun around in a panic. "What?"

"This place used to have thousands of kids in it and now look at it. I've never seen anything like it."

"I heard Michigan is worse."

"Well, that's comforting."

Tyler looked in another classroom, spotting nothing but knocked over furniture. "Look on the bright side."

"What's the bright side?"

"Least this isn't happening in a heavily populated area; imagine how that would be," Tyler said in a failed attempt to reassure his best friend. "You find anything?"

Sam moved away from the locked door and walked over to him. "No. A lot of these doors are locked, too."

Realizing he never checked any of the doors, Tyler turned and reached for the doorknob behind him. "Huh, I missed that."

Despite the small talk, Sam kept turning around, continually checking to reassure himself that nothing was there. His worry was persistent, with no sign of letting up. Tyler—while feeling the same—concealed his trepidation thanks to his years as a police officer.

"Which one is 413?" Sam asked, refocusing his attention to the hall in front of him.

Tyler pointed his rifle to the end of the hall. "Last door on the left."

Sam looked up.

The outlines of the doors lit up the dirty hall floors, but passed the unsettling shapes, nothing but blackness could be seen, creating large gaps with no light—perfect places to hide. But, unlike the other openings of light, the last one at the end of the hall was smaller in size—much smaller. From their distance, it was difficult for Sam to make out why that was, but his eye widened when he did. "The doors closed."

"Yeah, I spotted that too—"

A loud thump came from behind.

Tyler and Sam spun around, raising their weapons to the far end of the hall where they'd just come from.

A rush of horror shot through both of them so strong, it felt as if they were back outside. The loud thump lingered enough to remind them of the peril they were in. When the sound faded, Tyler spun around and started charging to the classroom of 413. "Come on. We need to hurry."

Following Tyler's lead, Sam started running after him but constantly kept looking over his shoulder, unable to shake the idea that they weren't alone. Despite the attempts to keep their footsteps muted, they created a vibration across the deserted hall that felt like the entire floor was shaking.

Tyler reached the door first, keeping his rifle and flashlight pointed at the center of the door. Any element of surprise they had was gone— Tyler knew that the second the hall door slammed shut. The only option was to go charging in and take out anything that was in their once joyful classroom. He placed his back against the wall and got into position. Sam went on the right side of the doorframe, keeping his weapon stretched out in front of him—Tyler pushed back from the wall and sent his foot swinging into the wooden door; snapping the old hinges off. The door flopped to the tiled floor. They rushed in.

Moving his flashlight all around the room, Tyler searched with his eyes as fast as—Sam spotted the outline in the corner of the room first. An audible shout exited his mouth. He aimed his pistol and fired three shots without any attempt to aim.

The figure came crashing down, violently landing on the floor with such a force, the classroom floor tremored. Startled by the deafening gunshots, Tyler turned his flashlight and weapon to see the figure crash on the ground. He lowered the light when he saw what it was.

It was an oversized desk globe that had taken the three shots directly in the center. Tyler immediately pointed the flashlight at Sam. "Jesus Christ, Sam."

Standing motionless—unsure of what to say as cool air entered his partially opened mouth, Sam lowered the gun, keeping his eyes on the antique glob that was now shattered to pieces. He finally found his voice. "Sh—shit."

Tyler continued with the search, hoping to find anything that resembled a clue, let alone an answer. But, he came up short; the room offered nothing but the same as the other classrooms. Dozens of old ill-fated student desks lined the room with a teacher's desk—Mr. Van Udan's desk—in the exact same spot it had been twenty-plus years prior. The sight brought a sense of déjà vu to him, almost as if he'd just found a time capsule he'd forgotten about.

"Nothing's here," Sam said in a flat-toned voice when he finished looking around. "He's not here."

Growing frustrated, Tyler lowered his rifle to the floor. A potent sense of uncertainty overcame him, leaving him unable to think.

"What other placed would there be?" Sam asked.

Taken back by the sudden question, Tyler shrugged. "What do you mean?"

"This is the classroom he was in the last time anyone saw him, right?"

Still unsure what Sam was getting at, Tyler acknowledged, but his answer lacked any truth. "Yeah…"

"So, where was another place in the school where something happened to him?"

Calmness reclaimed the room, leaving nothing but the ambiance noises of the night, allowing the two men to go back in time and search for an answer that wasn't guaranteed to be there. Tyler did his best to think back but found himself veering off in another direction. But, Sam stuck with it, using his excellent memory to guide him through the moments he's collected as life pursued.

Nothing struck him out of the ordinary at first; Russell Fritz was always getting made fun of. It got to the point where it just became an ordinary routine—at least for him, it did. The attempt he made to go back was a valiant effort, but agonizingly challenging. For nearly the entire first quarter of his life, he kept up his end of the promise he and Tyler made together back in the summer of 1997. Now that he was being forced to unearth those suppressed memories, it was mentally exhausting. And because of the lack of an answer, he found himself going back further than he wanted to.

When was it—when did we first meet you? It was second grade...no! It was first grade. Yeah, first grade because we had Mrs. Wright together. Even then you were quiet, but when did people start targeting you? A rush of memories combined with emotions from a much simpler time titled over Sam, leaving him a strange sense of limbo. But, he pushed through, keeping his mind at bay. *The year we started here you were in our classes...history with Van Udan, health with Miss. Jarry. And gym with Mr. Vashon—gym!*

"The gym," Sam finally said.

Stopping at the doorway, Tyler paused. "What about it?"

"That's where we need to go; that's where he'll be. I guarantee it."

The confidence in Sam's voice was admirable—even believable, but after coming all the way up to the fourth floor only to find nothing, Tyler was reluctant in following Sam's lead. "What makes you say that?"

"Fall of 1996, we had gym class with him."

Much like his best friend, Tyler had also driven the memories of his childhood as far down as possible—particularly memories with Russell Fritz. With the exception of a few moments throughout, he was just as effective in that effort as Sam. Over the years, he convinced himself what he and Sam did—or what they didn't do—in the woods was justified and anybody else their age would've done the same.

Tyler peaked his head out the doorway and looked down both directions of the dark hall. "What about it?"

"Remember he forgot to lock his locker and Cormack and the guys went in and soaked his clothes in the toilet?"

Oh yeah! Tyler thought to himself. *I forgot about that—yeah Cormack brought it into the accessible stall and soaked it in piss water.*

"So?" Tyler said. "Big deal, they got his clothes wet; that's nothing compared to some of the other shit that happened—"

"No!" Sam interrupted. "It's different. That one time was different from all the rest."

The firmness in Sam's voice revealed the passion of what he was saying, taking Tyler by surprise. Russell Fritz was the brunt of a lot of jokes and bullying—everything from soaking his clothes in piss-filled toilet water to being left for dead in the woods. And that was just the stories he knew about. All of them were terrible and proved the ugliness young kids have toward others who appear different, but that still didn't justify, in Tyler's perspective, why the gym incident would stand out above the rest.

"How is it different?"

"Because that was the first time you and I engaged in bullying him."

Tyler paused. *No, it wasn't, Sam. If anything it was—*

"Thank about it," Sam broke his train of thought. "We're the ones who took his clothes out of the locker, we're the ones who watched guard while Cormack soaked them and we're the ones who closed his locker back up. But, before we could finish—"

"He caught us," Tyler returned the favor of interrupting. "Just as we closed the locker door, he came walking back in."

"Yeah..."

Keeping the flashlight pointed at their feet, Tyler and Sam were unable to make out their expressions, but both mirrored each other's. And finally, after fighting it all night, Tyler could no longer do so and allowed the memories he'd been harvesting for decades to come flooding in like an angry ocean during a severe hurricane.

Within a matter of a split second, Russell Fritz was slithering across his mind, allowing the icy feeling to return and fill his arms with goosebumps. But, despite the variety of cruel memories he carried, Tyler focused on the day in the locker room and the look on Fritz's face when he spotted him and Sam engaging in acts of cruelty against him.

"He thought we were always nice to him," Tyler thought out load. "He didn't have a clue that we also made fun of him until that day—he always thought we were nice."

Sam stepped back into the dark, foul-smelling hall. "Exactly. That's why I said we need to get to the gym."

Assuming no response would come out of Tyler, Sam started for the end of the hall. While he wasn't confident how to get to the gym from the fourth floor, he had an idea—"Wait!" Tyler said as he sprinted to catch up.

"What?"

"We're just supposed to go to the gym, wait for him and then shoot him dead?"

Sam continued down the hall. "You seemed fine with that idea an hour ago."

"Yeah, well that was before—"

"Before what?" Sam stopped just shy of the doublewide doors to the stairwell. "Before you remembered how much of an asshole you and I were to him?"

Tyler didn't reply. He had begun the sentence even before he knew what he was going to say, but Sam's confrontational tone made it hard to try and find the right words to say. He kept quiet.

"He's killed almost a dozen people in case you forgot," Sam explained.

"Yeah, people that have done something to him, first," Tyler was finally able to say as he stepped up to Sam.

The sudden sense of remorse left Sam gobsmacked. For the entire night, Tyler's tone was the complete opposite and now his doubts started amplifying doubts Sam had himself during a time when they needed to be on heightened alert. The look in Tyler's eyes match what was coming out of his mouth; emotion occupied the corners in a way that Sam hadn't seen in years—let alone anytime during the night. Years of friendship had formed a bond between the two—a bond that allowed them to know how the other was feeling without saying a word. While there wasn't time to acknowledge it, the thought of that bond they formed as children still being there, after years apart, brought hesitation to Sam.

Changing his tone to a softer style, Sam made eye contact with his best friend and replied, "There's nothing we can do to change the past; if I could, I would. But, I can't and now this is where we are. Maybe on some deep twisted level, what he's doing seems justified, but that doesn't mean I'm gonna stand around and let him come find me. I know that's not the answer you want, but it is what it is. Maybe, in this story, none of us are good people. Maybe we're all just monsters and only the best one wins. Either way, it's out of our hands. Now, come on. We gotta get to that gymnasium."

With no time to rebuttal, Tyler lifted his flashlight to illuminate the hall, allowing enough light for Sam to step into the stairwell.

Slamming down on the breaks as hard as possible, Kimberly Wilson spun the steering wheel of the cruiser to the right and pulled up to the school as the tires squealed as if they were an animal bred for slaughter. Before the car was even in park, Kimberly pushed open the driver door, allowing a gust of night air to come rushing into the interior of the vehicle. A blank, emotionless look was across her face, matching how she felt inside. She was hurt, broken, but also enraged. She placed one foot out of the car but stopped before she got the other foot out. *I need a weapon—something strong to kill this son of a bitch!*

She began to frantically search the cruiser, starting with the center console and made her way to the glovebox. While she did hold onto hope that there would be a gun somewhere inside, she didn't hold her breath. Inside the center console was nothing but a CD and a container of mints. She slammed it shut and then went for the glovebox.

Yanking the handle down, the glovebox flung open. The small light inside on the right-hand side powered on, revealing the chuck full interior. Kimberly reached in, grasping for the first thing she could. Her fingertips touched a hard cold object, spooking her at first, but she wrapped her hands around it and pulled it out. It was a flashlight. An ever so slight feeling of relief rushed over her. The feeling was entirely out of place and yet somehow felt right in the moment—the thought of keeping the shadows away provided her with the sliver of resilience she desperately needed. She placed the flashlight on her lap and continued to loot the glovebox.

Because of how full it was, the light was mostly blocked, leaving much to the imagination. As she pushed deeper inside, she started guessing what she was touching. *More mints...napkins—*

She gasped as she froze in place. Even with her being unable to see what she was touching, the moment her hands felt the stationary object in the far back corner of the glovebox, she knew precisely what it was. Her heart began to thump like a Cherokee drum as her fingers wrapped around the object and slowly pulled it out.

The heaviness of the Ruger GP100 caught her by surprise. While she had used a gun several times when she was younger—mostly shooting targets in the back of her grandfather's house, a sense of trepidation bewildered her. Moonlight shined off the black colored barrel of the gun like diamonds on black velvet. She began taking deep breaths, hoping to calm her nerves.

This is it...Jesus Christ, this is it.

Goosebumps returned to her exposed legs and arms as the wind penetrated the interior of the cruiser. The fear within her was great; borderline devastating. But, the burning desire for revenge had built a foundation in her mind that not even a gust of wind could penetrate. And when memories of Mike trickled back in, the doubts—and goosebumps faded.

She stepped out of the car, slammed the door shut behind her and proceeded to walk to the front of the school.

Chapter 14

The wind howled, borderline roared as the majestic pine tree swayed as if their roots were about to give way and come crashing down. The sweeping reluctant force bent the branches of even the healthiest trees and snapped a few of the weaker limbs. The shadows of the branches danced in a haunting fashion as if they were trying to take hold of anything they could grasp. All night the howling wind had been picking up, but it wasn't until this particular gust that James Nelson realized how much it had intensified.

Staying true to himself, he pressed forward, keeping the flashlight aimed in front of him as he barreled through the thick woods. When a tree was in front of him, he dodged it, when a large rock was heading straight for him, he jumped it. And while the obstacles may have slowed him down, it couldn't shake the foundation of his determination as he charged through the thick brush and low hanging branches.

Holy shit, it's getting cold! Brrr! He grabbed the zipper to his jacket and pulled it straight up to his neck. Typically, he never zipped it that high—fearing he would choke, but the night air had broken through his motivation. His cheeks were rosy red; he could see the outline of them in the bottom corner of his eyes. His nose was also bright red, but it was his cheeks he fixated on as the coolness of them began numbing either side of his face. He began to shiver.

The sound of leaves crumpling under his shoes crackled and popped with every step. The attempts to dampen the noise got him nowhere—literally, and he determined it was best to run as fast as he could without ever looking back. *I gotta be close by now! It can't be that much further ahead…I hope—*

He stopped, coming to an abrupt halt, like that of a vehicle when the driver spots an object in front of them, with just a second to spare. A gentle exhale emerged from his breath and visibly lifted into the air—the temperature had finally dropped below freezing.

Remaining still like a deer caught in a set of headlights, James focused his attention to what was before him. Unlike every other time, when he was able to find the words to say, this time was different—much different. For the first—and probably the only time in his life, he was at a loss for words. His big imagination had finally collided with reality.

Below him, at the bottom of the hill, was the facility.

Just like it was when it was occupied, the building was lit up by bright overhanging lights that reminded him of the tall lamps you'd find in a parking lot of a grocery store late at night. The front of the building was lit up like a Christmas tree, but no light appeared to be coming from inside the building. When the sudden shock faded, which was much sooner than it felt, James shut his flashlight off and took cover behind a large fallen branch next to him.

His breathing began to pick up, allowing more cold air to go rushing into his lungs and throughout his body. Unlike every other child who found themselves in the situation, James smiled as a sense of euphoria overpowered anything that resembled fear. Using stealth and long shadows from the tree branches that hung over him, James raised his head carefully before taking off his backpack.

The sight of the facility mesmerized him—he couldn't take his eyes off it even if he wanted or needed too. Had it been up to him, he would've remained at the top of that hill and continued to enjoy the view while his big imagination ran berserk forever. The idea of living in a fantasy intrigued the young boy, but the thought of getting to see—or even meet some type of outer space visitor was far too tempting to sit and wait any longer.

Trying to stay quiet as he dropped to his knees, he pulled the straps of his backpack off his shoulders, reached around to the front and gently opened the first compartment. He stuck his right hand in and began reaching around. The first thing his small hand touched was the hunting knife he had stolen a couple of weeks ago back when the idea of extra-terrestrial—particularly hostile extra-terrestrial life—crossed his mind during one of his reading sessions. *No, not that. I need something else—something better!*

He dismissed the knife, pushing it aside and reached in further into the compartment. A hard object gliding up his arm, spooking him at first, but the feeling vanished as fast as it came. Without having to look, he knew the object he felt was his taser. Feeling like it was no better than the hunting knife, he shoved that off to the side and pushed his hand to the bottom until it landed on something cold and hard. His eyes widened with seriousness.

There it is.

Keeping true to his father's orders, James carefully pulled out the object, giving it the same respect he would give a real one. Grasped firmly in his hand was his matte black paintball gun; locked, loaded and ready for action.

Once he got the weapon out and carefully aimed it at the ground, James zipped the backpack up as quick as he could. Once he got it closed, he whipped the straps over his shoulders and placed both hands on the gun and re-focused to the facility.

A feeling of comfort surrounded him—almost as if the company of the weapon made him feel like a detective on the hunt for one of the world's most nitrous criminals. The idea made him feel gitty in a situation where any other person would be petrified. But, despite the euphoria, James kept his guard up and stayed true to his mission.

Using the stealth, the black sky overhead provided, he slowly rose from his knees and started downhill, heading straight for the main entrance, using only the light of the moon to guide him.

Keeping the gun and flashlight pointed straight ahead, Kimberly Wilson took the first step inside the abandoned school. Her breath was heavy, and panic loomed over her shoulder, but she hoped focusing on her anger would offset anything that would make her second guess her decision. Rather than sprinting to the side of the wall and blend in with the dark, she stayed in the middle of the large room, hoping the large spacious room would warn her of lurking danger.

Because the surrounding was so foreign to her, Kimberly had no sense of direction—the school was closed long before she was old enough to attend. The lack of familiarity kept her on guard, but she didn't let it stop her; the idea of focusing on the contempt inside was useful. She kept the flashlight pointed ahead and her finger on the trigger of the revolver.

Just like it had been for decades, the room was still. The wind howled outside as if it were an outer eyewall of a hurricane, but inside was dead calm. The windows in the front of the lobby shook—some even bobbing in their bracket, but none gave way to the overwhelming force of Mother Nature. The noise was brief, but it still spooked Kimberly when the clattering first began. She marched on, keeping her eyes moving about.

While much of the night had been a mystery to her, one thing was clear: the night wasn't over, yet. She relished in the idea of having the element of surprise, but being the rational, mature adult she was, she knew that was a double-edged sword. *If I have it, then so do they—them, whoever—*

Her eyes spotted something on the floor, bringing her to a complete standstill. She quickly looked around, twisting her head to the left and right multiple times, fearing something was about to lunge out at her and suck her into the shadows forever. No such lunge ever came; she was very much alone like she had been all night.

Looking down, she lowered the flashlight to her feet. Any sense—or even hope—of being alone evaporated when she spotted the footprints on the floor. Keeping the gun raised in front of her chest, she took another look around, making sure she wasn't missing anything. *Footprints...fresh ones, too. But, where do they go—*

She started walking forward, keeping the flashlight beam on them. With each step she took, her heart thumped in her chest like no tomorrow. And despite the cold air that claimed the night—or what was left of it— sweat started to form in the creases of her forehead. The heaviness of the pistol in her hand blunted the tension enough to where she could keep her panic to a minimum. She followed the footprints to the staircase but stopped short when the flashlight revealed something she wasn't expecting. *Oh, shit, they split up. The goddamn footprints split up...this is just great.*

Keeping in mind she now had proof of at least two other people inside with her, Kimberly moved the flashlight from one set of prints to the other. Because of the lack of time she had, she estimated the sizes were about the same with one pare made by typical regular shoes while the other set made by boots; possibly work boots. She fixated on those tracks not long after spotting them. *He had boots on—that's right! That son of a bitch had boots!*

It was a combination of debilitating fear and heartless rage that stretched her emotions to the breaking point. Doubt swirled in.

It was followed by anger.

Then fear.

Like the footprints in front of her, she was at an impasse. Everything that would happen next would all circle around the decision she was about to make. While she only debated it for nothing more than a few seconds, she was aware of the significance of the choice.

She kept the gun out in front of her and lowered the flashlight to the boot prints that ran the length of the entire hall.

Like the rest of the rundown school, the hall that lead to the gym was filled with trash, cobwebs and the smell of mold growing within the walls. The odor was so bad, it could make even the strongest stomach gag. The deeper into the hall Tyler Benton and Sam Rainey went, the more formidable the smell was, but both were able to control their nausea and focus on the decaying wall Tyler's flashlight revealed.

"It's gotta be close," Sam whispered.

"I thought we would've found it by now," Tyler confessed.

Because of his training at the police academy, Tyler guided with ease, but Sam shook with dread. Every step they took, he feared would be their last. He was so anxious, by the time he realized Tyler had come to a stop, he nearly banged into him. "Whoa, Jesus." He looked around before leaning into Tyler's ear. "Why'd you stop?"

Tyler answered by turning the flashlight to a large wooden door on the left side of the hall. The door matched its surroundings, but Tyler fixated on the bent blue sign that hung from the center. 'Men's Locker Room'

"Couldn't you get into the gym through the locker room?" he finally said, breaking the eerie quietness that compassed the area.

The sudden—almost random question halted Sam's nervousness to provide the right answer. It had been a long time since either had thought about the school, but for some reason, gym class always stood out in his mind. "Yeah, through the back door by the showers."

Tyler veered to the side of the hall and approached the large door. "Thought so."

Sam raised his gun and aimed at the center of the wooden door as Tyler took cover on the right-hand side. A steadiness in Sam's aim emerged for the first time all night, almost as if the fear of finding his murderous patient Russell Fritz had faded like the childhood memories remaining inside the nearby walls.

Tyler reached for the stainless steel handle and slowly pulled it open. Much too both their surprise, the door didn't make a sound as it opened. Had he not been looking, Sam wouldn't have even known the door was opening. The old door was in poor condition but was still just as heavy as it was twenty years ago, which forced Tyler to use his muscles. *This thing still weighs a fricken ton! Goddamn.*

As the gap between the wall and the door grew larger, an imperishable darkness emerged from inside. Standing at the distance he was at, nothing could be made out, but when the door was opened enough for the two to sneak through, Tyler shined the light inside. He stepped inside first and held the door open with his elbow. "Shut the door carefully."

Following Tyler—like he'd done for much of his life—Sam stepped through the opening and placed both hands on the door and relieved some of his force, allowing the door to close slowly and carefully. Paranoid they would lose their element of surprise—if they even had any left, Sam kept his hands on the door even after he felt it stop at the frame.

"You good?" Tyler asked after spotting Sam lingering at the door.

"Yeah, I'm good."

Refocusing, Sam lifted his gun back up and started to follow Tyler down the long-familiar hall that brought them to the locker room.

"Stay close," Tyler whispered.

The ominous silence of the building had followed them in. To the dismay of both, the unusual pink colored walls appeared the same as they did many moons ago. The smell, which consisted of mold with a touch of body odor, still lingered as if the scent had been trapped in the room for all this time.

The end of the narrow hall lead to a large room filled with isles of tall blue lockers and an office surrounded by walls made of windows in the far corner. All the lockers—at least in the first row—were wide open as if they'd been ransacked. The windows that made up the office were broken, too. When he noticed the damaged windows, Tyler tilted the flashlight to the floor and spotted glass covering the path forward. Tyler peaked over his shoulder and warned Sam to watch his step.

"Always something," Sam mumbled as a blue door at the end of the locker room came into sight.

Memories of their time in—not just the locker room, but the gym itself came flooding in like a broken dame. Everything from school assemblies to gym class itself rushed in with such force; it was staggering. For a brief moment, reality faded and feelings of childhood took over, reminding them of the earlier days in life when the stress of adulthood was unknown—the feeling faded as they walked passed the showers and approached the door. Keeping light on the blue door that had aged drastically well, Tyler reached for the handle and pushed it open with one mighty body slam.

They rushed out the doorway and onto the metal catwalk that overlooked the entire gymnasium. The two looked around, waving their guns in every direction with their fingers on the triggers. Along with his military-style rifle, Tyler shifted the flashlight from side to side, lighting up the dark corners of the large gymnasium. They found nothing.

Sam was the first to lower his weapon, letting out a frustrated sigh as he did so. Tyler soon followed with the same action, but held his flashlight at bay, keeping the hope alive that it would find something in the dark they might've overlooked. That hope diminished the longer they stood there in silence.

The old gym had taken the brunt of the harsh winter weather over the years. Large cracks covered many areas of the wooden floor with equally large cracks that sprouted up the walls on all four sides. The basketball hoops on opposite sides of the gym had fallen down decades ago, and the bleachers across from the metal catwalk had collapsed. All accompanied by two large holes in the ceiling that allowed moonlight to tickle in like a spotlights on a stage.

"Maybe he's not here," Tyler finally said.

"No," Sam yelled. "No, he's here."

Turning his fear outward, Sam snatched the flashlight from Tyler's grip and started running to the staircase at the end of the metal bridge that lead to the floor of the gymnasium. His feet stomped louder as his accelerated speed shook the bridge to the point Tyler grabbed the railing in front of him out of fear the entire ledge would collapse.

"Sam...Sam!" Tyler shouted but to no avail.

Ignoring Tyler, Sam ran down the stairs—jumping over the last two steps and rushed to the middle of the gymnasium floor with his arms stretched out like he was hanging from a cross. "Russel Fritz!" he shouted. "Russel Fritz! I know you're here!"

Panicking, Tyler tried to get Sam to stop, but the pleas were ineffective.

Sam raised his gun and fired two shots, the bullets blasting into the roof and bouncing off the metal beams. "Come on, Fritz! You want me? You want to take your shot? Well, here I am!"

The strength that rose from Sam's voice was pure and vibrant. He had reached the point where he was done chasing. Tyler was at that point, too—Sam fired two more shots in the air. "Russell Fritz! Come on!"

The empty space of the gym provided Sam's voice with an echo that pierced through the surrounding walls and rush throughout the nearby hallways, allowing anyone nearby to hear his voice

Spotting blood splattered across the back wall of the security hob directly in front of the opened gate, James Nelson stepped closer, hoping to get a better look and sense of what was going on. The sight of the blood brought his nerves to attention. The closer he got, the more blood he could see, but no bodies were visible.

The idea that something terrible—and dangerous for that matter, never entirely took effect in his mind; the idea of finding an extra-terrestrial loomed over everything else. Cautiously, he stepped to the hob and peered inside the front window. The blood across the wall had made its way down to the metal floor, creating a pool in front of the desk. The lack of any bodies was a welcoming sight for the young child. Once sure he didn't overlook anything, he entered through the barbed wire gate and started approaching the front entrance of the facility.

Whoa, it's even bigger than I thought it was...cool! There's gotta be a bunch of different things inside, and it looks like the front door is opened, too. I don't think anyone is around, though. Maybe I should try and find someone...?

A handful of Humvee's were sporadically parked between the gate and the entrance to the facility. All of them appeared to be empty. Choosing not to go searching for anyone, James approached the front of the building, his head bobbing in all directions, telling himself that if he spotted anyone, we *would* call out in the hopes whoever it was would help with the many questions he had.

Keeping his paintball gun aimed at the approaching door, James started up the three metal steps as quietly as he could. The closer he got, the more he realized the door *was* opened. A warmth of excitement rushed through him as if he'd just stepped outside during a scolding hot summer day. A smile grew on his face as the wind picked up again, but it didn't slow the young boy down. He stopped before the thick metal door and took in a deep breath of frigid nighttime air.

His heart thumped beneath his rib cage like never before; it was the moment he'd been waiting for since he spotted the lights with the telescope. The emotions running through him was almost too much for the young boy to bear, and they spiked more when he reached for the cold metal handle and began pulling it open.

The building was home for some of the highest level secrets the United States government had and such secrets required to be placed in something that would be nearly impenetrable to the outside world. The architectures who designed the facility knew that and therefore chose to make the metal of the building as thick as possible. That included the main entrance to the building, too.

James huffed, puffed and pulled as hard as he could with what muscles he had. *Holy crap, what's this thing made of? An elephant? Come on, open. Open, damn you! I said ope—*

A small gap started to form. It was an incredibly small opening, but James was an incredibly small boy. He eye-balled it and thought he might be able to fit in, but it was going to be tight. As he pulled, he could feel the resistance of the door fighting back. He didn't have much strength in his arms and knew he was only seconds away before the door drew back and—he let go of the door and dived in like a skydiver exiting a plane. *Crap! Crap! Crap!*

He landed on the metal floor with a mighty thump.

Less than a second later, the door closed shut, sealing him in.

Sweat billowed from his forehead when he realized he was in. His breathing amplified, matching the level of excitement still lingering within him. The sound of the door closing grumbled around him—a rumble so great, he immediately turned onto his back and looked up. When the sound evaporated, and tranquility reclaimed the building, James wiped the sweat from his face. *I made it. Holy crap, I made it!*

Typically, not one for being dramatic, James remained on the floor, trying to control his breathing as best as he could. It took some time, but once he did, he slowly got back on his feet and started looking around.

Whoa.

Just like the security hub outside, the lobby of the facility—or alien building he referred to it—was slathered with puddles of blood, but no bodies. The lighting of the lobby provided no safe haven for shadows of any type which allowed James to turn off his flashlight and conserve what life remained in the batteries. He raised his paintball gun and began taking small steps toward the blood that covered the front desk in the middle of the lobby.

Keeping all his attention on the desk, James didn't so much as blink. While he was making it up as he went, the plan was to try and find a map of the building—a spark came from his left side. James swung the paintball gun and his body in that direction. His eyes widened. Then, his knees started to buckle.

Off to his left was a long metal hall with blood draped across the walls and covering the floor. Like the lobby, no bodies were in sight, but the hall undoubtedly had more blood than either the lobby or the security station. Another spark snapped, apparently coming from a light that was dangling for dear life at the far end of the hall.

James took a quick look around, but found nothing; the sense of isolation loomed large. Along with the pools covering the floor, blood stretched across the white walls of the hall vividly. The sight was terrifying, but also mesmerizing to the young boy. And before he knew it, he found himself walking to the hallway, completely forgetting about the idea of trying to find a map.

The young boy stepped into the hall and took the safety off the paintball gun. Then, with a deep breath, he started down.

At first, she thought it was fireworks going off, but after the second bang, Kimberly Wilson was sure what she was hearing was gunfire. The realization brought a new sense of danger to the already dangerous path she found herself on. She shut the flashlight off and darted into the shadows on the right-hand side of the hall.

She bit down on her lip, forcing herself to breathe through her nose to keep her breathing silent. *You're okay, you're okay, Kimberly. You got a gun; you have control. You' re—oh shit. I didn't even check to see if the thing was loaded.*

Panic washed over her like a sailor spotting thunderclouds in the far horizon. Everything else on her mind slipped away, leaving her with only one thought: check and make sure the damn gun has bullets. She reached for the button on the bottom of the flashlight but stopped short of pressing it. Nothing had been going right so far that night, but the idea of attempting to blend in with the shadows seemed like a good idea to her, and the thought of giving away her position seemed pointless, especially now since she wasn't sure if the gun was loaded or not.

Kimberly placed the flashlight down on the floor gently, but close enough so she could remember where it was when she went back for it. Then, keeping her back pressed against the wall, she stretched out her hands and brought them into the moonlight coming in from the windows across from her. The windows were so dirty, much of the moonlight remained outside, but it was enough for her to get the revolver and bring it in the light so she could open the loading gate and see right away if there were bullets in it or not.

While she hadn't held a gun—much less shot one—in many years, the training she did receive as a young girl on her grandfather's ranch was never forgotten. Much of it had been basic, but it was enough for her to defend herself. And the thought of the Ruger GP100 being familiar to the type of weapon she'd practiced with as a child helped ease the anxiety she couldn't shake.

She reached for the clip to open the spin wheel, only to find she couldn't open it easily. *Of course, it can't be easy. Open you piece of sh—no!*

Her strength that emerged from the rage overpowered the nearly jammed clip and sent the spin wheel spiraling out and knocking out all the bullets inside. The sudden opening of the wheel spooked her until the sound of bullets plummeting into the darkness covering the floor forced her to look down at her feet. "Fuck!"

She reached down and started feeling around in desperation, hoping her hands would find something that resembled a bullet—*No, no, no!*

An icy metal object was at her feet, but it wasn't a bullet. It was a grate of a heating vent with multiple openings—openings big enough for a bullet to slide through. She stopped feeling around and threw her hands up in dismay. She knew every bullet fell in without having to waste the time looking.

The lack of light inside the hall hid the tears swelling in her eyes. The feeling of fear—a feeling she'd been trying to cope with, was breaking through in an insurmountable way. The idea of walking away and vanishing into the night came—she looked in the spinning wheel of the Ruger. She rose to her feet, keeping her eye inside the wheel, making sure what she saw wasn't just her mind playing tricks on her.

A single bullet remained tucked in one of the slots.

She pushed the wheel back into the middle of the gun and brought it to her chest, reminiscing in the luck—or as close to luck—she had. The loss of the other five bullets was devastating, but having at least one was enough to keep her mind focused despite applying sufficient pressure to the situation. *One bullet...but that's all I'm gonna need, goddamn it. One bullet to kill that son of a bitch. One shot, one kill.*

She resumed her walk down the hall, gripping the gun for dear life. But, the more she continued on, the more she knew another weapon was needed. As she pushed deeper into cluttered hall laced with dust, papers and old classroom furniture that hadn't been used in decades, she looked all around, hoping to spot anything that could be used as—*Ah-uh!*

Stopping in the middle of the hall, Kimberly fixated her eyes on something lurking in the dark: an emergency ax hanging peacefully in a display case. Like the windows behind her, the glass in the display case had been broken years ago, allowing a large scale of dust to form around the wooden handle and red tip. She grabbed hold of it and pulled it out of the wall.

She held the weapon up in the moonlight filtering in from behind her and glared at it as if she was mesmerized by its presence. While it may not have been as relieving as the bullets she lost, it brought her comfort. It also brought back the anger and rage she'd lost only moments before. Memories of Mike followed, and the lack of memories she wouldn't make with him fueled her feelings—another loud bang came from down the hall. She tightened her grip on the ax and the pistol. *This is it. This is where it ends. Right here, right now.*

Her entire life she'd never walked away from a challenge and always stood up for herself, just as she was taught to. The circumstances this time were much different—much more life-threatening, but her determination to keep going and get the final word loomed more substantial than any fear tugging at her. This was her moment to turn the tables and become the hunter instead of the hunted.

She continued down the hall and prepared to engage in the hidden truths that lurked around the corner.

Coming to a dead stop when she spotted Tyler's police cruiser, Lois Tangley shut the car off and got out as quick as she could. Yelling out for Tyler rattled in her mind first, but the lack of any presence around her suggested it would be a wasted effort. She closed the door to the police cruiser and sprinted to the front of—she spotted a police cruiser off to her left. *Goddamn it, Kimberly. Why in god's name—holy shit!*

She pulled out her pistol and twirled around, dramatically checking her surrounds. The feeling of nausea rushed from her stomach to her neck in a matter of seconds. But, she pushed past it and walked over to the vehicle keeping her gun aimed the blood-covered windshield.

At first, she couldn't see anything, but as she got closer, the outline of Agent McCann and Vitukevich emerged in horrible fashion. Stopping short of the blood oozing from the cracks of the passenger door, Lois knew by looking that everyone in the car was dead. Before she even realized, she found her eyes wandering from the blood dripping to something on the ground, entrenched in darkness. Keeping her eyes on the object, she pulled out her flashlight and pointed it at the object. The nausea feeling leaped high as she gasped and turned away at the sight of Mrs. Quimby's face.

She sprang into action and started running to the front door—a gunshot roared from her right side. She ducked and darted over to the cruiser Kimberly had stolen. Unable to control her breathing, Lois pressed her back up against the tail end of the car and braced for another gunshot.

No such gunshot came. Once enough time passed, she lifted her head and looked in the direction of where the gunfire came from. The more she thought about it, the more she started to realize the gunshot was too quiet to have been aimed in her direction; the sound of the shot came from the back end of the school.

The side was laced with darkness because the moon was on the opposite side of the building, but her flashlight was able to blast through the shadows and provide a bright enough path for her to see. Keeping her gun raised, she stepped onto the cracked sidewalk and headed down the side of the building.

Firing the gun again, Sam Rainey twirled around in the middle of the gymnasium, keeping his arms stretched out. From the balcony, Tyler Benton rested his assault rifle on the railing of the gallery while keeping his right eye in the crosshairs.

"Russel! I know you're out there!" Sam screamed at the top of his lungs. "Come on out. I know you can hear me."

Tyler's pulse thumped in his eardrum as a rush of sweat-soaked his undershirt.

Sam lowered his face as he kept looking around. Shadows loomed like skyscrapers, but he was confident the moonlight he was standing under from the crack in the ceiling was more than enough for him to be seen. He took in a deep breath of nighttime air.

"It's my fault, Russel. It's all my fault. I didn't help you that day in the woods—I didn't say anything when I found out what happened to you. And it's my fault all this is happening to you…I'm the one who allowed the experiments to go on." A sense of sadness arose from his voice like a criminal regretting his actions. The more he talked, the more regret found its way into his heart. "I'm the villain in your story, Russel. I'm the one you want."

Watching through the sight on top of his rifle, Tyler didn't speak, but as he listened, his own sense of regret emerged. It had been hidden for years, but the more he listened to Sam, the brighter those harvested feelings became. He opened his mouth to speak, but Sam continued before he got a word in edgewise.

"Nobody else needs to die, Russel. No one else needs to die, Russel!"

Tyler took the safety off his assault rifle—a loud bang came from the right side of the gym below the metal walkway.

Sam fixated on that area, preparing for the face of his patient to appear. Tyler kept his eye in the sights of the rifle with his finger resting comfortably on the trigger.

There was another bang.

Sam lifted his flashlight and turned it on.

Another bang.

The door at the far end of the gym opened.

Sam shined his flashlight. A figure entered.

His eyes squinted. "What're you doing here?"

"Who is it?" Tyler asked, unable to see who was below him.

"He's here," a voice said, keeping the pistol pointed straight ahead.

Tyler lifted his eyes away from the rifle. At first, he couldn't make out who's voice it was—the sentence was too short.

The door to the gym closed. "He's here," the voice continued. "I followed the tracks, and they stopped in here."

Sam was confused. "What do you mean tracks?"

"The ones from the entrance!"

A coldness of fear ran down Sam's body as he pieced together. He started looking around and shining his flashlight into the nearby shadows.

"Kimberly?" Tyler asked loud enough for her to hear.

She looked up to the walkway. "Tyler?"

"What're you doing—"

A shadow moved from his right side—a sudden thump struck the center of his back followed by pain so unimaginable; it took his breath away as his entire body jerked. A muted gasp shot through his mouth seconds before a bullet shot out of his rifle from his finger twitching. The gunshot made Kimberly jump and by the time Sam was able to react to the sound of the gunshot, the bullet fired already entered his stomach and shot out of his lower back.

Like Tyler, pain ripped through Sam's body before he knew what had happed. A sudden shock overcame him as his thoughts left his mind as blank as a fresh canvass. A warm sensation began slithering down the front of his stomach. His legs gave way, and he plummeted to the gym floor, landing on his back as the pistol in his right hand flung out of his grip and into the darkness.

A hand slammed down on Tyler's right shoulder and spun him around. Tyler's muscular body was heavy, but was no match for the strength of the hand on him. The rifle fell out of his hand and landed on the floor, joining Sam's in the dark abyss below. Groaning in pain, Tyler began trembling as he felt himself spinning around. His eyes were closed at first—not because he was scared, but because of the horrific pain. When he opened them, he let out a horrifying scream. Before he was able to do anything else, Russell Fritz pushed him off the metal bridge. Kimberly screamed.

Tyler gasped as he violently landed on his stomach as the sound of him landing on the floor echoed through the abandoned gym. The pain he was in expanded from his lower back to the rest of his body, the agony so great, it nearly brought him to tears.

Taking steps back as she screamed, Kimberly's eyes widened with fear as her body began trembling as if she was in the middle of an earthquake. It was too dark for her to see, but she was confident Tyler was hurt. She started sprinting over to him until a towering figure jumped down from the metal ledge and landed a couple of feet beside him. She froze.

The shadows of the gym were long and dark, but she made out the outline of the figure in front of her. Long legs, a muscular build, tall and broad animal ears resting atop of his head—she knew who was in front of her.

Straightening himself up, Russell Fritz looked down at Tyler as soft gasps ticked out of his trembling body. Like Kimberly, he was unable to see much detail of anything close by, but having a sense of where Tyler was, Fritz walked over to him, spread his legs and lowered them to either side of Tyler. Unable to do anything more than lift his head, Tyler groaned—two large hands grabbed his head from either side and began pulling up, and the foot that was at his right side came slamming down on his back.

The vibration of Fritz jumping from the metal balcony sent tremors throughout the gym and alerted Sam they weren't alone. The bullet wound in his gut had boarder line paralyzed him to the point where he was unable to move his feet, but Tyler's grunts—that quickly grew into screams—forced him to search for the pistol that was somewhere beneath the darkness surrounding him.

The pressure from the large hands covering the top of his head and face became overwhelming within seconds. Tyler did what he could to resist, but his body had little energy. Then, when his neck was pulled back as far as it could go, his grunting grew deeper.

Standing motionless, Kimberly watched in horror as Russel Fritz—the man who brutally slaughtered the love of her life—began finishing what he started. She was unsure if he knew of her presence, but she was sure once he was done with Tyler, she wouldn't be far behind. Her body trembled as she watched Fritz's ruthlessness at point-blank range. It brought back the memories of what happened earlier in the night as if they'd happened only moments before. But, passed that pain and fear, a void of steadiness occupied her mind—a void that would typically be filled with fear and desire to run.

She raised the pistol and fired the only bullet inside the gun.

A grunt came from the man behind the mask.

The sound of the gunshot jolted Sam, but didn't stop him from continuing his search for his gun; he knew a single bullet wasn't enough to stop Fritz. He noticed moments after the gunshot; Tyler screams stopped, allowing a sense of hope to the idea Tyler being okay. His heart began beating harder when they resumed.

From outside, the wind howled something awful. The temperature had dropped considerably due to the force of the wind, but as strong as the gusts were, it was unable to mask the sound of the gunshot from Lois Tangley as she proceeded down the side of the crumbling building. She spun around and aimed at the rusty door coming up on her left.

She was unsure if the gunshot had come from that part of the school, but she knew she needed to get inside if she was going to find the source of the sound. Keeping her gun pointed at the metal door, she reached for the handle. To her surprise, it was unlocked. She pulled it open and stepped inside the building, closing the door behind her.

Tyler's screams amplified as the pulling on his neck became overpowering. His neck was tilted back so much; he was now able to see the outline of the deer mask looming over him; he was no match for Fritz. He closed his head and prepared for—

Screaming as if in the middle of a medieval battle, Kimberly ran up to Fritz and swung the ax in his direction. The ax made a swooping sound as it cut through the air, but did not strike anything. A snapping sound started coming from the floor. Tyler's screams peaked. Kimberly lifted the ax again and swung with all her might.

A groan—familiar to the one after she fired the gun—emerged as the ax swung down and sliced through the left side of Fritz's mask. Despite being unable to see where she hit, the sudden stop of the ax halfway down proved she hit something.

She lifted the ax back up.

Fritz let go of Tyler and reached for Kimberly, but turned away when he spotted the ax swinging back down. He pushed his head away, which kept his face of out harm's way, but left his hands venerable— Kimberly swung the ax down, striking Fritz in the right hand and slicing off his pointer and middle finger.

A deeper groan came from the man behind the mask as his two fingers fell out of view and land somewhere at his feet. Blood squirted out and started collecting on the gym floor. The sudden pain forced Fritz to stop, but he recuperated fast enough to grab the ax from Kimberly's hand and smash the bottom of the handle into her face.

Screaming after she heard the loud snap come from her noise, Kimberly stumbled backward and fell to the floor, covering her nose with her hand. Using force, Fritz threw the ax across the gymnasium, leaving the teenager weaponless. Dampness began to collect in between the cracks of Kimberly's fingers as pain seeped from the nasal fracture.

Focusing on her sobbing on the floor, Fritz stepped toward her—

Tyler grabbed his leg.

The grip was mediocre but was enough to force Fritz to refocus on him. Tyler squeezed onto Fritz's leg and pulled it forward to—Fritz slammed his hands onto either side of Tyler's head and violently yanked up, snapping his neck as the tip of his spinal cord burst from the skin of his neck.

The sound of Tyler's neck bone breaking echoed, followed by the sound of his lifeless body flopping to the floor. Then, a sudden silence overcame the gym. Kimberly's screams became muted with shock as she watched Tyler's still body lay at Fritz's feet. An unexpected gasp fell out of her when she watched Fritz grabbed the handle of the hammer in Tyler's back and ripped it out. Then, Fritz turned to her.

She started crawling backward. "Oh, God! Oh, God!"

Squeezing the handle of the hammer, Fritz started walking toward her. The force of his boots slamming onto the ground vibrated the floor.

Kicking her legs back and forth in an attempt to get away, Kimberly trembled but was unable to look away from the horrifying sight of lose deer flesh heading straight at her.

Mimicking the same relentless speed, he displayed all night, Fritz clutched the hammer tight in his grip as he charged to Kimberly, preparing to seal her fate once and fur all—a gunshot rang out, followed by a sudden pain in the lower half of his gut. Fritz stopped his pursuit of Kimberly and turned to the direction of where the gunshot came. Much of the gym was still dark, but he was able to spot Sam on the floor, aiming a pistol at him.

He stepped toward Sam.

Sam fired four more shots into his chest. Each bullet struck his body; two of them blasted into his stomach on the right and the other two entering into his chest, ripping through the flesh and organs in their wake. Pain engulfed the masked murderer as a burning sensation expanded in his chest. Finally, he looked up at Sam.

Sam fired one more shot; the bullet striking the side of Fritz's neck and knocking him to the floor. Sam pulled the trigger again only to find no bullets remained in the gun. He dropped the gun as he lowered his head. Like his patient bleeding on the floor, Sam was struggling to overcome the pain from the bullet wound, but the sniffles from Kimberly were enough to get his attention.

At first, Kimberly kept her eyes on Fritz. He was so still, she could only conclude that her attacker—the person that took the love of her life away and shattered her future—was dead. The blood oozing from the nubs where the fingers used to be on his right hand only added to that speculation. *It's over…it's finally over—*

"Run," Sam coughed out.

Kimberly turned to him with a look of confusion. "But, but—he's."

"Run! Get out of here!" Sam repeated as he rolled onto his stomach.

What do you mean run? Why would I run, he's dead—no! No!

Beneath the gentle black drop that consumed the gym, Kimberly turned her head when a shadow among shadows started to move. At first, she thought it was her eyes playing a cruel trick on her, but when the shadow started growing and eventually stood, she realized the idea of it being in her imagination was folly.

Sam looked back at her. "Run!"

Fear forced her eyes to open wide as the outline of the mask formed in front of her. She took several steps back. "No…"

Blood dripped from the left side of the mask where Kimberly had struck with the ax. A large ear from the mask dangled at his shoulder, but Fritz's actual ear was nowhere in sight—Kimberly had effectively harmed her attacker, but by no means completed her task.

Fritz reached down and picked up the metal hammer.

Kimberly spun around and ran to the rusty doors on the far wall behind her as Sam warned her not to stop moving. Blood continued to drip from her broken nose, and the cool air stung the surrounding area of her face as she ran. But, despite the pain, she slammed into the doors with all her weight and charged into the narrow hallway behind them.

Unable to get to his feet, Sam picked up the empty pistol with his left hand and through it, striking his patient Russell Fritz in the arm. The sound of Fritz's feet stomping abruptly halted. A haunting stillness reclaimed the night, leaving Sam with only the sound of his breathing and the wind howling outside. He looked in the direction of where he tossed the gun, but was unable to see anything.

"Russell?" he mumbled.

He squinted his eyes, hoping to make out the outline of his patient somewhere in the surrounding area, but nothing seemed out of the ordinary. "I know you're still in here. Come on out, Russell. Come out and fac—"

A large boot slammed down from the darkness above him. A sudden snap followed by enormous pressure fell upon his neck, causing Sam to exhale in a way unlike he'd never done before. His body began twitching.

Thoughts raced through his mind at lightning speed, mimicking the nervous sweat that was starting to drip off his bright red face. He reached up and grabbed hold of the foot on his neck, desperately clawing on the ice-cold boot. Lacking strength, Sam did what he could to push the great weight off his neck. He started gagging when the pressure got worse. His legs flung up and down like a fish out of water, but the effort was useless. But when he lifted his eyes off the boot, he stopped moving. The pressure on his neck was so intense; Sam was unable to take in any air.

The outline of Russell Fritz loomed over him, but no details could be made out. When his body came to a complete stop, shallow breathing emerged from the person standing over him. All he was able to do was keep his eyes focused on where he thought Fritz's face was.

He stayed in that position for only a few seconds, but in those brief seconds, memories from his childhood—everything from meeting Tyler for the first time to watching Fritz get dragged away in the woods decades' prior—unexpectedly flooded in. The thoughts were brief and transitioned to memories of adulthood quickly, but they were enough to remind Sam of all the terrible things he's done despite the good intentions he's always had.

Unsure of what else to do, Sam loosened his grip on the boot and extended his right hand into the darkness. "Russel, I'm sorry."

When the words squeaked out, Sam dropped his hand on the cold floor and waited for the boot on his neck to press down harder. He closed his eyes and braced himself. The breathing that towered above him was calm and persistent, but loud enough for him to hear.

Suddenly, the boot lifted off his neck, allowing a large gust of cold night air to go swooping through Sam's body and fill his lungs back up with life. He took it in and started coughing. The pain from the boot striking him remained, but the feeling of air returning into his body briefly offset that pain. The coughs were loud and dry but dissipated quick. Once, he was able to catch his breath; Sam looked back up at the figure standing over him. He raised his hand again. "Thank you, Russ—"

The boot swung down again and slammed into Sam's throat; flattening all the bones in his neck and sending him into a void of darkness instantly. Remaining calm, Fritz kept the pressure on Sam's neck until the last jerks exited his limbs. Then, once sure no other movement would arise from Sam's body, Fritz turned back to the other side of the gym and started for the blue doors.

Stepping into another long narrow hall, Lois Tangley kept her gun pointed as she waved her flashlight from side to side. She was sure that she was heading in the right direction of the gunfire, but every hall she went through just brought her to another narrow, dirty hallway. By the time she got to the end of the second one, she stopped jingling the handles of all the doors she passed by. *If all of them have been locked up to this point, why should the others be any different?*

Exposed pipes hung above the cracked cement floor of the hall. She did what she could to avoid the large puddles of water that seeped through the cracked foundation, but she couldn't avoid the larger ones that covered the third hall. The more she thought about it, the more she started to question if these halls were leading her to the basement of the building.

At the end of the third hall, she reached a crossroads. On the left side was a staircase that headed up. On her right was a staircase cloaked in darkness that went down. *Fuck that.* She shined her flashlight to the left and sprinted up the stairs, keeping her gun at her side.

Complete darkness surrounded Kimberly as she ran down the long hallway. She couldn't see two feet in front of her, let alone anything she ran by. The mix of pain coming from her nose and the feeling like someone—or something—was about to grab her was front and center. She did what she could to retain control of her breathing, but a loud bang from behind forced a loud gasp out of her. She started running faster.

A sense of vulnerability came over her due to the lack of a weapon. She could fight with her fists and legs if need be, but because of everything she'd seen in the course of the night, the young teenager knew she was going to need some weapon to take down her adversary. Running profusely, she kept blinking her eyes, making sure her eyes were open when—a light appeared from the end of the hall.

It couldn't have been larger than the size of a peephole, but it stood out like a sore thumb in the dark hallway. At first, Kimberly wasn't sure what it was, but she fixated on it as she charged toward it. She had no idea what the light source was, but she didn't care—all she wanted to do was get as far away from the school as possible. The light source remained small for almost the entire length of the hall, but as she closed in on it, it grew from a small circle to a vertical line that started at the top of the hall and went down to the floor. *It's a door! Oh, thank God!*

Pain from her nose got worse with each step she took. It became so bad that it brought her to the verge of tears by the time she was down two-thirds of the hall, but she kept her focus on the approaching light. She picked up speed as she went charging to the outline of the door. Her fists tightened, she closed her eyes and charged into the door.

White light blinded her for a moment, leaving her unable to see more than a few inches in front of her nose. When she felt the weight of the door move off her shoulder, she extended her hands and started reaching out, hoping to latch onto anything nearby. The weight of the door had slowed her down considerably and even knocked her off her balance for a moment. She stabilized the jittery feeling in her legs quick, but by the time she did, she'd already stepped off the edge of the floor and was in freefall.

The suddenness of the fall was so quick; she didn't even have time to react. Her eyes blinked in a desperate attempt to get them to adjust—she landed face down with a loud bang as pain darted across her chest, and her clothes absorbed some of the water she landed in. Any breath she had left in her lungs unwillingly blasted through her like she had just been crushed by a great weight. She rolled over onto her back as she conceded to the idea of crying.

Her eyes had adjusted, but what she saw provided more questions than answers. At first, she thought she'd fallen into another dimension—where she was made no sense to her. She closed her eyes a few more times, opened them again, and then started looking around, trying to take in surroundings.

She had fallen into an abandon in-ground swimming pool. The light coming in from the large windows across the way gave ample amount of light to recognize where she was, but it was the large holes in the roof overhead that provided her with much details of her surroundings. She had landed in the middle of the pool—about halfway between the shallow end of the pool and the twelve-foot-deep end. Dirt, large sticky pile of leaves and other debris laced the entire floor of the pool to the point where much of the brilliant white that made up the pool floor was unable to be seen.

The coldness of the floor, along with the water scattered throughout, made her shiver. Goosebumps covered her trembling body while a burning sensation of pain came over her. She was hurt. Badly. Any strength she had was lost, leaving her with no way to—a loud bang emerged above her.

Pushing through the aches, she carefully rose her head. The pain she felt was so front and center, she couldn't think clearly enough to figure out where the noise came from. But, when another equally familiar noise echoed, she realized the sound was coming from the hall. The same one she'd just run out of. Her heart started to race.

Without thinking twice, she knew she had no energy—or even time—to try and make it to the exit of the pool. From her floor level perspective, she could see the nearest ladder looked very unstable. Another bang came from the hall, forcing her to look straight ahead. Panic started to set in.

She looked around frantically, trying to see if there was anywhere she could hide to rest up and regain any strength she could. She turned to the right, looking back at the rusty pool ladder and started second-guessing if she could try and make it. There was another bang; only much louder. And closer.

Her breathing started to increase, to the point where it felt like she was going to have an asthma attack. Tears began forming in her eyes as dark thoughts plagued her mind to the point where—she turned her head to the left.

Nearly the entire pool was empty, but out of the corner of her eye, she could see the reflection of the moon bouncing off what appeared to be water concentrated at the deepest end. Another bang roared from the hall and echoed into the large room. Kimberly rolled onto her stomach and started crawling to the deep end as quick as she could.

Because of the harsh elements and traumatizing winters Hunting, Pennsylvania—and much of the Rust Belt—endured over the decades, many of the tiles that made up the pool floor were cracked and broken with sharp edges sticking out like shards of broken glass. Another bang hurtled into the air.

Much of the feeling in her fingers—especially the tips of them—was gone, but the sudden sting of the freezing cold water when her hand made contact with it felt like a knife piercing through her skin. Her hand quickly recoiled; it was apparent she hadn't prepared for how cold the water was compared to how cold she thought it would be.

She started to look around, second-guessing her idea, but the sight of no place to hide reinforced her plan was the only option. Another loud bang entered the large room, louder than any of the previous ones before it. A sudden gasp came from her mouth as she nearly jumped out of her goosebump laced skin. Refocusing on the water in front of her, she placed both her hands in it and started crawling into it.

The dim moonlight coming in from the windows was mostly the only light that lit up the room, but it was enough for her to see the dirtiness of the water as she pushed herself into it. The water was pitch black and chuck full of debris—which included leaves, pieces of tiles and several dead birds—that added a foul odor to the water. The slimy texture of the water disgusted the wounded teenager as she felt the dirt beneath the palms of her hand, but when she spotted the dead bird, Kimberly gaged.

Trying to keep calm, she gently pushed herself into the water, hoping to keep the water as still as possible. Her body trembled the deeper she got as her clothing absorbed the thick brown water. Her gaging intensified as the smell of the water grew more potent with each inch the young woman crawled. By the time her entire body was in the water, she was in the deepest part of the pool, just below a broken diving board. Strands of her long hair draped into the water, absorbing the foul liquid faster than her clothing did.

Once she felt her shoes fill with water, she looked down, realizing her idea to blend in the water could work. She took a deep breath, but winced as she remained motionless. Without trying to, she glanced at the dead bird floating a few inches away. She groaned with disgust along with a bit of hesitation but forced her eyes shut and lowered her head into the water.

Her hair became wet first, followed with a rush of slimy water flooding into her eardrums. The gaging feeling she'd been struggling with ever since her fall into the pool grew with life as she feared for her own. *Just do it! Come on, hurry! He's coming! He's—*

Water reached her eyes while the back of her head touched the bottom of the floor. Her heart thumped in her flooded ears like a war drum, but she managed to control the urge to scream. She squeezed her lips closed as tight as she could, hoping to avoid getting any debris in her mouth. It required a great deal of effort—more than she thought it would. Water flooded across her face. Everything went silent.

Attempting to control her breathing, she took small inhales of air from her nose which was sticking out of the water just enough for her to breathe through as the rest of her body blended in with the black water she was submerged in—the door that lead into the room flung open. She kept still.

Despite her ears being underwater, the door being slammed open with such force it snapped in half was audible from beneath the water. So were the footsteps walking in. *Oh, God. He's here.* She squeezed her lips tighter. Then, the footsteps stopped.

The gusts of wind that were amplifying throughout the night had all be faded, leaving behind a calmness the night had yet to receive from mother nature. The blackness of space still engulfed the sky, but its shade wasn't as deep as it had been; dawn was approaching. The end of the night was close at hand.

Blood dripped onto the floor beside his worn-out boots as Russell Fritz stood motionless inside the large room. His breathing was calm and collective—almost as if no pain was coming from any of the wounds he sustained. He kept his head still and started honing in on the silence of the room, trying to hear anything that seemed out of the ordinary.

Ignoring the blood dripping down the left side of his face from where his ear was severed off, Fritz started looking around and took a few more steps into the large room. The blown-out windows and large openings in the roof allowed the night air to seep in and take a firm grip. Just by the goosebumps on his exposed arm, it was apparent the temperature was still dropping at an accelerated rate. A slight breeze allowed the air to bang up against the numbs of bone that were exposed on his right hand from where his pointer and middle finger once resided.

The deer mask had also sustained a significant amount of damage as well; nearly all of the left side of the mask had been cut due to Kimberly's attack with the ax. Nothing more than a thin piece of flesh by Fritz's chin kept the left part of the mask attached. But—unlike the man beneath it—the mask still had its left ear attach even though it dangled like a climber holding on for dear life.

The pool of blood at Fritz's feet had expanded to the point where it was only an inch or two away from the edge of the pool. If Fritz had stayed in that spot a few seconds longer, it eventually would've reached the edge, but he suddenly started walking away, keeping his head moving in all directions as a trail of blood followed at his side.

The ice-cold water that encapsulated Kimberly's body debilitated her physically and mentally while simultaneously numbing the wounds she'd sustained throughout the night. From beneath the water, she started to shiver uncontrollably. *Oh, shit! He's gonna hear me. And when he does, he's gonna fuc—*

The sound of Fritz's boots walking away pulled her out of her train of thought. The slimy water kept her mouth closed and body still, allowing her to hone in on the echoes of the steel toe boots walking away from beneath the water. She focused on them until they all but disappeared, leaving her alone.

The unsettling stillness returned to the large room; there wasn't even a gust of wind to keep Kimberly company. All she had was her thoughts and her hiding spot. Having been an avid horror movie fan for most of her life—and being pretty smart on her own—she resisted the urge to leap out of the disgusting slush of liquid and sprint to the exit. The coldness of the water may have numbed the wound on her leg, but it wasn't enough to make her forget about it. She was going to need some distance between herself and her attacker if she was going to have any chance of getting out.

Remaining as still as she could, Kimberly began counting backward from twenty; hoping by the time she got to zero, she'd be in the clear to emerge from her dirt nap and vanish into the night. *Nineteen…eighteen… you can do this, girl. You made it this far, so no reason you can't make it a little farther. Sixteen. Fifteen.*

As she made her way down to zero, a sudden—almost random— feeling emerged in her gut. She couldn't place it or even explain it if she needed to, but the immediate feeling brought a sense of warmth to her on a night where everything felt cold. The feeling mimicked happiness despite knowing it was impossible to feel that way given where she found herself. She tried not to focus on it, but the feeling became so overpowering, she couldn't avoid it. It was a warmth that reminded her of Christmas morning—where everything terrible in the world drifts away, and there's nothing left but a feeling of hope that tomorrow will be a better day.

I'm gonna make it. Oh, my God, I'm really going to make it. Okay…I got this…thirteen. Twelve. Eleven.

When she reached single digits, she started growing impatient with a bit of misplaced excitement; almost as if she was about to win a race, she'd put her heart and soul into. The feeling so was intense, the foul smell of the water no longer fazed her. And from beneath the water, she prepared to leap out and run. *Seven…six…five*—a gentle ripple glided across the top of the water. With her eyes closed, she was unable to see it, but she felt the bobbing of the water as it tickled her exposed nose.

Dammit, Kimberly, she said to herself. *You can do this—this is no time to start getting jittery. Your life is at stake—*

There was another trickle. She halted her train of thought.

Her pulse began to rise.

While she couldn't rule out that she might've unknowingly twitched; she was somewhat confident that she didn't move. She had been struggling to keep her eyes closed, but she wanted to make sure the coast was clear before she emerged from her hiding spot. She took in a deep breath out of her exposed nose and slowly opened her ey—a pair of metal boots came soring down and landed on her face, crushing her skull instantly.

One violent twitch erupted from her body—so fierce her feet rose from the water before splashing back in. Her mouth then opened, allowing a rush of thick slimy water and small pieces of decomposing leaves to flood her mouth and seeped in her throat and lungs. Blood rose from Kimberly's head and started to expand in the water, leaving her with agonizing pain until her lungs filled with water and the rest of her skull shattered like a glass plate landing on a hardwood floor, sending her into darkness that matched the darkness that's surrounded her the entire night.

Remaining still as Kimberly's skull and brain squished beneath his steel toe boots, Russell Fritz kept quiet, keeping his attention at his feet to watch the blood—and life—exit Kimberly's body. The splashes Kimberly's leg made as they squirmed for dear life slowly became overtaken by the gentle breeze slipping through the cracks of the ceiling above and the adjacent walls. The gust of wind was soft but enough to hide the sound of water costing up and down. Then, after a few moments—when he felt the last of Kimberly's skull shattered under his feet—the wind came to an abrupt halt, leaving the large room silent with nothing but the sound of blood dripping off Fritz's right hand and into the water above Kimberly's crushed face.

The scummy water—which contained more dead animals and bugs than one would care to know—slowly came to a standstill and everything became still. And for the first time all night, Fritz took a moment and embraced it. While no smile emerged from the man, a calmness took over as a slight draft of September air squeezed its way through the large opening on the left side of the mask where the ax sliced. It was by no means enough to stop the sweat dripping down his face, but the air hitting against his face was enough to cool him down. Then, once Fritz looked back down and saw—and felt—that Kimberly was dead, he squeezed the metal hammer with the remaining fingers on his right hand and made his way to the opposite end of the pool without a single emotion felt inside.

CHAPTER 15

Slamming the door open with all her weight, Lois Tangley stepped into the hall just beyond the blue door. She was out of breath from charging up the staircase, but she remained on guard as she pointed the flashlight in front of her with his pistol at her side with the safety off. Once in the hall, she spun around and looked in all different directions. The door squeaked behind her like a wounded animal until it slammed shut with locks clicking in place.

Unlike the previous ones she'd sprinted down, the hall had windows that looked outward which allowed light to drizzle in through the doorways. Like the others who entered the abandoned school before her, memories of a simpler time came rushing through her mind like a title wave after breaking through a floodgate. It was not the time for memory lane to come calling, but the atmosphere and memories held firm. Keeping her service revolver pointed at the ground, Lois started down the abandon hall. *Come on, Tyler. Where the hell are you?*

She picked up speed the further in she got while unable to stop the sound of the gunshots replaying in her mind. Her breath intensified. By the time she reached the end of the hall, she was in a full-blown panic. The stomps of her footsteps echoed like an Earthquake and evaporated any element of stealth she might've—a loud bang came from her right side. She stopped and shut her flashlight off.

Her footsteps faded into the air, leaving behind a stillness laden with foreboding. Her breath started to swell. *Stay calm; just stay quiet.*

Preparing herself for what was in front of her, Lois leaned back against the dusty lockers on the far right side of the hall and crept up to the edge of the wall. Her heart pounded, but she managed her breathing by forcing herself to take in long deep breaths of air through her nose. She tightened her grip on the gun, brought herself to the mindset she needed to be in and jumped out of cover and into the adjacent hall.

There was nothing.

The hall was completely empty.

The eerie silence of the previous hall followed behind her and expanded into the large hall she now stood in. To her right appeared to be dozens of doors that lead into classrooms scattered throughout. The sight brought a sense of isolation, especially when she focused on the darkness that rested at the far end. Part of her thought she should head in that direction; the idea seemed to stand out, but instead, she took a few steps backward, banging up against Russell Fritz after the second step.

An uncontrollable shout blasted out of her as she spun around to the see the outline of the deer mask glaring directly at her. Shadows draped across the hall, but the shape was precise: the man—the serial killer she and the rest of the town had been hunting for, was a foot away from her. She began to tremble.

From beneath the foul-smelling mask, Fritz fixated on the detective; gazing into her eyes before looking down and spotting the pistol in her right hand, which wasn't aimed at him at all. He watched, waiting for her to start that process—a parade of bullets blasted through his left shoulder, slicing through his bones and skin like warm butter.

Hunks of flesh hurtled through the air, forcing Fritz to jerk forward from the intensity and suddenness of the bullets as two of the buck shots reached Lois, striking her in the lower stomach. A terrible scream cried out from her before she spun around like a young ballerina and fell to the floor, landing on her back.

An agonizing burning sensation ripped up Lois's left side, paralyzing her as she felt the service pistol slip from her grip and into the shadows that surrounded her. The pain was agonizing, forcing her to let out a few low deep grunts. She reached down to the bullet wound only to feel the warmth of blood dribbling out.

Letting out a groan himself, Fritz looked at his left shoulder, spotting the large holes where the bullets had exited his body. Thick blood seeped out of the wounds and slid down his entire arm before dripping on the floor beside his blood-soaked boots. A numbing sensation began sliding down his arm, making it almost impossible for Fritz to move his arm, much less feel it. But, unlike Lois, Fritz focused on the anger building up inside him. He squeezed the metal handle of the hammer and turned around—

Another round of bullets struck him, blasting into his stomach and chest. Unable to remain standing, Fritz stumbled backward into another hall and plummeted onto his back. The sound of the hammer clanging onto the floor echoed throughout both halls before silence befell again. Everything became still. Not even the wind made a sound.

As light smoke coming from the barrel of the shotgun subsided, Jess Sowa kept the gun aimed down the hall with her finger on the trigger. She was a reasonable distance away from where her intended target had fallen, but the light coming in from the doors of the classrooms provided her with enough illumination to see. She interrupted the silence by cocking the shotgun. Then, very carefully, she started walking toward Fritz.

Blood collected around Lois' waist. She was in a great deal of pain, but she kept applying pressure to the gunshot wound, hoping to ease the blood flow as best she could. Moonlight shined off the glaze of sweat on her face like diamonds in the night. The trickle of light from the classroom across the hall was enough to reveal half of her face, but it wasn't enough for her to find her pistol. She knew it had to be close by, but where it was, she couldn't figure out. When Jess' footsteps drew closer—Lois looked and made eye contact with her.

Lois coughed. "You…you did this."

"It's nothing personal; just doing what I had to," Jess said in a lifeless tone.

Lois tried to lift herself, but the pain was too unbearable for her to do so. Only a soft grunt came from her efforts. Jess raised the shotgun in her direction as she closed the gap between them. The gesture was clearly an attempt to intimidate the wounded officer, but Lois—having been raised never to bow down—dismissed the move and continued.

"You're not going to get away with this!"

From the shadows, a villainous chuckle came from Jess. "A hero to the end; good for you. But, don't kid yourself. I've been getting away with this for years. And some rogue cop isn't going to stop what she doesn't know anything about."

The closer Jess got, the more apparent it became there was no reasoning with her; the look of desperation was front and center. It was a look Lois never used before, but even she knew it was a warning sign to not mess with someone who wore the look—especially a woman. The burning sensation in her lower stomach expanded, forcing Lois to let out a small grunt.

She was reasonably wounded and no longer seemed to be a threat Jess concluded. But, she was going to have to be dealt with. And as she approached the entrance to the hall where Fritz had fallen, she kept the shotgun aimed steadily at Lois.

Because of the large windows in the hall where Fritz seemingly was, the light was able to brighten up the floor for Jess to see in the hall once she reached it. She raised the shotgun and focused onto the entrance of the hall, ignoring Lois' soft grunts.

Despite being unaware that she'd be dead for quite some time, Jess continued to replay Mrs. Quimby's warning about being blamed for everything. Her words were clear and consistent—almost as if she was standing beside her and whispering in her ear. The thought—and fear— of becoming the face of the tragedy, brought Jess to a heightened sense of paranoia. It was a label she refused to accept. But, as she reached the entrance of the hall, she felt confident she would squeak by and never have to endure those consequences.

Doing what she could to muffle the sounds of her footsteps, she stopped at the corner of the hall and began to take a few deep breaths, bracing herself for what she needed to do next. Despite the light only revealing half of Lois' face, Jess could see the officer was still staring at her.

Jess steadied her aim at Lois. "No hard feelings—"

A bloody hand latched onto the barrel of the shotgun and ripped it out of her grip. Jess gasped as the gun slip from her fingers and got tossed to the side. Then, the hand slammed against her neck and started to squeeze, knocking the wind out of her. From the floor, Lois watched in awe as the hand started lifting Jess off her feet with little effort.

Raising her hands to her neck, Jess grunted and pulled, trying to get out of the grip. Her face started to get warm, and when more pressure was applied, the warm feeling transitioned to a burning sensation as she cried out for air. When her feet were off the floor, she started kicking them up and down like a fish that had been caught and taken out of water. She forced her eyes closed, hoping to hide the tears filling up around the edges when suddenly she started feeling herself moving forward, forcing her to reopen them.

She screamed.

The grip got tighter.

"No, no!" she pleaded for mercy as she looked into the cold black eyes glaring at her through the deer mask only a few inches from her face.

Ignoring the throbbing pain in her gut, Lois watched, completely taken back by what she was witnessing. So much so, the idea of engaging and helping Jess never occurred; she was mesmerized by the sight.

Standing still as Jess squirmed in his hand, Fritz remained focused on her. Throughout the night, a sense of anger had overcome him—a passion for revenge because of everything he'd been put through. It had guided him the entire night, providing him with a roadmap of where to go and that map always ended in the same place with the same person: her.

Straining to breathe, Jess mumbled out another plea for mercy. She could feel the vein that ran down her forehead, starting to bulge. A cracking sound started coming from opposite sides of her neck. She gasped, opening her mouth once more. "N...no, plea—

Fritz lifted the hammer and swung it down, striking her in the center of her forehead.

She gasped.

Lois jumped.

Blood splashed out of the wound as an overwhelming feeling of pain that mimicked a crippling migraine entered Jess' head, bringing her thoughts to a complete standstill. Her eyes drifted away from the deer mask and looked up at the claw of the hammer nested deeply in her skull. She groaned.

Fritz ripped the metal claw out the wound, revealing a massive crater deep enough to see the majestic pink of her frontal lobe in the center of Jess' skull. Lois remained motionless as blood continued to expand on the floor below her.

Jess' eyes grew heavy; the migraine sensation expanded, reaching the back of her head. The hammer swung down again, landing in the same spot as the first hit.

Lois jumped in shock, irritating the bullet wound in her stomach.

Blood started to drip on the floor beneath Jess' feet moments before her eyes started tilting to the back of her head. The hammer ripped out of her head again. Pain seeped through the hole in the center of her face.

The hammer struck again.

Then again. And again. And again.

With each strike, Lois' eyes widened, unable to look away from the savageness. With each blow, a stomach-turning squishing sound rose into the air.

Jess' pupils stretched out in both eyes.

A low growl came from beneath the mask.

Using all its might—the might it had been building up throughout the night, the test subject kept its crippling grasp around Jess Sowa's neck and squeezed tighter with each moment that passed. Refusing to look away, the test subject remained focused on her, watching as each strike of the hammer broke her face in more and more.

The head wound had become so large, nearly half the head of the hammer could fit in her forehead. Blood gushed to the floor and splattered its boots and pant legs. The test subject growled, ignoring the pain coming from its chest and missing fingers. It ripped the hammer out of the skull again, taking a chunk of brain stuck in the claw with it. Grinding its teeth, the subject leaned forward, making eye contact with its intended target.

A pale, lifeless look lathered its victim's eyes. It had seen the look before—in fact, all night it had seen that look. It first saw the look on its first victim—Old Man Claire—all the way up to its current.

Like with each killing, anger bewildered the test subject, but now that it found the person it'd been hunting for all night, it held nothing back. It swung the hammer down again, the tips of the claws scraping up against the back of the victim's skull.

The test subject could've stopped and Jess take her last breaths alone. It chose not to.

It raised the hammer one more time, holding it up as high as it could and swung it down, striking the victims skull and splitting her head down the middle as the hammer penetrated the back of the head and crashed into the wall behind her, the metal handle snapping in half from the force of the strike.

Blood sprayed out like a fountain, covering the walls, the floor and dusty lockers. In its grip, the test subject felt the resistance of its victim come to a standstill. Then, it turned and slammed the body onto the hard floor, effectively releasing the anger it's felt toward the victim for years.

Silence returned to the hall.

Mission: complete

*

A gush of dense blood oozed out of Lois' bullet wound, forcing her to unwillingly take her eyes off Jess' mangled body and look down at her stomach. The warm dark fluid covered both her hands, providing her with a sense of uncertainty. She tried to lift herself, but a ripping sound and burning pain stopped her before she rose more than two inches.

She cried out in pain.

Fritz looked away from Jess and slowly turned around.

The scream echoed in the deserted hall, bouncing off the metal lockers and cracked concrete walls until the night absorbed it as it had everything else. Keeping her attention focused on her stomach, Lois pressed down on the gunshot even harder, forcing out another groan. The pain was overwhelming, but when she saw movement in front of her, she slowly looked up. Her breathing intensified.

Standing in the darkness as still as the night air was Fritz, clenching the metal handle of his broken hammer and glaring in her direction. Blood dripped onto the floor beside his boot from his missing fingers mixing with the blood on the tip of the handle. The shadows in the hall hid much detail, but Lois could see Fritz still had the mask on.

The two remained silent, staring at each other.

Lois' body trembled profoundly as she waited for the sound of footsteps to start appr—

Fritz dropped the broken hammer; the handle crashing into the puddle of blood beside him.

After a long silence followed the hammer crashing to the ground, Lois nervously opened her eyes only to see Fritz standing in the same spot. Her heart pounded as thoughts of doom ensued her.

The two made eye contact again.

Lois was unable to see his eyes, but he was able to see hers—mostly due to the brilliant white that surrounded her pupils. He spotted the tears with fear mixed in. But, past the tears and fear, he was able to spot a sense of resistance in her dreamy eyes—resistance that reminded him of his own.

Remaining still, Fritz continued to look in her direction to make it evident that he saw her.

Rather than frantically start searching the shadows in the hope she would find her pistol, Lois kept still; keeping her eyes locked on the looming stranger as she unintentionally altered the threat level she posed. *Oh, Christ. I'm gonna die right here. Right here on this—*

Fritz suddenly turned away from Lois—a woman who never once harmed him or even raised a weapon at him.

Immobile and confused, Lois watched as the masked assailant walked away, leaving her in a pool of expanding blood, but unharmed.

Lois rolled onto her back and applied more pressure on her gunshot wound, moaning in agony while watching Russel Fritz push open the exit door of the school and vanish back out into the night.

*

Remaining focused on the moonlight raining down as it walked in the center of Mimic Street, the test subject marched on steadily as it replayed the events of the evening in its mind.

Clarence Grzywacz: Dead

Joe Catalano: Dead

Garrett Auclair: Dead

Tom Burke: Dead

Jonah Manning: Dead

Betty Quimby: Dead

Tyler Benton: Dead

Sam Rainey: Dead

Jess Sowa: Dead

And everyone else in between who harmed him throughout the evening: Dead.

They were all dead. No one remained.

Beneath the mask, the test subject grinned.

Mission: complete

CHAPTER 16

Standing at the doorway of the final hall, James Nelson stood motionless, glaring into the blackness before him. For nearly the entire night, nothing but excitement had occupied his bright mind—the hope of finally discovering an extra torrential overtook any trepidation he had. But, now that he was far enough in the facility to assume there wasn't much ground left to cover, his enthusiasm had deuterated, allowing a touch of reality to take its place.

Waiting for the feeling of hesitation to dematerialize, James continued to gently throw the fake handcuffs back and forth in his hands; he chose to holster the paintball gun a few halls back out of fear the weapon would make him come across as a threat. *I don't want the aliens to think I'm going to harm them. I just want to take one and prove to everyone at school that they are wrong. Then, they'll stop picking on me for sure!*

The harshness of reality subsided.

Excitement returned.

James powered his flashlight back on and stepped into the hall.

A strong dampness smell that mimicked the basement of his house was the first thing he noticed; it hit like the chilly night air when he first stepped outside. It reminded him of rain on a humid summer day—the type of day he never liked. But, moments after noticing the dampness, a hissing sound came from the end of the dark hall.

He lifted the flashlight from the floor. Reassurance allowed him to lower his guard when he saw the sound was coming from nothing more than large pipes on the right side of the hall. He found it strange, but didn't question it. Instead, he continued down the shadow-filled hall, hoping to find what he'd been after all night.

A mist of steam covered the floor like a gentle fog, hiding any objects resting on the floor. James—noticing the mist appeared to be rising—took note of his inability to see what was in front of him and slowed his pace. But, despite this reduction in speed, he eagerly turned the flashlight back and forth to opposite sides of the hall, hoping to make out as many details as he could. *Whoa, this place is a little—*

He left foot crashed into an object on the floor, causing him almost to lose his balance.

Uh-oh...Uh-oh!

His arms sprang out like a harpoon in a desperate attempt to get his balance or shield himself in the event he completely lost his footing and fell to the misty ground. It was close, but after a few stumbles, he finally stabilized.

Whoa! That was fricken close. He rocked his head back and forth, trying to shake off the stars spinning across his eyes.

Unsure of what he hit, James lowered the beam to the floor. The steam was so thick; he was unable to see what it was his foot had struck. He couldn't even make an outline of the object, but he knew it was heavy; he could tell by the way it felt when he hit it. Despite intense light of the flashlight, it wasn't able to penetrate through the mist. But, because of the excitement mixed with his abnormally high curiosity for someone his age, James refused to move on until he figured out what the object was. Thinking quick on his feet, he started swooshing his arms back and forth. At first, it seemed to be a wasted gesture, but slowly, the mist started to scatter around and reveal what it was he nearly fell on.

It was a door. A large metal door with large dents in it.

Wow!

The young was cursed with being a little slow to figure things out, but as he glared at the broken door, that disability all but faded. He moved the flashlight to the left, illuminating the room in front of the fallen door.

Like the rest of the hall, steam had engulfed much of the room, leaving it nearly impossible to make out any sense of detail as to what the room was. It took James stepping into the room for him to get an idea of what the room could be. *There's a bed or a cot I think is what it's called? There's a sink...and some metal thing—wait! This looks like a jail cell! Maybe this is where they kept them! But, why would they lock them in a jail cell? They must've*

gotten mad and broke down the door; I probably would, too! And I—hold on…
is this the only room here?

The sporadic thoughts roaming through James' head halted. Now
that he thought of it, he realized he never bothered to look down the hall
completely; he saw it was a dead-end, but never took the time to look at
the rest—a siren emerged from outside the cell.

Frightened by the sudden noise, the young boy spun around, spotting
that not only was a siren blaring, but a flashing red light was blinking
outside the hall. Because he could only see what the doorframe revealed,
he felt venerable. It was too late for him to turn back—he didn't want to
anyway, but he knew he needed to investigate if he was going to figure out
what was happening. He tightened his grip on the metal handcuffs and
crept up to the door frame.

Okay, here we go. One…two…two and a half…and…three!

James leaped out of the cell and back into the hallway. His feet landed
just over the collapsed door, making a thunderous boom when they struck
the cold cement floor. A puff of steam rose from his feet due to the air his
feet created when they landed, blinding him for a moment. He shined his
flashlight in front of him.

The red siren above the doorway he came out of continued to blare,
sending a terrible screeching sound down James' left earlobe—a sudden
light off to his left powered on, forcing him to spin the flashlight in that
direction and shine it up at the blaring siren.

Good lord!

Realizing the light was just another siren—which made sense when
he thought about—a soft childish giggle chuckled out of the young boy
followed with a smile—another red light came on further down the hall.
The smile vanished.

Wait, what the heck is that? Another one?

Another red light powering on the opposite side of the hall answered
for him.

It is followed by another one.

And another one.

As each one came on, splashes of red light pushed back the shadows
of the hall and created an eerie maroon ambiance in the hall—not enough
to overpower all the darkness, but enough, so James could see details of
the room with ease. It was even enough for him to shut his flashlight off,
which he ended up doing. The young boy's eyes widened.

Beneath every flashing siren was a door; a door that striking resembled the one that was broken on the floor. James didn't take the time to count, but from guessing, he figured there was close to a dozen, if not more. All the doors were closed, leading James to believe that someone (or something) was just behind the—a shadow emerged from one of the windows in the center of the door.

James flinched.

The red tint of the flashing sirens overtook most of the hall and surrounding walls, but a dim yellowish glow from behind the window in the door illuminated enough for James to see the outline of a figure—at least the head and shoulders of a figure. He wasn't able to make out a face—or even tell if it was a man or a woman (or even human; his mind was racing with scenarios), but he was sure it was the outline of a person.

He took a step forward.

Another yellow glow emerged from a door on the opposite side of the hall. His head snapped in that direction, spotting what appeared to be another figure behind that door; the figure bearing a striking resemblance to the first one he saw—

Another yellow light emerged.

Then another.

And another.

James stepped back, his eyes widening with surprise.

Thoughts of pulling out his paintball gun to provide him a layer of security popped into his mind. The idea gained traction when other figures from behind the doors stepped up to the windows. *I found them. Holy shit, I found them! They're all in here. I'm gonna be famous; people everywhere will know my name. 'James Nelson: the boy who discovered extra-terrestrial life on Earth!' Just wait until people read about this. I'm going to be remembered forevr—*

A shadow from behind him move. He only saw it from the corner of his eye, but he was confident he saw movement. Sweat started to build upon his cheeks; for the first time all night, he felt scared. The hairs on the back of his neck snapped at attention. *Somebody's in the doorway behind me. No, I haven't seen a single person here. Besides the front door closed; nobody else could've gotten in.*

James tried to convince himself that he didn't see anything—his eyes were playing tricks on him because of how late it was, but he was unable to accept the idea. Then, clenching his fist as hard as he could, the young boy slowly turned toward the direction of the doorway he entered from.

The handcuffs slipped through his fingers as his eyes widened.

*

Confused, the test subject—Russell Fritz—glared at the young child beneath the moist mask. At first, curiosity overtook the test subject, taking its mind off the lack of numbness coming from its missing fingers. With the only decent light coming in from the doorway he stood in, Russell Fritz found it challenging to get a good look at the child. He stepped forward.

As the patient had done with every victim throughout the night, it fixated its eyes on the young child. To its surprise, the child remained in place as it closed in. With each step, the light got dramatically worse, but Fritz was able to make out an object fall from the child's hand. He clenched his fist, preparing to do what was necessary.

The test subject stepped up to the child, looming over him like a skyscraper in the heart of a densely metropolitan area. More confusion set in when it noticed the boy was—not only unafraid but standing his ground.

Neither of them blinked.

The test subject noticed.

Brave.

*

Filled with fear, but taken back by what was before him, James focused on the dark outline of the person in front of him. Because the figures back was to the light, James couldn't make out a face, but the single ear standing up fueled his speculation that whoever—or whatever—was in front of him was not of this world. Suddenly, a nauseating smell that reminded him of rotting garbage fluttered into his nose, forcing him to let out a few coughs. *Could this be—is it? Holy shit—I mean crap, it is! And it's standing right in front of—*

Russel Fritz extended his hands and clenched them together. Then, he pointed down with one of the remaining fingers on his right hand.

Picking up on the subtle hint, James looked down, at first assuming the person was pointing at something on the floor. The mist of steam was still thick at his feet, but enough had exited through the doorway for him to see what was at his feet: the toy handcuffs.

Confused, James looked back up.

Fritz's hands were still clenched together and reaching out.

James looked back down, and frantically started looking around. Once confident that no other object was around, the young boy bent down and picked up the metal handcuffs, keeping his eyes on the figure towering over him.

Fritz extended his arms out as far as they would go.

To any other person, the fear of this gesture being a trap would've been center stage, but James never thought of that. While he made sure he was cautious—he'd read conflicting ideas about whether extraterrestrial life would be hostile or not—never once did he fear for his life.

Russell Fritz pressed his hands together tightly.

James Nelson opened the cuffs.

Sweat started glistening the boy's hair. The more he looked at the masked figure in front of him, the scarier it became, Suddenly, thoughts of the thing in front of him, allowing him to get close enough and then snatch him seemed to come out of nowhere. His breath picked up, but still, he never slowed down. He raised his arms to the person with the handcuffs stretched out, bracing for something awful—

Nothing happened.

He placed the cuffs across both wrists and carefully closed them.

Fritz remained still, keeping his arms stretched out. He glared at the young boy; taking in as many details as he could. The first thing Fritz noticed was how young the boy seemed to be. The second thing he noticed was how gentle he was.

The latches of the handcuffs made a ticking noise as they closed around the wrists. James had seen many police shows where the officers tighten the cuffs as much as they can, but the lack of movement gave him a sense of security; he figured if the person—or thing were hostile, it would've already attacked him. Wanting to not come across as hostile himself, James tightened the cuff only until the third latch. Once he heard it, he stopped and snatched his hands away and looked back up.

Continuing to take in foul-smelling air, Fritz tilted his head and looked at the handcuffs. Just by feeling, he knew they were fake—he'd been in handcuffs enough times to know the difference in weight. Nevertheless, once they were around his wrist, he lowered his hands, turned away from the boy and started to the doorway of the cell.

Without blinking once, James kept his eyes on Fritz, watching every step he took until the masked man stepped into the cell door and disappeared into the steam. Confusion overcame the boy. *Wh—wh—why would it go in there? There's nothing in there.*

Remembering the dented door on the ground, James carefully approached the doorway. When the tip of his converse shoe struck up against the top of the door, he stepped up carefully, making an effort to avoid tripping again. *Good, don't need to trip on that darn thing again. Now... where did it go?*

The steam that filled the room had grown so think, it mimicked a morning layer of dense fog. Much was still pouring out into the hall, but the floor of the hallway was nearly at capacity, forcing the steam hissing into the room to rise. James went for his flashlight but stopped when he grabbed the doorframe and pulled himself inside the room.

The floor was a mist of steam, unable to be seen.

Then it started rising up to his knees.

Then up to his waste.

Movement from behind forced him to spin around. A soft squeak came from him and his shoes.

Behind him was the masked figure. His head was eye level with the boy's chest, no longer looming over him. James blinked a few times before realizing the masked person—who he still believed was a visitor from another world or even galaxy—was sitting down on the cot.

Questions roamed through James' mind like a car itching for speed; every question he'd built up over years of obsessing about extra-terrestrials was flooding his mind, making it difficult to figure out which question he wanted to ask first. The feeling of danger got lost in that vortex of ideas and, to the dismay of Fritz, the young boy stepped back and sat down on the cot adjacent from him.

Steam hissed outside the hall and continued to rise from the ground, giving the two outsiders only a limited amount of time to take in all the details of each other. James used all his willpower to keep any movement to the bare minimum—Fritz's hands rose from his side and up to his face, pressing down on the deerskin.

Then, he started lifting the mask up.

James watched in astonishment.

A rush of misty air brushed against the mouth of Russell Fritz as he lifted the mask. Once it was high enough, he opened his mouth and took in a deep breath of air. Coolness raced down his throat in a welcoming fashion. He did the same thing when the mask lifted from his nose.

The steam rose higher, reaching James' stomach.

Fritz pulled the rest of the mask off and tossed it at his feet, the mask disappearing into the steam with nothing more than a soft splat from it landing on the floor. He opened his eyes to the sight of James still looking at him.

Scars and burnt marks—combined with the slime from the mask that mimicked the glaze of a donut—covered Fritz's face. Small sprouts of hair were starting to form on the top of his shaved head. But, unlike the rest of the night, a look of rage was nowhere to be seen. Nothing but a blank look was across Fritz's face; almost as if he was unsure how to react. The look on James' face was nearly identical, but the thrill of asking all the questions he'd been burning to ask kept his expression from staying blank.

The two of them—both victims of bullies throughout the town—made eye contact again, spotting they had the exact same eye color: brilliant hazel filled with hopes and dreams.

The hissing steam reached James' chest, leaving only seconds before he would no longer be able to see anything in front of him.

His small left hand rose out of the steam and gently waved. "Hi."

Steam reached the bottom of his chin.

A three-fingered hand—completely free of any wounds—emerged from the opposite side of the room and waved back.

"Hi," a low deep voice replied.

Steam overcame James' face, leaving the young boy in a blinding white fog, but not before spotting a grin on Russell Fritz's face—the grin of a winner.

That made two of them.

According to Independent UK:
"An effective cure for all types of cancer could be just 5–10 years away."

CPSIA information can be obtained
at www.ICGtesting.com
Printed in the USA
LVHW041155071019
633401LV00002B/246/P

9 781796 057928